Honey
in the
Horn

NORTHWEST
Reprints

A Northwest Reprints Book
Series Editor: Robert J. Frank

Honey
in the
Horn

H. L. Davis

INTRODUCTION BY RICHARD W. ETULAIN

Oregon State University Press   Corvallis

♾ This paper meets the requirements of ANSI/NISO Z39.48-1992 (Permanence of Paper).

ISBN 978-0-87071-768-0 (paperback)
ISBN 978-0-87071-769-7 (e-book)

Cataloging-in-Publication data is available from the Library of Congress.

 **Oregon State University**
OSU Press

Oregon State University Press
121 The Valley Library
Corvallis OR 97331-4501
541-737-3166 • fax 541-737-3170
www.osupress.oregonstate.edu

Introduction

In fall 1927 a small job printer in The Dalles, Oregon, issued a pamphlet entitled *Status Rerum: A Manifesto, Upon the Present Condition of Northwestern Literature, Containing Several Near-Libelous Utterances, Upon Persons In the Public Eye.* Authored by H. L. Davis and James Stevens, two ambitious but not yet well-known writers, the brief publication was a head-on attack on authors the two authors considered feckless, misguided, and romantic popularizers addicted to mindless claptrap. These writers, according to Davis and Stevens, were nothing but "posers, parasites, and pismires" turning out an "interminable avalanche of tripe." The printer even hesitated to print the pamphlet because it libeled several noted teachers and writers of the Pacific Northwest.

Status Rerum symbolized H. L. Davis's coming out as a regional writer. Earlier he had published a clutch of prize-winning poems in *Poetry* magazine and then collaborated with Stevens on short stories for the highbrow pulp magazine *Adventure.* But in the next three or four years Davis placed a half-dozen short stories in H. L. Mencken's influential magazine *American Mercury* and also in *Collier's,* one of the country's leading slick periodicals. The first-rate poetic works and the well-written shorter fiction attracted the attention and support of leading literary figures such as Harriet Monroe, editor of

Portions of this introduction appeared first in Richard W. Etulain, *Re-imagining the Modern American West: A Century of Fiction, History, and Art* (Tucson: University of Arizona Press, 1996), and Etulain, "Inventing the Pacific Northwest: Novelists and the Region's History," in Paul W. Hirt, ed., *Terra Pacifica: People and Place in the Northwest States and Western Canada* (Pullman: Washington State University Press, 1998), 25–52; and Etulain, *Oregon Historical Quarterly,* book review, 111 (summer 2010): 260–61. Used by permission.

Poetry, poet Robinson Jeffers, and Mencken, a widely recognized culture arbiter. These literary leaders supported Davis for a coveted Guggenheim Fellowship. When the application proved successful in 1932, Davis and his librarian wife Marion Lay headed off to Mexico. In the next two or three years he worked tirelessly—but under mounting duress—on his first novel. Published in 1935, *Honey in the Horn* immediately won national attention and major prizes.

The journey motif at the center of much of H. L. Davis's fiction mimics the peregrinations of Davis's family in his boyhood and adolescent years. Both his father James Alexander Davis and his mother Ruth Bridges Davis were of east Tennessee heritage. The southern backgrounds of his paternal grandfather, who lost his life at the battle of Vicksburg in 1863, and his Hard-Shell Baptist maternal grandfather remained alive in Davis's thinking and writing. In the second half of the nineteenth century both sides of Davis's family moved to Oregon, where Harold Lenoir Davis was born on 18 October 1894 at Rone's Mill, adjacent to Nonpareil, in Douglas County, Oregon.

Davis's immediate family remained on the move in Oregon. His strong-willed schoolteacher father, who had lost a leg in a youthful accident, was the dominant and dominating figure in Harold's early years. The itinerant teacher took his family to Looking Glass, Drain, Ten Miles, and later to Roseburg, Yoncalla, and Oakland, in the Umpqua and Willamette valleys. Then, in 1906, the Davises, now with three sons, moved east over the Cascades to the plateau grazing and wheat country of Antelope for two years and then finally north to The Dalles in 1908. James and Ruth and their sons remained in The Dalles after Harold (now H. L.) left in the late 1920s.

Davis's autobiographical statements about his early years must be used with caution. Even before the publication of *Honey in the Horn* in 1935, Davis had moved his birth date forward from 1894 to 1896. He also heightened his varied background by falsely claiming to have edited the *Antelope Herald* when, as a teenager, he only set type and perhaps wrote a story or two. He also spoke of entering the engineering program at Stanford University in the late teens even though he lacked the funds to enroll. Early on, Davis seemed bent on peddling stretchers in his life accounts or in his early writings that were patently untrue. He relished the much-embellished yarns of Mark Twain and the tall tales of southwestern humorists, adopting their yarn-spinning into his own writings.

Even after discounting these exaggerations, Davis's life provided rich, abundant experiences and information he adroitly shoveled into his early publications. His family members and early acquaintances remembered Davis as a casual, unenthusiastic student but a voracious reader, devouring classics and foreign-language works in his early years. After his graduation from high school in 1912, Davis served as an assistant to his father, who had become a county official. Harold also traveled throughout Wasco County as a deputy county assessor and later as a deputy in the sheriff's office as a tax collector. He was also drafted and briefly served in the army in 1918.

Meanwhile, Davis had begun to write. Toward the end of 1918 he sent a group of poems to Harriet Monroe at *Poetry* magazine. These poems, utilizing the places and peoples Davis knew in eastern Oregon, were promptly awarded the Levinson Prize in 1919; they were praised for their freshness of form and content. Some critics touted Davis as a startling, new poetic voice from the West.

In the next decade Davis seemed uncertain about his career—and about his future. Remaining in The Dalles in the early and mid-1920s, Davis published a few more poems in *Poetry* and worked at odd jobs. Those who knew Davis at the time spoke of him as a loner, a standoffish, morose man who preferred poetry and other literature to people. His obvious desire was to be left alone.

Then the breaks came in 1927–28. *Status Rerum* appeared, marriage to Marion Lay, and a move to Bainbridge Island in Washington.

Davis, gradually formulating his writing credo, backed into a literary career. In *Status Rerum*, he and Stevens harpooned writing teachers and some of their student writers of the Pacific Northwest as addicted to stylized, formula-ridden romantic literary forms and content. These literati didn't know enough even to "castrate calves." But Davis and Stevens "had a vision" and were ready to snatch the writing game away from these hopeless "mental weaklings, numskulls, and other victims of mental and moral affliction" of the Northwest. The two critics would rescue and then redeem the literary Pacific Northwest.

Davis, along with Stevens, came to believe, first of all, that writers of the region had to draw on local materials for their fiction. They also must avoid the superficial, stylized formats of eastern popular and pulp magazines. The focus of the new regionalists must be on the lore of the people, the culture of "the folks." The resultant regionalist writings would demonstrate how settings, how place, shaped character. In these prescriptions Davis and Stevens were following the fresh regionalist ideas flooding across the United States in the 1920s, especially in the South and in subregions of the West. In the Pacific Northwest, H. G. Merriam's magazine *Frontier*, emanating out of Missoula, Montana, was a major outlet for regionalist writing. By the late 1920s H. L. Davis had camped among these new regionalists.

In his first published short fiction, Davis drew on his wide reading, ancient and recent. He was particularly attracted to the pilgrimage or journey themes at the center of the works of Chaucer, Cervantes, and Twain. In addition, his reading in Mencken's new cultural periodical the *American Mercury* reinforced Davis's own tendencies to embrace sardonic, Rabelaisian satire and humor. Not surprisingly, several of Davis's earliest short stories appeared in Mencken's magazine.

In one short essay for Mencken's *Mercury* entitled "A Town in Eastern Oregon" (January 1930), Davis vigorously indicted newcomers to Gros Ventre, Davis's thinly disguised depiction of his hometown The Dalles. Those immigrants to the Columbia River town, Davis wrote, had "succeeded in whipping out of its corporate limits" enough "devilment and cusedness" to "line Hell a hundred miles." A year earlier Davis had set his short story "Old Man Isbell's Wife" in another eastern Oregon cowtown. "Ugly and little it had begun," Davis writes, "and ugly and little it stayed." The two major characters, Old Man Isbell, "slack-witted, vacant-minded, doddering, dirty, and a bore," and his young, three-hundred-pound, bearded wife, prefigure several of the less-than-attractive characters in *Honey in the Horn*. No one encountering first this essay and short fiction would have misrecognized the ironic, antiromantic tone of Davis's later regional writing.

Soon after these writings appeared Davis landed his Guggenheim Fellowship and headed to Mexico.

The next two or three years were especially tough times, perhaps the most difficult period of Davis's life. His personal, unpublished journals now on file at the Ransom Center at the University of Texas, Austin, overflow with Davis's manifold doubts, unhappiness, and even self-loathing as he struggled financially and tried to plan and write his first novel. At the nadir of his disappointment, in near despair, Davis recorded in his journal:

> Oh God has anybody, in honest and humility of heart, ever paid so high for so little free joy and self-satisfaction? Good flashes at the rate of one a month; bad—fear, dread, shame, grief, apprehension, horror from remembering reality has always been worse than I expected. Their rate is one a minute, and each lasts an eternity…When was I last anywhere near happy?

Davis's pressing problems were several. His marriage was increasingly stressed and unhappy. His income was insufficient, and he bore a truckload of guilt about that. In fact, his finances were so strained he sold his car and pawned and later sold his typewriter. He even worried about paying postage.

The worst of the headaches probably came from still other dilemmas. Davis's Guggenheim was actually for a proposed long epic poem, but soon after arriving in Mexico he gave up that idea, and, at the urging of Mencken, turned to writing a novel. The new project did not go well.

The largest challenges were authorial. What would be the subject of his book-length fiction? How would he open the novel, and what would be its plot? How could he organize the piles of information he had gathered and deal with the plethora of character types he had in mind? These large, troubling questions were, of course, not unusual for a first-time novelist; but, evidently, combined with Davis's upset about not being able, financially, to support himself and his unhappy wife, were almost more than he could handle.

Even when Davis decided on an Oregon story, he was not sure where to take it. As he wrote later, with more than a dash of hyperbole, "I didn't have much of an idea about what it was to be like . . . I had written the opening without the faintest ideas how it was all to come out in the end. . . ." Plus, although Davis's publisher, Harper and Brothers, promised and sent much-needed advances to the cash-strapped author, he soon learned that advances came only after he had written and sent in additional chapters. No new chapters, no further advances. But by July 1932, he had a start. It was, he recorded in his journal, not a "brilliant one or even an out of common one; but broad enough not to tie me to any blind-alley narrative. . . . Broad, fast, slightly sprung to feel with the country rather than with any of people in it." From 1932 to 1934, Davis pushed mightily to finish his novel. The manuscript was completed in early 1934 and published in August 1935.

Honey in the Horn exploded on the literary scene, much to the surprise of its doubting author. Days after its appearance, he received a most supportive letter from Mencken, who told Davis, "I needn't tell you that 'Honey in the Horn' has given me great delight . . . The book is beautifully written, the characters are thoroughly alive, and the underlying philosophy is shrewd and convincing. Altogether, it seems to me that you have done the best novel about pioneers that has ever got into print . . . You have done something really first rate." A few days later in a front-page review of the novel in the *New York Herald Tribune*, Mencken declared the novel the best first novel by any author and best American novel since Sinclair Lewis's *Babbitt* (1922). Robert Penn Warren, a southern regionalist launching what became a distinguished literary career, gave *Honey in the Horn* a resounding salute, with a strong second coming from literary critic Malcolm Cowley in the *New Republic*. Cowley also scored and denounced Seattlite Mary McCarthy's negative review in *The Nation*.

More pleasing and satisfying, certainly, were the much-valued prizes and mounting royalties. Delayed a few months to be entered into prize competitions, *Honey in the Horn* was awarded the Harper Prize ($7,500) in 1935, and then the top award in 1936, the Pulitzer Prize. True to his standoffish ways, Davis refused to go, in person, to New York to accept the Pulitzer because he did not want to become "a subject for exhibit."

Conversely, more than a few northwesterners reacted negatively to *Honey in the Horn*. One critic labeled the novel as profane, with far too many cuss words; another dismissed it as "a discredit to the true pioneers." Still another writer, a friend of Davis's, pondered privately why Davis found so few Oregon homesteaders he could praise. Most newspaper reviewers in the Pacific Northwest were more critical than praising in their comments about the novel. Davis was clearly at work at his typical leg-pulling when he claimed, in his headnote to the novel, that he had "no intention anywhere in the book of offering social criticism or suggesting social reform." Roasting second- and third-generation Oregonians, Davis had upset chauvinistic northwesterners and provided grist for critics throughout the region. Hearing of the negative reactions of the "Portland fictionists" and other like-minded naysayers, Davis thumbed his nose at them. "Nobody cares anything about those flatheads outside of Woodlawn" cemetery, he told one friend. And to another acquaintance he had written earlier and even more caustically about such matters. Obviously, he told the Oregonian friend his writings had "stir[red] a row" and "had scrapped some hide off a number of Eunuchs [sic] who resent being valued at any rate except their own."

These critics of *Honey in the Horn*, by in large, overlooked its first-rank contribution as a regional work of fiction. They may have been blind to its path-breaking approach to the Pacific Northwest region because they, or their friends, had been harpooned in *Status Rerum* and thus were unwilling to embrace anything Davis wrote, especially in the decade following the publication of the pamphlet attack. Gradually, Davis would gain more positive attention from his home region.

In several ways, Davis achieved in *Honey in the Horn* what many regionalists in the 1920s and 1930s were aiming for in their writings about the West. His novel, brimming with pungent descriptions of settings and lively characterizations, is a sprawling, picaresque work, portraying varied Oregon countrysides and overflowing with a full gamut of rural people.

From the beginning, Davis's intentions in the novel were historical—and perhaps autobiographical. In the novel's introduction, balancing seriousness and humor, Davis stated he "had originally hoped to include in the book a representative of every calling that existed in the State of Oregon during the homesteading period." If noted western writer Wallace Stegner is right in contending that the richest period in an author's life to draw on for later literary production ranges between the ages of five and early teens, H. L. Davis was doing exactly that in *Honey in the Horn*. During Davis's youthful years the peripatetic Davis family was moving through at least a half-dozen sites in the Willamette Valley, the eastern slopes

of the coast range mountains, the upper plateaus of eastern
Oregon, and finally The Dalles. If all the moving about in
Davis's novel seemed aimless rambling to alienated readers,
they might not have understood that Davis was dipping into
the redolent reservoir of his personal and family experiences
for these fictional nomadic wanderings.

Davis also takes a larger view of the past than did frontier-
focused writers such as fellow Oregonian Ernest Haycox.
Like the superb regionalist he was, Davis shows how human
experiences over time have shaped—even skewed—the lives,
communities, and work patterns of Oregonians in the early
twentieth century. Davis cast his work in the form of what
Germans call the *bildungsroman*. Here it is the coming-of-age
story of a young couple, Clay and Luce, who, suffering the
pangs of bittersweet love, wander over much of northern rural
Oregon. In their travels they encounter a panoply of provincial
character types. Telling his yarn in a rich, racy vernacular, shot
through with humor, tale tales, and more than a few touches of
exaggeration—thereby following the stated agenda of western
regionalists like Pacific Northwest editor H. G. Merriam and
Oklahoma editor and folklorist B. A. Botkin—Davis betrays
his strong debts to Twain, the southwestern humorists, and the
cultural influences of Mencken.

In evaluating the major contributions of *Honey in the Horn*,
Professor Glen Love, a noted authority on northwestern
literature, praises Davis's apt handling of nature. Love calls
this Davis's "ecological consciousness," his "awareness of
the primacy of the elemental natural world." In all ways, a
valuable observation. Davis was a superb delineator of the
environment: the ridges and rims, the sage and sand, the

coulees and streams, the bunch grass, the vineyards and wheat fields of the Oregon Country.

But Davis posited that something else was even more important in his writings. Twenty years later in an essay entitled "Puget Sound Country" (*Holiday*, May 1954), Davis asserted that "landscape counts in the character of a place, but people count more." Following his own dictum, Davis brings to life a wonderfully provocative cross-section of men and women and occupations. For the most part, Davis is intrigued with ordinary citizens; his regional portraits are drawn primarily from characters of all sorts: crop hands, Indian men and women, ranchers, sheepherders, hop pickers, and a variety of other nomadic folks. So much fresh vintage is contained in the novel, in fact, that the old wineskins of a traditional plot are stretched to breaking points.

Changing metaphors, one might compare Davis's novelistic organization to over-sized beads on a narrow string. His unending and expanding supply of satiric comments and his full run of lively character types continually threaten to overload and destroy the connecting story and turn it into a formless plot. Obviously, Davis had more places and figures than his already swollen beads could easily contain.

Although Davis's meandering plot bothered some critics and readers, the tone of *Honey in the Horn* may have raised even more controversy. Flooding over with hyperbole and satire, the novel lampoons the Babbitry and boosterism Davis saw widely displayed among Oregon homesteaders. As Davis's sardonic narrator repeatedly observes, life in Oregon had been too easy; carefree, lazy newcomers lived off nature's generosity, and they were little interested in staying around, putting down roots, and working out settled, unified communities. Too busy sticking their noses into the affairs of their neighbors, unwilling to stand up to the demands of pioneer life, and lacking the courage of tightly held convictions, Oregonians seem satisfied to rove, to drift on to new settings and occupations.

The main characters, Clay and Luce, try to lay out their uncertain route among these troubling experiences and troubled wanderers. At first the young couple seem thrown together before they understand the demands of commitment, to themselves and others. The slightest upsets and disappointments lead to disputes and unsympathetic attacks, and when Luce suffers a miscarriage and Clay rides to secure help for her, she warns him that his leaving will bring permanent separation. Separation does occur, accompanied by doubts and hesitations aplenty. But the teenagers also do some maturing. When unexpected circumstances throw them together again, they are older and wiser. Now they better understand their needs and seem ready to rely on one another—and in the closing scene they join a community ready to establish itself. Davis hints at, although recalcitrant man that he was he might not have agreed, that commitment and community-building challenge all humans. That theme, at the center of Davis's first novel, remained a major ingredient of his later stories and novels.

The strong sales of *Honey in the Horn* brought quick recognition and shored up finances, but the remuneration did not solve other lingering problems. Davis's dealings with his publisher Harper had descended into a decade-long vitriolic controversy over contract terms. As a result, the publication of Davis's second novel, *Harp of a Thousand Strings* (1947), was delayed for more than a decade. Although the royalties from Harper and his prize money allowed Davis to buy a small ranch in northern California, the absence of a new novel and fresh royalties for ten years forced him to take work as a researcher—and part-time script-writer—for one or two Hollywood movie companies. Not surprisingly, Davis loathed the necessary work. Meanwhile, his marriage, continuing to crumble, ended in divorce in 1943.

Then things seemed to turn. He found a new publisher in William Morrow, and with aid of that more accepting publisher, new novels came: *Beulah Land* (1949) and *Winds of Morning* (1952), the latter of which some consider even superior in merit to *Honey in the Horn*. In 1953, Davis married Elizabeth Tonkin Martin del Campo of San Antonio, and the couple moved to Mexico. Unfortunately, Davis's health, always precarious, worsened, and heightened arteriosclerosis led to the amputation of a leg. Throughout his ever-present health challenges, Davis continued to write, with the appearance of a collection of stories in *Team Bells Awoke Me* (1953), another novel *The Distant Music* (1957), and a collection of essays, *Kettle of Fire* (1959). But Davis's weakened heart finally gave way, and he died of a heart attack in 1960.

Many observers correctly cite H. L. Davis's *Honey in the Horn* as the epitome of regional literature in the Pacific Northwest. In that first novel Davis provided a model of what front-rank regional fiction could be: a provocative combination of one's personal experiences and knowledge of a region's past that avoided the straightjacket formulas of the popular Western. After nearly eighty years, *Honey in the Horn* stands as the first nationally important novel published in the Oregon Country.

Suggested Readings

Bain, Robert. *H. L. Davis*. Western Writers Series, No. 11. Boise, ID: Boise State University, 1974.

Booth, Brian, and Glen A. Love, eds. *Davis Country: H. L. Davis's Northwest*. Corvallis: Oregon State University Press, 2009.

Bryant, Paul T. *H. L. Davis*. Boston: Twayne Publishers, 1978.

H. L. Davis: Collected Essays and Short Stories. Moscow: University of Idaho Press, 1986.

Etulain, Richard W. *Re-imagining the Modern American West: A Century of Fiction, History, and Art*. Tucson: University of Arizona Press, 1996.

Kellogg, George. "H. L. Davis, 1896–1960: A Bibliography." *Texas Studies in Language and Literature* 5 (summer 1963): 294–303.

Love, Glen A. "Stemming the Avalanche of Tripe: Or, How H. L. Mencken and Friends Reformed Northwest Literature." *Thalia* 4 (spring-summer 1981): 321–40.

The bulk of H. L. Davis's manuscripts are on file in the Harry Ransom Center at the University of Texas Library in Austin.

". . . He met her in the lane and he laid her on a board
And he played her up a tune called *Sugar in the Gourd,*
Sugar in the gourd, honey in the horn,
Balance to your partners, honey in the horn. . . ."

NOTE

ALL of the characters in this book are fictitious, and all of the incidents are either imagined or taken from very old legends of the country. Some of the geographical names are real, but they are in general altered as to topography and location so that residents of the country will readily understand that they do not refer to any real places. None of the incidents are autobiographical, and there is no intention anywhere in the book of offering social criticism or suggesting social reform.

I had originally hoped to include in the book a representative of every calling that existed in the State of Oregon during the homesteading period—1906-1908. I had to give up that idea, owing to lack of space, lack of time, and consideration for readers. Within the limits set me, I have done my best.

H. L. D.

Chapter I

THERE was a run-down old tollbridge station in the Shoestring Valley of Southern Oregon where Uncle Preston Shiveley had lived for fifty years, outlasting a wife, two sons, several plagues of grasshoppers, wheat-rust and caterpillars, a couple or three invasions of land-hunting settlers and real-estate speculators, and everybody else except the scattering of old pioneers who had cockleburred themselves onto the country at about the same time he did. The station, having been built in the stampeding days when people believed they were due for great swarms of settlement and travel around them, had a great many more rooms and a whole lot more space than there was any use for; and so had the country behind it. Outside the back fence where the dishcloths were hung to bleach and the green sheeppelts to cure when there was sun was a ten-mile stretch of creek-meadow with wild vetch and redtop and velvet-grass reaching clear to the black-green fir timber of the mountains where huckleberries grew and sheep pastured in summer and young men sometimes hid to keep from being jailed.

The creek-meadow in season was full of flowers—wild daisies, lamb-tongues, cat-ears, big patches of camas lilies as blue as the ocean with a cloud shadowing it, and big stands of wild iris and wild lilac and buttercups and St. John's wort. It was well-watered—too blamed well in the muddy season—and around the springs were thickets of whistle-willow and wild crabapple; and there were long swales of alder and sweetbrier and wild blackberry clumped out so rank and heavy that, in all the years the valley had been settled, nobody had ever explored them all. When the natural feed in the mountains snowed under late in the year, deer used to come down and graze the swales and swipe salt from the domestic stock; and blue grouse and topknot-quail boarded in all the brush-piles and thorn-heaps by the hundreds all the year round.

It was a master locality for stock-raising, as all good game countries are. Why the old settlers had run stock on it for so many years without getting more out of it than enough to live on would

1

have stumped even a government bulletin to explain. They did get a good living regularly, even in times when stock-raisers elsewhere were wearing patched clothes, shooting home-reloaded cartridges, and making biscuits out of hand-pounded wheat. But in the years when those same localities were banking and blowing in great hunks of money on hardwood-floored houses and coming-out parties for the youngsters and store-bought groceries and candidacies for the Legislature for the voting males, the old people up Shoestring went right on living at their ordinary clip, neither able to put on any extra dog in the good times nor obliged to lank down and live frugal in the bad ones.

None of the Shoestring settlers had much of a turn for practical business, probably because living came so easy that they had never needed to develop one. What they had developed, probably unconsciously and certainly without having a speck more use for it, was a mutual oppositeness of characters; and it had changed them from a rather ordinarily-marked pack of restless young Western emigrants with nothing about any of them except youth and land-fever, to an assortment of set-charactered old bucks as distinct from one another in tastes, tempers, habits, and inclinations as the separate suits of a deck of cards.

Not that there was anything especially out of line about that. There used to be plenty of communities where old residenters, merely by having looked at one another for years on end, had become as different as hen, weasel, and buzzard. But the fact that the thing was common didn't make it explain any faster, and the Shoestring settlement's case was harder because the men's characters were so entirely different and all their histories so precisely alike. They had all started even, as adventurous young men in an emigrant-train; they had gone through the same experiences getting to Oregon, had spread down to live in the same country, had done the same work, and had collogued with the same set of neighbors over the same line-up of news and business all their lives long. It looked as if they had treated the human range of superficial feelings to the same process of allotment that they had used on the valley itself, whacking it off into homestead enclosures so each man could squat on a patch of his own where the others would be sure not to elbow him.

They had, of course, done no such fool thing. It was more likely merely something that had happened to them. Whatever it was, they had all come in for it, and it made both monotony and complications of character among them impossible. As far as personality went, they were each one thing, straight up and down and the same color all the way through. Grandpa Cutlack, who lived on Boone Creek nearest the mouth of the valley, ran entirely to religion, held family prayer with a club handy to keep the youngsters from playing hooky on the services, and read his Scriptures with dogged confidence that he would one day find out from them when the world was going to end. He was a short, black-eyed man with bow-legs and an awful memory for smutty expressions, which were continually slipping into his conversation in spite of him, and even into his prayers.

Next up the valley beyond him lived Phineas Cowan, whose inclinations, in spite of his advanced age, were lustful and lickerous. He had begotten half-breed children enough to start a good-sized town, kept squaws distributed around the country so that he could ride for two weeks without doubling his tracks a single mile or sleeping alone a single night, and was still willing to tie into any fresh one who failed to outrun him. Then came Orlando Geary, a tremendous man with a pot belly, a dull marbly eye, and a bald head so thick that getting the simplest scrap of information through it required the patience of a horse-breaker. Not having imagination enough to be afraid of anything, he was always retained to make arrests, serve legal papers, and sit up at night with dead people. He was also one of the several dozen early-day men about whom it was told that he had gone out single-handed after a bunch of horse-thieving Indians, and that he not only brought back all the horses, but also the Indian chief's liver, which he ate raw as a sort of caution to the surviving redskins not to do that again.

Beyond his place was a strip of open country, and then came a clearing which belonged to Pappy Howell, who promoted horse-races and gambled on them. Next to that was a deserted two-story ranchhouse where Deaf Fegles had killed himself in a drunk by jumping out of an upstairs window to get away from some imaginary snakes; and next to that a measly two-room cabin with a pole-and-puncheon roof which was Joel Hardcastle's. His passion was thrift, and he was so close and careful about saving money that he had never got round to making himself any. His was the last place up the valley except the toll-bridge station on Little River that was Uncle Preston Shiveley's.

The station was not of Uncle Preston's founding or construction. He was the scholar of the community, with a great swad of intellectual interests like writing and inventing and experimenting with plants and minerals and historical research, and no concern whatever about anything so low as charging a wayfarer a round dollar to cross a river on a home-made bridge. But he had taken the station over ready-built by marrying the original proprietor's daughter, and he ran it, even when it interfered with his more serious work, as a sort of tribute to her memory. On it, by way of reminding posterity that he skirmished that ground too, he had planted an apple-orchard, built up a band of coarse-wooled sheep, and raised a couple of bad-acting sons who got drunk, fought and trained around with thieving half-breeds until, to keep from being distracted from his studies by the neighborhood rows they got into, he called in Orlando Geary and had them formally kicked off his property for good.

None of Uncle Preston's studies had ever brought him in the worth of a mule's heel full of hay, but he was death on anything that distracted him from them. He had been known, while trying to write up a pamphlet on his pioneer memories, to sit watching a coyote chase three valuable lambs right up to the barnyard fence without lifting pen from paper until the women disturbed him by yelling for somebody to do something quick. Then he got up and killed the coyote with a shotgun; and, to make it strictly fair all the way round, he also killed the three lambs for having got themselves where a coyote could bushwhack them, and for bringing their troubles in to bother him with. He was a short man with long arms and tremendous shoulders and an alert glary eye like a fighting horse, and he was full of tall principles of justice about human rights and the sacredness of privacy. Horning in on a man's time, he argued, was stealing, and ought to be punished as such; and when his two sons got drunk and decided to come back on him after he had evicted them, he got permission from the district court to buckshot the pair of them the minute they set foot on his premises. They stayed away from him after that, a matter of ten years, un-

til one of them killed the other in a fight and took to the brush with
a reward up for his scalp with or without the ears attached. Uncle
Preston buried the dead son, closed up their house and hauled off
their furniture and effects, and gave the Indian woman they had
been living with twenty dollars to go home. Then he went back to
writing a history of the early statutes of Oregon, and he was still
at it in the fall when a fierce flood of early rain drowned the
country, hoisted the river clear up to the toll-bridge deck-planks,
and caught all his sheep to hellangone in the mountains with only
about a nine-to-eleven chance of getting out.

Even to a country accustomed to rain, that was a storm worth
gawking at. It cracked shingles in the roof, loaded the full-fruited
old apple-trees until they threatened to split apart, and beat the
roads under water belly-deep to a horse. Ten-foot walls of spray
went marching back and forth across the hay-meadow as if they
owned it, flocks of wild ducks came squalling down to roost in the
open pasture till the air cleared, and the river boiled yellow foam
over the toll bridge and stumps, fence rails, pieces of old houses,
and carcasses of drowned calves and horses against it. Uncle Preston sat locked in an old upstairs storeroom writing his history, and,
about dark, the young housekeeping girl got tired of being scared all
by herself and climbed the stairs to tell him how much of his property he had better get ready to see the last of. The sheep hadn't
been heard from and were probably stuck up in the mountains to
die; the toll bridge had slipped downstream two feet and promised
more; a couple of apple-trees had split at the forks; the house itself was not exactly as safe as the ark, because one of the trees
was liable to fall on it and cave in the roof.

"If it caves in we'll move to the barn," said Uncle Preston
through the door. "If it don't, I'll finish this chapter here. Did I hear
a wagon on the road toward Round Mountain awhile back?"

She said the roads were so bad no wagon could be out in them.
Then a tree cracked horribly and scared her downstairs; and he
went back to his writing. His chapter was about the first violation
of the state statute against polygamy. The transgressor had been,
not a Mormon, as one might have supposed, but an Indian in the
Kettle River country who was suspected of murdering a white
packer. There was no proof against him, but somebody discovered

that he had six wives, so they arrested him for that, and, camping overnight on the way in with him, burned him with a red-hot ram-rod till he got up and ran. Since that was legally an attempt to escape, they shot him, which was what he had coming in the first place. It proved that the old days had enforced justice strictly in spite of their roughness and offhandedness, and Uncle Preston hauled his books together and wrote fiercely to get done before the apple-tree fell in on the roof. It let out a crack like an explosion and came down somewhere with a thump that jolted the whole house, and the housekeeping girl climbed the stairs again.

"It fell," she said, breathing short. "It smashed through the granary. And they're burning the signal fire down on Round Mountain. A mile high, it looks like. But they've changed it and I can't tell what it means."

"You can, but you want an excuse to tell me about it," said Uncle Preston. Everybody in the country had been warned that a fire on Round Mountain would mean Wade Shiveley's tracks had been picked up and that the people in Shoestring were to look out for him. Everybody had expected that he would head back into the valley sometime because it was country he was most familiar with. It was almost a relief to know that it had happened at last. "He won't come here," said Uncle Preston. "If he does, I'll shoot him, and he knows it. You know it bothers me to hear about him when I'm writin', so what do you come hintin' around about him for?"

"There was to be only one fire if he came this way," said the girl, leaning against the door. The hallway was dark, with a lonesome smell of bitterish willow-bark that the rain had crushed outside. "There's two fires, right alongside of one another. I can't tell what they mean. And the sheep aren't in yet. I tried to send the Indian boy out to look for them, but he wouldn't go. He sassed me."

Uncle Preston said to let the sheep go to hell and let the Indian boy alone. In the old days, two fires on Round Mountain had meant that some lost youngster had been found and that all the searching-parties could knock off looking for him and come in. But no youngsters got lost any more—none, at least, that anybody wanted to find again—so what it probably meant was that Wade Shiveley had done something else. Not but what it seemed wasteful to light fires over an ordinary course-of-nature episode like that. If people held an illumination every time his son cut another notch in his hell-stick, the country's supply of standing timber would be used up before the lumber companies got round to stealing it. "Whatever he's been up to, he won't bother us," said Uncle Preston. "You can go on back—" He stopped, and the front legs of his chair hit the floor with a thump. Two horses were wading the wet leaves under the dripping apple-trees. "Go and see who that is. If it's him, shine a lamp through the back door so I can git a sight on him when he lights down. Damn his soul, I told him I'd shoot him if he come botherin' me at work!"

She came back and reported with her voice panicky; but it was only two herders from the sheep, after all. What jumped her was that the sheep were down at the edge of the timber, drowning, and the two men had given up and come in to find out about the fires on Round Mountain. The third herder, a drip-nosed youth whom Uncle Preston had inherited from his sons' abandoned household, was staying with them through ignorance and contrariness, but it was no use sending anybody to help him. When sheep decided to go down, they stayed down, and any effort to reason them out of it would be simply elbow-grease gone to hell.

Uncle Preston took it as if dropping four thousand dollars' worth of mutton down a mudhole was an everyday operation. "Well, we won't have 'em to winter," he said. "Go get supper and let me finish this chapter before some goddamned thing does happen. You men didn't hear a wagon on the road half an hour ago, did you?"

Chapter II

UNCLE PRESTON's list of intellectual interests ranged far outside the pioneer history he was muling away his time on. He knew Latin, and had books by authors like Sallust and Suetonius and Cicero and Leviticus which he could rip off by the nautical mile. He had high-toned truck by Hume and Jeremy Bentham and Volney and Gibbon as easy at his tongue's end as his own whiskers, and he could invent mathematical problems about the area grazed by a calf picketed on a ten-foot rope to a three-foot tree that nobody could work except himself. He had written a novel-length romance about that very neighborhood in which an Indian chief's daughter ran off with a high-strung young warrior from a hostile tribe, and how, when the vengeful pursuers were closing in, she hove herself over a bluff to keep from being parted from the man of her choice. It was founded on solid statistics, too. An Indian woman in the early days had gone over a promontory on Little River, though some of the older Indians claimed she got drunk and fell over, and a few mountain men told it that her parents backed her over, not to prevent her marriage, but in an effort to hold her down while they washed her feet.

Besides the romance, which was called *Wi-ne-mah: A Tale of Eagle Valley*, he had turned off a considerable raft of poetry. Most of it was for use in autograph albums, and was on the order of "May your joys be as deep as the ocean, your sorrows as light as its foam"; but there were also pieces in which he had got mad and cut loose against retail merchants in town when, to his notion, they had dealt a little closer with him than they should have:

> Oakridge is a pretty little ring;
> I say damn the whole damn thing.
> John S. Chance and R. C. Young
> And the whole damn bunch ought to be hung.

It lacked finish, but it helped his feelings. Probably it didn't miss the truth such a vast distance, either, for they were hard traders

8

in Oakridge, bred and nourished in the faith that old settlers had been put there by Divine Providence to be trimmed. But writing was only one of Uncle Preston's excuses to keep busy when he should have been licking lambs and midwifing ewes, and the fact that he didn't stay with it long was one reason that he pelted to it with such red-eyed devotion when he came back to it. With the same hell-bent consecration to research, he had invented a medicated soap-powder that would heal burns and poison oak. He had experimented diligently with native herbs and had discovered several that would make him sick, though none that would cure anything. He had the power, right in his own person, of charming away warts, and a man afflicted with the blasted things had only to mention the fact to Uncle Preston to have them disappear, leaving the afflicted member as smooth as a cat's stem-end. He had experimented with tobacco-culture and had produced several sample plugs of home-grown leaf, a sort of stagnant green in color and so rank in taste that even the Indians refused to risk their health by chewing it. He could play dance tunes on the violin, and call the figures with a wealth of lively new expressions that kept people alleman-lefting and do-se-doing till their ligaments atrophied, to hear what turn of phrase he had cooked up to order the next manœuver in.

Public-spiritedness about children who had been left orphaned or abandoned was another of Uncle Preston's off-and-on interests. He hadn't been able to raise the two sons of his own get to be anything but quarrel-picking drunks and community nuisances, but that didn't hinder his streaks of adopting loose youngsters to try his system on again. Mostly it consisted of turning them loose to range his premises as they pleased, and mostly it worked pretty successfully. A couple of his adoptions were children of a hired man who had died, people alleged, of trying to chew his experimental plug tobacco. They stayed in town during the wet season, going to school and behaving themselves as pious and scholarly as a lantern-slide lecturer on the Holy Land.

Another adoption was an Indian kid of about thirteen, with less behavior and more story to him. He belonged to a little community of fish-eating Athapascans in the lower valley, and he had been born with an extra finger on each hand. Among the Athapascans of Southern Oregon, it was an article of religion to destroy all deformed children at birth, and the youngster's mother had only managed to save him out by wrapping his hands in buckskin and pretending that they had been burned. The stall worked all right until a traveling missionary showed up, convoked a sort of mother's meeting in the tribe, and insisted on taking the bandages off to see what the burns looked liked and whether they needed medical treatment. He then left, after lecturing the squaw severely on the naughtiness of telling falsehoods; and she gathered the youngster up and carried him eighty miles across the mountains to Uncle Preston's station before the rest of the women could spread the news of her deception and organize a drowning-party in the interest of tribal eugenics. She never went back to the tribe, which got pretty thoroughly killed off in a measles epidemic not long after; and, though she lived with Uncle Preston's two sons until they swapped her to a sheep-shearing crew for a second-hand pistol, she never came back to see the youngster, either.

As well she didn't, for, probably because he was raised with whites, he grew up ten times more fanatical about Indian culture than any wickyup buck in the country. Everything the fish-eating settlement had ever believed in he believed, too, even to the by-law which had decreed his own extermination. He refused to have any truck with his mother because she lived with white men and because her saving his life had been in some way responsible for the tribe coming down with the measles. He wore his hair braided into a coon-tail on his chest, refused to wear shoes or go to school, and spent hours in the haymow, tootling tribal melodies into a flute made out of the drumstick of a turkey.

He was an unsociable little pint of willow-juice, with no friends among his own people because they blamed him for their tribal bad luck and wouldn't have him, and none among the whites because he wouldn't have them. One thing that made him worth keeping was his ability to handle horses, which few Indians of that country had. A colt in his charge never needed wearing down in the bucking-pen. Two days alone with the Indian youngster, during which nothing happened that anybody could see, and the animal would lead out as tame as a toy wagon and walk off under a saddle without even looking around to see what the blamed thing was. Besides horse-breaking, he amused himself in good weather by potting big red-headed woodpeckers in the brush because their scarlet top-knots had once passed among his people for money. When it rained he sat in the barn with the horses and practiced playing his flute by sniffling into it through his nose; and what happened to the station or any of the people on it cut no more figure with him than the tariff on beeswax or the new men's styles in embroidered suspenders.

The newest of Uncle Preston's adoptions was Clay Calvert, and he was the drip-nosed youth of about sixteen who had gone with the sheep to the mountains and refused to quit them and come in when the herders did. He had a knob-jointed godforsakenness of expression about him, and a mean-spoken sassiness that kept people from being pleasant to him even when they wanted to. Partly it was because he had been raised with people who didn't want to be pleasant, and partly because he had discovered that he could head off conversation about his personal history by being offensive with his personal character. His mother had borne him in some fence-corner, and when he was six years old had taken him with her while she cooked for an outfit of harvest-campers. The harvesters broke up in a row somewhere near the bush cabin where Uncle Preston's two sons lived, and she stopped off and married one of them—which one nobody had ever felt interested enough to look up. She hung on for nearly four years with them and then died, and her youngster stayed on with their fighting and helling and squaw-rolling for six years more, until the shooting. Then Uncle Preston closed the bush cabin up and took him home; and he got in a row with the housekeeping girl and the Indian youngster before he had been there two days. Both of them had taken the notion that he was only to stay there until the court decided what to do with him. He had set his head on living there a long time, and maybe for good, because it was the first place he had ever seen where things ran quietly and solidly. So, having called the Indian boy a grasshopper-eating Siwash and the housekeeping girl Pop-eyes, he went to the mountains with the sheep, where he could use all the hard language he wanted to without hurting anybody's feelings.

The housekeeping girl, who was Drusilla Birdsall, was the last on the list of Uncle Preston's adoptions. In point of time she had been on it longer than anybody else, for she was rubbing sixteen and her parents had been drowned fording a creek in the fall rains before she was old enough to talk. She was blond, round-faced, and not popeyed in the least, though she did swell and bulge a little in spots when she was excited. Another and unluckier failing was that when anything worked deeply on her emotions, her insides would register the fact by rumbling audibly. It prevented her from having anything to do with young men because the more she felt drawn to one the more distinctly she sounded as if her inwards were falling down a flight of stairs. Since it was a choice between repressing her natural instincts and feeling ridiculous, she let the instincts go over the tailboard and turned herself all over, from the heels as far up as she went, into a feeling of responsibility for the station. The loss of the sheep hurt her like a bereavement. She blamed Clay Calvert for it, because no sheep had ever been lost until he went along to help herd. That, by ordinary logic and considerable childishness in applying it, meant that he must be responsible. The two hired herders she didn't blame at all. They had never lost sheep before, and they had always done as she ordered without sassing back. She helped them guess about the meaning of the fires on Round Mountain while she rustled their supper.

The supper was all everyday victuals, but there were plenty of them. There was fried deer-liver with onions, a little greasier than it needed to be; beefsteak, excellent cuts but infernal cooking, with all the juice fried out and made into flour-and-milk gravy; potatoes, baked so the jackets burst open and showed the white; string beans, their flavor and nutritive value well oiled with a big hunk of salt pork; baked squash soaked in butter; a salad of lettuce whittled into shoestrings, wilted in hot water, and doped with vinegar and bacon grease; tomatoes stewed with dumplings of cold bread; yellow corn mowed off the cob and boiled in milk; cold beet-pickles, a jar of piccalilli, and a couple of panloads of hot sourdough biscuits. For sweets there were tomato preserves, peach butter, wild black-cap jam, and wild blackberry and wild crabapple jelly. For dessert there was a red-apple cobbler with lumpy cream, and two kinds of pie, one of blue huckleberry, the other of red. The country fed well, what with wild game and livestock and gardens, milk and butter and orchards and wild fruits; and no man was ever liable to starve in it unless his digestion broke down from overstrain. When the table was set, Drusilla went upstairs and called Uncle Preston. He was writing like the devil beating tanbark, his chair creaking like a walking-beam as he followed his pen across the paper and then reached to stab it into the ink-bottle, and he explained that he was in the middle of walloping home the moral of his chapter. He would rather eat cold victuals than look at the sheep-herders' table manners anyhow, so they had better go ahead and eat without him.

They were doing it, and he was still peeling off the snapper-end of his chapter, when a wagon pulled up to the carriage-block in front of the station. Two half-dead horses were on the pole, and they sagged down in the deep leaves, too fagged to need tying while two half-drowned men got out and came in without being asked. One was a dark, soft-featured little half-breed who was sometimes hired by the sheriff's office for hard trips because, though worthless for anything else, he could make horses go anywhere. He spread his hands to the stove, smiled apologetically as if he expected somebody to kick him, and began to steam dry. The other man was Orlando Geary. He wore a cartridge-belt with a gun, which meant that he was traveling on business, and, after a dullishly wistful invoice of the food on the table, he sloshed upstairs, mumbling to himself. Uncle Preston recognized his step and called his name and asked what was up; but he had his opening already made up, and he repeated it off as if he hadn't been spoken to.

"Press," he said. His voice was deep and mechanical, as if words were being blown through him by an outside blast of air. "This is Orlando Geary, Press. I'd like to see you downstairs a minute, if you ain't too busy."

He wanted, probably, to manœuver the conference down within range of the victuals in the dining-room. Uncle Preston refused to be so accommodating. "I'm a whole hell of a lot too busy," he said, without getting up. "What do you have to see me about? If it's got anything to do with Wade Shiveley, you're wastin' your time."

Old Geary took a heavy breath, rattled water on the floor from his wet clothes, and dug down after another prepared speech. "We want to see you about Wade Shiveley, Press," he recited. "He killed another man last night, it looks like. We found old Pappy Howell shot and layin' in the road yesterday mornin' on the way back from a horse-race. They claim he started from the racetrack with about eight hundred dollars on him. Wade's tracks was around him, so it looks like Wade killed him and took it."

"What do you want me to do?" said Uncle Preston. The news didn't seem to faze him. "Do you want me to help you find him? Talk, damn it! I got work to do."

Prepared speech number three sounded less as if it had hit the line of conversation by accident. Old Geary delivered it with one ear leaned downstairs for fear the noise of plates might mean that the table was being cleared. "This ain't got anything to do with arrestin' Wade Shiveley, Press," he said. "We wouldn't ask you to do that, on account of your natural feelin's. We don't need to, anyway, because we caught him ourselves this mornin'."

On the downstairs section, his artless announcement had about the same effect as if he had yanked the roof off the house and galloped away with it. Drusilla backed halfway through the kitchen door with one hand held over her mouth and her eyes dilated. The two sheepherders stared at one another, and Payette Simmons, the older of them, picked up a cream-pitcher and shook it carefully over his steak without noticing that it wasn't salt. None of them spoke, and even Uncle Preston was silent for some minutes. Then he brisked up. After all, he had never been able to do anything about his son, and there was still a lot that he could do on pioneer history if people would let him. "Well, you've got him, and as far as I'm concerned you can keep him," he said. "Did you swim all the creeks between here and town to tell me about it?"

Old Geary said no, there were three creeks that it hadn't been necessary to swim, and he had supposed lighting the old-time recall signal on Round Mountain would have told everybody about the capture. The thing was that the county jail was a little bit rickety to hold a man like Wade Shiveley, and the authorities had decided to ship him north to the state pen for safe-keeping until his trial. He had asked to talk to some one of his home people before his train left, and had mentioned Uncle Preston particularly.

The authorities favored the notion, figuring that, if he could talk out before a lawyer got to him, he might tell what he had done with old Howell's eight hundred dollars. Therefore, they had sent after Uncle Preston to come on the canter, and would he please get his coat and tell them where they could find fresh horses?

"I'll be damned if I go a step," said Uncle Preston. "I told Wade Shiveley a good long time ago that I didn't intend ever to see him again. You heard me, because you helped put him off the place. I've got work to do, and he's got no right to come botherin' me at it. Now you stand away from that door, Orlando, or I'll shoot the panels plumb through you!"

Old Geary stepped away from the door and stood dripping in the dark hallway. After five minutes, he tiptoed back. He hadn't been able to think up any offhanded reopening on such short notice, so he took the whole colloquy back where it had started from. "This is Orlando Geary, Press," he said, patiently. "I'd like to see you downstairs a minute. You've got a kid here that used to live with Wade Shiveley. I'll take him, if you'll fetch him for me."

Uncle Preston explained that Clay Calvert was out cheering the last hours of a band of sheep, and they would have to wait until he came in. "He'll be all beat out when he gets here, though, and he don't like Wade Shiveley any better than I do. If you yank him out for any all-night sashay on these roads, you ought to be ashamed of yourself."

"I ain't anxious to take him," said Orlando Geary, and edged toward the stairs. "I'll take you, if you'd ruther. We'll need some fresh horses."

Downstairs, he drew up to the table where the heat from the stove would strike him and hauled platters within reach of his fork. The two herders watched him enviously and wonderingly because he had caught Wade Shiveley and because of the forkfuls of food he was able to get his mouth around. He paid no attention when they volunteered that Clay Calvert was a hard-mouthed young hellfry who would undoubtedly make trouble about going to town. They themselves had bumped heads with him when they tried to persuade him to leave the sheep and come in with them. It was pure concern for his welfare, and instead of being grateful he had cussed and drawn a knife. Old Geary swallowed and wiggled his head in a double gesture of understanding and getting down a difficult mouthful.

The second herder, a long-necked man named Moss who turned all his gs into ds after the fashion of stump-country roustabouts, inquired how the doddam they had dot onto Wade Shiveley's tracks. He had been more than halfway planning to have a stab at the Wade Shiveley reward himself. There was a certain melancholy interest in hearing how it had been pulled from under his fingers. Old Geary cleaned his plate with a piece of bread, pulled the meat-platter close, and said well. "There was some buzzards circulatin' around the oak-grub country back of Roan's Mill," he stated, turning pieces of steak pensively. He had evidently told the story before, though the presence of food kept him from putting much spirit into it. "I laid somebody had been killin' a deer out of season, so I saddled up and paced over there to see what was left of the carcass. What's in this dish, preserves? So I hadn't any more than turned into the millroad when what did I see but the blood-curdlinest sight that— is everybody through with these string beans?—the blood-curdlinest mangled-up human corpse that a man ever laid eyes on. All shot up with a soft-nosed slug that had gone to pieces on the bone, and the rain and mud and all. Dogged if I didn't feel teetery to look at it. There ain't any hossradish to go on this meat, is there?"

Drusilla brought a saucer of fresh-scraped horseradish, and re-treated to the kitchen door, anxious to hear what had made him feel so teetery, but ready to leave if the recital got too strong for her. He horseradished his steak, ate a slice experimentally, and told on. The wet clay around the dead man held tracks, and some of them had been made by a horse with one broken shoe. He had no notion who it might belong to, but it made trailing easy. So with a few mill-hands to back him up, he followed it along into the mountains and up to a deserted trapline cabin. Wade Shiveley was in it. Getting him was no trouble, because they found him asleep. The money, of course, they didn't find. It was only after they got him in jail that they learned there had been any. But it was somewhere, and it was eight hundred dollars.

There was a difference in habits of thinking between the men of that deep-grassed old sweetbrier country and the women. It came out plainly when Orlando Geary pulled loose from the subject of the strayed eight hundred dollars. The two herders cheered up and lordamercied one another and talked about the amount of high-rolling a man could do who found where it was hidden. There was plenty of imagination among those stump-country men, because they had to depend on it for entertainment; but entertainment was all they ever got out of it. Putting it to grind on the meaning of life or man's mission to the universe or the problem of putting meat in the skillet was something they never thought of. They used it instead to picture the coming true of impossible make-believes and what-ifs that an ordinary roundhead would have been ashamed to squander his fancy on even in moments of desperation. They paid no attention when Orlando Geary reminded them that the money wasn't in the least likely to be found by them, and that when found it was not going to be spent on high-rolling, but turned over to the county authorities according to the law in such cases made and provided. To hear them talk, finding it would be no job at all, and the law would need a blamed sight more than making and providing to get it away from them when once they got hold of it.

Drusilla was a different cut of character. She didn't join in the herders' conversation. Carrying out empty dishes, she thought of the lost sheep and what the station was going to run on without its regular income from wool and lambs, and about Clay Calvert, who was elected to help the authorities find eight hundred dollars in cash, whether he wanted to or not. She brought a stack of hot biscuits to the table and put old Geary a question. "Suppose Clay does find out where the money is," she inquired, "and then suppose he won't tell you or show you anything about it? Suppose he digs it up himself and gives it to somebody or puts it in his wife's name or something? You couldn't make her give it back, could you?"

The problem was a little complicated for old Geary, but he handled it cleanly. "You mean that kid I'm a-takin' in?" he said, to have everything straight. "He ain't got any wife."

"He could mighty easy git one, with eight hunderd dollars in his hatband," said Payette Simmons. "Only he won't, because he won't go with you. He'll pull in here wet and tired and stubborn, and he'll balk and contrary you. I'll bet you money on it."

"He will, too, go!" Drusilla said. She shortened her neck challengingly. "He's no good around here except to lose sheep, and if he don't go Uncle Preston will have to. He's got to go. Don't you men put him up to hang back, either. If you do you'll never work for this station again, I'll promise you that!"

It was nothing to them whether he went or stayed. They promised not to put him up to anything, and then talked about Pappy Howell and the horse-race in which he had won eight hundred dollars and Wade Shiveley's foolishness in shooting him and leaving tracks. When Uncle Preston came down for his supper, they had the whole subject about talked out, so they dropped it and he told them stories about the country as he had found it when he was a young man packing a mule-train across the mountains to the Coast. While he talked, the rain stopped and the moon came out and plastered the great spread of soaked grass with foggy silver, so swift and blinding that the cattle came out of their shed and stood in it to see what it felt like. The big apple-trees around the house dripped so loud and threw such black shadows that nobody inside noticed the turn of weather until the Indian boy in the barn began tootling a sort of cat-fight tune on his turkey-bone flute to celebrate it.

About the middle of the tune—though it didn't have any middle that was exactly identifiable as such—they heard a tired horse come dragging through the deep apple-leaves. Orlando Geary took a last thundering swallow of something and got up to go out, but the two herders shook their heads and Drusilla motioned him back. It was Clay Calvert, all right, but they knew by the way his horse walked and by the way he slammed the barn door open without announcing himself, that he was packing a chip and hunting for somebody to knock it off on. Orlando Geary sat down again, and they waited while Uncle Preston told how he had come to inherit the toll-bridge station in the early days.

Chapter III

ON THE morning that the storm hit the sheep-camp in the mountains, a shortage of bedclothes waked Clay Calvert at the exact time when a big coyote paid a before-daylight visit to the sheep to purvey himself a feed of fresh mutton. It was a lucky circumstance, though at the time it didn't seem one, because the purveying process had such an outlandish half-dreamy solemnity about it that he stood and watched it from start to finish without interfering until the sheep was killed and the coyote settled down to load up on her carcass. But merely watching it that far made the mountain sheep-camp seem new and a little disagreeable, so that he didn't feel homesick about leaving; and he learned a couple or three things about the power of intelligence over instinct that stood him in hand a good many times afterward, not merely in handling animals, but in looking out for himself.

The sheep were bedded in a high mountain meadow that was half a swale of red wild snapdragons and half blue-flowering wild pea vine. There were a couple of square miles of open ground in it, walled on three sides by a stand of black fir timber that looked solid until you got within two yards of it, and on the fourth by a grove of mountain-ash saplings, fencing a chain of springs that were the headwaters of Little River. The sheep-camp was pitched close to the grove because it was handy to water; but the sheep insisted, principally because nobody wanted them to, upon picking open bed-ground in the middle of the meadow. There was no risk in it during the summer, but in the fall bears sometimes moseyed in to feed on the bitter scarlet berries of the mountain ash, and the herders took turns sleeping out with the sheep to see that they didn't get raided.

Guard duty was not burdensome in clear weather. A man didn't have to make any rounds or do any solitary vigils with his eyes propped open and a gun across his knees. He had only to keep his upper ear cocked for any unusual flurry or scuffling among the sheep, and to remember, whenever he turned over in his blankets, to reach out and lay a chunk or two of wood on the fire so it wouldn't go out. With a little practice one could do that without even waking up.

The herders kept a kind of off-and-on surveillance themselves when it was Clay's turn at it, because he was new to the responsibility; but they didn't watch one another because they were both veterans and touchy about it. Payette Simmons had herded sheep over thirty years, and Serphin Moss, the second herder, for considerably more than twenty. Between the pair of them, Clay got reminded of his inexperience and immaturity about every other time he turned round. It wasn't as if there had been any complicated mysteries about the business. The trouble was that they had both spent a good many more years learning it than their jobs were worth, and it hurt them to let on that anybody could acquire any understanding of it in less time than it had taken them. Their fussing and nosing and volunteering childish orders and supervising childish jobs made them hard to put up with. Clay got up with a chill when there was barely light enough in the tent to see by, and stole himself an extra blanket from old Moss. Before spreading it, he looked out the tent door and saw that the guard-fire was down to a couple of coals and that Payette Simmons had gone sound asleep with the bed-canvas pulled over his bald spot. The sheep were jammed together on account of the chill, and the close-packed yellowish fleeces pitched and heaved restlessly like the top of a forest catching the wind. Outside the pack, a few strays trotted uneasily, looking for an opening to crowd into. Not a sound came from them. They weren't wide awake enough to bawl, and their hoofs were cushioned on a couple of hundred years' accumulation of meadow-grass. The strays bored their way into the herd, which settled into drowsiness, with only one old ewe left moving around them at a worried sort of amble.

She raised her gait to a jog, glanced down at her side, and then put on still more speed, like an old lady being pursued by a cheap pitchman in the street. As she circled the herd she drew farther away from it, and, when her orbit brought her past the tent, Clay saw what ailed her. An old he-coyote was trotting beside her, his shoulder pressed against hers, holding a little back so she would keep trying to get ahead and rubbing her close so her shrinking from him would carry her out of range of the herd that she was working her best lick to get back to. He made no effort to hurry or hurt her; she was still so close to Simmons' guard-fire that he didn't dare to. If she had blatted or turned on him and started a rumpus, she would have been saved. But she was too scared to do anything but avoid him and try to outrun him. She trotted faster, and he let out another hitch of speed and rubbed her as if to remind her that he was still there. When they rounded the herd a second time, he had worked her a quarter of a mile away from it.

The promenade lasted a long time. Clay's legs hurt with cold. The light strengthened, and the sky bloomed full of light rose places where the dawn hit the bellies of black clouds. The sheep and the coyote trotted their round solemnly, pressed close like a pair of small-town lovers on Sunday afternoon, without noticing the daylight or each other. They went behind a stand of tall blue-joint grass, and Clay leaned a pack-saddle against the tent-pole and climbed on it to keep sight of them. When he picked them out, they had stopped. The sheep stood with her legs spraddled and her head dropped so it almost touched the ground, and the coyote stood watching her and waiting for her to look up. There was still time for Clay to have scared him off. A yell would have done it. But he held in because he didn't want to face a lifetime of wondering what the coyote had intended to do next, and because if he stopped the killing Simmons and Moss would claim it was all a yarn he had made up himself. He leaned against the tent-pole and waited, knowing perfectly what was going to happen, but willing to freeze his very liver to see how.

It was scarcely worth waiting for. As ceremonious as the preparation had been, the slaughter happened with no ceremony at all. The sheep lifted her head and the coyote trotted close and cut her throat with one swift open-fanged swipe. She knelt, folding her knees under her a good deal like the Lamb in pictures of the Holy Family, and died. It was so simple and she was so quiet about it that it scarcely seemed a finish to anything. But it was one, as the coyote proceeded to demonstrate sickeningly and unquestionably. He took a good long look around, and then dropped his muzzle and lapped the fresh blood under the sheep's chin.

The motion, as far as the coyote was concerned, was merely one of cashing in on a good morning's work. But it knocked the pictorial stateliness of the preliminaries plumb in the head. Clay didn't want to watch it, but he couldn't keep his eyes off it. To put a stop to it so he could go back to bed and get warm, he reached down Moss's rifle from the tent-pole and threw down and shot.

He didn't look at the sights, because he scarcely cared whether he hit the coyote or not. All he wanted was to make the brute leave. But the gun was a specially stocked one that Moss had bought for winter fur-gathering, and it handled so beautifully that it didn't need aiming. The bullet drove center with a smack. The coyote bounced a couple of feet in the air and hit the ground with his legs jerking slowly like a piece of machinery running down. The ordinary marksman's impulse would have been to gallop across and see where the bullet had connected and what damage it had done. Clay hung the rifle back on the tent-pole and climbed down from the pack-saddle. He wished he hadn't shot at all, because, in the moment that he pulled trigger, the coyote reminded him of Wade Shiveley, whom he had imagined he was shut of for good.

Both herders woke up at the shot. Serphin Moss reared up against the tent roof and grabbed his boots, yelling at old Simmons, who he supposed had done the shooting, to inquire what the dod-damn it was and whether he had dot it. Moss was long-faced and candid-looking, with an expression which long years of herding had subdued almost to what he worked with. He looked so much like a sheep himself that when he opened his mouth you half expected him to blat, and he generally half did it. Payette Simmons was an older man with a considerably better flow of language, though he didn't use it for much except to tell lies with. On ordinary occasions he talked faster than Moss, but in emergencies he didn't talk at all. He bounced up from beside the dead guard-fire, his bald head shining in the cold light, his shirt-tail flapping on his bare stern, and his gray whiskers hackled up behind the sights of his rifle, which he pointed at the tent under the foggy-minded impression that somebody in it had taken a shot at him. Clay gave him no chance to get his head back in working order. When Simmons' thoughts were all hitting the collar together, he could lie himself out of a three-ton safe.

"You can go back under the blankets if you want to, Santa Claus," Clay told him. "It ain't Christmas yet. A coyote just got a sheep, and I got him. Lucky you had your head covered, or he'd have eat your nose off."

He would have had Simmons cured of ordering him around for life if Moss hadn't stuck himself in the tent door to take a hand in gouging it into him. "Yes, pile on back into bed, for Dod's sake," he chipped in, all hearty and sarcastic. "Dit through dreamin' about them doddam women, or you'll lose us every tockwallopin' sheep we doddam well dot."

According to Simmons' own representations, which he spun off by the mile when he felt good, he was a considerable hand as a stud. His gray whiskers didn't match up with his claims, but he explained that they had been caused by the strain of watching women try to kill themselves over him. He also had one lop-lidded eye which, by his account, had been disabled by a female lodge-organizer to keep other women from falling in love with him. He could invent windies about his stand-in with the girls faster than a turkey could gobble grasshoppers. None of them had much truth to them, probably, for he passed among the stump-country roustabouts as a man who spent his leisure in Mother Settle's straddling-house talking about sheep-herding, and his work-season in the sheep-camp talking about the women who had hung onto his shirt-tail to keep him from abandoning them. Seniority made him the boss herder, and Moss had managed, by chesting his own authority down on Clay Calvert, to get himself resigned to it; but he still didn't believe that it was right. Moss himself was too bashful to patronize Mother Settle's riding-academy, and played the more expensive game of getting himself a wife through the Heart and Hand matrimonial bureau as often as he could afford it for as long as she could stand him. It came to about the same thing when you fractioned it down; but the fact that Moss spent his money on marriage brokers and preachers and divorce lawyers meant, to his notion, that he was moral and deserving of responsibility. Simmons squandered his on Mother Settle in smaller instalments, which meant that he was impure and shameless. Could anything be better proof of it than his having lost a sheep on a worn-out old coyote-trick? Moss thought not. "That's a hell of a fine fire you been teepin' up out there, ain't it?" he inquired, sarcastic and glad of the chance. "Dit back into bed or else put your pants on. You ain't on Front Street in town."

That was piling it on too thick. Instead of making Simmons meek and humble, it made him mad, and it started the day off in a row with Moss and Simmons digging on each other, and Clay, who had started the whole thing, shoved back into the position of referee; not that his opinion amounted to anything, but because it was the only one they had handy to work on. Simmons climbed into his pants, ordered the dead sheep skinned before the meat got to tasting of wool, and added that the next man he heard any back-talk from had better get ready to draw his time and walk home. Then he winked at Clay to indicate that the threat didn't apply to him and made a vulgar gesture with his fingers toward Moss which was Indian sign-talk to denote a simpleton who ran off at the mouth. Moss didn't get that, but he muttered confidential opinions about Simmons' debauched character and crumbling intellect all the way out to the dead sheep and all the time they were working the hide loose.

They were skinning out the forelegs when a few flakes of snow fell on the warm stripped meat between them, and Simmons yelled to them to give it up and run in the horses. They were going to pull camp and move before the storm hit, and there was no time to fool around about it. The air was as dark as twilight, and tree outlines a mile away had gone out in a black smudge like something scrubbed off a slate. But even in that Moss found an excuse to bellyache, because they had been hectored off to pelt out a dadblasted forty cents' worth of second-rate mutton when any doddamned fool might have known that there was a snowstorm working down on them.

The horses were forehobbled and easy to catch, and Simmons had the beds rolled and the canvas *alforjas* packed by the time they came crow-hopping in. The sheep needed only to be lined out and started moving, because the coyote had bunched them as competently as any herd-dog could have done. Each man singed a mammock of mutton on a stick and ate it in the empty tent, and then they struck

and rolled it. It seemed almost like stripping something naked to
expose the square of brown earth where they had come for meals
and sleep and rest and shelter until, because it was used for a different purpose, it had got to seem a different species of ground
from anything around it. Turning it back out-of-doors showed how
little difference their living on it had made, after all. None, except
that they had worn the grass down so the whirl of snowflakes
turned it white while the deeper-grown meadow was still only a
brindlish gray.

There was a good deal of cussing and yelling and chasing around
about leaving, but there was no regretfulness. The herders had
done it too many times, and they knew too well what they were
getting out of. A storm so near the summit of the mountains could
pile up snow from six to ten feet deep. As for Clay Calvert, the
place was spoiled for him. The sheep-killing and the dead coyote
had turned him against it. He felt every minute as if he was breathing a wind off Wade Shiveley. Clay hadn't felt any overmastering
surge of affection for either of the Shiveley brothers, but he had
liked the one who got killed the best, and he felt scared and sick-
ened of Wade for having killed him.

They got the sheep moving with an hour's spanking and kicking
and screeching and throwing rocks while the snow thickened. Then
they lined the pack-horses in front and plodded across the clearing
into the dark wall of timber, leading their saddle-ponies behind.
When they looked back at the meadow, it had turned all white,
and nobody could have told that they had ever been there. Even
the dead ewe and the dead coyote were white humps that might
have been snowed-in bushes. There was an easy and reassuring feeling about knowing that they were being put out of sight so peacefully. Wildness had destroyed them; now it was getting to work
to cover up the mess and all the messes it had made during all that
year in the mountains. Deer crippled by cougars, wild cattle hurt
fighting among themselves, hawk-struck grouse, stiff-jointed old
dog-wolves waiting in some deep thicket for death to hit them and
get it over with. The snow would cover them, more snow would
fall and cover them deeper, and when spring came it would melt
and the freshets would carry what was left of them away. Even

the bones wouldn't last, because the little wood-mice would gnaw them down to the last nub.

They trailed down through heavy timber all that day, and made camp, when it was too dark to see, by spreading the tent over some huckleberry bushes and crawling under it. The sheep lay down in their tracks, too tired to browse, because deep pasture had put more tallow on their ribs than they were built to pack. The trail hadn't been particularly hard, because the snow hadn't yet started sliding from the trees into it. There was not room under the tent for more than one bed, so all three men slept in it, Clay in the middle and Moss and Simmons on the outside, squabbling and arguing back and forth across him. Whenever he tried to sleep, they would wake him up to prove something by; and when he stayed awake and ordered them to shut up they would ignore him completely. Moss maintained that the sheep were going to be lost and that it would be Simmons' fault for not having started them out sooner. Simmons insisted that he had started in plenty of time and that if he lost them it would be Moss's fault for throwing off on him.

The second day's trail was harder. Trees dripping turned the ground into red greasy mud, and horses kept going down in it and having to be unpacked before they could get up. There were also clearings where the snow had drifted in a couple of feet deep, and the sheep, whenever they struck one, would either break back for the timber or give up and lie down. The two herders had to kick them up and keep them moving while Clay broke a trail across for them. He chopped down a small fir tree, looped his rope into the top branches, and rode through, dragging it behind him. Where the snow was wet and heavy, he had to drag back and forth three or four times to wear off a track that the sheep would tackle, and the herders would be almost worn out with work before he was ready for them. They would come wallowing across with the sheep, slipping and falling and crawling and cussing one another in a kind of windbroken cackle as if they were getting ready to cry.

Nothing but personal ill-feeling could have made those two herders put in the work they did to keep the sheep moving. They cared nothing about the sheep or about old Shiveley, and they were legally assured of getting paid off, whether they came in with all the sheep or ten or none. But they wanted to work each other down, and they fought brush and climbed logs and fell into stump-holes and carried broken-down strays into line on their backs, and, at a couple of clearings where the herd got halfway out and balked, they simply got down and boosted, like a couple of logging-engines horsing a string of flats up a grade. By the second night they had got to the small-timber belt well down the mountain. They camped in a deserted post-camp on Plum Creek. The sheep lay in wet snow and went for another night without anything to eat. The next day they dropped below the snowstorm into hazel-brush country where it was raining, and the sheep began to take spells of balking and lying down on the open trail.

It was about time. For two days they had traveled without food, their wind and strength were shot and their fleeces water-soaked and loaded with mud till their bellies dragged their tracks. Half a mile of shoving through dripping brush and soapy mountain mud fetched them to the ground as if they had been clubbed, and no amount of heaving and hauling could get them up again until they had blown and rested. The two herders tried plenty of it, and Clay helped until he saw that they were working merely because neither wanted to be the first to quit. After that he sat under a bush with the horses when the herd stalled, and let the two bull-headed old reprobates have both the work and the argument to themselves. It was hard to tell which wasted the most time, but the argument gave them the most satisfaction. Simmons brought up the string-halted old story about one of Moss's Heart and Hand wives, who, after comparing him with the photograph he had sent her, chased him down the road with a grubbing-hoe, explaining to everybody she passed that she was going to fix his face to match his picture; and Moss recalled the time when Simmons had made one of Mother Settle's veteran boarders a birthday present of a pink silk corset, and that she had raised considerable hell around town about it because it was of a design intended to disguise impending maternity.

That was the worst day of all, and the worst night followed it. The fir timber got small and then changed into alder and willow.

About dark they dragged clear of that and struck open country, with a last streak of watery light breaking circles in the flooded stubble before them. Beyond was a rise, with the black rails of a stack-yard corral making a rib-bone pattern on the sky. The stage-station itself was maybe eight miles off, but it was all open going. They could see the yellow dot of a lamp in one of the windows, and Clay had to grab ropes and mill the pack-horses to keep them from stampeding for it. Even the sheep brisked up, broke line, and jounced into the water, ignoring the herders who tried to hold them and hunt up a shallow place to cross. Both men jumped in after them. Moss grabbed his chaps from his saddle and whacked heads, trying to drive them back before they got in too deep. Simmons yanked a limb off a tree and spanked tails with it to get them across with a rush before they got time to think how deep it was. Clay fought the horses to a standstill and jumped down to help, but he was too late. An old ewe let out a resigned blat and knelt, and, with the trustfulness of wild geese settling to a pond behind their leader in the night, the whole herd caved down around her. They lay still, with the muddy water swishing as it roiled round them and worked into their wool.

This time they meant it for keeps. Moss and Simmons flogged and kicked and whacked the water to scare them, and Clay tried throwing them out bodily. But the ones who were in stayed in, and the ones who got helped out simply came back in and lay down again. It was jesusly hard work, waist-deep in mud with the rain and dark and weariness. Nobody would have minded if it had shown signs of getting them anywhere, because it would have been something to brag about afterward; but it was all useless. The sheep had decided to die, and there was no way of scaring them out of the notion, because there was nothing worse that they could be scared with. Moss made the first break toward giving up, not because he wanted to, but because he was too tired to keep his balance. He fetched a wild swipe with his chaps, missed, and fell flat in the water with a splash like launching a ferryboat. Simmons dragged him to the bank and sat down with him. He needed a rest pretty bad himself, and Moss's breakdown made the time right to recommend one. He was diplomatic about it, because the least touch of twitting might sting Moss to get up and go at them again.

"No use killin' ourselves for nothing," he said, emptying mud out of his boots. "I hate to lose the blamed helpless idiots after the work we put in gittin' 'em this far, but churnin' 'em around in the mud won't help any. What do you think we better do?"

He hit the right tone and the right moment. Moss rolled his head wearily in the mud and said maybe he had better send the kid to the station for help. Personally, he thought that he and Simmons had got the sheep a hellsight farther than anybody else could, but if there was anybody within call of the station who thought he could do more, it was time he was getting started. Simmons said he felt the same way about everything, and stuck Moss's chaps under his head for him to rest on. They called Clay, who was still in the water throwing out sheep, and he came, hot, winded, and bleeding where a ewe had laid a hoof-cut across his forehead when he lifted her to throw.

Clay had taken up the job of fighting the sheep loose from their suicide partly because he was green enough to imagine he could and partly because he had shirked working with them before. During the trip down the mountain he had taken no hand with them because they seemed a personal set-to between Moss and Simmons. Now they turned all their solicitude on one another, the sheep could drown and be damned, and they boosted one another's dignity by letting on that Clay himself didn't amount to anything. "Run on in to the station and tell Shiveley we need some help," Simmons told him. "You're no use here. Me and Mr. Moss will stay and see that nothing happens."

That was expressed badly. Clay was hot and fightable, and it insulted him to be ordered off his work like an errand-boy playing stick-horse. He told them, plain and pointedly, to kiss where he couldn't reach. "What help is there at the station? There's an Indian kid that wouldn't come, and an old man that wouldn't work, and a girl that would try to boss everything. If you want anybody in that layout, go after 'em. Let me alone."

They didn't want to go themselves. It would look like a throw-down if they both went, and there was that much of their feud left that neither wanted to leave unless the other did. "Dit your horse and dit started," Moss ordered, raising his head. "You dot no business bein' impident to Mr. Simmons."

"It was your idea in the first place, so he's impident to you, too," said Simmons generously. "Now you look here, boy. Do you want to go to the station decent, or do you want me to tie you to the saddle hind side to and turn your horse loose to take you?"

He got up, ready to move fast if Clay selected the wrong alternative. Clay pulled a knife. It was an Indian-made gouger, with a haft cut from an old wagon-spoke and a blade ground down from a barrel-hoop, but it looked mean. Clay balanced it in his hand, ready to throw underhanded. "I ain't goin' to any station," he said. This kind of run-in was old business to him. He was accustomed to having one with the Shiveley brothers at least three times a week. "If anybody goes, it'll be you, and if you take ary other step at me you'll go packin' your innards in your hat."

Simmons took a couple of steps backward, put one hand over the place where he evidently judged his innards to be located, and sat down. Clay went back in the water again and wasted his time and strength trying to make the sheep take an interest in having their lives saved. Simmons and Moss took turns arguing with him from the bank. They proved, right up to the hub, that if he went to the ranch it would mean health, fame, and prosperity for all of them, and that if they went it would cost Simmons his entire future and Moss his life. They built up an awful case against his staying. Unluckily, the signal fire on Round Mountain took hold while they were clinching all their points, and all they had worked for and squabbled over and argued about got buried under their curiosity about what the double blaze could mean. Moss got up from his prostration, put on his chaps, and said they needn't count on his company any longer. He had counted on getting the Wade Shiveley reward money himself, to get married on or some similar treat, and he felt obliged to keep tab on the developments in the case. He got on his horse and left, and Simmons, not to be left out of anything gossipy, climbed on his to follow. He pulled up for a minute in the water to excuse himself to Clay for not staying. "I got to find out about them fires, or I won't sleep a wink," he explained. "A man's got to think of his health first, and when I don't sleep, mine goes plumb to hell. If it ain't anything excitin', I'll be back. I'd think you'd want to find out about this yourself, livin' with the Shiveleys as long as you did."

The fact that Clay had lived with them was exactly the reason he wanted to hear nothing more about them. Too much was plenty. For downright interest and excitement, the problem of keeping eight hundred head of sheep from immolating themselves out of damned contrariness had any case of homicide looking like a game of tit-tat-toe. It exercised the ingenuity and it cured spiritual uneasiness. When Simmons was gone, trotting to catch up with Moss, Clay put the signal fires out of his mind and flaxed down to try the sheep again.

This time he went at it differently. He found a pitchy pine stump, hacked a chunk off of it, and lit it for a torch. He waded among the sheep, waving it while it roared and spouted flaming drops into the black water. When they didn't move, he pounded them with the fiery end and jabbed their noses and whacked them across the eyes with it. They flinched, but none of them moved, so he threw the thing away and kicked them, not to prevent them from dying, but to punish them for wanting to. He worked at that till he was tired, and crawled out on the bank and lay down to rest. In the quiet, he heard a horse coming on the trail from the station. He sat up, hoping it was Simmons and that there had been no news of Wade Shiveley, after all.

It was only the Indian boy from the station. He was riding a big red colt bareback with a halter, and he had come out to take the pack-horses to feed and shelter for the night. It was like him to have ridden away from news of a fugitive that the whole country had been hunting for and gabbling about for weeks, and to ride through the middle of eight hundred sheep in imminence of death without thinking of anything except some ten-dollar pack-horses that might chill if they stood out in the wet. The sheep-herders, he admitted, had got in, but he hadn't paid much attention to them when he found they hadn't brought the pack-horses. There had also been some visitors in a wagon, but he hadn't spent any time finding out about them, either. He knew nothing about the fire on Round Mountain except that it had nothing to do with him. "Now I'll take them horses," he said. "You better come, too. You won't have nothing to ride on if you stay here."

"Like hell I won't," said Clay. "I've got to get these sheep out of the water when they drown, and do you think I'm goin' to pack 'em

out on my back? Leave them horses alone or I'll cut your whang off.
I'll bring 'em in when I'm through with 'em."

The Indian boy didn't know for sure what a whang was, but
he didn't want his cut off. He elected to wait for the horses, and
Clay helped him build a little fire to keep warm by. They sat by it
watching the water slop around the sheep and white frost hair out
on the grass in the moonlight, and the Indian boy turned sociable
and told his favorite story, which was about how Big Beaver had
licked a wicked spirit with eight sets of eyes and claws like a hay-
rake who lived at the bottom of Camas Lake and kept hindering
him whenever he tried to build the world. There were several pas-
sages in the narrative that didn't stand to reason. For instance, if
there wasn't any world, how could there have been any Camas
Lake? The Indian boy said that the world wasn't a necessary ingredient of Camas Lake. It was simply a place for Camas Lake to
sit down on, like the rawhide chair that Heavy Annie McCurdy
carried to all the school entertainments because none of the ordinary
seats would hold her.

"Well, what did Big Beaver want to make a world for?" said
Clay. "He was doin' all right without one, wasn't he?"

It wasn't on his own account, the Indian boy said. It was so people could have a place to live. Up to then they hadn't had anything
—no ground to walk on, no feet to walk with, no mouths or eyes
or anything to feel with. They were nothing but loose toots of vapor
that went rocking around in mid-air, getting all mixed up with one
another and wishing, without knowing exactly why, that they could
get sorted out again. So Big Beaver flaxed in and fixed them a
world for them to keep themselves apart in.

"A blamed sight better if he'd left 'em mixed, to my notion,"
Clay said. "What good did it do him to fetch out a lot of people
to hell around and fight and make fools of themselves? Why didn't
he mind his own business and let them mind theirs?"

"Well, them sheep in the water," the Indian boy said. "You
been fightum and kickum to make 'em come out, hey? Why didn't
you mind your own business and let them mind theirs?"

"They belong to somebody else," Clay said. "He's hired me to
take care of 'em. Or help, anyway. And if I let 'em do as they

please they won't be worth anything to him. They ain't anything to me."

"That's the way it was with Big Beaver," the Indian boy said, and got up as if he had settled the whole argument. "Them sheep ain't goin' to die for a long time. Why can't you drag 'em out now?"

"Because they'll walk back in again," Clay said. "Hell, if they'd stay where I put 'em I'd have 'em all started for the station by now."

The Indian boy had to have that explained to him, and then he took ten minutes to think it over. "Them horses is goin' to take cold if we don't hurry," he said. "You could start draggin' them sheep out and put 'em in the hay-corral yonder, hey? Then they couldn't walk back. I'll help you."

It showed how much could be overlooked by depending on men who handled sheep according to the teachings of experience. Moss and Simmons had sat looking at that hay-corral for more than an hour, and neither of them had once imagined that it could be employed in the profession of sheep-tending, simply because they weren't accustomed to having such a thing handy when a herd stalled on them. Clay mounted his pony, dropped his rope on an old ewe, and dragged her out across the stubble. She stood being towed like an old bobsledder, but when he kicked her through the gate she trotted around inside, bawling uneasily. The Indian boy had come off without rope or saddle, so he unloaded a pack-horse and climbed on the pack-saddle with a swing-rope that had been cinched round the tent. They worked together, hauling sheep out of the roily water and wearing a trail with them across the mud and hoarfrosted grass to the corral.

Practice made the work go easier. The horses learned to pick their sheep and sidle to the right and hit for the bank at almost a derrick-horse jog when the rope caught. The old ewe bawling through the fence grew to twenty and thirty and then to a shape-less mob, churning and blatting, impossible to count except in terms of the area they covered. The signal fire on the mountain burned down and went out, new windows lighted up in the station, and the unused horses stamped and shivered in the cold wind. They re-minded the Indian boy of his original errand. "I got to take all them horses in," he said. "They're takin' cold to die. We can't haul out all these sheep."

Clay begged him to hang on for a few dozen more. He was loose-ribbed and logy, and there was no more life in his muscles than in a cut of wet rope. The sheep were cold, slimy and back-breaking to put through the corral gate. But he remembered how they had mobbed together when the coyote jumped them, and he knew that if he worked at them long enough they would mob again. How many it would take he didn't know. He might have to haul out all but three or four to get them in the notion of joining the bunch in the corral, in which case he was licked. But a few more dozen turned out to be enough. The penned sheep didn't represent over a fourth of the herd, but every one bawled fit for fifty. The sheep in the water, having composed themselves to die, weren't bawling at all, and the shoreward blatting roused their curiosity. They lifted their heads and moved restlessly, and a few scrambled up. Then, in a waterlogged scamper, they all came out and went crowding to the stackyard with mud dripping from their bellies and hoarfrost gathering on their fleeces in the moonlight.

The Indian boy untied the pack-horses and hit for the station, leading them, without waiting to see whether that was all of it or not. He was playing his turkey-bone whistle when Clay came dragging in behind him from turning the herd into the corral and wiring the gate shut on them. He stopped and let Clay into the barn and stood close to him in the dark while he unsaddled. "People in that house makin' business against you," he muttered. "I don't know what, but they leave their team standin' in the rain all night, and you better not stay here. Put your saddle on the red colt, and pack your camp outfit on one of the wagon-horses and go back to the mountains. Maybe in a day or two they'll be gone. Then you come in."

That was childish. Clay didn't know what kind of business they were making against him, but he couldn't think of anything it could be that wouldn't be written off by his getting the sheep safely penned on dry land. To duck off to the mountains without claiming credit for saving them would have been acting like old Luke Phipps, who cut his own wages from a dollar and a half to a dollar a day because fractions made his head hurt. Clay went on into the kitchen. Drusilla Birdsall stood by the door, waiting for him. She grabbed his arm and ordered him in a whisper to be still and not to go into the dining-room.

"Go clean the mud off yourself and put on some dry clothes," she said, with her mouth against his ear. It was bossiness, but she didn't act bossy. She acted almost giggly, like a school-kid fixing up some trick to spring on teacher. "Your good clothes, do you hear? And then come to my room. I want to tell you something before you talk to those men."

She pushed him to the stairs, holding her hand over his as if she already owned him. When she let go he tried to tell her about the sheep, but she shook her head and pointed for him to hurry upstairs. Then she went back to the dining-room to make sure nobody had heard him come in.

Chapter IV

NOBODY had heard him, or at least nobody dared to let on they had, because Uncle Preston disliked being interrupted when he was telling a story. He had got into the swing of his narrative, which meant that he was through the stages of recollecting middle initials and which bush old man So-and-so had camped under and whether he owned a white mare or a gray gelding, and that he was cracking down on what things had happened and what people they had happened to.

The main argument of the piece concerned his father-in-law, a long-faced old widower named Joab Meacham, who had come to the country away to hellangone before any of the early settlers. To start with, he had been a carpenter attached to one of the Indian missions on the lower river. The mission blew up because the brethren in the East stopped sending money and the Indians refused to start. So old Meacham helped himself to some horses and a stock of groceries and truck and lit out, with one ear cocked for intimations of divine guidance, to hunt up a new location for himself. He came to Little River in the season when a hot spell was fetching the snow out of the mountains, and he lost two of his horses trying to swim the high water with their packs on. They floated ashore downstream, and he went down and salvaged the packs; but the freight in them was all watersoaked, and it included all his corn-meal and forty hymnals and two bundles of tracts that he had taken along to make up his back wages.

He couldn't do much about the reading-matter, though he did take a few copies to pieces and dry them off for his personal use; but he kept the corn-meal from spoiling by building an oven and making all of it into bread. It took him three days, because his oven would chamber only one loaf at a time. On the third day, when the last loaf was baking and he was rolling his packs to go on, a mysterious voice came out of the air and called him by name and told him to stay where he was. It was perfectly distinct, though of course with a kind of unearthly scrape to it, and it repeated

36

several times, "Meacham, stay!" Nobody ever questioned that he actually had heard something, but nobody ever ventured to hint that it might have been less supernatural than he made it out. A couple of drowned horse-carcasses left three days in a hot sun will always generate internal gas, and eventually will burst and let it out with a sibilant wheeshing noise that, if you're not expecting it, can sound like almost anything your conscience will let it.

The messenger, whether equine or heavenly, didn't suggest what old Meacham was to subsist on, but he worked that out without any help. He unpacked his chest of tools and started hewing stringers for a bridge across Little River before his last loaf of bread was out of the oven. Afterward he joined up with travel by building a pack-road from the settlements across the mountains, and got it done in time to catch the Orofino gold-stampeders. With that to run on, he built his overnight station and sent East for his daughter. Not to enjoy his new-found prosperity. The notion of a woman enjoying anything would have hurt old Meacham as much as seeing a man win money on a horse-race without getting struck by lightning afterward. What he wanted her for was to do the cooking for his overnight boarders. When Uncle Preston came through on his first freighting-trip over that road with his mule-train, she was running the kitchen and tending a grab-and-gallop lunch-counter for an average of forty men a day, and wishing that the divine voice would toss the old gentleman a hint about the amount of work an eighteen-year-old girl could stand seven days a week on six hours' sleep a night.

That was one prayer that got answered. The night Uncle Preston laid over with his mules, the divine voice turned loose in the night and said several times, loud and commanding and awful, "Meacham, go preach!"

At least that was what he claimed it said. Uncle Preston's mules had done considerable trumpeting in the corral during the night, but if a man wanted to make a summons from the Almighty out of hee-haw-hee, it would have been foolish and unfeeling not to let him do it. Nobody tried to argue with him, and he packed a couple of saddle-bags and went forth to call sinners to repentance, and nobody ever heard poop nor twitter of him again. Uncle Preston married his daughter and stayed on, and the business throve under his management till the newer road over the mountains let all the steam out of it. She had been a good wife. He said that looking at Orlando Geary as if he wondered whether the neighbors had formed any different opinion, and Geary brought himself to and studied the matter for several minutes before he committed himself. He said yes, she had been all right.

"She's dead now," he said, as if everybody didn't know it. "It's a good thing, probably, with them youngsters of hers comin' to what they have. Her pa was red-eyed on Bible-bangin'. I remember well. He heerd heavenly voices, or claimed to. He throwed up his business here and went off preachin' on the strength of 'em. After he left, old Grandpap Cutlack come down with religion. I knowed Grandpap Cutlack when he couldn't have told a Bible from an Ayers' Almanac."

Uncle Preston agreed that old Cutlack hadn't been any vessel of grace when he was young, and began remembering other old men and old tombstone inscriptions in the country. The year Deaf Fegles died with snakes in his boots was the year Ira Humason started coming home with them in his; and the year Warnick Martin chopped a tree down on himself and left fifteen kids was the year Ross Morningstar's wife started having another youngster every time he shook a pair of overalls at her. The year Anse Tucker got dragged to death by a wild horse was the year the Indian kid at the station started learning to break horses, and that seemed to have been the regular order of development for the people around there, take them straight through. Some of them never developed any definite character at all. None of them did until somebody died and left one vacant.

The hypothesis didn't much interest Orlando Geary, because it soared into regions where law-enforcement and his digestion couldn't circulate. But the names of people he had known reminded him that Ellis Yonce had got killed in a scuffle with some mongrel Indians the same year that Wade Shiveley's girl threw him over and married a young school-teacher who had won several championships for digging potatoes. On her wedding night Wade rode his horse back and forth in front of their house, yelling and cussing and throwing rocks at the windows and keeping the happy couple scared within an inch of their lives till the mail-carrier came along in the morning and ran him off with a gun. And in the fall of that year Orlando Geary had come over and helped Uncle Preston put both his sons off his place.

The conversation was heading toward ticklish territory, and Payette Simmons hastened to volunteer that he remembered that Ellis Yonce, having worked with him on a post-hole contract one summer when Big Mary Grove rode over on her old white mare to invite him to marry her daughter. She was all primed to screech and pull hair and raise a rumpus if he refused, but all he did was to haul off with a shovel-handle and hit her square in the Adam's apple. It not only quenched her cries of ladylike reproach then, but it fixed her so she hadn't been able to talk above a whisper since. That occurrence was familiar to everybody, but, being warmed up, Simmons went ahead with one that wasn't. The year that Ellis Yonce took to packing a chip, he said, was the year his own oldest brother got killed in an Indian raid up the valley. His oldest brother had been considerable of a fight-banterer and a devoted hand at breaking community dances up in a row, and his death was an outlandish piece of business. It might make material for a smart man to write a piece about.

The compliment was pointed enough. Uncle Preston looked pleased but not overwhelmed. He was used to trade-lasts from the ignorant, and he had a considerable swad more Indian-raid material than he could use. "You couldn't use your brother's killin' to prove anything, I expect," he said. "He couldn't have been much loss, to judge by the little that got wrote about him at the time. He didn't leave any young bride or anything like that, did he?"

Simmons admitted that no, he didn't, and there hadn't been any red and white rosebushes springing entwined out of his grave, either. And the story his father used to tell before company about his death was an ordinary kind of recital, for it was the old one about the Indians having caught the youngster and his having turned up and run them off too late to prevent them from killing him. But that wasn't what had happened. The straight of the business, which Simmons remembered because he had been an eyewitness and five years old, was that the Indians were burning the ranch-house, and old Peg Leg Simmons was hiding with him and the rest of the kids in the brush, waiting till they got through and left. All the kids had been forbidden to move, no matter what happened; but the eldest was full grown and high-spirited and hard to control, and when the barn took fire and the horses started screaming inside, he broke cover and made a run at the Indians, shooting and whooping to try to scare them. He emptied his gun and fell over a bunch of bucks on outpost at the edge of the clearing, and they knocked him down and dragged him to the house and tied him to a tree. They started piling brush around him, thinking that if they warmed his legs he might tell where the rest of the family was hiding. He was so close that the kids could see his face twist when he tried to pull loose from the ropes; a foolish thing to waste his strength on, because even if he got loose the Indians would merely have tied him back. It showed how scared he was that he even tried it. To make it worse, a young squaw stepped in and started embroidering designs on him with a butcher knife. That caved him in completely. He shut his eyes and opened his mouth and screamed, and one of the kids in the brush started whimpering under his breath, and Peg Leg Simmons raised up easy and took a rest with his rifle.

"I remember that," Orlando Geary said, coming in at the wrong time. "I was with the men that went out and fetched the kid in to the buryin'-ground. The way them squaws could work a man over was a caution. They ought to got worse than shootin', the whole bunch of 'em."

Yes, Simmons agreed, they ought. Two minutes of that squaw's performances that day had scared him so his liver hadn't recovered its natural color even yet. But his father hadn't shot her. He had aimed at his son, and the bullet took him right between the eyes. There was so much smoke from the burning house and barn and horse meat that the smoke of his shot didn't show, so they all laid close and the Indians whacked brush trying to find them for a couple of hours, and then left. That was all of it. Maybe it wasn't worth writing, but it was a little out of the ordinary.

Uncle Preston opened and shut his hand, and wrote flourishes with his finger on the tablecloth. "Yes," he said. "I don't recall a case exactly like it. He shot his son to keep the Siwashes from torturin' him."

"To keep him from breakin' down and tellin' where the rest of 'em was hid, more likely," said Orlando Geary. "None of them high-spirited men can stand pressure. You take Wade Shiveley rippin' up and down the county road the night his girl got married, or the way Ellis Yonce used to cave and rip around in court when he was on trial. I've seen him yell and bawl and buck till two men had to set on him when somebody was testifyin' against him. Likely that's how it was with Peg Leg Simmons' kid. I knowed Peg Leg Simmons well, and I remember his kid well because I helped bury him. And that was the year that Ellis Yonce and a carpenter down at Civil Bend tied their wrists together with a handkerchief and fought with knives. The carpenter bled to death."

Uncle Preston sat studying his hands. He asked what Peg Leg Simmons had died of.

"He overet," said Orlando Geary. "There was a barbecue and shootin'-match down the river a piece, and he got to feelin' good and bet his team and rig that he could outeat any two men in the crowd. So he did. I was one that eat against him, and we didn't give up till we'd made him stretch himself. He like to busted before they could git him home. I never to this day seen a man come so close to eatin' a whole steer without any help. Afterwards I went over and laid him out. He was clear-headed up to his last breath, and admitted that he oughtn't to have tackled such foolishness at his age. Pomp and vanity had been his downfall, he said. He was around seventy-odd then."

"And that was all?" said Uncle Preston. "This shootin' his son didn't work on his mind?"

"Not that I ever heard of," Orlando Geary said.

"Not that I ever noticed," said Payette Simmons. "It worked on mine plenty, I can promise you. The place went to hell after pa died because none of the kids would ever go back there. I wouldn't."

Orlando Geary said that was foolishness. "Your pa done right, and he knowed it," he said. "What would you have done, left the blamed disobedient young pup to tell where you was hid, and torment a lot of innocent people along with himself? That's all you'd have accomplished. What good would it have done him, or you, either?"

Payette Simmons said he guessed it wouldn't have done any. But he would have turned loose on the Indians, and enjoyed the satisfaction of taking a few of them to glory along with him. Old Geary said it was no wonder he had remained a sheep-herder all his life, with principles like that, and Uncle Preston got up and said he would have to be getting back to his work. There was some writing to turn out before bed-time, and the loss of his sheep would take some thinking over. "When that kid comes in, send him up to my room for a minute or two," he said.

In his room, he spread his papers on his table and unstopped his bottle of ink, but he did no writing. He hadn't known before that the traditions of pioneer times in that country required him to be not merely a chronicler of history, but a partaker in it. He had known, though he had never admitted it to anybody but himself, that you didn't get rid of responsibility for a son by throwing him off the place and advertising yourself as no longer answerable for his bills. But he had not known what to do about it, and now he did. He got down a pistol from its nail on the wall, took out the cartridges, and set to work with a pair of wire-nippers to pull out all the bullets. Once or twice he sat back from his work, thinking whether what he was doing was what he ought to do. Then he felt ashamed of himself and went on. Peg Leg Simmons hadn't hesitated, though killing one son had meant throwing a scare into all the others that lasted them for life. And in that he was better off, because he had no others to throw a scare into.

Upstairs there was no noise except the shearing up and down of great overgrown apple-boughs as the cold wind pressed through them. He heard Drusilla and Clay Calvert talking down the hall, so he opened his door to call when Clay passed to go downstairs.

Chapter V

THERE were no bathing accommodations in Clay Calvert's room except a graniteware washpan, a wooden bucket of cold water, and a baking-powder can full of soft soap made of wood-ash lye and coarse lard. He made out with them, and rubbed himself down hurriedly because of the chill and the soft soap, which, if left on over a minute, was liable to take the hide off with it. Then he put on dry clothes and lay back on the bed to rest and read the inscriptions which earlier lodgers at the station had whittled into the rafters overhead. Mostly they were comments on the quality of grub the station set out for its patrons under old Meacham's management, and they contained a considerable amount of flavor which the bill of fare in those days had apparently lacked. He turned his eyes away from them when Drusilla came in, and he made a face to indicate that it would have suited him all right if she had stayed away. She ignored it, and sat down on his bed. He hadn't come to her room as she had asked him to, but she was so excited and hurried that she ignored that, too. "We can't talk long, because the men are waiting for you downstairs, and they heard you ride in," she said. "This is something you've got to know about before you go down. Wade Shiveley has killed old Mr. Howell and stolen eight hundred dollars. Eight hundred dollars, and they've caught him. They've caught him and he's in jail and the money's hid where they can't find it. He wants to see you, and they think he wants to tell you where he hid it. So they've come to get you, and you'll have to go with them. Don't talk so they can hear you."

"I'll talk any way I damn please," said Clay. "What right has Wade Shiveley to git me hauled all the way to town because he wants somebody to talk to? I've worked ever since sundown, or mighty near it, puttin' your blamed sheep into a corral where they wouldn't drown themselves. All the thanks I git for it is to have you tell me I'm dirty, so go away and let me alone."

The news about the sheep did make her stare. Her face got round, and she repeated his announcement over to herself, which

43

was a habit of country girls then when they wanted to fix something in mind. She said thoughtfully that it was smart of him to have saved them when experienced hands had given them up, and she hoped the corral was a safe place to put them. Her plan had been built on the supposition that they were all dead, but she went on with the job of explaining it to him because it was so good she couldn't bear to give up trying it. After all, he was going to be taken to town, whether he liked it or not, so the only thing he needed persuading about was what to do when he got there. "They'll let you talk to him, and then they'll ask you where he hid the money," she warned him. She was so solemn about it that she looked childish, which made the whole thing seem a piece of make-believe. Children are always solemner about make-believe than about reality. "Then you're to tell them you don't know. You're to let on he didn't tell you anything about it. They can't do anything to you for that. They'll try to make you tell, and when they can't they'll have to turn you loose. Then you can go get the money yourself and bring it here, and I'll put it away for you. That's all you've got to do."

"That's plenty," Clay said. "Wade Shiveley don't like me well enough to tell me about any money, and I'll bet you a pretty he ain't got any. Maybe he's killed another man, but he never killed one with any eight hundred dollars. He wouldn't have that much sense."

She said a lot he knew about it, and picked his towel up from the floor and tossed it over a cross-beam overhead. It was one with a specially flavorsome inscription, but she didn't notice it. She had lived so long with those old signs of people who had been there before her that she paid no attention to them. The way to make a place mean nothing to you was either to live in it too long or not to live in it at all. Suggesting that the money might not be where she expected made Drusilla as cross as if he had done something to turn it to a pile of leaves. "The men downstairs say he's got it, and they ought to know better than you," she said. "What could he want to see you for except to tell you about it? It isn't as if you could suit yourself about going; you've got to go. And we could buy more sheep with it."

Clay said they had more sheep already than they could tend to, and he didn't have to go. He could step out of the window into the apple-tree, coon down, and hit for the brush as the Indian boy had recommended. If she said very much more, he would, too. He hoisted himself on his elbows, and she grabbed him and pushed him flat. "Don't you do it!" she warned, holding him. She was strong. Ordinarily he could have out-wrestled her at even holds, but he was fagged and logy, and she kept him pinned like a hog to be ear-marked. "You keep still or I'll call those men. They'll either kill you or they'll hurt you. You'll go to jail, and what good will that do any of us? You've got to go, I tell you!" She really believed it. Her plan had grown so big and fiery in her that she forgot that Clay was being taken to town merely as an alternate to Uncle Preston. All her arrangements depended upon his going; therefore, he blamed well had to go. She put one arm across his neck and caught hold of the bed-rail and straightened it flat, holding him as one holds a rattlesnake with a stick when one has a taste for such knicknacks. They lay side by side, and whenever he tried to get up she clamped down and shut off his wind; and in that romantic and unescapable position she made him her offer of marriage. "When they get through with you in town you can come back here with the money, if there is any, and stay as long as you please. Maybe we won't buy sheep with it. We could use it to fix up the buildings and put up a new granary. After Uncle Preston dies we can have this place for ours. Look at me. Do you want to do that, or don't you?"

She eased up the pressure so he could turn his head, and he looked at her close. With the candlelight on one side of her face and the moon on the other, she was pretty. She wasn't trying to be pretty, either, for she lay ready to grab if he tried to duck from under her arm. She was good and dependable and respectable; she was better than he could have expected to get, with his raising and his name in the community. She made no offer of sentimental demonstration, but that was all right too, because he associated such gentle manœuvres with road girls and shearing-camp followers, who had kissed their dependability and respectability a determined good-by when they left home. He still didn't believe the trip to town was going to mean what she expected it to, but if he climbed out and skipped now, she would think it was because he didn't want her. "I'll go," he said. "It won't do you a lick of good, but I'll do it if the old man thinks I ought to. There won't be any money; I'll bet you a horse and bridle on it."

She let him go and got up and smiled down at him in a fine humor. She had been half afraid that he wouldn't understand her offer, and half afraid that he might understand more from it than she intended. There was no flirtatiousness about him; he didn't even appear to realize that the occasion called for any, and that was one fine thing about him. Keeping their deal on a sort of collar-and-elbow basis, she wasn't embarrassed by internal noises. "I'll tell Uncle Preston you want to see him," she said. "Don't tell him we've been talking about fixing the station over. There'll be money. Don't let those men get it away from you, and come back as soon as you can."

It was disturbing, parting on the renewed assurance of something he felt certain wasn't going to pan out. He sat on the bed for a minute or two after she was gone, wishing he hadn't promised her anything. Then he got up and went down the dark hall. Uncle Preston's door was open, and Uncle Preston called him in and shut it behind him. He didn't look like a man about to be humiliatingly bereaved of his only surviving son. There was a kind of pointedness about him, a kind of consecrated resolution something like old Lorne Jessup when the manure-chute trapdoor fell on his neck and his grown sons got so weak haw-hawing over the picture he made that they could't lift it and turn him loose. It made Uncle Preston look better than usual, because it wasn't usual for him to decide to do anything about anything. "You're goin', I hear," he said. "That's good. Somebody has got to, it looks like, if we're ever to get shut of Orlando Geary. I told Wade Shiveley ten years ago that I wouldn't ever look at him again, and I'll stand to that, by God, if they hang me along with him. So it's lucky you're here. There's something I want you to help me with when you talk to him."

Clay mumbled all right. He had respected Uncle Preston, and he tried to make a quick splice between his respect and Uncle Preston's selfishness in sending him off to town without even an apology for the extra work he had done already. He had hoped somebody around the place might see how beat out he was and insist, as a matter of politeness, on his not leaving till he was rested. But they were all too concerned with their own business to notice. Bereavement made Uncle Preston selfish; concern over the station made Drusilla selfish;

devotion to duty made Orlando Geary selfish; fear or contrition or some damned sentiment or other made Wade Shiveley selfish in jail. It looked as if nobody could feel anything, good or bad, without being stingy and inconsiderate of others along with it. Uncle Preston did think to mention the sheep, but he might have been talking up a trapeze act in a circus for all the genuine gratitude he put into it.

"Drusilla told me about it," he said. "It shows you're dependable, and that's more than that son of mine will ever be in a hundred years. If I'd wrung his neck the night he was born, everybody would have been better off. And his brother wasn't any great sight better, except that he didn't last as long or bother as many people."

"I liked him better," Clay said. "He wasn't as set on devilment all the time."

"He wasn't set on anything that ever I heard of," Uncle Preston said. "A drink of water, that's all he ever amounted to. Well, this son of mine that's in jail bellerin' for somebody to rush in and hear how bad he don't want to be hung. I want to do something for him, and I want you to take this gun. Pack it somewhere out of sight, and if you can slip it to him when nobody's lookin', I want you to do it."

He slid the oily black pistol across the table into the lamplight. Clay picked it up, noted that it was fully loaded, and laid it down. Compared to this, Drusilla's notion about a monetary return from the trip to town wasn't childish at all. It was downright philosophical. He wondered if Uncle Preston could be ignorant of what was certain to happen if his son got hold of anything to shoot with. "You're certain you want him to have this thing?" he asked. "He'll kill somebody with it."

"He'll try to," said Uncle Preston. "The cartridges ain't got any powder in 'em. I pulled all the bullets and emptied it out. Don't tell him that when you give it to him."

Clay sprung the cylinder and looked at one of the loads. The base of the bullet was flattened slightly and marked with bright dents in the lead. It had been pulled and reseated, sure enough. He dropped it back and shut the cylinder. "What do you expect him to do with a gun that won't shoot?" he inquired. "If he tries to use it, he'll git hurt."

Uncle Preston said yes. "I remember the night he was born," he said. "I suppose every man's mind runs back like that when he's in a situation like this. I want him to get hurt. I want him to get killed. It'll be better for him and better for everybody. You take this gun."

He pushed the gun across the table. He was as solid and placid as an oak stump. Still Clay felt doubtful. He had been around enough to know that it was easy for anybody to feel brave about a killing before it happened. The only way to tell how you were going to feel afterward was to kill somebody and see, and you didn't always come out of it nearly as high-headed as you went in. To judge serious things by trifles, Clay had killed a thieving coyote raiding the sheep, and his mouth had tasted of blood and burnt powder and guiltiness for an entire day. "I won't do it," he said. "You're liable to take to studyin' about it afterwards, and you might decide I'd been to blame for it."

"No," said Uncle Preston. It was his nature to study over things he had done, and he knew it. But he knew that this time he wouldn't because what he was doing had been done and pronounced right before he ever dreamed of it. He had found Peg Leg Simmons' character vacant and he had moved into it, and as long as he stayed there he could never look back or feel doubtful. He wasn't creating a judgment of right, but copying one that had been carried to a successful finish long before him; and while the determination lasted in him he intended to stick to his model. "What I study about after this is over is my lookout," he said. "You can either take this gun to town and do as I told you, or you can turn in your time and quit. You won't be the first disobedient kid I've put off this place, either."

Clay took the gun and stowed it, cold and drippy with oil, under his shirt next to his skin. There was a possibility that he might get into trouble trying to slip it into the jail, but Uncle Preston was too determined upon his plan to let that perturb him, and, to tell the truth, it didn't perturb Clay much, either. He had seen too much rowdiness and illegality around the Shiveley brothers' establishment to be scared of a little more of it now. How he was to slip the gun through he didn't know, but if caught he could work himself loose by proving it was harmless. It did strike him as not only selfish, but inconsistent, that Uncle Preston and Drusilla should both have started by feeling suspicious of him on account of his disreputable upbringing, and that now they should both be offering to herd him with the family for life if he would misappropriate stolen property and smuggle deadly weapons into a county jail. It gave him a naked-backed feeling of loneliness and misgiving to think how childish both their plans were and how little likely it was that things would work out as they calculated. But if he tried and fizzled, they would have to put the blame on the plans, whereas if he refused to try, they would blame him. Trying was best. It might even teach them sense. "You'd better send somebody out in the morning to bring in your sheep," he said. "I'll have to tell him this gun come from you. If he thought it was mine, he'd test it out before he tried to use it. Is there any word you want to send him with it?"

For all his literary experience, Uncle Preston had trouble thinking up a message that sounded at once fatherly and natural. "You can tell him I wished him luck," he said. "And you might say I expect to see him later on. Maybe you'd better not, though. He knows blamed well I'd whip the devil and bust out of hell if he was there ahead of me. Tell him anything that'll make him feel good. You know him better than I do."

He sat scrawling aimless flourishes on his paper with his finger, and stared out the window at the wreckage of the apple-tree that had fallen on the granary. The under sides of the leaves were white in the moon, and it looked like something new that had been brought in by some lodger overnight instead of an old growth breaking away after nearly fifty years. Too many things planted in that country grew bigger than you expected them to, and some prospered by it while others destroyed themselves. Sweetbrier and evergreen black-berries, that went wild from old women's plantings and turned acres of bottom-land into impassable tangles of thorns; morning-glory and bachelor-buttons, that jumped flower-garden fences and choked standing wheat out of existence, got along better in their rankness than they ever had by being homelike and ornamental and harmless. Nothing could kill them out or keep them down. But the apple-trees, which had turned rank and flourishing, too, were so ridiculously underrooted and overwooded that any heavy rain or wind was apt to knock them flat through their own extravagant topheaviness. They were not only dangerous to themselves, but to everything within reach when they fell. Once they might have been pruned back. It was too late to do anything about them now except cut them down.

Uncle Preston hated to do that because he was used to them around the house and because he remembered how much work it had cost him to plant and tend them from sprouts. He preferred having them around to look at and listen to, even though he did have to stand ready to move to the barn whenever a storm hit them.

That carried his thoughts back to his son, who had also cost him trouble to raise and uneasiness to keep. There was illogic in his determination to get rid of his son and his persistence in not getting rid of the trees, but it didn't bother him. He knew the cases were different, though he couldn't settle in his mind what the difference was. He sat studying it over, and Clay slipped out and went downstairs, buttoning his coat over the pistol and pulling in his abdomen so the bulge wouldn't show. When he entered the dining-room, Orlando Geary heaved to his feet like a slumbering cow hit with a rock, and the two sheep-herders slid behind the table to be out of range if it came to a fight. Clay stuck his tongue out at them and made a disrespectful gesture with two fingers and his thumb because the occasion didn't seem appropriate for expressing his opinion of their sheep-herding in words, and told Orlando Geary that he was ready to start. Geary put on his coat and explained in a speech that sounded got-up that he wasn't to consider himself under arrest. He was merely assisting the legal authorities to locate stolen property. It was a mighty fine thing to be engaged in, and he ought to feel proud to be called on, and where could they find fresh horses?

Chapter VI

THEY went out all in a pack to skirmish up a fresh team. The whole valley had turned sleek and glittering with frost and moonlight, and, though colors were not strong enough to get through it, every shape was outlined against its shadow as if it had been nicked deep into a hard rock. The long grass of the meadow, too heavy to take movement from the wind, was white as if it had been snowed on. Against it the clumps of thorn-bushes threw shadows so black that it seemed a man couldn't step in one without dyeing his clothes and, probably, having to sit down and empty inky substance out of his boots. The high-centered flood-waters of the river were brindled intensely black and throbbing gray and blinding silver, and they piled and foamed and hell-roared through the motionless meadows like a wild train making up time through a country where everybody was asleep. For all its gleaming thunder, meadow and mountains actually did sleep, for the frost stopped all growth in the grass and struck all life from the trees and bushes above the roots.

What was happening struck Clay Calvert for the first time clearly and too sharply ever to forget, because his mind kept warning him that he was never going to see the valley like that again. There was no reason for such a warning that he could think of. It was caused, probably, by involuntary uneasiness about the errands that he had undertaken to do for Drusilla and Uncle Preston in town. But it lasted in him from the start of the journey until its finish. All the shapes of the valley and of all the people in it struck into him as permanently as if they had carved themselves in the inside of his skull-bone right over his eyes. It was not because they possessed any special virtue that they deserved being remembered by, but because he was fixed to remember them. He was so ready for it that he thought of them as a mass of people while he walked under the apple-trees to the barn. A mass of people, separate as blades of grass in the meadow and as firmly part of one patch of ground. Set-charactered men, hardened by the valley into shapes they could no longer break any more than the grass could break through the frost.

51

Under them, he thought, were the forms of older settlers who had come there before them and died; bigger and vaguer shapes, breaking up and rejoining and separating and rushing out of memory like water in the flooding river; and sometimes jarring the ground like the river though there was seldom anybody to notice. Behind was the snow-fog ripping and rocking and drifting out of the mountains, and that represented still earlier lives. It represented what all people had been, if one took the Indians' word for it, before Camas Lake had any place to sit down and before people had bodies that would hold anything that they could be told apart by.

That, of course, was running to foolish notions. If they had been even halfway sensible, no Indian would have bothered to believe them. Clay didn't waste much time with them because there were more practical things to think about. The Indian boy had foreseen that there would be a requisition for fresh horses, and he had objections to lending any of the station nags for such a trip. Instead of owning up to his prejudices and letting himself be argued out of them, he had sneaked the barn open and turned all the horses out into the open pasture. Signs of them there were none, for the cold wind was certain to have driven them into the bushes where they couldn't be seen, and the frost had covered their tracks so they couldn't be trailed. The Indian boy had taken himself out of sight as thoroughly, and he refused to show up even when Orlando Geary lifted up his voice and charged him to present himself quick or incur the serious displeasure of the law.

He repeated his summons several times, but he got nothing from it except a competitive crow from the old rooster, so the little half-breed driver hunted up a rope and trudged out into the haze of moonlight to shack in the horses by hand. He didn't look at Clay when he left, and Clay felt glad to have him out of the way for a spell. There were peculiarities about his family that made conversation with him embarrassing. He had a great raft of sisters and aunts who wallowed around his house a good deal of the time and ran loose around the roads the rest, prospecting for money when they could get any and for fun when they couldn't. There were few youngsters of Clay's age who hadn't seen more than the law allowed of at least one of them, and the little half-breed knew it and felt ashamed of it. Clay had, and he knew and felt ashamed of that, too, though he had no

reason to. It was no bark off his tail how his female kin behaved;
or any bark on it, either, for he made nothing out of them. But
telling him so would only have made him worse, and it was a lot
better to have him turned loose on horses, about which he didn't
have to be told anything.

He came back with a team in less than an hour, and looked sheep-
ish when Orlando Geary turned the lantern up to see what he had
picked out. They were the result of hard luck rather than bad judgment, for he had taken the first span he came to; but he couldn't
have drawn worse if he had done it on purpose. One was a sway-
bellied old mare from the wagon-team, named Doll. She was gentle
and a good puller, but she had feet as big as nail-kegs and a gait like
moving a brick church. The other had no name, because she was
too mean and unworkable to need one. She was high-sprung, bony
and glary-eyed, and a bad runaway when she was a two-year-old
had bunged her up around the hindquarters and left her not quite
right in the head. The feel of anything touching her rump turned
her maniacal with terror. Even an ordinary set of harness-breeching
was enough to start her throwing handsprings and waving her heels
in the air as if she was using them to demonstrate toy balloons at a
country fair.

The layout, with one horse that wouldn't hold back and one too
clumsy to do anything else, and a road to travel that had been ruined
by a flood, made it look likely that Wade Shiveley might have to do
his confidence-volunteering to some stranger's ear, after all. The
little half-breed felt both horses over experimentally, and the crazy
mare kicked at him in the dark and barely missed braining him. He
brought the harness, and Orlando Geary said maybe he hadn't better
try to put it on. It might be better to put back the tired team and pick
up a fresh one at the first ranch. Clay said nothing, because he felt
that he would be about as well off whether they ever got to town or
not, but the little half-breed said the tired team needed a rest too
badly to be worked any more. What old Doll and the crazy mare
would do together he couldn't guarantee, but he had found them
eating grass, and any animal that ate grass was within his ability to
drive. He put on the harness, and left off the breeching because the
crazy mare raised hell and almost tore the fence down when it

touched her. They wouldn't miss it, he explained. Breeching was for people who drove slow, and they were going to drive fast.

Orlando Geary said they had better, and helped Clay in and wedged himself on the outside. The half-breed put out the lantern and got in hurriedly, holding the reins easy so he wouldn't be dragged if the crazy mare undertook a jump-off on him. He eased the bit to her mouth carefully, and then fetched the wagon in a wide swing through the corral gate and into the road. The lower floor of the station was dark, but there was still a light in Uncle Preston's room and one in Drusilla's, and she raised her window and waved to them as the horses broke into a trot on the straight frosty road. Clay didn't wave back, because he had both elbows clamped firmly over his belly to keep Orlando Geary from nudging him accidentally and discovering the pistol; but he looked back and saw her against the light and saw the light go out.

The first five miles of road went clippingly. It was gravelly with a half-slope between it and the meadow, and the rain had drained from it into Little River almost as fast as it fell. The horses drummed it flatfooted as if they enjoyed the sound of their hoofs; frost glittered beyond the neck yoke and a long way ahead in the moon as if it was a tape they were starting out to print full of hoof-marks and wagon-tracks. The horses looked straight ahead and kept time without looking at each other. There was driving back of that, for they were built and gaited differently and they had never worked together before. The little half-breed's driving didn't look like anything. He merely held the lines out of the way and let the horses sashay along without even letting on to them that he was there. He didn't need to let on. Horses under his management always knew he was there, and, unless they had been irremediably ruined by bad handling, they always shed every trace of their ordinary loginess and contrariness and acted so self-conscious and anxious to please that they were almost ridiculous.

The first mark of the road that gave trouble was the crossing of Drift Creek, a couple of miles from the lean-to where Joel Hardcastle lived, dedicating himself to thrift, patched overalls, and the use of molasses-treated sawdust as a substitute for coffee, if there was any truth in the stories people told about him. In ordinary seasons, Drift Creek carried scarcely enough water to lay the dust on a frog, and a man could step across it without wetting his feet. But it had broken loose now, and the horses had to plug through water for a full mile before they got to the place where the creek was supposed to be. Alder trees shadowed it ahead, but the roaring of swift water stopped them, and the little half-breed cocked his ear, prodded the water with his whip-handle, and shook his head. There was a pole bridge over Drift Creek, and on the trip in they had crossed on it dry-shod and solid. Now it was flooded under. They had either to strike for it by guess and pray it was holding, or else dive in where they were and swim. Orlando Geary pulled his hat down and laid his gun behind the seat, to be rid of the weight in case. "Strike for the bridge," he ordered. "If it's gone, the horses'll go through it first, and we'll have time to git the kid out before the wagon goes."

Clay said that a man of his weight would do a blamed sight better to think of getting himself out. The little half-breed said nothing, and took the team ahead into the dark. They could feel the water slapping the wagon-bed under their feet as it rippled back from the horses. The crazy mare stepped too hastily and went in clear over her head, choking and plunging and struggling fit to have upset the wagon if old Doll hadn't planted her feet and held the tongue steady. The half-breed swung old Doll off to the right and dragged to a belt of moonlit shallow water. He stopped to let the crazy mare get up. "Lost the road for a minute," he explained, talking across Clay to Orlando. His way of putting it showed he was a good driver. A bad one would have said the gad-blamed horses lost the road, and have damned their hides to seven kinds of hell for doing it. "I'll find it now. It goes around the butt of the hill on a curve."

They pulled across to the butt of the hill. It was a course that took the ground crossways, and they rode submerged ridges that sometimes hoisted them high and teetery, sometimes dropped them so low that water splashed their knees, and sometimes threatened to stick them entirely. The horses had trouble finding ground that their feet would hold in, and Clay suggested, while they floundered and fell down and got up again, that maybe the two passengers ought to get out and wade, to save weight. He started to get up from the seat, and Orlando Geary took him by the shoulder and pressed him down again. "You'll stay here," Orlando ordered. "The authorities owe you free transportation for this trip, and yu're goin' to git it every step of the way. Set still."

The ground smoothed off and the water shallowed. The team stopped, smelling ahead of them and shifting their feet in the water nervously. "This is the bridge," the half-breed said. "Give 'em a little time to figure it out."

"What figurin' can they do when they can't even see it?" Orlando Geary said. "Throw the whip to 'em. We got to move."

The half-breed shook his head. You whipped a horse to punish him for doing wrong, not to stimulate him to do right. He handed Orlando the reins, climbed down onto the doubletree, and walked the tongue forward. He stepped off into the water and felt the ground ahead with his feet. It was the bridge. The flood had cut down the road so the approach was a three-foot step up. He took the horses by the bridles and waded ahead in the dark, leading them. The crazy mare caught her knees on the jump-off and backed sideways, but old Doll dragged her back into line and the half-breed held her to the collar. Both horses mounted the step and lay down and pulled, and the wagon mounted it. They could see nothing, but they knew it was the bridge because they felt the vibration of the wheels scraping on the guard-log and the bumping of the floor poles that rolled and gave under the weight of the wagon. The water in them made them springy. The current was so strong that it drove the horses sideways, and the half-breed had to let his feet go and dangle from the bridles like a snagged salmon. Then the water calmed and deepened till it ran into the wagon-bed again, and they went off the bridge with a cracking jolt that broke the seat loose from the brackets and almost wrenched the coupling-pole in two at the kingbolt. After a long time they came out into the moonlight where the water was shallow again, and the horses stopped. The crazy mare blew loudly between her knees and shivered. Clay and Orlando Geary fixed the seat back in place, and the little half-breed came back and climbed into it. He was completely soaked, but he took the reins from Orlando and pushed the team to a walk. "Nothing busted," he said. "She went bad for a minute or two back there. These horses could be made into a good team."

Orlando Geary pried his hat loose and put his gun back on. They came to solid ground where the moon shone against them and a cold wind, smelling of wet stubble and rain-bruised wild gourd and mountain laurel, blew on them and pinched the mortal life out of their wet feet and legs. The road was walled close with trees; first alder, then vine maple and dogwood, then a black stand of little second-growth firs. That fell away into a side-hill patch of gray buck-brush and then to a level hay-meadow, half-mowed, with an old hand-scythe and a wooden-toothed rake leaned against the rail fence so they stuck up into the sky. It was Joel Hardcastle's place and the beginning of the settled section of the valley.

All the men were sitting up, waiting for the wagon to pass. Joel Hardcastle stood by his gate, holding a lantern which, economically, he only lit when they got close. He was a heavy, club-jointed man with a croupy voice and a long gray beard with the end braided and tucked into the waistband of his pants. The beard was the only sign of age about him. His face was unwrinkled and the only expression in it was one of smallness, as if he had pulled all his features close together to save space. He held his lantern up and inspected Clay from his head right down to his wet boots, leaned over and read the manufacturer's name on the straps, and admitted that he might furnish a fresh team if they would leave him the one they had. Then, his instinct being never to give anything without getting something back, he turned his lantern on Clay again. "Press didn't come?" he inquired, as if they might have Uncle Preston hidden under a corn-shuck somewhere. "I knowed he wouldn't. How old are you, boy?"

Clay didn't answer, and the half-breed put in that he didn't want fresh horses just yet. He didn't say why, but everybody knew that Joel Hardcastle's horses were underfed, badly shod, and skates to start with. The fact that Joel Hardcastle was willing to make the swap was a sure sign that something was wrong with it, so it was only good sound sense to decline. What he would like, the half-breed said, was an old bed-quilt or horse-blanket or something to keep himself warm with. Joel Hardcastle found an old woolsack in the barn which he was willing to part with for thirty-five cents. He stood turning the money over in his hand until they started, and then he waved them to a stop and came running after them. One thing he had forgotten. He had intended to find out how old Clay was.

"Tell him," said Orlando Geary. It was odd how those old men of the same generation favored one another's peculiarities. "Tell him, and none of your lip, either. He's asked you polite enough."

"I won't do it," said Clay, and took the loose near rein and whacked the crazy mare on the tail-end with it. She kicked the double-tree resoundingly and went away from Joel Hardcastle at a gallop, dragging old Doll alongside. Orlando bellowed back that he was something over sixteen, but it was doubtful if his words carried, and he sat stiff and turned his head away offendedly. It was uncomfortable to be cold-flanked on both sides, and Clay remarked, by way of improving things, that Orlando had got his age a little low. It didn't work. "I don't give a damn how old you are," said Orlando, without looking around.

The streams that headed in the mountains were not hard to cross, because the high-altitude frosts were holding back the water. The bad ones were those that drained the valley itself. At Bird Creek, the whole crossing was gone into mud so deep the wagon-bed dragged in it, and the bridge had floated off the stringers and hung by one nail. They picked a downstream crossing and went in, the two horses swimming and the wagon half-floating and half-dragging on the bottom. This time they did have the moon to see by. They needed it, for halfway across the crazy mare tangled her feet in drifting brush and balked, with muddy water sloshing in the wagon-bed and the wheels settling into the mud while she reared and strangled and stood on her tail. Orlando Geary took off his gun again. "I told you," he said to the half-breed. "You ought to changed teams when you had a chance."

The half-breed handed him the reins and got down on the tongue with water smacking him around the hips and the mare threshing and wallowing and trying to sit on him. "I'll git her loose," he said. "I hate to. That would be a good horse if I had time to work with her. Loan me that gun of yours a minute."

He took it and walked forward with the tongue bucking under him. The moon was setting and the rush of water carried its light in great rounds and plates and circles past them. It looked sometimes as if the crazy mare was struggling in a bath of dull fire. The half-breed caught her by the headstall, sat back when she reared, and got up and cocked the gun when she came down. He set the muzzle carefully, holding her tight, and shot the tip of her ear off. "Now come on," he said, and climbed on her back and slapped old Doll with his hand.

The wagon lifted from the mud with a jerk, and dropped into deep water till nothing stuck out but the seat. Both horses were swimming, and the half-breed had slipped off the crazy mare's back and towed alongside her by hanging to the hames. It looked bad while it lasted, for they seemed to make distance only downstream; but it was over in a couple of minutes. The round backs of the horses came out sleek and shining into the yellow moonlight, the dark water went on without appearing to know how close it had come to getting them, and the half-breed let go the hames and climbed into the wagon as it caught bottom and rolled past him. He wrapped himself in his woolsack and took the reins without saying anything. Orlando Geary let go his hold on Clay, and the team climbed the bank and thumped across the frozen sand, blowing and trying to shake themselves dry between thumps. Getting them through that flood had been a real piece of work. Clay said so, forgetting, in his natural elation over having learned something new, that in that country things like rescuing drowning livestock seemed to be taken for granted once they were over with. "I'll remember that trick," he said. "That shootin' a horse's ear off to cure balkiness."

The half-breed said it was a trick you had to be doggoned careful about trying. Some horses would stand it sometimes, others wouldn't. "You be careful how you use it," he said, and swung the crazy mare sideways so the moon would show how she was traveling. His unsociability hadn't been any grudge, but simply doubtfulness whether Clay might think he was responsible for his female relatives. He knew now that he stood better, because he knew he deserved to. "This mare may come out of this all right. But I took a chance on ruinin' her for life. Sometimes that shootin' business makes 'em as crazy as a buck."

At the place where old Pappy Howell had lived they pulled up for a minute and talked to the sour-faced old hostler who had trained Howell's race-horses. He was not one of the old settlers of the country, and Clay noticed little about him except that his hat brim was cinched down over his ears with a blue handkerchief and that the rims of his hard black eyes were red from crying. "This is the kid that's to locate the money, is it?" he said. "I wouldn't trust him too damn far, if I was you. I got a fresh team harnessed for you, if you need 'em."

The half-breed said, apologetically, that he believed he could get more out of the team he had. He knew better, because old Howell's horses were first-class stock, with every team he owned matched and gaited and grained twice a day. But work was getting the crazy mare over her nervousness from the shooting, and he cared a whole lot more about that than about whether they ever got to town at all. The trainer looked the outfit over and whacked the crazy mare contemptuously on the rump. She kicked, and he jumped back only in time to keep her from ripping him open with her hoof. "That's Press Shiveley's breed of livestock, all right," he said. He was fierce and hateful. Grief, instead of making him mellow and forgiving, had soured and hardened him. "Anything of Press Shiveley's is bad and man-killin' and treacherous, you can count on that. I'd watch this kid, too, if I was you. No tellin' when the little feist'll turn on you."

They left him growling and threatening in the frosty road before the dark house that death had left him in reluctant charge of. Orlando Geary explained that the reason he took on so was that he had always lived relationless and pretty near friendless, and that this was the first time death had really meant anything to him. An old man in his first bereavement is wilder and less reasonable than a child in his. He didn't address himself to Clay, but he made Clay feel glad his own first bereavement was over with and even that he had had one. You saved nothing by putting it off except to make it harder to stand at a time when you were less able to stand it. You didn't even save anything by avoiding it altogether. People who never lost anything that hurt got like Joel Hardcastle, who had always been too stingy to involve himself with anybody whom it would hurt to lose. The upshot of that system was that little losses nicked him about as deep as big ones would have done, and he mourned in the middle of the county road because Clay had refused to tell how old he was.

The moon was gone, but the country was still light from its reflection against the mountain fog. They climbed a grade through red mud and a fringe of hazel and oak and open grassland. At the top the wind struck hard and steady, the road turned to firm gravel, and there was a little graveyard inside a picket fence. There was a white headboard which, Clay knew, was for Uncle Preston's son, dead that summer, and an indistinct gray-green stone for Uncle Preston's wife, dead a long time. Drusilla's parents were buried there, and old Simmons' father and eldest brother under a long thatch of unpastured grass side by side as they belonged. Deaf Fegles, dead of overdrinking, and Ellis Yonce, dead of overfighting, were there through their own faults; Clay's mother was there through hers, and other women were there, some with little headstones, some with big, and some with none, through no fault of anybody's. There were not fifty graves inside the picket fence on the hilltop, but every one of them represented work on the part of the living; sickness, doctoring, galloping the country for help in a relapse, watching the death, calling neighbors to watch the dead, funerals, mourning, rearranging the house and dividing the property and the children. Every grave had represented that much or more, even the old ones that were so untended that they had become mere low spots in the deep mat of grass. There was no more need to tend them. They had done what they were supposed to do. Every one of them had brought some of the people in the valley closer to becoming men and grown women, because practice in standing death was a step in one's growing up. How big a step depended, of course, on one's backbone and understanding. Clay asked Orlando Geary if the graveyard contained any relatives of his.

"Two kids," said Orlando. His voice didn't break, and he didn't hoist a hard, rough hand and bat a drip of moisture out of his eye. It didn't mean as much to him, by the looks, as the condition of the grade ahead, because it had happened too long ago. But he was more of a man than old Howell's hostler or Joel Hardcastle because it had happened to him. "Both girls," he explained. "They died in the early days here. Well, now we've got a downgrade to run, and there ain't any holdbacks on the harness."

The road ahead of them pitched down through scrub-oak and blue-brush into a flat valley. Beyond were mountains, and beyond them daylight, running broad white streaks through the sky like milk spreading through water in a glass. Fog from the valley gathered and turned white going up to meet it; but all the way down the mountain it was still half-dark. The little half-breed stowed his hat under his leg and set the wagon-brake to see if it worked. "She'll hold," he announced, as if that made everything all right. "I can slide the hind wheels with it."

"On a grade like this you could drag the wheels and still be goin' like the milltails of hell," said old Geary. "We'd better pull in at my place and put in a new team and a set of breechin'. Can you hold it on the brake that far?"

His place was on a shoulder of the mountain a little over a third of the way down. They could see where it was by a faint yellow glow which was a lamp that his wife was keeping in the window for him. The half-breed laid his foot to the brake and swung into the road. "It's a poor team that can't outrun a wagon," he remarked. "You do the ridin' and I'll do the drivin'. We'll go fast."

"Drive on," old Geary said. "We got to move. I knew you'd git in trouble hangin' onto this damn team when you could have had a good one."

They went over the pitch like diving off a springboard. The front wheels dropped, the hind ones kicked up, and the team lifted to a trot and then to a half-canter. Behind them the brake shrieked and gaggled without seeming so much to slow the wagon as to provide its acceleration with a musical accompaniment. The half-breed set it up another notch, took a curve and two mudholes at a gallop, and grinned at Clay. "Too early to get scared yet," he said. "Too early to get scared and too late to get out if you did."

Clay told him to watch his driving. The crazy mare was trying to keep tab on the wagon behind instead of the road ahead, and she needed a close rein to hold her where she belonged. The half-breed pulled her head straight and cut her with the whip to remind her to keep it so, and they went faster. There seemed no relation between the brake and their speed except that the faster they went the louder it squalled. The horses lengthened their stride, and the crazy mare stopped sashaying and showing off because there wasn't time for it. The scrub-oak changed to willow and that in turn to black-leaved alder, loaded with unshed rain, that swiped across their faces like being hit with a fence picket. They bounced through streamers of light fog, and lunged through mudholes that wrenched their backbones and bogged the horses so the wagon several times

threatened to run them down. The trees dropped away and they
whirled between cleared fields toward a gate where Orlando Geary's
wife stood waiting. They passed her in the same breath. She was
short and heavy-set, with a red face and eyes that, in her effort
to flag the wagon down, bulged a little like Drusilla's when she
mistook somebody's refusal to see any sense in her notions for an
inability to understand them. She had on one of Orlando Geary's
coats, and she flapped her apron and yelled something as they went
past with a rip and a snort that almost blew her backwards through
the fence. The half-breed yelled to Orlando that he had to keep
going or pile up on a tree, and Orlando yelled back that it didn't
matter, because all she usually stopped him for was to order a spool
of thread.

The road ahead of them lay in a kind of three-quarter twilight
because the fog was coming up between them and the sky. Underneath was yellow mud in which a wheel skidded and hubbed a
stump with a bang that almost took it off the axle. A big blue
grouse waddled out in front, and spread his short wings to fly, but
they knocked him down and ran over him before his feet left the
ground. They rounded a turn mostly in the air, came down with a
whack and a ripping noise of iron straining on wood, and bounced
again when the off front wheel ran high on a tree-root. The wheel
cramped back for an instant, the tongue swung and hit old Doll,
and she fell down and lit on her side. The crazy mare galloped on
alone, dragging her.

Orlando Geary planted his feet and held onto his hat with one
hand and Clay with the other. "You'll kill the whole damn shootin'-
match of us!" he yelled. "Pull into the bank so we can jump!"

The half-breed turned his head. A big hoofload of yellow mud
had hit him in the face, and his grin through it was upsetting,
like a man trying to look offhanded and reassuring with his nose
cut off. "I ain't got but the one rein to pull with," he yelled. "I'll
git us down. This is goin' to make a good horse."

It was a load to put on even the makings of a good horse,
expecting her to keep ahead of a runaway wagon and drag a
fifteen-hundred pound draft-mare down a mountain grade without
getting either herself or the wagon out of the road. Old Doll, coast-
ing along on her side in the mud, had probably the easiest end of

the two, though there was nothing soothing about it. Several times
the wheel rammed her, and once or twice the crazy mare stepped
on her in shying from the doubletree at her rump. For a piece of
luck there were no bad turns. The road went straight down like a
flight of stairs, and with about the same average incidence of
bumps. They piled down it, ripped through a stretch of muddy
water that rose up in front of them like a sheet of dirty window-
glass, and dragged to a stop in axle-deep black mud between two
plank-and-wire fences. Ahead there was a big shabby house and a
haystack and some lean cattle. Phineas Cowan's grown sons were
keeping a fire of old fence rails in the road by the gate, and they
ran and helped old Doll to get up. They paid no attention to the
little half-breed, being mostly of the same complexion themselves
and touchy about standing comparisons. He got up and stiff-legged
it over to the fire to get warm, and it was odd to see how little
and forlorn he looked humped over the coals with his dirty woolsack spread out to catch more heat like wings on a bat. Coming
down the grade with a runaway team and wagon that threatened
at every bounce to kill him, he had been masterful and offhanded;
he had looked right down the barrel of immediate destruction, and
it hadn't made him back an inch. But before a bunch of big-
mouthed Cowan offspring trying to be hard and show their dis-
respect for the legal authorities, he backed into himself like a dry-
bellied steer expecting to get knocked in the head. He sat meek and
lonely and took the heat hungrily as if he expected to be chased
away from it any minute, as if it was only through somebody's
oversight that he had been allowed near it to start with.

The wind now had gone down. Blue-white drifts of fog lifted
from the meadow and from the ponds of rain water beyond it and
the rust-red bracken beyond that. But it was day; all the cattle were
up from their bed-grounds and all the deer back in theirs; the
whole meadow moved with grass-stems shedding water and springing erect from the mat into which the rain had beaten and the
frost fastened them. Water dripped from the hazel bushes and the
wild-rose thickets speckled with scarlet rose-hips and from the
clumps of wild crabapple along the fence. The night was over and
the dangerous part of the road was over, and Orlando Geary
climbed down from the wagon and stretched and looked over the

scenery, which, considering how much trouble he had taken to get exactly that view of it, might have been considerably better. Clay tried to get down after him and couldn't. His legs had gone to sleep and the cold had numbed them all the way up to his knees. Three of the Cowan youths helped him down in silent envy because he was enjoying the distinction of traveling in the custody of an officer without having to undergo the discomfort of being jailed for it afterward. They led him to the fire to thaw out and limber up, and the biggest, who had a loud voice and long black hair and was named Zack Wall, spit tobacco juice and inquired of Orlando Geary if this was the shooter's kid. "The old man wants to see you on business, if that Siwash woman of his can git off his shirt-tail long enough fer him to git down here," he said. "This kid ought to have some dry clothes. Strip off, bub, and a couple of you tads go rustle him a change from the house."

That was a hard one to get out of. It would look idiotic for Clay to refuse a change of clothes when his own were wet to the waist. But if he stripped he would expose the gun under his shirt, and he had kept it concealed so long that fetching it into view now would certainly get him into bad trouble with Orlando Geary. He would have to lie out of accepting the dry clothes. He was tired and frazzled and sleepy, and daylight had changed the trip from its night current of swiftness and courage and new things to see and learn into something thin, humiliating, mendacious, confused. The night had called on good things: patience and nerve and courage. Now it was time to let go all that and to start two-facing and side-stepping and mixing ends with the truth. "I don't want any dry clothes," he said. "That driver yonder needs 'em worse than I do. You can see he's soaked plumb to his hair."

Zack Wall said shucks, those half-stripe Siwashes could stand cold that a white man would stiffen out and die in, and that it didn't interest him whether an understrapper from the law-enforcement section of the county froze up or not. With Clay, now, it was different. "You're goin' to a hell of a lot more trouble to see that guardeen of yours than I'd stand to see mine," he said, and spat a load of fine-cut sap in the direction of the house. "By God! If they tried to haul me around the country on anybody's say-so like they're doin' you, I'd fight 'em. But you ain't got that kind of a nature, and there ain't any use of killin' yourself when you don't need to. Come on, I'll help you peel off."

He caught Clay's coat and undid a couple of buttons. Clay pushed him off. "I ain't goin' to change clothes till that driver does, I told you," he said. "I can git dry from the fire. Stand away from here and let me alone, or I'll take this fence rail and knock you end-ways with it."

A couple of youths came from the house with dry clothes. They were youngish, and they appeared to expect considerable more of Zack Wall's fighting nature than he was quite ready to deliver. One of them picked up a rock and stood ready to hand it when the engagement was declared open, and the other yelled "Fight!" in a hoarse dieaway bawl like the chorus of a hymn. Zack Wall cuffed them both, yanked the pile of clothes away from them, and tossed it in front of the driver. "Climb into 'em, buckskin," he ordered. "Be damned sure you remember where you borried 'em." He stood watching while the little driver shuddered into them. They were three times too big for him and they made him look meeker and scareder than ever. They may even have made him feel so, for he didn't let out a peep when a bunch of the Cowan youths hooked a fresh team to the wagon. Zack Wall nodded at Clay as if that was the effect he had hoped to achieve. He was less loud than he had been at first, but friendly. "We'll fix you up over in the bunk-house," he said. "You can't peel down out here now. Too many women around."

That sounded more practical. Clay had no objection to switching clothes if he could do it without witnesses. Orlando Geary had. "This boy is in legal custody," he said, holding his wet pants leg out with his fingers so the steam wouldn't scald him. "You got no right to take him anywhere without I go along. He ought to stay here, anyhow, to be on hand when we're ready to start."

It was easy to see why he was so firm about Clay staying. He didn't want to leave the fire. Zack Wall spat and slapped a couple of youngsters who had stolen a harness-snap and were fighting over it. "Put that team in the barn," he ordered. "You throw that cow-chip at me, Pick, and I'll cut you into steaks and feed you to the hogs! Here comes the old man, Mr. Geary. He wants to see you on some business."

Phineas Cowan was a tall, bony old man with wandering blue eyes, one lock of white hair distributed around a peaked bald head, and an intensely red nose. He was wrapped in a yellow blanket, and as he opened the gate the youngster with the cow-chip threw it at him and ran. It hit the gate-post and burst, and he came down brushing pieces of it off himself with one hand while he greeted Orlando with the other. "Damn me if I ever see such a set of younguns in all my days," he apologized. "There ain't a day passes but they either try to kill me or each other. I'm blamed if I wouldn't be better off sendin' the whole bunch to the reform school, they've got so bad. Children is an awful trouble to a man, damn it."

He was a querulous, nagging-voiced old man, and the light strengthening made him squint so he looked as naggy as he talked. It seemed curious that such a scrawny and fretful and dried-up-looking specimen should have done so much damage among the women. But there were the children to prove that he had, and, according to Zack Wall, he was still doing it. Orlando Geary, of course, knew him too well to see anything strange about it. He said that the reform-school idea might be a good one, but it would require certain formalities, and that he was in too much of a hurry to go thoroughly into them.

"That ain't what I wanted to see you about," old Cowan said. "As long as these kids stay inside my fence, they don't bother anybody but me, and I can stand 'em. Press Shiveley tried kickin' his two sons off his place, and look what happened to them. No, this is another kind of a thing." He lowered his voice, and watched one of the youngsters knock another one off the fence with a rock. "There's a family of hobo horse-traders camped three-four miles down the road, and they're inside my land. I want 'em moved off."

Orlando Geary changed position to steam another section of his pants, and ran the details over in his mind. He would be glad, he said, to undertake the eviction if the law sanctioned it. But it would be necessary to prove that they were doing something they oughtn't to. Trespass was out, because if they were camped on the county road they were on nobody's land but the public's. Could there be anything else?

"There ought to be," old Cowan said, sternly, and sank his voice again. "The man of the bunch is a gambler. It was him that Pap

Howell won the purse from the day before he got killed, so you can tell he bets 'em high. That would be bad enough to have around a bunch of growin' boys all by itself, but it ain't the worst. There's a couple of women with him—his wife and daughter, he claims—and as long as they stay there I can't keep these kids of mine at home after dark to save my life. They'll jump every damn fence in the— Zack, you take that tobacker out of your mouth and quit makin' faces at me or I'll wear a switch out on you. Where did that tobacker come from?"

Zack muttered that he reckoned it came from Kentucky, and added, mostly to Orlando Geary, that while they were talking would be a good time to take Clay to the bunk-house and get him into dry clothes. Orlando Geary said it wasn't sanctioned by law and that he had no assurance that Clay wouldn't keep right on going, and old Cowan said he would stand good for that, and for God's sake to go on and quit standing around being disrespectful. Zack Wall took Clay's arm and they went up the muddy path together. Once inside the bunk-house, Clay thought, he could pick a corner to change clothes in and smuggle the gun back onto himself with his back turned. He could even, if that looked too risky, turn on Zack and order him to step outside for a minute or take a flogging. Whichever way it went, he would have dry clothes and he would be done being pestered about them.

It went neither way. The bunk-house had two dirty windows, which Zack carefully hung blankets over, and one door, which he locked. Then he sat down on a bunk and stared at Clay and took a chew of fine-cut out of a paper package. "You've got some nerve, bub," he said. He couldn't have been over two years older than Clay was. "That's the way I like to see 'em. What are you goin' to do with that gun?"

Clay stared and said what gun, which was a waste of time, and bad manners to boot. But Zack Wall was not offended. Excitement had hold of him too strong.

"I felt it when I tried to help you off with your coat," he said. "I could have out and split on you to old Belly out there, but that ain't my cut. You remember how straight I kept my face? I said to myself right then, there's a boy that maybe I can help, and that's what I planned this out for. What are you goin' to use that gun for? Do you aim to shoot up the jail?"

Clay said no. Discovering that Zack had known about the gun all along made him uneasy, and Zack's friendliness and enthusiasm didn't reassure him a particle. There could be no reason for his anxiety to help except the pleasure of bragging about it afterward, though probably he hadn't thought himself out that far ahead. But he would almost certainly brag, and bragging was dangerous. Clay thought of throwing the gun into the brush and not going back to the station at all. Still, if it worked out as Uncle Preston had calculated there could be no risk. There wouldn't even be anything to brag about. "It's for somebody else," he said. "I ain't goin' to use it myself at all."

Zack nodded approvingly. "That's what I reckoned. Yes, sir, I guessed it out right to the hair line. You're goin' to slip it to Wade Shiveley through the jail door. He'll shoot himself out of jail, and they'll put up another reward. Lordee! How do you aim to slip it through?"

"I don't know," Clay said. He was too tired to stall and side-step any longer.

"That's right where I can help you," Zack said. "Yes, sir, the minute I heard Wade Shiveley was in jail, I says to myself, some-body's goin' to slip him a gun to bust out with, and if it was me, how would I do it? And I set down and figured it out, and it'll work right down to a gnat's tail. Shuck your clothes while I rustle you some more, and I'll show you."

The clothes he brought were almost as much too big for Clay as the little driver's had been for him. The trousers were almost big enough to have fitted Orlando Geary. In the legs they were wide enough for him to have jumped through, and so long that they covered his feet completely. "That's the way they've got to be," Zack Wall said. "Put these boots on, and let's have your gun."

He tied a cord firmly around the gun from the inside of the trigger-guard to the face of the hammer. He wedged the gun into the leg of Clay's right boot and strung the cord up through a hole in the right-hand trousers pocket. Pulling lifted the pistol free of the boot. Paying out lowered it to the floor, where the folds of extra trousers leg concealed it. "Now pay attention," Zack Wall said. Clay remembered that Drusilla had led off the same way and with the same consecrated enthusiasm. "I went to that jail once with the old man to see one of his squaws that had got drunk. There's a door with cross-bars that you talk through to the prisoners, but the bars is so close together you couldn't git that pistol through 'em. But down in the right-hand corner is a place where the cement floor has got a chunk cracked out of it, and a hole goes through under the door about as big as your two fists. You stand there when you're talkin', and you plant your right foot at the edge of that hole. These pants will cover it, and you'll lift the gun clear of your boot with this string and then you'll ease her down a little at a time. It'll slide right through that hole, and all you'll have to do is let go the string and take your hand out of your pocket. I'll clamp a buckshot on the loose end so the string'll fall clear, and you can climb on this bench and try how it works."

They tried it twice. Both times it worked perfectly. If the gap in the cement was still there and if it was big enough for a gun to go through, Uncle Preston's plan was halfway accomplished already.

"It's there, and it's plenty big," Zack said, unblanketing the windows. "I seen it not over two months ago, and I could git my whole foot into it. One of the kids was along, and he tried to poke his head down it. These kids ain't anything but a bunch of wild hogs."

"What did your old man go to see the squaw for?" Clay asked "Did he pay her out, or something?"

"Him?" Zack Wall said, and spat. "She'd been helpin' here in the kitchen, and he went there to find out where she'd put the flour-sifter." He unlocked the door and they went out. The fog was burning off into cold orange sunlight. All the mud-puddles up the road were dark gold with it and the leaves as far as one could see waved and glittered with a sudden access of life. A squaw came out of the house with bed-quilts to air, and a mob of youngsters caught an old hen and tossed her up to watch her frantic wing-work on the way down. Zack Wall threw a clod at a post. "I wish I was goin' instead of you," he said. "There ain't anything around this wild hog's nest except when the old man gits sick and all the squaws come high-tailin' in to prove they're married to him so they'll git his property. That's worth watchin', if you never seen it. Amongst these damned Siwashes, a man's wife is supposed to howl and hack herself with a knife when he dies. So they all set around here in the yard, and pretty soon one of 'em whittles a hunk off herself and lets out a squall, and then the next one whittles off a bigger one and squalls louder, and so on plumb around the ring. Then the first one cuts herself harder to even up, and around it goes again with all of 'em rockin' and screechin' and lettin' on they wished the old man wouldn't die, when all they wish is that all the other squaws would. None of 'em ever do, though. One reason they git themselves so fat is so they can cut themselves up without any damage. You ought to watch 'em at it here one of these times."

It sounded more exciting than entertaining, but Clay said he might arrange some time to take it in. He was younger than Zack Wall, and his raising in the Shiveley brothers' house had been of the same hog's-nest stripe as this. Yet he felt himself the maturer of the two. He had seen no more of the country, probably, than Zack Wall had; but he had seen his good work with the sheep turned into nothing by a little selfishness and the half-breed driver's work with the horses turned into nothing by the impersonal class-contempt of youngsters who were nothing but a bunch of wild hogs. Clay shook hands with Zack Wall and reefed his borrowed trousers into the wagon-seat between Orlando Geary and the little driver. He tried to feel friendly to Zack for having helped him, but all he could feel was distrustful and sorry. Zack thought faster and looked farther than the youngsters who were like wild hogs, but right at the gizzard he was exactly like the rest of them.

"I'll see you again," Zack said. "Maybe we'll fix up something together when you're through with this. I don't intend to stay on this damned tomcattery much longer."

This was the last stage of character in that old-settled grass-country; to bring in so many children that there were not even enough little shacky things like frugality and lechery and drunkenness for them to harden themselves around; and so they all took on the same one and the easiest, which was to be like a bunch of animals—wild hogs, with each trying merely to be the biggest. Zack Wall, lying awake nights thinking how he could slip a gun to a man in jail whom he had never seen; and helping eagerly to do it without any more knowing what he was doing than a hog who roots a dead tree down on top of himself in pursuit of a sowbug.

The road was good and the new team went fast, though the little half-breed drove dejectedly and mourned for the team that had been taken away from him before he could finish making the crazy mare into a good horse. Orlando Geary sat up straight and legal-looking, having cautioned Clay to keep his pants folded under so he wouldn't look ridiculous if they met anybody. There was a shot-up-looking spike-tent by the roadside, and a wagon with twenty-odd horses grouped around it, eating hay out of the back. Nobody was in sight except a tall colorless-haired man in carpet slippers hacking stove wood off a stump. Orlando Geary stopped the team and leaned out and explained who he was. The tall man let his ax trail on the ground. He was scared, and scared bad. He stuttered and trembled at the mouth and stared off to one side as if he was searching for a hole to hide in. He didn't even get over it when Orlando explained that this visit was merely to deliver an official recommendation.

"I don't know what the legal aspects of the case is," Orlando recited. "But Mr. Cowan complains that havin' these women of yours this close is a bad influence on his children. The horse-feed down the road is as good as it is here, and up the road it's better. So if you was to hitch up and pull on a few miles, it would be a favor to the authorities."

The man said, trying vaguely to get his wits started working again, that he would study about it. A girl came out of the tent, twisting her long black hair into a braid down her shoulder. The dark gold light of the meadow behind her was so strong that her face was only a soft blur against it. She had gray eyes, and she was barefooted, and she laughed at Clay and spread her hands out at her sides to indicate that his pants were too big for him. She was about Clay's age. He had a thought, the irony of which didn't strike him till long afterward, that she wouldn't look so gay and sociable if she had as many cares on her mind as he had and that her sweetness and high spirits came from her having never known the grimness and messiness behind the world. She finished braiding her hair and flapped it at him, and a sun-burnt woman with a long chin came out of the tent and inquired what in the name of time they were being hectored about now.

She had the tone and set of a scrapper, but when Orlando Geary explained that his business was the preservation of moral elevation in old Cowan's brood, she laughed. "That old mink has been down here to try to haul me up to his haymow every night for a week," she said. "When he couldn't corner me he picked on Luce, here, and twice he's even tried to come into the tent after her. He's afraid for his kids, is he? If any of them big-mouthed he-mules of his comes prowlin' around here, I'll take a club to 'em. You tell him so. Maybe it'll ease his mind."

The girl didn't look at all self-conscious or embarrassed. She turned so the light caught her face, and Clay saw that her gaiety was not so innocent and plum-bloom as the shadows had made it look. Her gray eyes held him and took his measure without flinching; she knew that he was taking hers, and she was neither eager about it nor afraid of it. Her jaw muscles under the young flesh were flat and hard, and Clay knew that, against her, Drusilla and her masterfulness would look like mere childish bullying, like a miller-moth batting against a lamp chimney without ever touching the flame inside. The man, who may have been her father but didn't look it, said that they didn't want trouble with old Cowan. They had intended to move on three days ago, but had put it off on account of the rain. Now that it had cleared, they would be on their way as soon as they could get packed.

"Maybe we will and maybe we won't," said the woman, sharply. "We move when we please, mister, and if we take a notion to stay here for the next six months, we'll do it. Luce, go in the tent and put your shoes on."

Orlando Geary opened his mouth and shut it and flapped his coat back to show the badge on his suspender. "I don't know what the legal aspects of the case is," he said again. "You've been gamblin' on a horse-race, I hear, and it's made considerable trouble for the authorities. Gamblin' is against the law."

"That was this fool here," the woman said, and yanked her head at the thin man. "Go ahead and arrest him for it, if you want to. He won't do any more of it around here, I can tell you that. Will you?"

The thin man fidgeted and said he guessed not. Clay noticed that the woman and the girl both watched him hard as if he was a nervous child doing a school recitation before company. Orlando Geary said that the law didn't allow him to make arrests for gambling unless the offense was actually in act of being committed or unless he had a warrant formally sworn out by a responsible person. "If you'll pull along a few miles, it'll be a favor to the authorities," he said. "We got to be movin'. Glad to have got acquainted with you."

The horses swung into a trot, the man picked up his ax and went back to hacking the stump, and the girl came out of the tent with her shoes on and stood in the road, looking after them. When she was out of sight, Clay could call to mind nothing about her except her gray eyes and big braid of hair and the hard easy strength he felt when she looked him over. She had not spoken one word to him and he never expected to see her again. But he felt as glad over having seen her as he had when the little half-breed brought the scared horses out of the flooded river-crossing into the moonlight. She was like an action; she was something that made mankind seem bigger and more creditable than he had imagined; she was like one of the things that had happened in the night before he had to start thinking of lying and smuggling firearms and listening to Wade Shiveley in jail.

She lasted in his mind all the rest of the way to town, and even after he had fagged out and gone to sleep she was like a new possession that he had put away for the night, intending to wake up to. The signal fire on Round Mountain still drifted black smoke against the sun; half-dozing, he saw Grandpa Cutlack as a fierce little gnome with white whiskers glittering in the sun like porcupine quills. He saw nothing more. When he came to there was no girl and no valley. They were in front of the court-house, and Orlando Geary was shaking him, and his right hand in his pocket still had the pistol cord wrapped around it. "We're on time," said Orlando. "Go in natural and shake hands with him, and talk to him friendly.

If you see he's about to tell you anything important, kind of tip your head at us, and we'll let on not to be listenin'."

There were three men in the sheriff's office around a desk. Orlando nodded to them and sat down. None of them said anything. It was exactly like a party sitting up with a dead person. Wade Shiveley was standing at the jail door, with his hands grasping the cross-bars. He was fresh shaved, with two cuts close to his mouth where the razor had slipped. His face was swollen across the cheek-bones, and perfectly bloodless except his eyes, which were red. He pressed his face closer to the bars and gagged twice before he spoke. "The old man didn't come," he said, hollowly. It sounded a little as if he was putting some of it on. "He's against me like the rest of 'em, I suppose. Well, he's got a right to be, but he ought to give me a chance to speak for myself, hadn't he? I wanted to tell him something particular."

"He ain't against you," Clay said. "He said he wished you luck and maybe he'd see you later. If you've got anything to tell, tell it to me."

The hole in the cement floor was still there. He sidled to it and planted his foot on it. The gun came out of his boot crosswise, and he wished Wade would untrack himself and talk up so the men would stop watching him. He nodded at them and they looked carefully away while he fumbled the gun with his foot so it would go through. "I didn't kill Pap Howell, Clay," Wade said. "I swear to God, if they hang me for that they'll be committin' murder. You got to help me prove it. If they'd let me out of here for a week I'd find 'em whoever it was that done it. That first killin' of mine was self-defense, and now they git me for one I'm innocent of. By God! it makes a man—" He cried, resting his forehead against his hands on the bars.

"There wasn't any money?" Clay said, softly, and paid out another inch of string.

"None of his," Wade said, with his head still on his hands. "There was a few dollars of mine hid in a brush lean-to about three miles above the cabin where they nailed me. It's at the head of the bed. And my rifle is there, and two or three trinkets that belonged to your mother. Take my horse when they stop watchin' you, and go git 'em. Fetch the rifle back here and give it to a good lawyer. Listen to me, Clay." He bawled a little more, and muttered that it wasn't right, that it was wrong. "That gun that shot old Howell split the bullet-jacket. You can shoot mine at anything you want to, and it won't ever do that. That ought to be something towards clearin' me. And I want you to tell the old man that I'm sorry for all I ever done to him. I want you to tell him that if I ever git out of this, I'll be a good son to him and make up for——"

"He sent you this," Clay said, softly, and let out another loop of the cord. "Look down. When it's ready, pretend to drop something and pick this up with it. A pencil or something. I'll tell you when."

"All right," Wade muttered. "You don't need to go after them things, I guess. If you see the old man before I do, you tell him thanks for this, and I'll see him in a couple of days. Yes, by God! and tell him I'll kick the stuffin' out of his low-down old hide for the way he's treated me, too. He owes me a damn sight more than this, and I'll collect it, too. And you let them things and that brush lean-to alone. Do you hear me?"

Chapter VII

It was worth noticing how the mere sight of that doctored pistol coming down into the jail with him honed up Wade Shiveley's faculties along with his courage. Some men can do their fastest and sensiblest thinking when there is no way out of their difficulties except head-work. Wade Shiveley's wits didn't work that way. They were more like a pack of cur dogs around an Indian camp, all hot to fight anything as long as nobody particularly wanted them to, but liable to hit for the brush and hide when anything showed up that really needed fighting. The gun on the jail floor lifted the heaviest worry off Wade's mind. Having no longer to think what he was going to do to get out, his brain emerged from its retirement, unfurled its tail, and began to handle chipmunk-sized game as fiery and efficient as hell. He edged the gun in between his feet so he could clap shut on it if any of the prisoners got up and came scouting in the corridor. Then he took out his tobacco and spilled about a handful on the floor trying to hit a cigarette paper with it. "That's how a thing like this conquers a man's nerves," he said so everybody could hear him. "Roll me one of these things while I rake up this heifer dust I spilt."

Clay took the makings through the bars and rolled a cigarette, standing so the men at the desk could see him do it. He had some trouble keeping his own hands steady, but it didn't interfere with the construction of the cigarette, and that seemed to be all the men were interested in. He licked it and passed it back, holding it high so they could all see what it was. Wade Shiveley had finished scraping the tobacco from the floor. He had the gun in the side pocket of his coat, and he prodded his finger into the cylinder chambers to make sure it was really loaded. "All right," he mumbled, and brought out his hand to take the cigarette. Apparently he had intended to give the gun back if he found anything lacking about it. But he could feel the bullets in the cylinder, and the only thing that worried him now was Orlando Geary. He had been afraid of Orlando Geary from his earliest childhood, and even the possession of a deadly weapon wasn't enough to overcome his deep-set timidity of that thick-headed old knot whose very lack of intelligence and sensitiveness made him impossible to be argued with or scared. "Well, you tell the old man what I told you," Wade said, raising his voice. "That business about my rifle and the split bullet will prove that I never killed old Howell, and that other killin' was self-defense and you know that your own self. You tell the old man he's got to help me with this. He's got to hire me a good lawyer. By God! if he don't I'll sue him for a settlement on that toll-bridge property he had me run off of. I'm part heir to that place, and I can make him ante up on it. You tell him so. I mean it, too."

He meant that he wasn't talking merely to impress the men at the desk. "I'll tell him," Clay said. He felt sneaking. Through his treachery, those men at the desk were going to get the scare of their lives and this big bloodless-featured man with the nervous blat in his voice was going to have about fifteen minutes more to live. Clay remembered how he had felt over the dead coyote, because his feeling was exactly the same now. Not worse, not profounder, though now it was a human being whose light he was scheming to put out, but simply the same feeling that he was interfering with something bigger than himself, that he was killing another wild animal for doing what nature had intended. It seemed wrong. Yet everybody else did it and saw nothing wrong in it. If you let an animal get away with a killing, you let down your employer, you exposed valuable property and helpless creatures to suffering and wrong that they had done nothing to deserve. Whichever you did was about half right and half wrong. "I'll tell him," Clay said. "He said if you knew where the Howell money was, you'd better tell me."

"I've told you as solemn as I could talk that I don't know a damn thing about old Howell's money nor old Howell, either," Wade said. His voice lifted with irritation, not all of it put on. "Now shut up about it. You're all against me, the whole damn pack of you. Git out of here and let me alone."

He sat down on a bench and covered his face with his hands. The men at the desk nodded among themselves. They had expected the interview to come out something like that, but they had consented to it to make old Geary shut up dinging about it. Orlando

Geary, giving up hard, demanded what Wade Shiveley had done all that muttering about, and Clay explained that it had been some testimony Wade had wanted him to swear to if he was called as a witness in the first killing. His character, the relations between him and his brother, and a lot of similar foolishness.

"That's about what I allowed for," one of the men said. He was pale and fat, with a curled mustache and a prominent blue eye which he walled triumphantly at old Geary. "Well, Orlando, we tried it. What do you think we ought to do with him next?"

You could see there was considerable disharmony between the two office men and Orlando Geary. He was slow and steady and obstinate. They were faster and smarter, less apt to be wrong and less apt to stick to their first conclusions when they were right. It was considerable of a treat to them to catch old Geary in a bad guess, despite his refusal to admit that it had been bad. He opened his eyes and let on that he had been doing some deep thinking about it, and said his notion had been good. The only thing wrong with it was the timing. If the kid hadn't kept him waiting half the night at the station, if a fool driver hadn't dawdled the other half away on the road trying to make a show-team out of a span of crow-bait horses, they might have got Wade Shiveley with his contrition still on him instead of giving him time to rest and get over his scare. "I'd watch this youngster for a week or so, anyhow," he recommended, hopefully. "Maybe he don't know anything, but all you've got is his word for it. You're fixin' to marry that light-haired girl at the station, ain't you, bub?"

Clay said no, with an unintentional emphasis that made the two office men laugh. "Watch him yourself, if you want to," the curled-mustached man said. "You've hauled him away from his work and run him to a frazzle for one of your hell-bent notions, so you might as well go on and finish him up. Did he come with you willing, or did you have to serve papers on him?"

Orlando Geary said, with dignity, that no papers had issued in the case yet, and that anybody he went after came willing. "You watch him," he repeated. "I'd do it myself, only I can't be away from home that long. My wife hailed me on the way in and I got to git back and see if there was anything wrong." He edged for the door to pull out before they poked any more sarcasm at him.

"There's a bunch of horse-traders camped on the road a piece below Phin Cowan's place. He's asked me to make 'em move."

The curled-mustached man said let him swear out a complaint, damn his rooty old liver, and then took thought. Old Cowan had the voting of some eighteen grown sons, and it was worth while expanding formalities a few holes to oblige him. "We've got no right to move 'em till they do something," he said, "but you tell 'em I've been hearing reports about 'em and that they'll save themselves some trouble by edging along a few miles. All these horse-traders have got some old crookedness behind 'em. If they hadn't they wouldn't be horse-traders. Tell 'em that and see if it don't work."

Geary said all right and went, moving his lips over a speech to deliver to the horse-traders on his way home. It restored all his dignity. The office man turned to Clay and said he had better chase along and catch up some sleep. "Go down to the Orcutt House and tell 'em I said to give you breakfast and a bed. When you're rested, take this note to Cartwright's livery-barn and tell 'em you want Wade Shiveley's mare and saddle to go home on. There's no sense making the county board her when Press Shiveley's got a pasture where he can keep her for nothing. We'll send for you if we need you any more."

It had seemed, when Clay entered the town, as if almost a full day had passed since sunup. But along the street it was still early morning, with a pleasant smell of stores unfurling their newness for another whirl at the country trade. Smells of new bolts of cloth, bales of overalls, fresh-painted farm tools and sheep shears and axes, cigars and coils of derrick-rope and kegs of sheep-dip and new harness, coffee and kerosene and candy, barber-shops and drug-stores and frosted-windowed saloons with empty barrels corded along the street outside. What made it stronger was that the clerks were scrubbing out and all the odors came out with the scrub-water into the open air. It was a temptation to stop and gawk inside some of the places, for the smell of fiery newness is always an infernal sight more seductive than any flavor, however fragrant, of long and useful service. But Clay didn't stop. He was set to hear shooting in the court-house, and desperate to get where nobody could find him before it banged loose. Not that he was afraid of being arrested. What he wanted to get out of was being hauled back after the rumpus was over to look at Wade Shiveley's dead face. The crack of a teamster's whip behind him almost struck him down in a faint, and he covered the next four blocks at a trot, holding up his extra length of pants leg so people laughed at him and twittered pleasantries after him. He turned into the great dark-arched Cartwright stable like an old sow going for a hole in the fence with all the dogs ripping at her flanks.

Nobody was in sight in the stable. There was a hostler in the harness-room to take night calls, but he had locked the door on himself and was doing something inside with a couple of girls that made them giggle and whoop fit to split. There was a familiar twang to their gleefulness, and Clay recognized them for a couple of girls from the little half-breed driver's household, winding up a late skirmish or beginning an early one. It was scarcely any use knocking for service while they kept that up, so Clay went through into the feed-lot, found Wade Shiveley's mare among the loose stock, and dumped Wade's saddle and bridle on her. He rode back past the harness-room door, and the hostler stuck his head out, all rumpled and rosy and foolish-looking, holding the door so nobody could see past him inside. Clay handed him the sheriff's ticket. "Takin' her home for the old man to keep," he explained. "You don't need to be so particular about that door. I've scratched myself on them two rubbin'-posts a many a time. Where's the back way out of town?"

The hostler stared, stuck the sheriff's ticket in his pocket and took it out again, and directed him. There had still been no shooting, though it was well past time for it; and there was none as he turned into an alley dropped full of storm-fallen plums and apples and yellowing cabbage roses spoiled by the rain. Clay knew Wade Shiveley's mare as if she had been his own, every gait and every turn of speed she had in her. He itched to take her out on the fly and be done with it, but he didn't dare. A horse traveling at a gallop through town would be certain to fetch everybody to the windows to see if it was a runaway. He tightened his knees on her and she racked through the drying mud and rain-struck fruit

at a trot. The alley ended, the houses got farther apart and ended
in a line of gardens, a juicy-earthed dairy, a field of red clover,
and then a stretch of pasture with clumps of hazel brush worn out
at the base by cattle. The road in front of him had not been used
since the rain. There was not a sign of anybody on it or near it
except a squad of hoboes who waved to him from a coffee-fire a
few jumps off the road. He waved back without slowing up. They
were moving into the lower country for hop-picking, probably, and
their camp would have been a place to rest, maybe even to eat.
But the temptation didn't hurt much. Any set of short-stake hoboes
would be apt to steal his horse and maybe his shoes while he slept,
and a bunch of them that big was certain to contain several sexual
perverts who might attempt to do worse than that.

The ground rose, and the road went through a scattering stand
of oak-grubs, the leaves already turned coppery and a herd of
lively-looking hogs already nosing among them for fallen acorns.
The town now was only a gleam of wet roofs in the sun, with the
rain burning out of them into a great thin pillar of blue vapor.
He was too far away to have heard the shooting even if there had
been any. It was certainly over now, and men would be out hitch-
ing up for another trip to Uncle Preston's toll bridge to peddle the
news and fetch somebody back to town to hear how it had happened
and tend to the funeral arrangements and go over the details with
the coroner's jury. This time, Clay told himself, they could have the
job to themselves, all for their very own. Not until the whole
business was done with and the funeral over and the grave filled in
and the responsibility for the doctored gun hung on Uncle Preston,
along with the thanks of the community for having thought of it—
not until all that was finished did Clay intend to give them another
chance at him. It would be two weeks, maybe. For that time he
could stay camped at the brush lean-to where Wade Shiveley had
stayed hidden so long before they caught him.

The road before Clay was only a wagon track for wood-haulers.
Nobody had been on it for months, and, unless a general raking-
out of the whole country was called on his account, nobody was
likely to. But he played it safe by steering the mare, not between

the dim wheelruts or in them, but off to one side in the brush where his tracks were less apt to show and less apt to be noticed if they did. The mare had played that kind of game before, for she followed the road without missing a turn or setting foot in sight of it. There was another advantage besides concealment, for whenever Clay went to sleep in the saddle the oak boughs scratched his face and woke him up.

He rode so all day, heading away from the sun into the gray-white backbone of mountains, and he knew he was pointed right because the farther he went the more eagerly the mare traveled and the surer she was of her road. In the afternoon he struck the snow line, and a mild piece of luck with it. The warmth was going out of the sun and his stomach hurt with emptiness; and in the shallow black water of a rain pond he found four duck's eggs. He climbed down and roasted them in a twig-fire while the mare pawed dead grass from under the frozen snow and ate it with the bit still in her mouth. She was a real trail-horse, that mare. In color she was dark buckskin, with cream mane and tail, a good stretch of legs and body, a long, easy action, and a perfect readiness to hit any clip you called on her for and the ability to hold it until she heard from you again. Clay buried the egg shells, piled mud on his fire, and shinned back astraddle of her, and she went on as willing as if she was only pacing out to run in the work-stock before breakfast, picking her trail at a lifting walk through the last daylight and right into the dark, with Clay getting numb and sleepy and chinning the saddle-horn to keep the loose branches from raking his eyes out.

By the feel of the loose branches he knew that the oaks had left off and that he was going through second-growth fir. Then it changed to vine-maple, with leaves that were white even in the darkness against the snow, and that meant he had entered big timber. Vine-maples grew only under tall trees or in full sunlight, and wherever the sun struck them they always turned as scarlet as geraniums. There was a sound of water running in the dark, and when they got close to it the mare stopped. Clay got off and she pushed past him and stood with her nostrils against what, by sense of touch, he made out to be the door of a cedar-bark lean-to. He opened it and she went in by herself and rattled her bit in an empty feed-box while he struck a match. That she knew her way around was one good sign. Another was that a horse had occupied the lean-to recently, and a load of clean hay in the pole-rick on one side was another; but what made identification certain was that the place seemed never to have been cleaned out since it was built.

That settled it for sure. Only Wade Shiveley would have thought of keeping a good horse in such a stall without ever shoveling out the manure. His cabin must be poked somewhere around the adjoining brush, but Clay was too fagged to hunt for it. He peeled saddle and bridle from the mare, tossed her a feed, and, ignoring her polite astonishment, gouged himself a hole in the ricked hay and crawled into it.

It was better almost than winning a hard fight against sleep to have put up an agonizingly hard one and then to give up and let go and let it have him and be damned. He hurt too much with fatigue to let go all holds in a minute, so there was a short, aching interval in which, one by one, all the tracks of consciousness and conscious memory smoothed out on him. The jail and Wade Shiveley; the trip to town and the half-breed driver and Zack Wall; Uncle Preston and Drusilla and Orlando Geary; the drowning sheep and Moss and Simmons and the sheep-trail down the mountain and the dead coyote. All those things lifted from his brain until only two were left. One was the gripe of weariness tightening his muscles against the blood trying to get back into them; the other was the barefooted girl who had looked at him in the horse-trader's camp below old Cowan's. He expected that she would lift from him next and that the last tussle would be between his soreness and sleep. But the soreness went away and she still held an exultant small spot inside his skull until he was sound asleep and the mare, having cleaned her feed-box and chewed all the seed-heads out of her hay, had lain down and gone to sleep too.

Even against hunger and sleepiness, against the memory of all he had been through and seen and the fear of all he had started and run away from, she was strong enough to last. He didn't feel that it was any credit of his in holding onto her, but as if it was hers for having thrown so deep a hold into him. It was as if she had won a hard race or done something praiseworthy out of her own strength and merit. Clay felt proud of her in his sleep and without knowing that he would ever lay eyes on her again.

He slept through that night and all the next day, and roused only to a kind of painful half-dreaminess in the twilight because somebody had come into the shed and was trying to tell him something urgent and important that he couldn't get through his head. It was about Wade Shiveley, and he mumbled the name over, trying to raise some feeling inside himself with it. But no feeling came, and he slept again and woke up in the dark with hunger blazing through him from heart to groin and the panicky realization that he had been slipped up on and was being watched. By the sound of breathing he knew that there were two horses in the shed with him—the mare and a new one, not unsaddled. He could hear the leather creak. He shed the hay off himself cautiously, getting ready to climb down and run. A voice spoke in the dark and his liver turned a complete handspring with fright and shame that he had let himself get treed so easily.

"You come on down now," the voice suggested. "I waitin' here from to hellangone back. We got to talk."

It was the Indian boy from the stage station, the one with the crippled hands who had helped Clay pull out the sheep. The extra horse was Uncle Preston's big red colt, which he had brought into the shed for concealment. He leaned against the wall, waiting, as he had waited there without moving for over five hours. "I make one hell of a ridin' to find you," he said. "Lots of people wantin' to put you in the jail now. I stoled this horse and come to tell you. Come on down."

Chapter VIII

CLAY got down in the dark and knocked broken hay out of his hair and spat to clear his mouth of the ammoniacal whang the barn had planted in it. "Did you come all the way up here to tell me there was people lookin' for me, damn it?" he inquired. "If I hadn't knowed it already, I wouldn't be here. Now they'll have two sets of tracks to trail me on instead of one, and I'll have to find some place else to duck to. Did you fetch anything to eat?"

The Indian boy cautioned him to talk lower. Men, he repeated, were hunting Clay all over the country and around the toll-bridge station and through the brush and everywhere, because they were mad at him. Wade Shiveley had broken out of jail. Now he would have to be caught all over again. It had got around that Clay slipped him the gun to make his break with, and the solid citizens were all madder about it than fire. If they caught Clay they would raise hell with him.

"They're welcome to, if they can catch me," Clay said. He had felt at the start that there was something infirm about that determination of Uncle Preston's. An old man, trying to be brave and unsentimental without having the least idea how to, was bound to do some misfiguring somewhere. "You've opened up the trail in here. I'll have to load up and git out. How did Wade Shiveley come to break jail? The gun I slipped him wouldn't shoot."

The Indian boy explained scornfully that Wade Shiveley hadn't found it necessary to shoot. He had merely pointed it at the two men in the sheriff's office, and they had trotted over and unlocked the door for him as eager as pet puppy-dogs. He took their guns away and locked them in, and then walked out and hit for Uncle Preston's toll bridge to deliver his thanks and enroll himself as a steady boarder. The floods had gone down so he had little trouble getting there, and Uncle Preston's fit of early-day firmness had got turned hind side to overnight, so the arrival, instead of being taken as a calamity, had been merely an occasion for a lot of bawling and apologizing and swapping broken assurances of contrition and damp

promises to do better in future. Uncle Preston had fixed him a
hideout in one of the blackberry thickets in the meadow, and the
way they all twittered around over him and lugged victuals to him
was enough to make a man think he owned the place and that
they were all trying to stand him off for the rent. "So I got out,"
the Indian boy said. "That man go tellum people what to do, he
don't do no tellum on me. I stealin' one horse to ride on, I askin'
people in town about you. Man say your horse packin' one busted
shoe, I ride out easy and look for tracks. Lookum, lookum, lookum.
Rideum, rideum, rideum, rideum. Whoosh! I come here."

"Much obliged," Clay said. The Indian boy didn't seem to have
left much unaccounted for. All his prospects, everything he had
worked and lied and swum creeks and run his neck in peril of the
law to get was knocked spang in the head. Nothing was left. The
curious part of it was that he didn't feel particularly swept away
by it. Sometimes a man would go into a gambling-house and dump
every dime he owned on the flop of one card and stand there waiting and suffering and praying for the card to show up until he
wore himself out at it. And, thinking desperately what the devil he
could do if he lost, an inspiration would strike him right fresh out
of nowhere, and it would seem so exactly the thing he ought to do
that he would watch the wrong card fall and his money go into the
bank with almost a feeling of relief that it was off his mind so he
could chase out and run down his inspiration without any holdbacks to bother him. It wasn't like losing your bet when a thing
like that happened. It was more like paying it over on a swap for
something better. "What's that wall-eyed girl at the station doin'
about all this?" Clay asked.

The Indian boy said she was doing pretty much what the others
told her to. She had taken it into her head that Wade Shiveley had
an armload of money hid somewhere, and that if she threw pancakes
enough into him he would dig it up and give it to her to patch the
station buildings up with. Nobody was bothering much about catching Wade Shiveley, because Orlando Geary had claimed that job
for himself. But there was a whole swad of men out after Clay
because the story had got out that he had come one on them by
dropping a gun into jail from his pants leg, and it made them look
foolish.

It was Zack Wall's bragging, of course, that had let out the pants-leg tidbit. If that had made them feel foolish, it was past imagining how they were going to feel if it ever came out that the gun wouldn't shoot. "They may catch me," Clay said. "If they do, by God! they'll need to go some. I got to haul out of here before they pick up that trail. You didn't bring anything to eat, I suppose?"

The Indian boy managed to dig up four soda biscuits, a small square of fat pork which he had stuck in his pocket after greasing the bucksaw with it, and a few sticky pieces of candy which he had bought with his last nickel on his way through town. "You don't need to worry about that trail, though," he said. "I findum, sure, but I rode all your tracks out comin' in. Nobody findum but me. Maybe there's goin' to be something to eat in the house. You lookum?"

Clay admitted that he hadn't got round to lookum yet. He finished the biscuits and pork, and they lit a splinter of fat pine and went out in the snow to hunt the shack up. The Indian boy found it, after a long search, by locating Wade Shiveley's water-hole and feeling with his fingers under the snow for old foot-marks. The place was inhumanly well hidden, being simply two big cedar logs thatched over with fallen rubbish to look like an accidental hurrah's nest, and the outside entrance carefully disguised with bark, earth and red huckleberry bushes. Inside, the bulge of the logs had been hewed down into straight walls. It was warm and dry, and there was a bed of fir-boughs, deep and still fresh. There was also a rock fireplace, a pile of clear pitch for torches and kindling, some odd tinware, and a covered can a third full of dirty uncooked rice.

"He ridin' out to scout more grub, I guess," the Indian boy said. "He scout plenty now, damn to hell! What you diggin' after?"

Clay gouged out the dirt at the head of the bed and fetched out the things Wade Shiveley had first entreated him to find and then ordered him not to lay hands on. The first was a tobacco-sack containing a little garnet ring, a woman's-size gun-metal watch on a breast-pin, and a pair of shell side-combs filigreed with a frugal quantity of what looked like gold. Clay's mother had not lived to any ripe age, but she had worked hard while she lived, the very hardest she knew how at anything she could find to do. All her work, over and above what she and Clay had needed to live on, had got her this. Eight dollars would have bought the whole layout and perhaps would have set up a good dinner at a first-class restaurant out of the change. Clay's mother had spent her life on work. The work was gone and her life was gone, wasted, worn out, and forgot about. The only thing about her that still held its existence and identity was this little handful of her frivolity, and it was worth something less than eight dollars.

The next thing in the hole was a tobacco-can with some loose silver and a sprinkling of five-dollar gold pieces; in all a little over forty dollars. Under that was an old copy of *Coriolanus*, the covers warped by the damp; and last, wrapped in the tail of an old oil-skin slicker, was Wade Shiveley's rifle, the muzzle carefully plugged with tallow, and a handful of loose cartridges, greased with the same substance. That was all. Of food there was not a sign. Not, of course, that anybody with a gun and cartridges in that country needed to feel uneasy about starving to death. It was merely inconvenient, because the job of finding something to shoot required time, and a shot was liable to attract some settler's attention and inquisitiveness. Clay dug the grease out of the rifle muzzle with a twig, wiped the cartridges on his shirt-tail, and poked a handful into the magazine, and said that they would chance it. He added that as far as he was concerned the toll bridge and everything around it, all the people with bad consciences and tottery resolutions and obsessions and habits of beating youngsters around to their way of thinking and then crawfishing out of it themselves, could all dip their haberdashery in butter, set themselves afire, and go flaming plumb to hell.

"We'll kill a deer the first thing in the morning," he said. "I know this gun. Anything you point her at she'll hit. We'll go out about daylight."

The Indian boy considered and said they had better go out right now, while they had the dark to cover them and the country to themselves. A shot at daylight was liable to be heard by somebody on the road, and to lead to investigation and poking around. Now the road was empty, the settlers were all feeling too warm in bed to get up for a stray shot even if they heard one, and it was easier to shine a deer with a flare than to hunt him down legitimately.

"It ain't easier to pack him in," Clay objected. "Them white-tails is heavy, and it's so dark in the trees you can't see anything except straight up. If you keep your flare goin' on the trail, somebody's liable to see it. I'd sooner wait till morning."

He was talking partly off the four soda biscuits and the buck-saw pork. The Indian boy was emptier and consequently in more of a hurry to get started. Night hunting might be twice as hard, he agreed, if you counted packing the game in; but it was ten times as safe. By burning a flare maybe three minutes, they could have a deer downed, packed in, dressed out, and a hunk of venison cooked and eaten before it got light enough for a stray traveler to see ten feet ahead of his face. By daylight they could not only get caught at their hunting, but at their cooking. Suppose some-body noticed a smoke coming from timber where nobody lived, and came rooting around to see if the brush was on fire? The Indian boy voted to go now, and squatted on the dirt floor and fixed a night-hunting flare by splitting Wade Shiveley's pile of kindling into fine splints and filling a tin bucket with them. He hung the bucket on the end of a stick so the heat wouldn't scorch him, hung Wade Shiveley's wash-basin back of it for a reflector, and stuck all his matches into the thick part of his hair-braid so they would keep dry and be handy. "You bring the gun," he said. "Deer comin' close, I pointum and touchum off, and you shootum. Come on."

They went out. The moon was high and frost-white, and the cold had set the snow so it crunched underfoot like an old horse wading into a big feed of dry oats. It was necessary to get to high ground because that was where the deer fed at night, but all the high ground was across the road and they didn't dare cross it for fear of leaving tracks in the snow. In fresh snow they could have crossed and raked their tracks over with a bundle of brush, but this was old snow, too frost-hardened to rake. They trudged through the dark brush parallel to the road, hoping to find a watercourse where the snow hadn't stuck. None turned up, so they followed the road high up the mountain where the trees still held their loads of snow, and that did as well. They picked a limber tree with a good deal of snow in it, walked across under it, and jiggled it so the snow shed down in a soft rushing smack and buried their tracks four feet deep. Clay remarked, mostly to see if the cold had done anything permanent to his voice, that it had been a smart fetch, and the Indian boy whispered back that he would have to shut up. Deer would run if they heard people talking. Being able to see pretty well in the moonlight, they were liable to scare all too easily, anyhow. They could have meat or they could have conversation, but they couldn't have both.

They went through the big timber and into a belt of firs that were snow-stunted and wind-gnarled and mean to get through. Several times they stopped, trying to hear whether deer were moving, and twice they heard branches crack and rustle as some animal ran. But nothing sounded close or unsuspecting enough for the Indian boy to waste his flare on. Their crunching snow and wallowing brush made too much noise. Everything could hear them coming, and everything got out of the way for them.

The stunted firs ended and they came into a great spread of waist-high salal, all even-topped and dull-bright like tarnished silver except where a bead of ice glittered at the end of a bunch of purple berries. There were deer trails through the salal, which made the going easier. But the hunting didn't improve, for the moon struck full on them and there were no shadows now to hide in, so all the deer could see exactly what they were up to. It was so light that they even saw the deer in a gray cloud like blowing vapor lit with a flash of white as the herd tail-flagged it down over the hill and out of sight. The place had been silent enough with them in it, but, now they were gone it was as soundless as a homestead-claim right out in the middle of the empty sky. Frost rustled, settling against the stiff salal leaves. A tree somewhere let off its load of snow with a flap-plop. The Indian boy sat down in the brush and stuck his fingers in his mouth to get them warm. "Look out now," he breathed. "They tryin' to smell us. Pretty quick they comin' back to see what we are."

Neither Clay nor the Indian boy thought any more about the toll-bridge station or about the luck that had changed them from honest young work-hands to hideouts and fugitives sneaking through the cold brush to steal venison so they wouldn't starve. They were too young and too little afflicted with social conscience to feel any of the uneasiness of the hunted. As long as nobody caught or crowded them, dodging people was a game, like bull-pen or wounded soldier, only a good deal more gratifying to be ahead in. As to having to stalk and skin their dinner before they could eat it, that was no comedown. There were plenty of respectable households where that happened, and the only disgrace about it was in going out after a deer and failing to get one. The air turned colder while they waited. A light wind was setting from the east. In the direction it came from nothing was visible except the gray-black saw-toothed ridge of mountain against the totally black sky. But beyond that were grass plains where people lived and ran cattle; mountains where they lived and worked mines; cities where they lived and kept books and sold things and ran steamboats and street cars. Millions of people working at trades that the people in Shoestring considered so unessential that they didn't even know what a tenth of them were. The wind came off all those places; all those people had felt it and breathed it and turned it loose again, and one would have expected it to carry some flavor of second-handedness from them; some touch of restlessness and trouble, maybe, considering how much disorder and uncertainty and fierceness an infinitely smaller number of people seemed to make out of living together in Shoestring. But there was not a trace of human use or passion about the wind at all. There was only a faint wildish whang, musky and bitterish and elusive, that almost blew away and then steadied again plain and unmistakable. Clay eased a cartridge into his gun and the Indian boy lit his bucket of pitch-splints and got stealthily to his feet. The deer were coming back.

The return was no special shakes to look at. At first there was nothing at all except shadows at the edge of the salal. Then the pitch burned high and the Indian boy got a better focus with his wash-basin, and Clay saw a faint scattering of little luminous dots against the black timber. They looked a good deal like the phosphorescent worms that children used to dig out of rotten stumps; but they moved, went out, and blazed up plainer than before. They were the deer's eyes, glowing with the reflection of the flare. "Here they come," the Indian boy said, playing it on them. He spoke in an ordinary conversational tone of voice. Holding deer in a strong light makes them forget to be afraid of anything else. "Pretty

soon you shootum. The green eyes is bucks and the red ones is
does. You hurry up. This thing she gittin' hot."

The flare was consarned hot. It frizzled Clay's hair as he brought
his rifle into the light to find his sights. The hind notch was merely
an opening in the dark, but the front-leaf settled into it as big and
plain as a stick of chalk. He picked the biggest pair of green sparks
because they looked the easiest to hit, held between them and a
little below them, and let go. Smoke blew back and stung his eyes
so he couldn't see, but the Indian boy tossed his flare-bucket into
the brush, blew on his scorched wrist to cool it, and said that had
done it. "You got him," he said. "Dead center. What the hell you
pickin' out the biggest one for? You think we got freight-train to
packum in on?"

The dead buck, when they searched out the place where he had
hit the ground, looked as if he was going to need some kind of
steam-transportation. He lay in the snow, stretched out long, as if
he had started after something he couldn't quite reach, and he was
as big as a colt. Even dressed out, he would scale close on two
hundred and fifty pounds; and they didn't dare dress him out to
pack because the viscera in the salal would draw buzzards, and
buzzards would fetch Orlando Geary with his tail up to find out
about the killing and trail the killers. As to the deer's death, neither
of them regretted that. There was a difference between killing a
coyote for spite and killing a buck deer for something to eat. "We
could chase back to the lean-to and fetch a horse for him," Clay said.

The Indian boy kicked snow over the blood around the deer's
head. "Too long gittin' here with a horse," he objected. "Hard
trail for a horse to travel in. Hard to find it in the dark without
hollerin' back and forth. We got to pack him ourselves. Find a dry
pole to string him on while I skin his feet out."

He knelt down in the snow with his knife, and he had all four
lower leg-bones out by the time Clay got back with a dead sapling
which, being heavy enough to hold a big deer without bending, was
a moderately uncomfortable weight in itself. The Indian boy tucked
the leg-bones into his pocket, tied the deer's feet together by the
ends of loose skin, and strung the pole through them. They shouldered it between them and headed down through the gnarled timber
for the road. The deer was so heavy that they had to stiff-leg their

way along to keep their knee-joints from folding up under the weight. Clay, who had the rifle and the front end of the pole, got the worst end of the lug because they were pointed downhill and the carcass kept sliding down the pole on top of him. The job of holding the thing off the ground used his strength so totally that the mere weight of any loose weed-stem against his ankles or any stick underfoot was enough to make him stall and totter before he could get over it. He kept going because it was easier to do that than to dump the load and then have to lift it up again. He said nothing because his muscles burned up all his wind, and he worked himself into a slow and uncomprehended state of anger waiting for the Indian boy to volunteer at least some apology for having got them into such a bone-grinding job by suggesting the night hunt to start with.

The Indian boy volunteered nothing. Breath was also a scarce article with him, for, though he had the light end of the load, he was the smaller of the two, and he had to keep his gait timed to Clay's when it was too jerky and irregular to make any rhythm out of and impossible to watch in the dark shadowing timber. It was an odd circumstance that the very success of their hunt should have started the two hunters building up a grudge against one another, alone under the white moon in which the naked bushes stood bright and made shadows on the snow like marks traced with a wet black pencil. Nothing moved. There was no wind, there were no birds. If the road had been closer, the feeling that their work was getting them somewhere might have worked their anger away before it had a chance to set. But the slope lasted and lasted. The Indian boy dropped the pole and had to lie down and rest before he could lift it again. He rolled his head in the snow and fought air into his blood desperately, and Clay lay and blew with him, despising him for having bull-headed them into something he couldn't stand up to. They got up and lugged on, and Clay fell down himself, had to rest, and felt madder because he had been rawhided into a hunt that showed up his lack of endurance so embarrassingly. When they neared the road they were taking fifteen minutes to go a hundred yards and falling down to rest every twenty steps. The pale shrubs against the snow turned black, and their intense black shadows turned pale. The sky was lightening for dawn. They were almost in sight of Wade Shiveley's lean-to, too exhausted to move another step; and they heard the stamping of horses and the grate of sled-runners in the road below them. Daylight had overtaken them, travel on the road had overtaken them; the necessities of their own bodies had caught up with them like a band of squalling children hanging onto a man's shirt-tail when he was trying to win a foot-race. They threw the deer down in a vine-maple thicket, sat on him, and began to run through the list of grudges they had thought up against one another while they waited for the sled to pass in the road so they could go on.

To Clay's insulted surprise, the Indian boy was able to dig up as many things to complain about as he had. He opened by mentioning that the whole trouble was the Indian boy's fault for having promoted the night hunt instead of waylaying the deer when they drifted down to their bed-grounds at daylight. The Indian boy retorted that it was no such damned thing. It was simply that Clay, instead of using a fingerfull of sense in picking a deer they could manage, had elected to butcher more meat than they could use in six months or carry home in six years. Clay pointed out that he couldn't weigh a deer that he couldn't see, and that what had brought them to this pass was simply the Indian boy's empty belly, and the Indian boy observed that his belly was empty because Clay had hogged his four biscuits, which was a wicked come-back if he had known enough about scolding-match technique to have pressed it. But he took the argument into serious ground by explaining that there was no sense talking about how much better it would have been to do their deer-killing by daylight, because it was impossible to kill one then. By daylight in this season, the deer carried a medicine that could only be whipped out of them by a lot of initiation ceremonies before a hunt started. You had to go without eating for twenty-four hours, to scrub yourself in running water a disagreeable number of times, to purify your clothes and gun in the smoke of several specially prescribed kinds of wood, and a whole lot of similar truck that there hadn't been time for. Whereas after dark Big Beaver took the deer's medicine away from them and used it for purposes of his own. He delivered this theological exposition with a touch of impatience, as if anybody ought to know that; and Clay said it was all foolishness. If he hadn't already worked all the spring out of himself, he could scout up a deer-trail and kill a deer on it in an hour. Big Beaver had nothing to do with it because there wasn't any Big Beaver. The Indian boy said that was a lie, because he had seen Big Beaver himself.

That was a fool thing to be arguing about, because there was no way by which either side could be proved. But they disputed back and forth about it as spitefully as if they genuinely despised each other. They didn't at all. The trouble probably was that, after the excitement of meeting and of hiving meat had died down in them, they had room to start sizing up their individual intentions and prospects, and that each, in the back of his head, realized that they would have to split up and go it alone.

It was a good thing for them to have realized. Their partner-ship from the beginning had been accidental, a little superficial. Both disliked Wade Shiveley; both, on his account, had taken to the brush so they wouldn't have to stand him; but outside of that there was nothing between them. Underneath they pulled in entirely different directions, and it made understanding and sympathy im-possible. The Indian boy pulled to his own people, whom he scarcely knew anything about except by hearsay and guesswork; and Clay, with even less actual information to go on, pulled to the horse-trader's camp, which, if Orlando Geary hadn't lost his cunning, would by now be piling around the country somewhere on the move like himself. As far as will and intention went, the separation be-tween the two youngsters was already completed, and the sensible thing would have been to speak up and say so and split. They couldn't do that. The loneliness of the mountains imposed some kind of extra necessity on them, so that mere feeling and under-standing didn't seem enough to separate on. There had to be some-thing solider, something more familiar and obvious, and the most reasonable thing they could think of was to rake up a squabble. They raked one and sat passing it back and forth across the dead deer until old Flem Simmons came driving his sled-runner wagon-bed up the road and pulled up almost in front of them without noticing them. He hooked his lines on the jacobstaff, climbed out stiffly because he was wearing four or five pairs of pants against the cold, and unstrung a deer's carcass that had been hanging in a tree about forty yards away from them. If they had waited till daylight they would have seen it and they could have swiped it and packed it to the lean-to as easy as spitting off a horse.

Flem Simmons was the oldest of the Peg Leg Simmons get of sons. Like the rest of them, he amounted to nothing, but in a slightly individual style. He was hard-working, good-natured, and extremely sociable, but he had lived by himself in the high mountains longer than anybody could remember, and the pressure of sociability with nobody to exercise it on had got him in the habit of talking to himself; not because he had anything to say, but for the purpose, apparently, of keeping up his practice with a monotonous formula of cusswords. He shouldered his deer—a small female, with part of her red summer pelt not shed yet—and it looked for a minute as if he might get back to his sled and pull out without seeing them. But the Indian boy's carelessness gave their hideout away. He raised up cautiously, putting his weight on the dead buck, and the carcass, startlingly, let off a deep spooky-sounding quack. Old Simmons stopped, glared nervously, and fumbled under his armpit for his pistol. The doe's head peeking over his shoulder gave him an arch appearance, but the old cuss was dangerous. Those old mountain settlers were so unused to people around them that they were liable to bang half a dozen shots into a suspicious clump of brush merely to see if there was anything hiding in it. Clay spoke up, and old Simmons uncocked his pistol and dumped the deer off in the snow and started his cussword formula working loud and amiable, with the cold condensing it in little drops on his grow-and-be-damned gray whiskers.

"Well, God 'n' I thought I heerd somebody a-colloguin' around here when I come up the road," he proclaimed. "Damn, though, you blamed nigh fooled me a-layin' low on me. God 'n' I see you got you a buck, and, Christ, he's a whacker, ain't he? Damn, you boys ain't tryin' to pack a critter that size? Christ, he's bigger'n the pair of ye. Where you takin' him?"

"Down the road a piece," Clay said. "We got horses stalled up in the brush, waitin' for us. Did you night-hunt that doe?"

He was after the Indian boy's theory about Big Beaver and the deer's protective medicine, and he got it. "Damn, no!" old Simmons said. "God 'n' I shot her right from the road here in broad daylight, and a couple more along with her! Damn, I had to ram home and fetch out the team to haul 'em all in. Load your buck into the wagon-bed, and God 'n' I'll haul down to your camp fer you. Or up to my place if you'd sooner. You can't stay camped out in this weather, because, Christ, it'll kill ye!"

He glared at them sociably out of pale-blue eyes that must at one time have been able to see what other people were thinking about behind what they did and said. But living off by himself with wild animals that thought and acted all at the same clatter, and wild mountains that never thought or acted at all, had thickened the brain behind his eyes until a good half of what he saw never got through to it. The mountains did that, as they had made Clay and the Indian boy unable to separate without stirring up a quarrel to do it on. "We'll go to your place," Clay said. It would be better than having the old cuss find out where Wade Shiveley's lean-to was, and it would also make more of an occasion to separate from the Indian boy.

"I'll go, but I ain't goin' to stay there," the Indian boy said. He was sulky and sullen, as he had always been around the toll bridge station. He had taken a dislike to old Simmons for having killed deer in the daytime against Big Beaver's medicine. One would have expected him to pitch his spite against Big Beaver for putting out a grade of medicine that failed to take hold, but religion doesn't work that way. "I goin' rideum across the mountains," the Indian boy said. "I findin' reservation across the mountains to live on. This ain't good people here."

"They ain't people that take any stock in this damn fool business about medicine," Clay said. "A reservation will be a good place for you. I hope you find one. Go fetch the horses while I help pack this deer to the road."

The Indian boy went, and old Simmons remarked that God and he didn't know whether it would be possible to get across the mountains so late in the season or not, the way the snow had been drifting into the passes. "Damn, a wagon-outfit went past yesterday morning to try it," he said, boosting his shoulder under one end of the carrying-pole. "But, Christ, he had a string of forty-odd extry horses to help break out ahead, and a couple of women to help with the drivin'. A horse-tradin' outfit, that was. It ain't come back, so maybe they made it. But, damn, the trail's all blowed over ag'in at the summit by now, and the snow's settled so I wouldn't back a horse to stand up on it. You headin' somewheres, or do you aim to stay around here for a while?"

"Headin' somewhere, I guess," Clay said. It looked as if he wasn't going to shake the Indian boy, after all. "If that horse-tradin' outfit got across the mountains, I got to git across, too. If I can't make it I'll go somewhere else. I can't stay here. It's a hell of a place."

Old Simmons laughed proudly. "God 'n' I thought so too when I first struck it," he said. "But damn, I've stuck it for fifty years nigh about, and it ain't killed me. Yonder comes your horses. We'll git where it's warm."

Chapter IX

FLEM SIMMONS' land-holding was a half-mile-square homestead claim astraddle of a creek bottom full of devil's-club stalks and skunk cabbage and wild-currant bushes and alder saplings. There was a round hundred and sixty acres of land in the claim, as provided by the Act of Congress of 1864 to encourage settlement on and development of the public domain; but old Simmons had never got round to using anywhere near all of it, and there were parts of it that he had never even had occasion to set foot on. A six-acre strip of beaver-dam meadow below his cabin produced sufficient hay to winter his horses, and he had fenced that in with an enclosure of dried brush, less because it would hold livestock than because the government required a certain portion of a homestead to be fenced as a symbol of permanence. His cabin was also laid according to land-office regulations, for it contained two rooms, two glass windows, and one stove, all of which the homestead inspectors required a settler's cabin to have, whether the settler needed them or not. There were several stools made by sawing rounds of a log and driving pegs into them for legs, a table topped with split cedar shakes that weren't nailed down and were therefore liable to rise up and slap a man in the face if he leaned too close to the edge, and a bed made by joining four small logs in a rectangle and filling the enclosure with the tips of fir boughs. Above the bed were two enlarged family portraits in black and white. One was of Grandma Simmons, who had been made by the artist to look like an iron-chinned old wampus with her hair done up so tight that she appeared to be keeping her mouth shut against the pull by bearing down with all her strength. The other was of Peg Leg Simmons, a large old gentleman with a hat pulled square across his eyebrows and a godly scowl set on his countenance as if it had been nailed there by a professional horseshoer. The bed was covered with an elaborately-pieced quilt which was a family inheritance, and there was a big grandfather's clock in a corner that must at one time have been considerable of a machine. The dial was rigged to register not only the hour of the day, but also the seconds, and there was an outside scale that kept track of even the days of the month and the phases of the moon. There was also a charge of mysterious liquid in a glass tube attached to the case, and it was supposed to cloud up ahead of any important change in the weather, and there was a set of directions lettered alongside so a man could read off exactly what kind of change it presaged. The liquid had turned sulky from overwork or lack of appreciation or something, though, and it was stalled on "Violent Storms." Old Simmons said it had stayed there without budging for fifteen years, and that it was a blamed sensible thing to do, because, instead of working itself limp trying to keep up with the weather, it simply got a long way ahead and waited for the weather to catch up.

The timekeeping department of the thing was badly used up. The second hand was gone, the minute hand was bent so it pointed out accusingly into the room instead of at figures as it should, and one of the weights was missing. Simmons had taken it to kill a skunk, and it had got lost before the smell wore off so it could be brought back. So the clock didn't run. But it was handy to hang things from and lean things against, and old Simmons couldn't have kept house without it. His father had freighted it all the way across the plains in the early days, and any clock that had been that much trouble to import was too good to throw away. It did give a comfortable feeling to the homestead cabin, the light from the stove shining against it in the half-dark that represented warmth because the dawn in the snow outside was so eye-hurtingly dazzling and white.

Simmons had planted fruit-trees and berry-bushes in the yard outside his door. They weren't of any particular use to him, but he kept them because he had always been accustomed to seeing such things around places where people lived. Some of his nursery experiments actually were doing well. A couple of rows of currant-bushes had borne so heavily that the birds hadn't managed to strip them in a whole summer of hard work. But old Simmons never picked any of the currants, because they required cooking and canning to be any good, and he had no time to fool away on such squaw's business. He had also set out a patch of strawberries, and, now that the frost had killed the weeds in it, you could see the red leaves shining under the snow as clear and pretty as flowers; and he had several runty peach- and apple-trees which he had installed before discovering that the season at that altitude was too short for them to mature their fruit. Closest to the door, within easy reach in case of unexpected illness, was a chittim-tree, the bark of which, boiled in a tea, was a reliable and violent purgative if the patient was man enough to get it down.

There were certain rules for barking a chittim-tree for physic, and a good deal of hard luck was apt to hit the constipated sufferer who guzzled a dose that hadn't been peeled carefully from up to down. If stripped on the bias, or round and round, the bark would take one's innards in that direction too, and grind the patient back and forth and sideways like gravel in a stamp-mill without ever turning anything loose. If peeled up, it was liable to fetch his entire system up, like turning a sock wrong side out, and there was a story to the effect that somebody in the country had once actually hauled his own toe nails plumb up into his ankles trying to heave up a slug of chittim that had been peeled the wrong way of the limb. Chittim-trees grew wild on that slope of the mountains, and Simmons made a considerable chunk of extra money every year by peeling the wild bark to ship to patent-medicine manufacturers in the East. Sometimes they didn't pay him much for it, and then he evened up, not by sulking and refusing to deal with them any more, but by selling them a shipment of bark that had been peeled round and sideways and hind side to. The thought of the patent-medicine factory being jumped by indignant customers who had heaved up the insoles of their boots getting rid of the medicine, and by others who hadn't been able to get rid of it at all, gave Simmons more genuine entertainment than he could have bought himself by getting a decent price for his chittim bark.

The entertainment, of course, was purely a matter of guess-work and imagination. Simmons had no way of knowing whether his mis-peeled laxative had worked on patent-medicine users as awfully as it was legendarily supposed to. His snickering himself through a whole winter with so little actual information to go on showed how easy he was to entertain. Even his own conversation was enough to hold him spellbound, and he could take the measliest little episode that had happened to him and string it out and wool it around and supple it and driddle it along for hours as joyful and preoccupied as an old squaw tanning a stolen buckskin. He couldn't simply state what had happened to him, exhibit the scars to prove it, and then start talking about something else. He had to start with the way the weather had looked when he woke up and what he had thought about it, what fuel he had started the fire with, which sock he had put on first, what he had had for breakfast and how it tasted, whether he had left his team in the barn or turned them out to pasture, and the most infernal rigmarole of particulars that had no purpose whatever except to keep Clay and the Indian boy from squabbling about whether they were going over the mountains together, separately, or at all. The most they could do, while old Simmons cooked breakfast and talked, was to make faces at one another across the table.

They did so, and old Simmons set instalments of victuals in front of them and told a story that began with his getting his boots wet so he had to grease them with tallow before he could put them on, and how on that identical day he had trapped a red-fox pelt worth every nickel of eighty-five dollars. It wasn't very easy on the ears, but breakfast made up for it. There were fried bacon and onions and potatoes, sliced venison-liver and big saddle-blanket pancakes with sugar syrup, country sausage and brown flour-gravy and eggs fried with their eyes open, and a plate of fried head-cheese because old Simmons had recently killed his hog. There was also coffee. He didn't fry that, but boiled it in a tin bucket with a rag in it. When the rag rose and floated, the coffee was strong enough to drink, and Simmons, cantering along with his story, set it on the table.

According to the story, he had set his trap out on the sidehill in the middle of a line of tracks which he thought belonged to a coyote. He had been delayed visiting it by the arrival of a horse-trader's outfit heading across the mountains with a big string of medium-grade saddle stock and a couple of women. While the women got down to use old Simmons' backhouse, Simmons undertook to persuade the man not to risk taking them on over the mountains in such weather. Simmons said that God and he had argued high and low with him, but the horse-trader was a stubborn kind of character, soured on the country and suspicious of any advice he got in it, so Christ, he stuck to his notion of going on, and God and old

Simmons couldn't budge his determination a single peg. The women
came out and backed him up, so Christ and they all got in and went
on, and God and old Simmons remembered that he had intended
to chase up and look at that damned trap. Well, and then ——

"It was yesterday they come past here?" Clay inquired. "They
didn't mention whether there was any news from down in the valley, did they?"

Simmons said that God and he had asked them what was going
on down below, but to save his gizzard he couldn't recollect whether
they had told him anything special or not. His own thoughts and
concerns had grown on him with isolation until he couldn't take
enough interest in outside events to remember whether there had
been any. The one thing he felt sure of was that they hadn't told
him anything out of the ordinary run. "Well, God and I moseyed
along up to the trap, not expectin' to see anything except a blamed
chicken-stealin' coyote, and Christ and this fox was nabbed right
down into it. And me without anything to shoot him with, and I
didn't dast leave for fear he'd chaw his foot off and slope on me.
Well, God and I picked up a club and peeled him one over the
head, and Christ, he squalled bloody murder and halfway made to
pull loose, and God and I edged around to git him by the tail. . . ."

He laid the frying-pan down in the middle of the floor and stalked
it dramatically to show how he had edged around the fox. Then
he got down on his hands and knees and showed how the fox had
glowered up at him. To complete the performance, he picked up
the frying-pan and whacked himself across the head with it and
keeled over with his eyes walled up and a big black patch of soot
on his bald spot where the frying-pan had landed. It was spiritedly
rendered. The Indian boy remarked that a fox dying usually kicked
his legs, so Simmons lay down again and kicked his. Then he got
up, put more wood in the stove, and set a tin cup full of melted
bacon grease on the table to serve as butter. "Set up to her, boys,"
he invited. "Well, when I see that fox was dead, I got out my knife
and opened the little blade and set down to pelt him out. So God
and I ——"

"Them horse-traders didn't mention anything about Wade Shiveley, did they?" Clay asked. He did his best to sound offhanded,
but he might as well have saved himself the trouble. Simmons never

noticed overtones in anybody's conversation except his own, and not any hell of a lot in that. He said he hadn't heard a word about Wade Shiveley since Adam was a cowboy, and what was the newest cussedness he had been up to?

"They put him in jail," Clay said, cautiously. "But he busted out on 'em, so now he's loose again." The statement sounded flat and scrawny, cut so close to the bone. He felt slightly disappointed to realize that what had cost him so much strain and so many tall emotions to live through could be put into words so simply and with so low an emotional content. There wasn't enough in it to get old Simmons interested, and he didn't care enough about it to feel disappointed. So he said uhuh and tied into his breakfast, combining it with a long story about how he had figured on having honey for his pancakes from a swarm of wild bees he had caught, only a damned thieving bear had sneaked in and raided the stand the night before he was ready to rob it. It was even longer-winded than his stories usually were, because the only real action came off right at the start, and the rest was a painstaking catalogue of the things he had done about it, the upshot of the whole business being that he hadn't managed to do anything. He shot at the bear in the dark, and when daylight came he found blood on the ground, so he feathered up and trailed it across the mountains onto the headwaters of Wokus Creek. There the trail petered out, and from then on the story went sort of wallowing along without being about much of anything.

One thing kept it mildly entertaining. It was nothing to listen to, but it was rather worth watching because old Simmons could eat and talk at the same time. Most of the settlers who had slung down to live in the Cascade Mountain passes into eastern Oregon could do that, and most of them did as often as they could get hold of anybody to listen to them. One thing that had kept those mountain people from developing any sort of community life, probably, was the fear that they would all talk one another to death the first time they got together. Loneliness is supposed to make people reserved and taciturn, but it didn't work that way with them, except when they happened to be of Scandinavian stock and therefore unable to think up anything to say. What solitude had lost them was the habit, not of talking, but of listening. They did so little listening themselves that they actually didn't realize what kind of a job it was, and so it never struck them that their seven-year-itch style of bush-beating narrative was any less fun to hear than it was to perform.

It was no use undertaking to explain to them about it, either. Either they refused to believe it or else they got mad about it; and in either case they went right on talking. Old Joel Farlow, who trapped cougar at the Dog River Meadows, had actually brought permanent scandal on his family name by refusing to let his daughter's marriage ceremony proceed until he had told all his life experiences to a bashful young preacher whom he had imported from the lower valley on a rush call to take charge of the splicing. He forgot all about the emergency under the witchery of being able to tell about himself, and he took up close to two days doing it, with the bride fidgeting herself into a sick spell, the groom being detained under guard in the smoke-house till they were ready for him, and the young preacher twisting and trying to get started on the wedding and being yanked back into his chair by the necktie as often as he got up to find his Bible and call the witnesses. Before it was over, the guards had got tired and left, the groom had escaped through a hole in the smoke-house roof, and the bride had taken to her bed and given birth to a prosperous infant that, according to the squaw who attended as midwife, didn't look like the vanished groom at all, so there was no chance of ever shotgunning him into acknowledging it. And besides old Farlow, there was also Mrs. Yarbro, who raised bees in the fireweed slashings on Upper Thief Creek. She was so enslaved to the practice of unbosoming herself before strangers that she deliberately worked into a lawsuit regularly every year so she could explain to the jury, from the witness-stand, what a hard life she led, and how worthless her last four husbands had been, and how much trouble her children had given her to raise, and how her roof leaked and her cow had run off with a stray bull and her bees swarmed when they weren't supposed to and stung her when she went after them, and how her female disorders (which she described in minute detail) gave her hell all the time and no doctor in the country had been able to do them a lick of good.

Sometimes Mrs. Yarbro's lawsuit would come off before a strange judge who would undertake to make her confine her testimony to the lawsuit instead of rambling along about which intimate organs were almost killing her. But no judge ever tried that more than once. It merely made her get mad and yell, and when that was over she would be unable to recollect where she had left off, so she would have to back up and start her story all over again from the beginning. The only way Mrs. Yarbro could tell anything was to start from taw and tell everything, like a school-kid who has learned the multiplication table but can only tell what nine times eight is by starting at nine times one and singsonging his way up to it.

It would have been unreasonable, of course, to blame the mountain air or water or scenery for the talkativeness of Mrs. Yarbro and old Farlow and Flem Simmons. But there did seem to be something about the section that drew long-winded people to it, because, out of the fifty-odd lone trappers and hand-loggers and wild-cattle-skinners scattered along that slope of the divide there was not one who couldn't talk the hind leg off a mule with ease, fluency, and relish. In one sense it was a good thing, because it made them better able to stand the only kind of life they were fit for. But there was something out of gear about a life that people could stand up to only by becoming a set of windies. It wasn't the right way to be, even if they did like it and even if it did keep old Simmons from taking any interest in news from the lower country and from being suspicious about Clay and the Indian boy and the circumstances under which he had found them.

As long as the light outside remained a cold shadowless glare against the snow, old Simmons' cabin seemed a pretty good place to stay shacked in. But the earth went on revolving, and the light turned to a clear rose-tinged flush as if the snow had started to run full of life. The air itself was too clear to take color from the sun, but it moved as it always does about dawn, and little blades of frozen vapor drifted through it from the creek, glittering as the light struck through their facets with light red and hard blue and fire-yellow that hurt the eyes. Black shadows laced out against the powdery snow, and the bare fruit-tree twigs turned from dead black to a metallic blue like the burnish of fire-tempered steel. There was no warmth in the new sun. It gave only light,

and it knocked blinding little rainbows out of the frost-beaded
cobwebs in the currant-bushes without thawing them even at the
edges. But with it the day seemed to untrack itself and start moving,
and it was hard to watch it from the Simmons wickiyup without
wanting to start moving, too. The Indian boy pushed back his
plate and said he would have to be getting saddled up. He couldn't
count on any horse feed on the upper slope of the mountains, and
he wanted to make the summit before night and get down to open
pasture the next day before his horse began to pinch up around
the backbone.

Old Simmons urged him not to rush off until he was rested, and
Clay not only urged, but ordered him to stay where he was and
not go skallyhooting around the country wearing down his horse
when there was no use in it. Clay himself hated to think of pulling
out so soon, because the evening's exercise had sprung his muscles
and cost him some sleep, and he hadn't got any great sight of re-
cuperation out of listening to old Simmons. Now, having taken
aboard all the hot food he could hold, he would have liked to climb
into the haymow, pull some hay over his head, and sleep till his eyes
grew shut. He would have done it, in spite of the Indian boy's determination and the risk of being caught by a search-party from
town, but a dull and unaccountable feeling of jealousy took hold
of him when he thought of letting the Indian boy go on over the
mountains alone. Not that he wanted the blamed Siwash stringing
along with him. What he wanted was to prevent him from sashaying
on ahead to catch up with the horse-trader's outfit and have that
all to himself. And he knew that was a fool thing to feel jealous
about. A girl like that horse-trader's wasn't apt to be in much danger, as far as her affections were concerned, from a little hair-
braid buck Indian barely old enough to be out of knee-pants if
he had ever owned any. But the lack of sense didn't make Clay
feel any less earnest about it, and it did make him meaner about
arguing. "You don't need to go across the mountains," he said. "I
do. I'm goin' alone, and if I catch you taggin' after me I'll lay for
you and shoot your horse out from under you. Why can't you
load up and go on back home where you belong?"

The Indian boy said bullheadedly that there wasn't any home
that he belonged in. He didn't intend to follow anybody, and he

didn't feel uneasy about having his horse shot, because he didn't think Clay could stay close enough behind to hit him. He grabbed his coat and started for the door, and his bone flute fell out of one of the pockets. Clay grabbed it, dodged the Indian boy's attempt to knock it out of his hand, and backed to the stove with it. "You come back here and set down, or I'll bust your whistle and throw it in the fire!"

He knew that some Coast Indians treated their flutes to some kind of religious initiation ceremony, with fastings and visions and protracted-meetings to make them hit the right key or something, but he didn't realize how much rumpus a really well-consecrated instrument was capable of stirring up. The Indian boy reached Wade Shiveley's rifle from behind the table and trained it on him. "You wantin' git killed, huh?" he inquired. "Giveum back!"

He pumped a cartridge into the chamber. His hands and his chin trembled, which, in an Indian, is a sign of serious intentions. Clay opened the top of the stove and held the flute over the coals. "You shoot, and your whistle will fall into the fire and burn up," he said. "I ain't goin' to give it back to you, so put that gun back where you got it and set down."

The Indian boy kept hold of the rifle, and they stood glaring at one another. It was a nice, lively start for a bad fight, all boiled out of ingredients that both the youngsters were ashamed of, and, therefore, touchy about. The Indian boy didn't want to admit that his flute was his warrant of audience with the supernatural powers. Clay didn't want to let on that he had a case on a girl he had seen for two minutes in the middle of the county road. Neither wanted to go on with the set-to and neither was able to stop, because it would have necessitated some kind of explanation. It was a relief to both of them when old Simmons put in and settled it. "He won't shoot," Simmons said. He leaned back from the table, holding a slab of fried liver on his fork and squinting over it at them with disapproval. Their dratted argument had broken in on his story about the bear that raided his bee-stand. "Give him back his whistle. Neither one of you's goin' to leave till you've skinned out and cut up that deer of yours. Godamighty, you lay out all night in the snow to kill him, and you might' near break yourselves in two

packin' him in, and now you want to leave without findin' out
what he eats like? Is that the way they train kids nowadays?"

"We've decided we won't need him," Clay said. He had totally
forgotten they had a deer. "We'll give him to you."

That ran him up against another discovery about mountain settlers' characters. Old Simmons depended on wild game for most
of his living, and he looked on a deer as property too valuable to be
shot merely for the hell of it and given away like a dead blue jay
in the barnyard. He refused the donation because the three deer
he had killed for himself made all the meat he needed to winter on,
and any extra would go to waste. "He's your game, it don't matter
a damn whether you need him or not," he said. "You ought to
thought about that before you killed him. This ain't no time for it,
and this business of butcherin' good meat and then throwin' it
away is a bad habit for boys like you to be encouraged in. You go
on out to the barn and start peelin' the hide off of him, and do a
good job of it, or blamed if I won't begin to think you're both
run away from the reform school or something. I'll be out when I
clear up the dishes."

It was warm in the stable-end of the barn where the horses were;
but mighty little of the warmth circulated as far as the wagon-
shed where the dead buck had been dumped among piles of rusty
scrap-iron, broken-down furniture, old nail-kegs and coffee-barrels
and tin tobacco-signs, bottles of poultry-conditioner and horse medicine and whisker-revivifier, old gun-barrels and shoes and hoops and
wire bustles and pieces of buggy-harness, wornout horseshoes and
deer antlers and eagle wings, old catsup-bottles and lard-pails and
baking-powder cans, miles of rusty wire and decayed rope binding
the whole smear into one monumental unit of uselessness. Building
it had taken old Simmons years of serious application, and he never
made a trip to town without raking the municipal dump for something else to fetch home and pile on top of it. He considered it a
mighty useful collection, because there was scarcely an article needed
by man that couldn't be found somewhere in it if you looked long
enough. The trouble was that it was too blamed comprehensive. Old
Simmons could never feel right about dumping his bread-sourings
into the wrong-size bottle, because he felt so positive that there
must be a right-size one somewhere in the pile. So he would spend

sometimes as much as a week hunting it out, and in the meantime his sourings would have gone flat and he would have to make up a new batch and look out another-size bottle to fit them. But time was of no value to old Simmons, and it did keep him entertained when there was nobody around to talk to.

The dead buck lay in the short chaff close to the junk-pile, his legs poled out as if they had frozen in the middle of a jump, his head stretched back helplessly because the impact of the bullet had strained it back against the neck-joints. Both his eyes were wide open, with bits of dry chaff sticking to the naked pupils. Old Simmons' three smaller deer were corded against the side wall, the cold having stiffened them so they handled as easily as so much wood. Clay and the Indian boy drew no reflections about death from the line-up of carcasses because they were accustomed to think of deer meat as something to eat and not any more to associate it with mortality and dissolution than if it had been a quarter of beef. They did think, somewhat as a man might in the shank end of a hard marriage, that it was a good deal of a joke on them to have been so anxious not to lose the buck and then to discover what a slew of trouble and backache their success had let them in for; but neither of them did any talking about that. They tied a rope to the buck's hind legs and hauled him up to the cross-beam overhead. Their breath froze into hoarfrost on the thick slate-blue hairs as they peeled the wet skin down from the cherry-red flesh, and the cold griped their hands so they had to lay off every few minutes and get warm on the horses to be able to hold a knife to skin.

When the hide was off they cut up the carcass, taking out the top loins first, then the hams and shoulders, and lastly the ribs, separating the two sides by chopping straight down through the back-bone with Simmons' kindling-hatchet. Simmons was a lot better at such work than Clay and the Indian boy put together. He came out from his dish-washing before they had finished skinning their deer out, and he had all three of his peeled clean and knocked apart before they were through with their one. By that time the morning was too far gone for them to think of starting across the mountains, and they were too tired even to squabble about it. They watched

Simmons while he dug a big hole in the frozen ground and built a fire in it to fix his venison so it would keep over the winter.

There were several original wrinkles about old Simmons' meat-preserving system. He claimed that it had all been his own personal discovery, which he had accomplished by sitting down and turning his intellect loose to grind on it. He also claimed that nobody else in the country knew about it because they were all too stubborn to ask him and too sluggish-minded to figure it out for themselves, which was only partly true. Every settler in the neighborhood had a different process for putting up venison, and no settler ever used anybody else's because he considered his own to represent the very last stretch of human intelligence and cunning. Simmons' took harder work and more equipment than most of them, but it was a good system and he enjoyed showing it off.

He began by cutting his three deer into hunks about two inches square, without any fat or bone or gristle. Then he packed it into half-gallon tin cans with a half-handful of salt and pepper at the bottom of each, and pressed it down solid with his hands and his full weight. It took almost a hundred cans to hold all the meat from the three deer, and he filled every last one of them before he started his cooking, because he got mixed up when he tried to do two things at once. There wasn't room in the cabin for a man's feet when he got all the cans loaded and set out ready to cook. The table, floor, chairs, and even the bed and stove-mat were jammed with them.

He started his cooking by packing a load of cans into a tall wash-boiler partly full of water, and settling it down into the hole in the ground where the fire was. The water didn't come high enough to get into the cans. One beauty of the Simmons' process for preparing venison was that the meat furnished its own syrup, and the water merely supplied the heat to cook it out with. When the boiler began to heat up, he clapped on the tin cover, put a blanket on top of it and a big load of dirt on top of that, and let her simmer. The boiler chambered twenty cans at a time, and each load took about three hours to cook done. The meat, when cooled, was a dish to make a man climb out of bed and go trailing the odor down the middle of the road in his sleep. The steam cooked it to a fine, fiberless paste suspended in a clear jelly that, for frag-

rance and drawing-power, could have licked the stuffing out of all
the perfumery-counters on the Coast. Clay and the Indian boy
tried to persuade old Simmons to dish up one of the cans for dinner so they could see whether it ate as good as it smelled; but in
that they bumped into another of his notions. It wasn't right, he
felt, to put up venison to keep and then bust it open without giving
its keeping-powers a chance to show themselves off. There was
something profligate about it, like staying up all night at a party
when you were paying for a bedroom at a hotel. They pointed out
that their own deer had enough venison to refill the can and fifty
more like it, and they offered to swap him the whole carcass for a
couple of his cans and to move clear to the summit of the mountains before opening them. Even that didn't move him. It was
childish, he held, to eat canned meat that would keep when you had
fresh that wouldn't, and the outrage was the same whether you ate
it at a distance or right in your tracks. He sealed the batch of
finished cans with melted deer-tallow, stowed them on top of the
cabin-rafters, and put a fresh boilerful into the fire-pit, breathing
hard through his nose like an indigent mother who has been advised to put her child up for adoption among strangers. Having
won the argument by refusing to pay any attention to it, he didn't
allow it to cool his hospitality. He set his guests as big a line-up
of victuals for dinner as he had done for breakfast. In fact, they
were the same victuals: fried bacon and onions and potatoes, sliced
venison-liver, saddle-blanket pancakes, country sausage with flour-
gravy, fried eggs and a plate of headcheese, and coffee with a rag
floating in it to show that it was plenty powerful. It was all good
food, though liable to get monotonous; and so was old Simmons
with his long-windedness and his notions about dressing venison
that you didn't need and saving bottles and scrap-iron and waiting
to eat something you wanted until you had stopped wanting it.
Simmons' life and location were such that he could have done
pretty much anything he pleased. He had cut himself off from
society to be independent of rules and restrictions, and the only
thing he could think of to do with his freedom was to get up
other rules and restrictions of his own which weren't a lick more
sensible than the ones he had escaped from.

When they finished dinner Simmons droned along into another

of his God-and-I stories about something, the Indian boy retired to
the barn to do some practicing on his flute, and Clay leaned back,
facing the enlarged portrait of Peg Leg Simmons, and thought
that it might be a good notion to take up a homestead claim in the
high timber himself when he got old enough so the government
would let him. It looked like one sure way for a man to live strictly
as he pleased without bothering anybody, though it did strike Clay
as a little suspicious that none of the mountain people did live as
they pleased and that most of them did bother anybody they got
the smallest chance at. He dozed, thinking over all the timber-line
settlers he knew or had heard of, and the sun climbed down from
its meridian into the lower valley, thawing the snow a little so the
roof dripped and the shadows took on a blue cast and the air turned
dark gold with the smoke and vapor hanging low in it. Simmons
tallowed meat-cans and told how he had been attacked last spring by
Christ and a buck deer which God and he had stood off with a
pitchfork and finally clubbed to death. Along in the high fever of
the tale he stopped, noticing that Clay had gone to sleep on him.
The roof dripped and the Indian boy's flute tootled, and he was
about to jolt Clay awake and resume his recitation when he heard
a wagon rattling from the road up the mountain. He let Clay alone
because he wanted the pleasure of meeting whatever traveler it
might be himself. He set his tallow carefully off the fire and eased
the door shut behind him. Then he shaded his eyes and saw that
what was coming was the horse-trader and his outfit, bucking back
from the summit which he had warned them they would never
be able to get across.

Simmons felt pleased that they had been able to make it back.
He didn't stand to gain anything from them, one way or the other,
but he couldn't have collected much credit for his good advice if
they had all frozen to death on the road. He was also tickled because he had predicted a tough trip for them and they showed
signs of having had one. They had left the place with the horses
all trotting, the horse-trader sawing on the lines, and the two
women sitting with him in the seat to yank his elbow when he overlooked a turn or threatened to outpace the herd of led horses
behind. Now the horses walked and made hard work of even that.
The hard-voiced older woman drove in the wagon-seat and she

had it all to herself. The horse-trader rode a big old sorrel stallion with harness-galled shoulders. He traveled ahead, working the wagon-team along with a quirt so the wagon wouldn't run forward on top of them. The girl, on a long-legged black gelding, followed the herd of led horses and made them keep up by whipping them with the hondo-end of a rawhide rope. Several of the horses had bunged their knees falling on ice in the high meadows where springs had frozen in the road. Almost all of them went lame, having got sore-footed in the fields of broken black lava that stuck out of the snow on the last pull below the summit. Snow was packed inside the wagon-hubs and on top of the coupling-pole, so you could tell the horses had been dragging their bellies in it before the outfit gave up and turned back.

The horse-trader halted his sorrel stallion by the gate and sat waiting for the wagon to catch up. He didn't look at old Simmons or the cabin. That would have indicated that he favored stopping to rest, and with the two women bossing him so close and rambunctiously, he didn't care to assert his own feelings that far. They asserted themselves in spite of him. His yearning to get down and rest up showed through him even as he sat with his back turned. Even the horse felt it, and had to be checked to keep him from turning in through the gate against the rein. Longing for a rest and timidity about owning up to it were all the horse-trader had in him. He was not anxious about the amount of road they still had to get over, not concerned about the time they were making, or how the horses were holding up, or about anything except the frostbite in his feet and the sag in his muscles and his bones aching with chill and weariness like a raw burn. It wasn't that he hurt worse or broke down easier than anybody else. Plainly he wasn't a very powerful character; but weak men are often able to carry a tremendous amount of hardship simply because their weakness prevents them from doing anything to get out of it. He thought only of himself because the two women had taken the responsibility for everything else away from him. They had left him nothing but himself to think about.

The woman in the wagon didn't signal the team to stop. She didn't need to. They dragged to the gate where the sorrel stallion was, and, remembering that they had stopped there once before

without getting licked for it, they stopped again. They spraddled
out to keep themselves from falling over, and blew melted patches
into the snow between their forefeet, shedding a pale cloud of
vapor into the blue-white sky, while the led horses, not quite so
badly done up, nosed one another and shifted and fidgeted, trying
to tangle their lead-ropes and start a fight. The whole layout looked
something like one of those old parlor-chromos entitled "Home for
Christmas," though the hard-voiced woman considerably weakened
the resemblance by reaching a hog-whip from behind the seat and
handing the two horses a flogging with it. She had no notion of
making them pull on. All she wanted was to punish them for being
unable to. She was not insensitive to the horses' weariness as her
husband was. She knew exactly how bad off they were, and she
hated the living hell out of them for it. Her lips were peeled back
from her teeth, her eyes glary, her face dark red, and she hauled
and shot the lash as if nothing would have pleased her better than
to cut the team into mink bait with it. The horses lunged sideways
and crowded her husband's sorrel into the brush fence, and she
aimed a couple of side-throws at him before she saw old Simmons gawping at her from behind the gate-post. The sight certainly
sprinkled her down. She put the whip behind her, contrived an expression of neighborly amiability, as if she had only driven down
for a minute to borrow a bootjack, and said she supposed he hadn't
been expecting to see her again so soon. She had her eye on the
tracks in the snow where Clay and the Indian boy had taken their
horses in through the gate in the morning, and she could hear the
Indian boy in the barn handing the winds and zephyrs a flute solo
that sounded like an ungreased wagon-wheel, so she didn't feel any
too easy in her mind about what she was steering into. But she
made a good job of not letting on. "You've got company, I see,"
she said, as if she suspected old Simmons of using his cabin to entertain light women in. "Well, we only stopped here to blow the
horses and pass the time of day. Then we'll be moving along to some
place where we can put up for the night."

Even when she was cowhiding the horses and her husband, she
had been a fine-looking woman. Repose showed her off even better.
She knew how to look a man up and down as if she were taking
stock of all his capabilities and concealing her admiration for them.

Some women in that part of the country were able to do that, too, but a man couldn't feel so generously complimented when they did it. Too many people of the neighborhood knew how easy their admiration was to get and how little it amounted to. The horse-trader woman's was far stronger medicine because old Simmons knew nothing about her. She turned it on him, and he folded his claws and keeled off his perch as helpless and fluttery as a quail hit with a rock. His visitors, he explained, were nothing; a couple of runaway kids whom he had picked up in the brush that morning with unwiped noses, no place to go, and a fresh-killed deer that they didn't know what to do with. "Drive on in and we'll cook up a bait of it for you," he offered. "There's slews of it and plenty of room and a whole damn barn-load of horse feed hollerin' to be et. Dog it, I could put your whole outfit up here for the whole damn winter if you wanted to lay over that long!"

The news about the visitors was all the woman had held back for, but when her husband turned his horse to ride in she shook her head at him. It wasn't good manners to accept invitations all at a gulp, only a tramp would do that. "We wouldn't bother you to cook up anything for us," she stipulated, as if that had to be cleared up before she promised anything. "We can't eat fresh-killed venison. We tried it coming up the mountain and it made us sick."

She didn't mention what the nature of the sickness had been. Venison eaten too fresh hits some people harder than croton oil, and that may have been partly responsible for her ill-temper with the horses and for her husband's look of dragged-out suffering. Simmons didn't need to have the matter explained to him. He knew about it, and her mere allusion to it was an intimacy that knocked him loose from his last hold on his life-long principles. "God, I've got deer meat here that won't make you sick," he assured her, and boosted the gate open as wide as it would go. "You come on in, and I'll open you some of this canned venison of mine. I got a whole houseful of it, and you could feed the whole business to a suckin' baby and have him hollerin' for more. Whip up and drive on in, dog it to hell!"

The noise of the wagon rattling as it turned through the gate woke Clay in the cabin. He got off the bench and took a sight out through the window, and, seeing that it was not Orlando Geary come after him again, he went to the door and watched the horse-trader's outfit make its entrance. There was a considerable pitch uphill from the gate to the barn, and the wagon-team, in spite of their rest and having the led horses untied from behind and the woman's standing up to heave the leather into them, had such hard work to pull it that the horse-trader hung his rope on the end of the wagon-tongue and put his sorrel stallion to work pulling with them. It got the wagon moving, but it left the girl to manage the loose horses alone, and she had her hands full doing it. They were still roped head to tail, and the smell of feed from the barn made them all try to get through the gate at once. The opening couldn't be expanded to accommodate them, so they jammed up in it with their ropes crossed and crowfooted so they couldn't get loose. A couple of light nags slipped down in the snow and got stepped on, and the rest of them started rearing and kicking and biting hunks out of one another. The mess couldn't be worked loose by crowding the tail-enders, so the girl backed her black gelding and started him at the brush fence for a jump. She was so far from the house that Clay could make out none of her features clearly, but he recognized her. She was dressed for the weather: a man's felt hat cocked back on her head, a long red blanket looped on her shoulders like a cloak, and high Indian moccasins of un-tanned beef-hide to turn the snow. In politeness, he should have gone down to help her with the horse-herd, but he didn't want to be too fast about it for fear something about him might show her how much closer she stood to him in his mind than she did in reality.

She scarcely needed help, as it turned out. The trip had worn the horse-trader's wife into hating the horses' weakness and it had worn the horse-trader into feeling sorry for his own, but she was stronger than either of them. If it had worn any of the life out of her she was easily able to spare it. She pointed the black gelding at the fence, and when he reared and refused to jump she gouged her spurs into him and stood on them and gave him a whaling with her rope that almost caved him under her. It wasn't so much spite or cruelty as that she was intolerant of weariness because she didn't know what it felt like. And it was the right kind of treatment for the gelding. A horse should never be called on to do anything beyond his strength; but if you do call on him you must make him come through or rupture himself trying. Otherwise he will get the notion that he can quit on you whenever he wants to, and he will start wanting to most of the time. The black gelding was too tired to jump the fence, but he jumped into it and scrouged his way through it. The girl turned him back at the pack of horses in the gate, and Clay ran out in the snow and started untangling tie-ropes to help her.

He had not expected this first meeting to do more than get an acquaintance started. When the horses had all been picked loose and kicked and dragged into the corral, he pulled the gate shut and looked at her and tried to think of something to say. She was leaned over her saddle-horn, staring down at him with her gray eyes wide open against the hard glare of the snow. "I know you," she said, low. "You came with that big fat sheriff to put us out of our camp. To tell us we had to move. You had on those same pants."

Clay said yes. It struck him a little aback that she should have remembered him, too, and that the thing she remembered him for should have been Zack Wall's donated pants. Also, what kind of notion must she have of him, from having seen him in the custody of an officer of the law? He explained that to her, how it hadn't been an arrest or anything he had done, only a case they had wanted him to testify about. He made it emphatic and said it over two or three times in different forms of words so she would be sure to understand how it was. For the first time he felt uneasy about the Wade Shiveley jailbreak. With that on his slate, the business of convincing her that he had only been going with Orlando Geary as a witness was not in the least different from lying to her. It was bound to make her believe he was not in trouble with the law now, and he was. And still, as long as they didn't catch him, what difference could it make?

She believed him. Her name, she told him, was not Lucy, as he had thought, but Luz, which is the Mexican word for light. The Mexicans and Vascos in the sheep country across the mountains called it Luce and claimed that was the right pronunciation in their language, so she had taken to writing it one way and pronouncing it another to accommodate them. Her having a Mexican name didn't mean that she was Mexican. It was only that she had been born one night in a horse-trapping camp in the Malheur Desert and there was no place for her mother to lie except in the back of the wagon, and no light except a broken-chimneyed lantern with willow-moths batting into the wick by the hundred. So the Mexican sheep-herder's wife who tended her mother kept saying not to be afraid because it wouldn't be long till daylight. There seemed no reason why that should have helped things any, but she kept repeating over and over in her Spanish—*"No tiene miedo, niña, no tiene miedo! Ahi venga la luz!"* and praying to herself, *"Ay Dios, que se venga la luz!"*

She said that so much during the night that it got to sounding as if she was praying for the baby to be born and get it over with, and the girl's mother got to thinking of her by that name, so they called her by it. Nowadays, the girl said, they didn't trap wild horses any more. It was too hard and dangerous and the horse-market wanted bigger horses than the wild herds usually ran to. What they lived at now was trading for horses east of the mountains to sell to farms on the Coast. Sometimes they trained racehorses on contract, and sometimes they took work-teams that had got jaded with overwork and ignorant treatment, and doctored and fed them till they were worth money again. "My father knows everything about taking care of horses," the girl said. "If he tells you anything about a horse, you believe him. But if he tells you about anything else, don't believe him."

She seemed to feel no need to explain why she wanted him to know all about her. She went on talking because there were certain things he needed to know and she wanted to get them out and done with. Horse-swapping was not their only trade. Sometimes, when wages were high enough to make it worth the trouble, they worked harvesting; sometimes when the demand for horses was slow they traveled around, working at whatever there was. Her father had been a spur-maker when he was young, and sometimes he worked at that. Some day soon they were going to take land and settle for good; they had been traveling and working around for longer than she could remember. During all that time, Orlando Geary's visit was the first hint they had ever had that they were doing anything against the law or that they weren't wanted. So they had decided that a country that treated them like that was a good country to get out of, and since they couldn't make it across the mountains they were heading back to pull south and work in the hop-fields where people didn't come in for insult and suspicion because they lived by traveling around.

All that she told in a kind of unstemmable rush, without giving Clay any chance to put in anything. But it was not mere gabble-itis. It was not the kind of scrambling blurt that Mrs. Yarbro galloped her testimony to in her annual appearance in court, to get it all in before anybody could head her off. The girl was not of the same stripe as mountain settlers like Mrs. Yarbro and old Simmons, who would talk all day for the pleasure of hearing their heads roar. She told only as much about herself as she had to, and it was only on Clay's account that she told anything. When old Simmons bore over within earshot, she stopped talking and didn't begin again until he had gone back to the wagon. When the Indian boy ran his flute solo to the end of its string and came out to see what was going on, she stopped again. The Indian boy observed that the road up the mountain seemed to have given them a tough time and that their horses looked bad.

"They ought to," she said. She was tall, with a face rather wide across the cheekbones, a fair skin that seemed transparent so the movement of her blood colored it, and large hands. She lifted the heavy roping-saddle off her black gelding with one hand, stripping the bridle loose with the other. "No feed on the road, no track across the summit except over the bare rimrock, and when the horses' feet were ruined we had to buck ten feet of snow in the pass."

The Indian boy said rimrock was bad for horses' feet. "I goin' to go over the mountains," he said, looking at Clay. "I goin' now, and ride tonight with the moon. I thinkin' it's better luck you come, too."

It was liberal of him, considering that Clay had threatened to shoot his horse out from under him. Probably he had received some hunch from heaven in response to his flute-concert that made him think having Clay along would bring good luck. And of course there was no longer any reason for Clay to go with him. Old

Simmons was telling the horse-trader and his wife about a road that would fetch them in to the hop-fields by a back way that nobody lived on, so they could pasture their horses at night without bothering private property. It turned off south at a cattle-salting grounds in the oak timber and crossed the low divide into Gate Creek and followed that across the county line a little below Elkhead. "You won't bother anybody and you won't see anybody," Simmons guaranteed. "Nobody's traveled it for fifteen years except Wade Shiveley when he was hidin' out up here. You might have to cut out a few logs, but it's a good grade and grass till hell wouldn't sneeze at it."

It sounded secluded. "I can't go across the mountains now," Clay told the Indian boy. "I'm leavin' with these people tomorrow for the hop-fields. Or wherever it is they're goin'."

"You mustn't come with us," the girl said. She spoke low and looked at him close, as she had done when she remembered having seen him with Orlando Geary. She meant it. She had honestly wanted him to know about her, and now that he was getting ready to, she remembered some prospect about it that scared her. "Not with us. You mustn't. We can't let you. Promise you won't."

"I can't stay here all winter," said Clay. "Where do you want me to go, across the mountains?" He knew she didn't. She had only got through saying the trip was impossible and dangerous. But he felt injured, as if she had implied some promise to him that she lacked nerve to stick to. He had half a notion to horse up and go across the mountains to spite her. The Indian boy wanted him strong enough, and said so again. "I been findin' out about this," he said. "You ridin' with me, it's good luck. You go away by yourself, it's bad for both of us. Maybe we git arrested, maybe killed. I don't know. You better to goin' with me. I bring your horse, huh?"

"You can't cross the mountains!" the girl said. "It'll kill your horse and you'll die! You could just as well go somewhere else, down the valley or somewhere—" She saw that the Indian boy wasn't listening to her and that Clay hadn't listened to him, and gave up. "All right, go on if you're bound to," she said. "You'll die in the pass, and they won't know what became of you till spring.

And you'll go alone. You heard your friend say he was going down to the hop-fields with us in the morning, didn't you?"

The Indian boy went to get his horse, and Clay held the gate open for him to ride through. He had no road rig except a shoulder of venison hung in a long flour-sack at the fork of his saddle, and he rode out without saying good-by to anybody. His red colt hit a stretching walk to keep warm, and he went out of sight in the snowy firs as if he was not merely escaping notice, but hurrying to avoid any. Clay shut the gate and leaned on it, talking with the horse-trader's girl while the sky cast yellowish and turned cold and the fir trees moved their upper branches in a sort of oratorical motion as they always do about sundown. She explained that the horse-trader's wife was not her mother, but a woman that he had married since her mother died, and that they were on the move because they were ready to move and not on account of Orlando Geary's eviction notice, when a few flute notes drifted back from so far up the mountain it sounded almost like a late bird. It was the Indian boy playing for luck. Luce remarked, feeling partly to blame for letting him tackle the mountain alone, that he would need considerable more than luck to get a horse over that road; and Clay, pretending to feel easy about it, said that if he couldn't make it he could turn around and come back, and maybe it would cure him of showing off his stubbornness.

He didn't feel guilty about letting the Indian boy go it alone. There had been times that he could hardly have got through without him—the night with the drowning sheep, the night in Wade Shiveley's hide-out. But he didn't believe there were any times ahead of him that he would need help with—not that kind of help, at least—and the only sensation he felt was relief because the faint flute-twittering supplied a little extra material for conversation with the girl. Couples in that country made an important point of keeping up talk about something when they were alone together. Not that they underrated the beauty of wordless communion of spirits, but because merely sitting and lallygagging always brought to mind the case of the Scandinavian hired man in the lower valley who, after a fourteen-hour working-day, would tog up and hoof it nine miles to sit up with his girl, a quarter-breed cook for a neighboring farm. According to the story, they would sit from seven till past midnight on opposite sides of the kitchen without ever getting any further into the realms of practical discussion than—"Maybe I better go now, huh?" "Huhuh." "Uhuh, I better." "Huhuh, don't." "Why hadn't I better?" "'Cause." "'Cause what?" "Oh, 'cause." Which ritual of reciprocal devotion was followed by another two hours of admiring silence and then the same rigmarole all over again. It seemed to fill all emotional requirements when the hired man and his girl did it, but it got out on them and people laughed at them. So other couples avoided such interchanges for fear of being considered like them. Clay and the horse-trader's girl talked at the gate and said everything they could think of without saying exactly what they wanted to till dark, and then they went in to one of old Simmons' company suppers. The difference between it and his company dinners and breakfasts was that there was lamplight to eat by and that instead of sliced venison-liver he had opened two cans of his preserved deer meat. He bragged on it a good deal while they ate it, but he was entitled to. A man would have had to do some reaching around to find a better way to cook deer meat than that.

After supper Simmons got sleepy. He always got up at four in the morning, though it wouldn't have mattered to anybody on earth if he had lain in bed till the next sundown. He spread down on the fir-bough pallet in his living-room. The horse-trader's wife and Luce brought their own beds in from the wagon and set them up in the kitchen, and the horse-trader and Clay went out to sleep in the haymow. Clay lay awake a long time, watching the moon through the log-chinks. The Indian boy was riding by that moon; probably he was knocking the feet off his red colt in the lava-beds below the deep snow already. Nobody would know till spring whether he had died in the pass or made it across. If he did die, the word would be sure to get around, because he could be identified by his crippled hands. But if he got through he might never be heard of again, because that eastern Oregon was so big a country. A man almost had to die in it to attract any notice.

Clay remembered that Luce had looked at the Indian boy's crippled hands, though she had made no mention of them then or afterward. Maybe that was because she had been around enough to be used to such things, or maybe it was because she wasn't sure enough of her standing to volunteer remarks about the deformities of others, or it may have been that she merely forgot about it through having so much else to talk about. He tried to decide which it was, because on her account he was undertaking a new way of living, among people of a kind that he had worked most of his life to grow away from—the homeless, dissatisfied wagon-campers who went eternally cruising around the country, looking for a place to light without ever finding one—and he wanted to prove to himself that she was going to be worth it. It was less dignified herding with wagon-camping people than with a man like Wade Shiveley. Property-holders were afraid of Wade Shiveley, whereas of the wagon-campers they were merely disapproving and inclined to keep movable property locked up while the travel season was on. A good year for prices was usually a bad one for wagon-campers, which proved that they could settle down to regular work when there was inducement enough. But they never stayed put long, and as soon as prices slumped and ranches started cutting down on hired help and contract-farming, the roads filled up with them again. Throwing in with them was almost a guarantee of variety, but there were drawbacks. It couldn't be all fun, because Clay's mother had been so desperate to get away from them that she had been willing to go live with the Shiveley brothers rather than stand any more of it.

He ended by deciding that Luce was worth all he was giving up for her and that he wasn't giving up much, since his alternatives had been wintering on a reservation with the Indian boy or going to jail. In the morning, saddling to start for the hop-fields, he discovered that his decision was costing him higher than he had expected, and he also understood why the Indian boy had pulled out so summarily without stopping to say good-by. The leather-hided little runt had stolen Wade Shiveley's rifle to take with him. He had it stashed in the flour-sack with his deer meat, probably, and he didn't want to stop for fear he would be caught with it and compelled to give it back.

Clay searched the whole place for the rifle before he could bring himself to realize what had gone with it. He even searched the horse-trader's wagon when nobody was looking, and he found a rifle of the same caliber hidden carefully under a folded tent and some spare harness and a great pile of cooking-utensils. But it was a much older model and it had seen harder use. He covered it back carefully and left it. The rest of Wade Shiveley's unearthed property he packed around in his pockets, and he decided that the next man who got any of it away from him would have to move a blamed sight faster than the first one had, and be a blamed sight bigger.

Chapter X

IT TURNED out that Simmons, probably overstimulated by the presence of bold-eyed womanhood, had given the back road to the hopfields a good deal better name than it deserved. He had mentioned that there might be logs to chop out, and there were several hundred of them. Besides, the rain and melting snow from the mountains had caved off sections that had to be regraded before the wagon could get through, and in places the mud was so deep that after they had hand-boosted the wagon-team across they had to hitch onto the loose horses and pull them through, too. Instead of making the county line in one day's travel they took three, and they didn't even have the road to themselves as old Simmons had promised. The head of Gate Creek, when they pulled down into it about nightfall, was occupied by One-Armed Savage's sawmill and the five sons who worked it for him. The shadows under the heavy trees were beginning to run together and make darkness when they struck the bottom of the canyon. A fog was rising and they could make out Gate Creek only by the noise and by white spumes of foam where there were rapids. But the mill was still lighted and old Savage's sons were at work running tie timber through it with lanterns hung overhead to see by. The horse-trader's outfit pulled right up against the mill platform in front of them, but they went on working and paid no attention except to squint sideways, as if they had got too big to waste working-time on such arrivals and halfway wished they hadn't.

One-Armed Savage's five sons had worked for him ever since they were old enough to keep out of the saw. Not because they liked his employ, but because he kept them so whipped down and dominated that they had never dared quit him. He didn't even pay them wages, though they outworked any set of hired mill-hands in the country. They ranged in age from twenty-five to around forty, so they had both age and experience enough to have quit the old man and gone to work somewhere else if they had wanted to. But the most they ever got up nerve for was to strike him, every few

127

months, for a new headsaw to work with and a few regular wages, both of which he always managed to talk them out of. Whatever he paid them, he would point out, meant that much less that they would inherit when he died, which he was liable to do almost any minute. If they were low down enough to want to poison the last hours of a failing old man over a few measly dollars, all right, he would pay up. But he would also see that they didn't get a cent of his estate, and he would run them off his property and hire himself a crew of really high-class mill-hands who could cut lumber with any blamed saw they found. At that point the sons would all lope back to the mill and start ripping out boards as if they had been turpentined under the tail, all for fear the old man might chase them out to earn their living among strangers who didn't know how well-meaning they were.

None of them had ever married or had a girl, and since they had never known either the frivolities of youth or the responsibilities of maturity, they all looked about the same age—the youngest as blocky-featured and as muscle-bound as the oldest, the oldest as wide-eyed and underdone as the youngest. The old man had kept them scared down for so long that they were able to be afraid of him without even thinking about it. Working as late as they did was risky, the light was so bad and the machinery old and treacherous. But they bucked logs into railroad lengths and squared them on the saw and piled them in the dark and risked losing a hand or arm at it because the old man didn't come and tell them they could knock off. Being watched by strangers embarrassed them, and they nosed down to their work as if it had a deep and solemn interest for them; not pleasurable, maybe, but impossible to tear their attention away from.

The sawmill looked big in the dark, with the lanterns flaring into the cold fog, the belts jarring and gear-shafts grinding and the engine snorting steam and sparks into the loose-piled sawdust and the big saw going spang when it ripped a flank slab loose from a log. Actually it was a small outfit, the frugalest possible layout of machinery enclosed in the flimsiest kind of shed. It was kept modest, not because modesty suited One-Armed Savage's character, but because the shebang caught fire and burned down about every other year, and the less there was to it the less had to be replaced.

One-Armed Savage was not a good species of landed proprietor for Clay to start his enlistment at wagon-camping on. He was wealthy, as he could scarcely have helped being since he worked his sons without pay and got his raw timber by manoeuvering homestead boundaries around on government land where the trees grew plentiful and unwatched. He was high-tempered and overbearing, partly because of his wealth and partly because most of his timber-cutting was against the law and he could keep people from asking questions about it by hackling up and yelling at them. The timber he helped himself to didn't amount to enough to make him worth bothering with; but he thought it did, and believed the whole system of government land laws was a piece of spite work against him personally. He was a bull-built old man with a rattly voice that had been developed by talking above the noise of the sawmill, a hedge-formation of white whiskers which he kept trimmed, it was said, by fanning them out on a stump and hacking them off with an ax, and cheeks so red that the color seemed to have been burned into them with a blow-torch. Ordinarily he stayed clear of the sawmill because it reminded him of the accident with a loose driving-belt that had lost him his arm when he was young and forced him to stop working for wages and get hold of a sawmill of his own. But having looked the horse-trading outfit over through his window without recognizing anybody in it, he gave way to his curiosity, unlocked himself from the board shanty where he kept books and slept, and came out to see who it was. He climbed to the mill platform, unhooked a lantern from an overhead stringer, and turned the light the full length of the horse-herd before he said anything. Then he blew a chestful of fog through his nose into his ax-trimmed whiskers and inquired what was wanted.

The horse-trader and his wife knew how to size up a man they were asking a favor of. With old Simmons, he had sat modestly back and let her beam the outfit into a night's free lodging. Now, though they didn't so much as look at one another, she did the sitting back while the horse-trader, with a broken-down quaver in his voice, explained that they would like permission to camp somewhere on the sawmill property for the night. He wouldn't be asking such a concession except that he had women along, and they were too road-worn and delicate to stand traveling farther without rest. For a finish, he volunteered a full though slightly retouched account of himself and outfit, where they had come from and by what roads, what their business was and where they were going and what they intended to do when they got there. He didn't offer any separate explanation about Clay. It was always well to introduce yourself with a good deal of detail when you were traveling the upper country, but it was also well not to make the introduction too complicated. It put too much strain on the listener's attention. He was liable to get absorbed trying to straighten everything out in his head and forget what you were asking him for.

The horse-trader did about as well with One-Armed Savage as anybody could have. Nevertheless, Clay felt irritated because he made himself sound so humble and pitiful about it. Clay knew nothing of the art of front-gate solicitation, and he saw no sense in so much agony about asking camping privileges on a patch of stump-land that wasn't being used for anything else. He crowded his buckskin mare forward into the light and pulled her close to the horse-trader so One-Armed Savage could see that at least one of his petitioners wasn't half so faint and woebegone as report made out. The two women stayed back, the horse-trader's wife drooping in the wagon-seat and letting her husband run the program because he could always sound a great deal worse off than she could. Luce kept still farther back, among the trailed horses in the shadows. Even when she was completely tired out, she could never manage to look it, and front-gate negotiations usually went better when she was out of range. She would have kept Clay back, too, but he got the spur to his mare before she could reach him. She watched him uneasily as he pulled up in the light, wishing that there could be some way for him to travel with them without having to learn about this meek-fronted business, and hoping, since he still had it to learn, that he would have sense enough to keep out and let the horse-trader tend to the talking. He was between her and the lanterns, and he shadowed black and gigantic against them. Behind him, One-Armed Savage showed so pink-mapped and dwarfish that she felt afraid, knowing the unpredictable temper of these headwaters land-proprietors, that the old badger might realize how insignificant he looked and fly into a mad spell about that.

It was only her nervousness, of course. One-Armed Savage was a good many years past the stage of imagining that he looked small in comparison to anything. He studied the wagon and the horses all over again, and said they couldn't camp on his property. They were too liable to get careless with their camp fire and let it spread into the timber. The timber was so soggy with rain that it wouldn't have caught fire in a coke-furnace, but the horse-trader knew better than to mention that.

"We won't build any fire," he offered, respectfully, and kneed his sorrel stallion a couple of steps sideways. Luce could see, though old Savage couldn't, that he hooked his toe across Clay's stirrup leather as a caution to hold in and keep still. It wasn't time to feel discouraged yet. All these old moss-necks began by saying no to whatever you asked. They didn't really mean no, merely that they wished you would argue your case a little more fully while they thought it over. The way to handle them was not to argue at all, but to sit still and look hopeful, whereupon, not getting it from you, they would start an argument with themselves, answer it point by point until they had got every possible expostulation knocked in the head, and then feel so good over their triumph that they would tell you to go ahead and camp wherever you pleased. The horse-trader followed that system, keeping his foot against Clay's leg, and Clay kept still. Luce felt proud of him because he had picked up the hint without understanding its purpose. She could see that he didn't want to keep still at all. His shadow against the lanterns was so magnified that she could see the small motions he made and tried to hold down. He was fighting a case of fidgets. He didn't feel meek or submissive, and it plagued him to have One-Armed Savage think he did. Luce was glad of that, too. Courage, independence of spirit, openness of character, were all creditable things to have. Any woman was entitled to expect them of the man she set her mind on. She had not admitted to herself that her mind was set on Clay, but she was glad to know that much about him in case events took her farther than she intended.

Not, of course, that he could go on talking up to people if they did come to live together. In this wagon-camping life it was im-

possible to be frank and haughty without getting into trouble, and
that was one thing she had foreseen when he first announced that
he was coming with her to the hop-fields. He would have to learn
to be meek. She had wanted to save him from it because she knew
how hard it would be. It had been hard for her, though she had
started young and learned a little at a time. Children who yelled at
her and complained to the authorities when she yelled back or threw
rocks; flirtatious spirits like Phin Cowan, stubbornly officious ones
like Orlando Geary; horse-race promoters like the old man in Shoestring who had won a pile of money from her father and got himself shot in the road going home with it. They were the worst
of all because of her father's weakness. He couldn't resist betting
on a horse-race, even when he was bound to lose. And since he almost always did lose, they would insist on working him into one even
when they knew he was gambling with money that wasn't his and
even when they had been asked not to. Often enough he had bet
and lost money that belonged to Luce's stepmother and to Luce
herself. It was nothing that he could help, though he invariably
promised to afterward; and it was dangerous. It was something
that Luce thought about only when she had to. If Clay never had
to go through anything worse than a little tactful management of
One-Armed Savage, he could feel thankful. And so would she.

There was nothing especially wounding to the self-respect about
managing old Savage. Not knowing that a system was being worked
on him, he walked right into it. He proved by good solid argument
and knock-down rebuttal that they hadn't a lick of business camping on his land, and then he not only gave them permission to, but insisted that they build a fire to go with it. He even gave them directions about a camping-place. "There's a spring branch crosses the
road a couple of miles from here," he explained. "It ain't fenced,
but the grass is good, so your horses won't go far if you turn 'em
loose. We can keep on eye on you there, and I might be down in the
morning to price up one or two of your horses. How old is that
buckskin your kid's ridin'?"

Clay stiffened and yanked his stirrup loose from the horse-
trader. Luce spurred her horse to reach him, but she didn't start
soon enough. "This mare ain't for sale," he said, all on the peck.
"This man wouldn't have any right to sell her if she was. She

ain't his, and I ain't—" He was about to correct old Savage's misunderstanding about his parentage. Luce headed that off, with a long reach and a jab with her spur that caught the buckskin mare in the flank. The mare jumped in outraged astonishment, and tipped Clay backwards with a jerk that almost dislocated his neck. By the time he got scrambled back into the saddle and worked the mare back into the light, the conversation had got away past him again.

"She's a little off five," the horse-trader said, guessing at it and pretending not to notice the rumpus. "Plenty of life, easy action, gentle-broke, a good puller, and works single or double. I can see you know how to size up a horse or you wouldn't have picked her out. I'd hate to let her go, because she's a pet and the kid's attached to her, but of course if a man offered me a fair bid I'd feel obliged to turn her off. You got any price in mind?"

He had no intention of parting with the mare at all. Not wanting to create ill-feeling by a flat refusal, he was playing to boost her for all he was worth so old Savage would get suspicious of her. Clay sat up, all fixed to spoil it, but Luce held him down, and whispered to him and he let his weight off his stirrups again. Old Savage climbed down from the platform, hung his lantern on the stump of his arm, and sprung the mare's mouth open for a look. He let out a pleased grunt, and inspected her feet and the brand on her hip. "Five years old and a kid's pet, hey?" he inquired, sarcastically. "She's on eight by her mouth, she ain't any more of a pet than I am, and I can tell you why you wouldn't like to part with her. She ain't yours."

Clay yanked the mare's head away from him. "I told you she wasn't his, didn't I?" he demanded, and wheeled back so Luce couldn't get hold of him again. "I told you she wasn't for sale, too, so git out of here and let me alone!"

"She ain't yours, either," One-Armed Savage said, and peered across the lantern to see how he took it. "I've seen this mare around Elkhead for over a year past. I never seen you there, and she wasn't with any tradin'-herd, because she's worth too much money to trade. You stole that horse, bub."

The accusation had too much truth in it for Clay to argue it off calmly. The horse-trader took it better, being more accustomed to such difficulties. He looked hurt and offered to produce a bill of sale attesting that he had purchased the mare as a colt from a Warmsprings Indian named, he couldn't exactly recall what. One-Armed Savage said the name didn't matter. If there really was a bill of sale and if he could see it, he might be willing to modify a few of his statements. "I ain't sayin' you stole her, mind you," he stipulated. "All I claim is that she's been in this country before, and that she's been stole. Any man's liable to buy a stole horse, with all these damned Indians stealin' the country blind. Let's see your bill of sale."

He was beginning to crawfish, and it looked as if things might all be smoothed out again. The horse-trader wasn't four-flushing about his bill of sale. He carried several dozen with him, all signed and filled out, covering horses of every known weight, color, and description, with nothing left to insert except the brand. They were all in indelible pencil, convincingly dirty, and his wife usually put the right brand in while she was digging the document out of the luggage. Clay didn't know about such practices, and he judged the horse-trader had talked himself into a hole and Wade Shiveley's mare into a confiscation. "You go to hell with your bill of sale," he told old Savage. "This mare ain't stole and she ain't for sale and she ain't any of your damn business! Stand away from that bit and pull your nose out of this, or I'll fix you so you won't be able to!"

About all that accomplished was to convince old Savage that he had been right to start with. He let out a victorious aha without budging from the mare's head. "Goin' to shoot your way out of this with a big gun full of hard bullets, is that it?" he queried, indulgently. "You're startin' this business young, kid, and if you go to pull any firearms on me you'll end it young, too! Any man that would raise a kid to cave around like you ought to be drug out of the country by the hamstrings!"

There might have been room for an argument about that, considering the example furnished by old Savage's five sons, all raised to such excessive submissiveness that they didn't even perk up when their old man was being threatened with extermination. The horse-trader let that pass, in the interests of concord. "He ain't goin' to pull any gun on you," he promised. "Where would he git one? There ain't a single firearm in this whole outfit, and we wouldn't let him pack one if there was. That's the truth."

One-Armed Savage lifted the lantern and inspected Clay, the horse-trader, Luce, and the woman in the wagon. That done, he agreed that everything the horse-trader said might be true, but that for a kid who was riding a stolen horse with nothing to back his meanness up with, Clay was acting suspiciously forward. "If he ain't got a gun on him he knows where he can find one, and, by God, I don't know whether I want a specimen like him camped in range of my property or not."

"The horse ain't stole," said the horse-trader, desperately. He would have liked to knock Clay in the head, though timidity prevented him from saying so. "I can show you a bill of sale!"

"He certainly can!" his wife put in from the wagon. She had been born to this kind of life. Pulling an injured tone in front of men like old Savage hadn't cut her spirit, as it had her husband's. She enjoyed it and made a game out of it. "We can show you the papers on that horse, and what's more there's not a gun in this whole outfit, his or anybody else's! You can come up here and go through the wagon, if you want to make sure. We had a rifle, but this fool bet it on a crooked horse-race and lost it for us."

"I didn't—" the horse-trader began.

"You did!" his wife said. "Are you going to keep us here palavering all night? If this gentleman"—she meant old Savage, who looked startled at the tribute—"if this gentleman wants to see the bill of sale, come and get it for him and be done with it; don't sit there and gawp. And if he can find any gun in this wagon, I'll give it to him for a present."

It looked as if their lack of shooting-irons was being insisted on a little more than was strictly necessary. Old Savage ignored it and refused to be sociable. "I don't know a blamed thing about you, madam," he observed. "Your mare may not be stole and you may all be unarmed like you say, but what's this kid raisin' so much hob about? He threatened to lay me out, didn't he? What for and what with?"

"I wouldn't need any gun to lay you out, you old fool," Clay said. Since they couldn't talk the old digger into acting friendly, he could see no more use wasting friendliness on him. "If you think I stole this mare, look! Could you do this with a horse that belonged to somebody else? Hold still!"

He gouged his toes into the mare's shoulders and tightened the reins. She reared straight up and lunged forward till old Savage was standing right under her forefeet. Wade Shiveley had drilled that trick into her, and for anybody who didn't know how incapable she was of meanness it was a scary one. Old Savage's mouth fell open. Instinctively, cowering, he caught his lantern close to his bosom and clasped his arm around it as if his only fear was that the chimney might get busted when she lit on him. It scorched him, and he dropped it. Clay backed the mare and brought her down. The lantern was out so he couldn't see how mad old Savage was.

"All right, now git your damned outfit to hell out of here," old Savage said in a voice blurry with rage. "Clear off my land, do you hear? If I catch ary one of you this side of my line-marks by tomorrow morning I'll swear out a warrant for the whole damned crew of you and hire me a sheriff's posse to serve it! Move before I take a shotgun to you!"

He climbed to the platform and walked back inside his shack, leaving the lantern where he had dropped it. His five sons watched after him till his door slammed, and then went back to ripping out ties. It wasn't so much being scared that had raised his spite as the fact that he had been scared with them looking at him. Clay felt rather pleased at having done it. It had stopped the argument, which was getting nowhere, and as far as camping privileges were concerned, he favored camping where they pleased without asking old Savage anything about it. He said so, and the outfit got ready to move. The horse-trader's wife gathered up the lines, the horse-trader pulled his quirt and started the team, Luce woke up the herd-horses and bunched them behind to cross the creek. None of them said anything, but they passed grass and water and good camping-places without stopping, they traveled the red-clay road between a tumbled wall of dead slashings until long after the moon was up, and they must have covered a good twelve miles before they found a belt of standing timber that showed where the sawmill property ended. In the middle of it was a patch of open grass, with a troughed-in spring that ran off into a wooden watering-trough. The grass was too old and strawy for good horse feed, but they pulled in and unharnessed and made camp in it. The two women slept in the tent, the horse-dealer shook down under the wagon, and Clay, realizing that he had been brash in the wrong place and being anxious to make up for it, stayed up to stand guard over the grazing horses.

He had little guarding to do. The horses were too tired to range much, and after he had broken them out of the bunch and spread them around in the grass he had only to stay awake and keep them picked out against the stringers of fog that came dragging through the dark timber half-shadowing and half-glittering in the moon. He unbridled his mare and held her by the neck rope so she could graze, and to keep himself awake he took to thinking over the run-in with One-Armed Savage. He had started it and spoiled everything, and though he could see nothing wrong in what he had said or done, he could see that his doing it had put the outfit to a twelve-mile trip after dark that could have been avoided if he had kept his mouth shut. Probably it hadn't been necessary; probably there wasn't enough harm in old Savage to justify their trouble. But though these people might not know as well as Clay did what was harmful they knew what they were afraid of. And, being afraid of old Savage, they had been right to try to get along with him before he got mad, and right to travel twelve miles to get out of his reach afterward. Clay's bravery and uppitiness had done nothing to old Savage except, maybe, to put a fresh curl in his whiskers when the mare reared up over him. All he had accomplished was to inflict a lot of extra work and inconvenience on the outfit he belonged to. The lesson in that was that bravery in the wrong place was nothing but a blamed nuisance, which Luce could have told him before the rumpus ever started, except that he wouldn't have believed her.

Having settled that, he thought of the rifle that he had found in the horse-trader's wagon when he was searching for his own. Nobody had taken it out, he had watched them pack their beds and bedding in with it, and nobody could possibly have smuggled it off without his seeing it. Then it was still there, and why had the horse-trader and his wife denied having it? There was nothing suspicious, in that country, about traveling with a rifle. If anything, it was the other way round, and there was a slight presumption of suspiciousness against people who traveled the mountain roads without one. The woman had explained that away by volunteering that theirs had been gambled off on a horse-race. Could it be, then, that the rifle Clay saw had been hidden in the wagon without her or her husband knowing it? He was in the habit, by what they had let out, of gambling away things that didn't belong to him. Could it be that the rifle belonged to Luce and that she had cached it under the camp-rig to keep him from finding and gambling it, too? She hadn't said anything when they were denying up and down that there was any such article in the outfit. It was true that they hadn't given her much chance to, but she could have put in a denial on her own account if she had wanted to. The likeliest explanation was that she hadn't wanted the wagon to be searched, because she knew the rifle was in it.

The horses were getting rested and beginning to spread out. He could hear a few livelier ones poking into the brush, hunting for lichens that always sprouted when the moist night-fogs began to drag over the sea-face of the mountains. Then he heard a snort and a crashing of brush and they came back to the clearing on a run. All the horses packed back into a herd, their round backs glittering with fog-drops as they crowded together, snorting and backing. Something had scared them. It had been after them and it was coming closer. Clay could hear it walking through the brush. It sounded like a mounted man, but that couldn't be, because the horses would have whinnied instead of snorting and acting panicky. It sounded about the weight and blunderingness of an elk, but that couldn't be, either. There were no elk on that slope of the mountains, and elk didn't pursue horses. The next likeliest possibility was a bear, though it would have to be a big one to make all that racket and a mean one not to be more cautious. An old silver-tip, maybe. Clay hauled his mare in and hooked her to the wagon-wheel so she wouldn't try to stampede with the herd, and then dived into the wagon after the rifle. He remembered where he had seen it— well back in the wagon under the deepest part of the load. But he moved harness and nose-bags and tinware and heavy baggage until he came to the bare floor-boards, and it wasn't there. The horses were milling and drifting toward the road, and he gave up searching and went into the tent to wake Luce. The moon shone in on her bed when he tossed the tent-flap back. She turned over, still asleep, and moved her bare arm to keep the light out of her eyes. She was so round and young and white that he stood staring at her for a minute before he remembered what he had come for. Then he touched her shoulder, and knew that she had come awake, because her body straightened and tensed under his hand. She opened her eyes, saw who it was, and lay back relaxed again, covering his hand with her own to hold it against her. "Talk low," she warned him. "What?"

"Something after the horses," he muttered. "Can't tell what, but they're about to stampede. If I can take your rifle ——"

She went rigid all over. He could feel her body turn cold before she shook his hand off and sat up. She remembered not to raise her voice. "Where did you see any rifle? We've got none. What were you prowling into? Tell me."

It was less a pretense of ignorance than an accusation, instinctive, fierce, hostile. The swiftness of her transition from welcome to terror shocked him. Her hand on his had been nothing; there was one thing she hated him for knowing about, one thing in which she trusted him as little and feared him as much as old One-Armed Savage.

"I don't—I didn't see any," he denied. "I thought ——"

She lay back. She didn't ask why he had waked her instead of her father outside. The horse-trader was not the kind of man to whom people ordinarily thought of turning in an emergency. "There's no rifle," she said, and shaded her eyes from the moon so he couldn't see them. "Nothing to shoot with at all. What does it sound like was after the horses? It might be only wild cattle. I'll be up to help you in a minute."

"No wild cattle this low in the mountains," Clay said. He might have been talking to Drusilla at the toll-bridge station, for all the intimacy and understanding there was in it. "Bear or timber wolves, more likely. Build up the fire when you come out. I'll try to herd 'em in close to it."

He went out and unfastened his mare from the wagon-wheel. The job seemed scarcely worth bothering with. The horses couldn't mean much to her if she wouldn't even unearth a rifle to defend them with. But she was getting her clothes on in the tent, the horse-trader's wife had waked up and was asking what the matter was, and the horse-herd was surging and crowding and trying to decide which way to run. He boarded the mare and pulled her head toward the cracking brush. She didn't want to go, and danced around, trying to avoid starting until, having worn the neck rope half out on her without any result, he hit her on top of the head with his fist. She caved at the knees and then ran straight toward the noise as hard as she could buckle. The neck rope wasn't enough to hold her in, and the brush didn't make her miss a stride. She went through it, jumping logs lickety-bang. Clay ducked forward on her neck with brush flogging his ears and ripping at his face, unable to do anything except hang on and hope she wouldn't disembowel herself on a snag. She reared, ramming the bridge of his nose with her head, and wheeled sideways and rammed something with her off shoulder that knocked her down. Clay fell off to keep his leg from being caught under her. It was too dark in the brush to see what she had rammed, but it seemed to have had some influence on whatever had been scaring the horse-herd. The brush-cracking was still audible, but it got fainter and fainter, and finally stopped. The camp fire was beginning to blaze up behind him, and he caught his stirrup to mount and go back when the leaves moved not ten feet from him. The fire had improved the light or his eyes were getting used to it. He saw that there was a man close to him, lying on one elbow in a patch of rabbit brush. He struck a match and saw that it was one of One-Armed Savage's sons. Which one he couldn't tell, because they all looked alike, but as to species the identification was positive. Nobody else had that look of combined maturity and unlickedness, and nobody else, in that soggy tangle of foggy undergrowth, would have opened with a warning about forest fires.

"Be mighty careful where you put that match," young Savage cautioned. His voice was a little shaky, but earnest. "Some mighty valuable timber has been lost around here on account of people droppin' matches. You make sure it's plumb cold before you let it out of your hand."

"There's been a lot of timber lost because sawmill operators swiped it and sold it, too, ain't there?" Clay said. "How did you git out here, and what for? This ain't where you sleep, is it?"

Young Savage sat up. The camp-fire was taking hold big, and

the light, catching him full, showed several scratched and bunged places on his head. "I sleep up at the mill, gener'ly," he said. "Pa sent me to scout down the road after you and fetch back word where you was camped. So my mule went lame and I took an old wood-road of ourn to catch up with you, and then I got brushed up and you come pilin' along and run into me. Dang, you people do have a good time, ridin' around the country and stoppin' where you please, don't you?"

Clay said the pleasures of traveling around the country depended a good deal on the people who lived in it. "You blamed near lost us all our horses, wallerin' around here on that mule. They ain't used to the smell, and it scared 'em. Where is he now?"

"Back at the mill, I guess," young Savage said, hollowly. "I fell off of him when you run into us, and he got away from me. Dang, I hate to ride around on a mule like a blamed old woman peddlin' butter, anyhow. I wouldn't trade a horse for a dozen of 'em. You people have got the only kind of livestock that's worth havin'."

"It's a good kind to git in trouble with," Clay said, feeling his bumped nose. It hurt devilishly, but the skin was unbroken, and the discovery that he had come out of the collision without any damage that would show made him feel better. "How are you goin' to git back to the mill? You can't walk twelve miles in the dark."

That, young Savage said, vaguely, was something he would have to do some figuring on. He didn't intend to walk, but he also declined Clay's offer to try to run in the lost mule, explaining that it would be hard to overhaul him in the brush and that he had ridden the warty old brute as much as he wanted to already. He wouldn't go in to the camp, either, and he gave two explanations for that. The first was that on account of his torn clothes the meeting might embarrass the women. The second was that he wasn't accustomed to female society and that it might embarrass him. "That's a fine girl, that one of yours," he added, as if his predicament was so hopeless he didn't even like to worry about it. "She's stuck on you, too. All of us noticed it up at the mill. Dang, if I had a girl like that to go lopin' around the country with, you couldn't buy me out with a mint. Good horses to ride and a good layout to travel with and that girl, what more could a man want?"

"The layout ain't mine," Clay said. He didn't attempt to clear up the misunderstanding about Luce, or to explain that he had ridden into the woods mad and resolved to have nothing more to do with her. To hear her praised and himself envied for having her, even by this overworked papa's boy of forty, took away all feeling of estrangement and distrust against her. The trouble about the rifle was nothing. After all, what had she said? Only that there wasn't any rifle there, in a voice that, probably due to his own imagination, had seemed alarmed and resentful. How could he feel sure the rifle hadn't been moved or that it was hers? And if it was and she had lied about it, he could hardly claim a much honester score for himself. He hadn't told her that he was wanted by the Oakridge sheriff's office for having abetted a jail-break, and he didn't intend to. She probably had as good a reason for her reticence as he had for his, and she certainly had as much right to it. Having run out that line of reasoning, Clay felt better. It relieved his mind of considerable unpleasant matter that he had been brooding on and feeling mad about, and it turned him to thinking of Luce herself; how she had looked when the moon shone on her asleep, how she had put her hand up to cover his when he woke her. That was worth considerable, and he owed it all to young Savage's wistful admiration. But he didn't press his suggestion about going in to the camp, because he felt easier keeping such compliments at a distance. "You can't set here all night," he remarked. "You can't walk that mud road back to the mill in the dark, and you won't come over to the fire. What are you goin' to do?"

Young Savage did considerable side-stepping before he could be brought to admit that he contemplated doing anything. Finally, having hedged back over his preference for a roving life, the beauty of horses to ride as compared with the ugliness of mules, and the taking appearance of Luce, he owned up that he counted on bargaining for one of the horse-trader's horses. His father, having cooled down from his mad spell, had decided that the horse-trader would camp his outfit on saw-mill property. He had determined to catch them at it, to threaten them with arrest for trespass, and then to offer to let them off on condition they would sell him the buckskin mare. He had taken a shine to that mare, and the more he thought about her the more determined he was to have her. Mostly, young Savage thought, it was because her rearing trick had made him look foolish before his sons. He wanted to get hold of her so he could show them that he wasn't really afraid of her at all. Clay asked why he hadn't come after her himself, if he was that bad off.

"He won't ride anything but a horse," young Savage explained. "We got all our horses out haulin' ties to the railroad. They wasn't anything at the mill except this lame mule. He won't ride a mule because he claims it makes a man look foolish."

Clay said it was a shame, thinking how much more agreeable it would have been to dump One-Armed Savage on his neck in a brush-pile instead of his son. "How much did he aim to pay for this mare? Or did he figure we'd give her to him to keep out of jail?"

"He give me some money," young Savage admitted. He felt to make sure he hadn't lost it in falling off his mule. It was still there. "He told me to offer fifty dollars for her. That's a good big pile of money. Travelin' around and livin' off open land like you do, that would last you a long time."

"I might let him have her pelt for that when she dies," Clay said. "Or if he wants a cheap horse I can git him an Indian cayuse that wouldn't run him much more than fifty dollars."

"He said I could go as high as eighty if I had to," said young Savage. "I'll catch hell for doin' it, though."

"How much money did he give you, all told?" Clay asked, curiously. "You won't git to spend any of it, because this mare ain't for sale, so you might as well tell me. How much was it?"

Young Savage studied to himself and confessed that the old man had given him a hundred and fifty dollars. "I told him you wouldn't be camped where he could hold you and that it wouldn't be enough," he complained. "But he said it would and that if I come back without that horse he'd cowhide me. But I couldn't pay you all of it for her."

"You won't have to pay me any of it," Clay assured him. "Why couldn't you?"

"Because he said if I did he'd cowhide me for that," said young

Savage, in a voice like a man telling a ghost story. "You don't know what it's like, workin' for an old snorter like that. It ain't like this boomin' around the country on a fine horse with a girl taggin' along to keep you livened up, I can tell you that. If you was to hang around that mill a week or— What's that in the brush?"

He reared up and dug an old single-action pistol from under the bib of his overalls. Clay caught his hand and held it down. The noise in the brush was far off because it sounded faint, and human because you could hear twigs dragging against cloth. "Somebody comin' out from camp to look for me, I expect," Clay said. "Put that thing away. Does your old man know you've got it?"

The old man had donated it personally, young Savage claimed, to defend his hundred and fifty dollars with. He didn't usually deal out firearms so prodigally, but there was a report going around about somebody who had got killed and robbed on the road above Oakridge, and it had impressed him. Clay offered to buy the pistol, but young Savage was as stubborn about selling it as Clay had been about selling his mare, and for the same reason. It wasn't his. They were arguing about it when the horse-trader came poking through the brush with a lantern. "Come out to find what you'd run into," he explained, staring at young Savage. "The girl thought you might be hurt."

He continued to stare while Clay told him what the run-in had amounted to and what errand young Savage had been entrusted with. He asked no questions, but when Clay mentioned the hundred and fifty dollars his expression became noticeably less uneasy and more cordial. "Well, come on in," he invited, picking up his lantern. "If your pa sent you out here to talk horse, he sent you to the right place. Come on in and I'll set you on a saddle-horse that'll make this mare look like dog feed. You won't want her when you see some of the other mounts I've got."

Young Savage objected that his personal preference wasn't an element in the deal, that his father had commissioned him to buy the buckskin mare and nothing else, and that he didn't want to go where the women were because his pants were torn. But the horse-trader refused to be put off his game.

"The women will be gone to bed when we git there," he promised. "Your pa stuck for this mare because she's the only one he looked at. You won't have to buy a horse if you don't want to. It won't hurt you to look at 'em, will it?"

They went, Clay riding and the horse-trader and young Savage walking ahead with the lantern. Nearing camp, it took considerable persuasion to keep young Savage from breaking back for the brush, out of bashfulness. They talked him out of it, and it was unjustified, because the women actually had gone to bed. The fire had burned low again, and the horse-herd was scattered about the meadow, pasturing peacefully. Clay pulled his rein, intending to skirmish around and make sure they were still all there, but the horse-trader called him back.

"The girl won't believe I found you unless she sees you," he said. "Go let her look at you, and then you can roll in for the night. Me and this gentleman will tend to the horses."

Going inside the tent was not as easy or offhanded as it had been. The knowledge that Luce was expecting him made it seem a kind of ceremony that he wasn't prepared for. A kind of buck ague took hold of him, and he stood by the tent door, trying to cast it off, until Luce saw his shadow against the canvas in the moonlight and called to him. Then he went in, and there was little ceremony about it, after all, because the horse-trader's wife woke up and insisted on chipping in on the conversation. Clay sat on Luce's cot and explained, without pointing his narrative at either of them, particularly, what had happened and how he had accidentally unhorsed young Savage. The horse-trader's wife said what a fool, and added that she didn't mean Clay. It was dark in the tent and Luce ran her fingers lightly over his face when he finished talking. She felt the swollen place where the mare had rammed the bridge of his nose, so he explained about that. "You did get hurt, then," she said. "I thought you had when you took so long coming back. I thought I was to blame for it."

The horse-trader's wife put in that she didn't call a man hurt when he got his nose bumped, and Clay said it didn't amount to anything.

"She waited up for you," the horse-trader's wife said. "Like a simpleton. It's more than I'd do for any man on earth, with all the traveling we've got in front of us tomorrow. I made her come to bed."

Clay couldn't think of any polite response. He got up and said it was late; and Luce agreed, meaning, as he did, that it was no use trying to talk, with the horse-trader's wife pitching her white chip into the middle of everything that was said. "I was afraid I'd said something you took offense at," she said, "when you came in about the horses stampeding. Did I?"

"Why, no," he said. But that was a lie, so he changed it. "Well, for a minute or two I did, maybe. But I thought it over, and it wasn't anything. It was all right."

She said all right and lay down. The horse-trader's wife asked if her husband was selling the visiting pilgrim a horse. "If he is, you listen and find out how much he gets," she said. "He'll hold out half of it if he can, and I want it out of him."

The horse deal was grinding along without getting much of anywhere when Clay went out, and it looked, from young Savage's skittishness, as if it might last the rest of the week. Clay rolled under the wagon and went to sleep, not expecting that it would come to anything except talk. But when he woke up at daylight it had. Young Savage was gone, and so, when he counted in the horse-herd, was Luce's black gelding. The horse-trader turned over a hundred dollars in gold pieces to his wife. Being urged and threatened, he sweetened it with forty more, which, he swore, was every dime he had got. He called on Clay in the hope that he might have overheard the final bargain, offered to fetch young Savage back to bear witness for him, offered to let them search him to the skin, and ended by digging up five dollars more. Then he retired behind the wagon, claiming to have been insulted by their suspicions, and they let him alone. Afterwards, while they were packing, he called Clay back under the hind wheels and spoke confidentially. "That sawdust hog that was here last night said you offered him twenty dollars for his gun."

"I offered him sixteen," Clay said. "It ain't worth that."

The horse-trader said despairingly that it looked like everybody you met these days was either a swindler or a liar. A man who dealt aboveboard and told the simple truth didn't stand a chance, and it made him feel sometimes as if it wasn't any use to try. "Can you beat that blamed young scoundrel makin' me believe you'd offered him twenty?" he demanded, with indignation. "Well, take it for sixteen, damn it! Give me the money. The gun's in the jockeybox on the front of the wagon. You can git it when the women ain't lookin'. That mare of yours has got a busted shoe that ought to be fixed. I noticed it last night when that one-armed old crow was lookin' her over. You want to look out for him."

"I'll have it fixed when we strike a blacksmith," Clay said. "I ain't afraid of that old fool. It's you that had better look out for him, sellin' his kid a horse he didn't order and takin' everything he had for it. He'll be red-eyed."

The horse-trader cheered up and said maybe he would, but what could he do? "He can't claim it was a swindle, because that black gelding is a good horse. So there won't be anything he can go to law about, and if he comes after us himself he won't catch us. We'll be all mixed up with the crowd down in the hop-yards by the time he gits here. The only thing he could do would be to trail us, and he can't do that if you have your mare's shoe fixed. I got a horse-shoein' rig here, and I can fix it for you while we're packin' up if you'll give me that other four dollars. Give it to me now, while the women ain't lookin'."

Clay gave him the four dollars. It was rather more than a blacksmith would have charged to shoe a whole horse, but it did seem worth something extra to get the broken shoe out of circulation. He felt curious to know why the horse-trader had run up such a fever about getting hold of money. Five dollars that he had knocked down on the sale of the black gelding, sixteen from the pistol, four for putting a new shoe on the mare. It looked as if there must be some kind of game running down at the hop-yards that the horse-trader was saving up to buy a stack in. Clay asked if there was, and the horse-trader took a tone of offended rectitude and said there were several, but he never used them. "The only good money is money you work for," he announced, righteously, and dropped the coins, one at a time, down a rip in the leg-lining of his boot.

"All I'm puttin' this away for is because a man don't feel like a man without he's got a few dollars to knock together, and the women take every cent they catch me with. If you want to avoid a lot of trouble you'll stay single."

"And be like that roundhead you sold the gelding to?" Clay asked. "He's avoided trouble by stayin' single. I suppose you'd like to trade places with him. Would you?"

The horse-trader said there were times when he would be willing to trade places with anybody. He got out his horse-shoeing rig and caught the mare, and he had the shoe about half shaped by the time the women and Clay got the wagon packed and the team harnessed in. Waiting on him, they didn't get started till well after sunup, though a morning fog that clouded low in the wet arrowwood and wild-lilac brush made it seem earlier. Clay and Luce rode together with the horse-herd, talking about old Savage and how they had got the best of him. He kept expecting her to mention the rifle again, and felt disappointed because she took his word that it was all right and didn't say any more about it. But she didn't ask why his mare had to have a shoe changed when they were in a hurry to get across the county line, either, and since he wouldn't she evidently didn't feel like telling him.

They followed the fog all the way across the county line at Elk-head. When it began to lift and burn off they were on the main road in the rich alder-bottoms along Mud River, traveling between miles of dark-green arbors hung with long bunches of pale-green flowers. Hop-driers stuck out every few miles, great barnlike structures four stories high, with a blind belfry on top. They came to places where the arbors had been torn down and ripped to pieces, the strings cut and the poles lying on the ground, and places where there were tents and wickyups and blanket lean-tos and corrals of parked wagons. People were eating breakfast on the ground; women were cooking and hanging out clothes on the wild-lilac bushes and hauling water from the creek; men were cutting wood and currying teams and sloshing cold water on themselves; children were yelling and scuffling and putting their clothes on or running around the camps without any. There were no people in sight except the campers. Nobody was supervising them, nobody was there to inquire who they were or where they came from or anything about them. This was the hop-fields, where all the homeless and jobless and worthless people in the country were camped to pick hops at a cent and a half a pound, and as long as the hops needed picking nobody cared whether the pickers belonged anywhere or amounted to anything or not. If all the people in that country had been solid and respectable, there would have been nobody to get the hops picked.

Chapter XI

THEY picked a camp-site a couple of hundred yards off from the main scramble of hop-pickers' tents and wagons and clothes-drying rigs, on the bank of a spring branch under big alder trees, adjoining somebody's winter stock of high-class oak cordwood. There was no grass; the alder leaves had killed it all out; but it was clean and convenient to water, the woodpile was handy to borrow from, and across the spring branch was an old orchard with a good rail fence and a meadow-grass pasture under the unpruned old fruit-trees. It wasn't extra-good feed, being seedless and badly fouled up with acrid dog-fennel, but it was sustaining enough for horses that didn't have to work, and it was easy to watch against thieves. They turned all the horses into it except the horse-trader's sorrel stallion, keeping him up on account of a childish notion of the horse-trader's that he had to be fed twice a day on grain. Then they pitched the tent and made camp, which was easy, and then they circulated around where the picking was going on, sizing up the pickers and the work.

There was plenty of sportiveness and high spirits around the hop-fields that fall. Hops were fetching thirty-five cents a pound at the drier, and the hundred-acre patch where they were camped stood to return its owner a profit of sixty thousand dollars, clear of all expenses for planting, plowing, poling, stringing, picking, drying, and baling. The owner walked around between the rows, looking solemn and responsible about it, though that may have been due to his wearing all his best clothes, including a stiff-bosomed shirt and a funeral-model stand-up collar. His hops were going to make him rich, and since they couldn't be cashed in on till they got picked, he felt bound to tog himself out uncomfortably by way of showing his pickers how much he appreciated their being there. He had even taken care to see that everybody got camped decently. All the camp-sites were laid off with shade, clean water, brick fireplaces, straw for bedding, and free clotheslines out in the open pasture where the women could hang their washing. There was a small commissary store handling fresh meat and common groceries and gloves and work clothes, at which Clay bought a pair of new overalls to replace Zack Wall's ten-acre pants. There was a little clearing in the brush beyond the hop-yard fence where the men could get action on their day's earnings at chuckaluck, which, according to the long-chinned old Civil War veteran who ran the table, was the game that had been used to put down the Rebellion; and there were lanes and trails in the deep dog-fennel of the old orchard where young couples could go walking after work to watch the moon come up and go down.

Both the gambling and the moon-watching ought to have done business to an extensive clientele. Picking hops was not grinding toil, and a young man could easily get through several weeks at it without having his emotional reflexes worn down a particle. Also, it was fairly profitable. A man with his mind on it could weigh in from three to five dollars' worth of picked hops in a day. But the men among the hop-pickers didn't show much interest in getting a play either on their emotions or on their earnings. Mostly they preferred to sit around camp and gas while the women flagged to and fro, doing up the camp chores for the evening. To the general way of thinking, of course, hop-picking was a kind of squaw's job, and though the men did get out and work at it, they kept their dignity by letting on not to be interested in it or anything connected with it. They were disappointing when you came to know them, for there wasn't enough adventurousness in the whole bunch to kick a breachy hog through a hole in the fence. They lived on the move, all right, but it wasn't the kind of moving that people did who sashayed out into unknown country to see whether it could be lived in or not. They followed the same line of travel year in and year out, from the California prune-orchards up the Coast to the Calgary wheat-fields and back again as regular and undeviating as a man tending a suburban milk route. A lot of them let on to have been blooded gamblers in their time, and some of them had a good deal to say about fights they had been in and towns they had left where women followed them several miles down the road, bawling and begging them not to leave. Some of them even claimed reputations in other sections of the country as dangerous desperadoes, and allowed that a common short-pod hell-raiser like Wade Shiveley might look pretty mean to a hayseed community, but that he wouldn't constitute over one mouthful for them if they ever took a notion to cut loose. None of them ever did cut loose. The nearest they ever got to it was sitting around the fire, devouring tobacco and blowing about what they had been through, as if the old Civil War veteran's chuckaluck board and the couples in the dog-fennel had worn off all interest for them about the time they stopped crawling under the barn to smoke cigarettes. The horse-trader looked rather creditable alongside of them. He sat and chewed and blew about his experiences, too, but at least it wasn't because he considered it any ideal recreation. It was only because his wife watched him so close he couldn't buy in on the chuckaluck game with the money he had knocked down on her.

At Flem Simmons' homestead in the high mountains it had been full winter; at old Savage's sawmill on Gate Creek, full autumn; but in the low hop-raising valleys it had not entirely stopped being summer. The sun by day was hot, and the rains had laid the dust so that at night all the smells of wild asters and flowering grass and blackberry blossoms came in on the moist wind as strong as spring. Clay felt restless with it. He couldn't stand to spend his evenings bragging with the older men; chuckaluck in the brush didn't tempt him because he didn't need to win and didn't want to lose. The couples in the orchard were what bothered him. He could hear them talking after he had gone to bed and ordinary noises had quieted down, and though he knew they weren't saying anything worth listening to or laughing at anything very funny, he would come wide awake straining to hear them, and not be able to get back to sleep. How much of that was his being in love with Luce and how much his distaste for being classed with the circle of blowhards who spent their evenings rooting for themselves he didn't know, but it was bad for his nerves. He didn't let on about it to Luce because, though she seemed restless, too, he saw that she was keeping deliberately shy of him. Couples in the hop-fields usually stripped their hops into one basket for sociability and the fun of watching it fill up faster. The horse-trader's wife followed that system, usually with the assistance not only of her husband,

but of the yard foreman and a whole troop of stiff-jointed old
bucks who had traipsed out from town to watch other people work
and had fallen under her eye before they could get away. But Luce
worked by herself, and carried her basket around to the far side of
the vines whenever Clay edged close enough to talk to her. In the
evenings after work it was the same. She acted afraid of him, and
took such elaborate pains to keep him from catching her alone that
he stopped trying to. It was a strain, having to want her and dislike
her at the same time, but it did teach him something about what
love could amount to—that though it could be a tremendous sight
better than planning station improvements with Drusilla, it could
also be a thundering sight worse. The knowledge was of no particular use to him, and it certainly wasn't worth the wearing down
he went through to acquire it. But he learned nothing else from it,
and what finally brought matters to a showdown was the sociability
of the woman who had the camp next to the horse-trader's.

Where that woman had floated in from nobody knew. None of
the hoboes knew her, and none of the crop tramps had ever seen her
along the road they followed regularly. She was not so tall as Luce,
but older; somewhere, maybe, between twenty-five and thirty. Her
eyes were light blue, and her face was strong and hard-fleshed, but
with a curious look of uneasiness beneath its strength. She had
little camp equipment—a cup, plate, and bedding were about the
size of it; and she had a little short-bodied guitar of the kind that
Mexican sheep-herders used to carry around behind their saddles to
entertain the woolies with on dull afternoons. Of evenings she
played it to herself; sometimes tunes, sometimes merely whanging
the strings and humming to them. She brought it over in the dark
to where Clay was sitting watching the moon's track through the
mist and wishing he could sleep. "You've got it all to yourself,"
she remarked. "Nobody to keep you from being as mournful as
you please. There's a song goes with that." She fingered a chord
on the saddle guitar. "Do you know Spanish?"

He said not if it was poetry, and she explained that it was about
a lonesome *vaquero* jaybirding it out on the corral gate with his
head on his brisket, and how the foreman came along and told him
not to be so down in the mouth. Then she stroked the guitar easy,

muting the thrums with her thumb, and sang *"El Vaquero Desfortu-nado,"* with the pretty turn at the end——

> *"Su mayordomo le dijo*
> *No te attriste, Nicolás,*
> *No te attriste, Nicolás!"*

"You know enough Spanish to understand that, if you know any," she observed, picking the strings one at a time. "I'm not Mexican, though."

Clay said he hadn't supposed she was. Her voice was deep, and she sang low so as not to wake anybody. It made it sound as if she was thinking the music over to herself. He felt a little uneasy lest Luce might hear it and make it an excuse to cold-shoulder him harder, but it was so pleasant he couldn't ask the woman to stop. "Do you know 'Cumberland Gap'?"

She stroked the strings softly. "Sing it," she urged. "I'll catch the tune as you go along."

He held his voice down and sang it.

> "Lay down, boys, and take a little nap,
> We'll wake up in Cumberland Gap.
> Cumberland Gap, it ain't my home,
> I'm a-gonna leave ol' Cumberland alone!"

The guitar ran on with the tune after he was done. "That was a good tune," she said. "I'll sing 'Edward Hallahan'."

It was one of those long gallows-ditties in which a condemned criminal recounts, with ill-concealed relish, all the wicked things he is about to be strung up for, and ends by warning his hearers not to try to have as much fun as he had. A lot of it was monotonous, though the verses about the ship were pretty. The ship's name was the *Flying Cloud*.

> "The *Cloud* she was the fastest ship that ever sailed the seas
> Or ever hoisted main-topsail afore a lively breeze.
> I've often seen that gallant ship with a wind abaft her keel
> And topsle royals set aloft sail nineteen by the reel."

The old tune was so wistful and lovely that it seemed to have displaced not only the words, but the woman who sang them, the camp behind her, all the white tents and wagon-covers in the moon-light, and the moonlit orchard beyond. It stopped and the guitar stopped. Clay realized almost with a jolt that she was speaking to him. "What else do you know?"

He knew several other songs, but the beautiful tune had driven all of them out of his head except a couple of ditties of the dog-house school. One was "Old Mother Kelly's Got a Pimple on Her Belly," and it was too high-power to be possible. The other was in the aggregate almost as bad, but it did have spots that weren't too rowdy. He started, ready to pull up the moment it began to slip.

> "Out on the range of Montana
> In the shank of a cold winter night
> An old cowpuncher lay in his blankets
> A-wishing he'd been brung up right.
> Above him the bright stars were shining,
> Around him the tired night-herd lay,
> As the night-herder rode by the camp fire
> He heard that old cowpuncher say,——
>
> "Oh I am a mean old cowpuncher,
> I never was brung up just right,
> At eight I was cursing and drinking,
> At ten I would ——"

He stopped short. The guitar had led him almost too far. "That's all there is of it," he said, shortly. "Anyway, it's all I ever learnt. You sing one."

She laughed, guessing what the trouble was, and sang several—"Take the Two Best Horses Your Father's Got" and "Lowlands Low" and "The First Come Down" and "Swannanoa Town"——

> "Swannanoa town, O!
> Swannanoa town, O!
> That's my home, babe,
> That's my home.
>
> "I'm a-goin' back to
> The Swannanoa town, O!
> Before long, babe,
> Before long.

"Look for me till
Your eyes run water,
I'll be gone, babe,
I'll be gone.

"O Lord, Emma,
What's your trouble?
Hain't got none, babe,
Hain't got none!

"Swannanoa town, O!
Swannanoa town, O!
That's my home, babe,
That's my home!"

"That's enough," she said, and ran the tune over on her guitar
as if she hated to let go of it. It was her best song, and when she
had sung it she never sang anything more. "You sing one, and then
we'll quit. You know more than two songs, don't you?"

He still couldn't think of a very good one, but he didn't want the
recital to stop at exactly the point when he was beginning to feel
improved in spirit from it. He sang one that he had never liked
because it put him in mind of the Shiveley brothers.

"One day as I was a-rambling around
I met up with Wild Bill Jones.
It's walking and talking with my Looloo girl,
She bid me for to leave her alone.
I said that my age it is seventeen years,
Too old for to be controlled.
I pulled my revolver from my side
And destroyed that poor boy's soul!"

The guitar muffed a couple of notes at the end and shut off with
a clack. "I've heard that one before," she said, and got up. The uneasiness was in her voice and in her face again. "It's late, and I've
got to work tomorrow. Do you sit up out here every night?"

Clay said not always. Sometimes he sat in the wagon, or over
in the horse-pasture. She laughed, understanding more than he had
intended her to. "A kid your age getting edged over a rumpus with
your girl!" she said. "Well, if you're bound to go on with it, you

might as well come over and sit with me as off by yourself. I don't expect to be around here much longer, and I ought to be getting more out of my spare time. If you want to."

He said all right. The singing had made him feel so much better that he didn't feel sure he would need to go on being restless. He might even have turned in and slept, but before he could get up Luce came out of the tent and sat down beside him. "I heard you," she said. Her voice was a little strained with effort not to sound accusing, and she pulled her riding-blanket down on her bare shoulders with a temperish jerk. "You ought to be getting some sleep. Then you wouldn't be so restless, and you wouldn't be sitting up keeping other people awake till all hours."

It was a good deal like telling an overworked man that the way to fix himself was to work a lot harder and make money enough to retire on. Clay said, trying not to sound sulky, that he saw no use lying in bed wondering what was going on when he could as well sit up and see that nothing was. He couldn't help it if people happened along to visit with him.

"You didn't try to help it," she said, sharp and short-tempered. "You don't know anything about these stray women in the hop-yards. You have to be careful how you take up with them."

He said he hadn't done any taking up. "Neither did she, if you come to that. She stopped in and played over some music. I listened because there wasn't anything else to do. I thought when we got down here to the hop-yards everything would be different."

"So did I," she said, unexpectedly. "Or else I wouldn't have let you come here with us. But I was foolish to think so. I've got no business to tell you who you're to talk to and visit with, because we can't be any different than we've been. We just can't."

She sounded a little as if she had been downing too many Bertha M. Clay novels.

"Why can't we?" Clay demanded. "And why do you say you can't tell me who I'm to visit with for? You just got through tellin' me to let that woman alone, didn't you?"

"I said you ought to be careful," she corrected. "Because I know these hop-yards better than you. That doesn't mean we can be any different from the way we've been. I can't tell you why, exactly, but I'll tell you as much as I can. There's something against me, something that might make trouble for me any time if it came up. If we were together it would make trouble for you, too. That's all I can tell you. I'm afraid of it all the time, and I ought to have told you sooner. I can't always be sensible."

He didn't see why she needed to be sensible at all. If being afraid of one's past was any item, he had about as much in his to be afraid of as anybody in the country. He was not afraid of it, and he didn't feel obliged to retire into a cave and shun humanity on account of it. It might never hit him at all, in which case self-denial would be a total waste of valuable time. And if it should hit, any enjoyment he managed to get beforehand would be clear profit. It seemed unjust, since he had got his own conscience out of the way so successfully, to have Luce come bothering him with hers.

"If you don't want to tell me what this trouble amounts to, all right," he said. "I won't nag you about it. But you can tell me what kind of thing it was, can't you? Is it—is it anything about a man? Or is it anything that happened around that old mink of a Phin Cowan?"

She said scornfully that it wasn't that or anything in the least like it. "If I could tell you what it was, there wouldn't be anything about it to be afraid of. We could be together and everything would be all right. But I can't. There's nothing wrong about it, but it's trouble, and I'm afraid of it. I oughtn't to have let you come this far with us."

"You tried to keep me from it," he reminded her. "Well, now you want me to leave?"

"No," she denied, anxiously. It seemed important to her to have him understand the exact shade of difference between what she felt and what she considered advisable. She dwelt on it childishly. "I don't *want* you to leave. Please don't think I do. Only, I'm afraid ——"

"Only you hope I will," he said, impatiently. "Why don't you say so and be done with it? All right, I'll leave. I'll move over to this next camp tonight, and you'll be shut of me. Or else—" It struck him that his acquaintance with the guitar-playing woman wasn't advanced enough to warrant a visit so late at night. She might get scared and start throwing cordwood at him. "Or tomorrow morning," he added, haughtily. "I'll need daylight to pack up by. Now go on back to bed."

She sat still and outraged. "Over to that woman?" she demanded. "You think that'll spite me, I suppose. Don't you see I don't want you to go at all? Haven't I explained how I feel?"

Clay said rudely that as long as she couldn't do anything about her feelings he didn't need to have them explained. "You've told me to leave and I'll do it. Where I move to is none of your business. You said that yourself."

"But you don't know who that woman is!" She wasn't far from parting with her temper. "You don't know anything about her!"

"I don't know anything about you, either," Clay informed her. He felt injured over her refusal to tell him anything about what was on her conscience, and he wanted to jag her about it. Instead, he made her mad. She rose and bunched her blanket around her with a pop. "If you can't tell the difference between me and that—" She tried to think of the word, and probably succeeded; but she didn't say it. She went into the tent and stayed there. She didn't even come out at daylight, when Clay rolled his blankets and hauled them and his saddle across to the adjoining camp-site where the guitar-playing woman was breakfasting on a board laid across two chunks of firewood. She stared at him questioningly. "I'm movin'," he explained, and dropped his blankets in front of her. "Let me know if I crowd you."

She watched him while he hung his saddle in a tree under the creek bank. "I usually let 'em know when they crowd me," she said, unsmiling. "I wouldn't have asked you over if I hadn't meant it. Sit down and have some breakfast."

She might not have been a professional crop-follower, but she set out what was the standard line of fodder for one. There was bakery bread, store butter, packing-house bacon, eggs fried with a tough crust on the outside, and package coffee; all store commodities, with no special virtue except that they were easy to cook. Having fixed and set them in front of him, she nodded inquiringly at the horse-trader's camp. The horse-trader was welding a toe weight onto a racing horseshoe. His wife was getting breakfast. Luce was still in the tent, and the tent door was tied down. The guitar-playing woman looked at it and then at Clay. "You had it

out with her, I see," she said. "About time, I suppose, the way
she's been treating you. I wasn't to blame for it?"

"No," Clay said. The woman's uneasiness seemed to have dropped
into the ground. She didn't look gay, exactly, but she looked sure
of herself. "You kids!" she said. "As if it wasn't hard enough to
be one, without all this squabbling and cold-shouldering and breaking up housekeeping to make it worse! You're going to start working by yourself?"

"I'll work with you," Clay said. He had thought that all out.
"You can have whatever we make, to pay for my keep. It'll only be
a few days, probably."

She took the cup and bucket-lid plate from in front of him and
said probably it would. "Your girl will be as mad as fire," she said.
"Not but what she's got it coming for her foolishness. So have you,
for putting up with it. Do you want to start work today?"

It was a pleasant change working with her. She was unshirking,
lively, and good-humored with a kind of here-goes-nothing reckless-
ness about her, though that might have been caused by the amount
of notice their partnership let them in for. The hop-field had seemed
a place where people minded their own business and let one another
alone, but it wasn't any such thing. It was a good deal like an
inquisitive-minded village, that had kept its identity, its social levels,
and its inquisitiveness unaltered through all the moving around it
did in the course of the year. Women left their work and came
clear from the other end of the field to see how Clay and the
woman looked since their consolidation. Men went out of their
way to stroll past and look them over, and then carried the news
to other men and strolled back with them to prove that they had
told only the gospel truth. The rush of sightseers let up at noon
because most of the pickers went back to camp for dinner. Clay
and the woman ate theirs in the field under a hop-vine. It consisted
of bread, butter, and corned beef out of a can, and while they were
eating it Luce passed on her way in to camp. She got close before
she noticed them, and she walked past without speaking. Clay had
expected that, but he hadn't expected that it would make him feel

so dejected and out of spirit. He stared after her with his chin hanging. The woman frowned at him and then laughed.

"You didn't expect her to act pleased about this, did you?" she queried. "You've made her mad, and it's good enough for her. What'll you do next, go back to her?"

Clay said he couldn't do that, because Luce had asked him to leave for good and he had announced himself as intending to do it. He should have added something about finding the new arrangement too pleasant to quit, but he didn't think of it and the woman didn't appear to expect it.

"If that's how it is, maybe you're right," she agreed. "It won't hurt to hang around like this a few days to make her wish she hadn't spoke so quick. It can't last very long, though, because I don't know when I may have to pull out of here. Or where to."

"We might pull out together," Clay said, more out of regained politeness than because he wanted her along. He tried to imagine what their exodus would look like, himself leading the buckskin mare and her riding and hanging onto the saddle-horn like Sunday-school pictures of the Flight into Egypt. To his relief, she said no. "I might not want to leave when you do," she explained. "This is a kind of vacation for me and I want to make it last as long as it will. And then, I might have to leave before you're ready to. I won't know for sure till the time comes. Let's not bother about it till then."

She disliked talking about anything that had to do with unpleasantness, even when it was something that needed only a little ordinary fixing. Clay noticed during dinner that she kept one foot out of sight under her skirt, and when they went to work again he saw her sit down and do something hurriedly to her right shoe when she thought he wasn't looking. She changed the subject when he asked her about it, but, returning from cutting loose a fresh pole ahead of them, he found her fitting a hop-basket slat inside the shoe for an emergency insole. The original sole was broken completely across. Clods and gravel had worn through it and her stocking, and a blister was threatening on her foot. The skin where she had rubbed the dust off was scarlet and inflamed. "You can't wear that thing any longer," he said. "Wrap this handkerchief around your foot, and I'll go over to the commissary and buy you a new pair. Why couldn't you have done that instead of tryin' to cripple yourself?"

She said he was talking like an old granny, and that it took a good deal more than that to cripple her. She tried to get the shoe away from him so she could put it back on and go on working. "The commissary hasn't got any shoes I could keep on," she said. "This one only wore out this morning, and I can make it do the day out. Give it here."

It was true that her foot wasn't built on the standard hop-yard pattern of feminine sub-structures. Hop-picking women, mostly from having gone barefooted till they were ready to marry, ran to large orders of meat below the ankle, with a good, substantial spread of toe. Her feet were narrow, high-arched, and slim at the heel. It was doubtful if even the stores in town could supply her exact size, but they would at least have something she could walk in. Clay wanted to send the broken shoe in by one of the hop-hauling wagons and order a pair, with it as a sample. She wouldn't let him. She couldn't pick hops barefooted, comfortable though it might be. She didn't want to lose the afternoon's work on the very first day of their partnership, and she didn't want to buy shoes to work in when she didn't know how much longer she would be able to work.

"But you've got to have shoes, whether you work or not," Clay argued. "You can't even walk with this thing on."

"Oh, give it back and quit harping about it!" she said. "Didn't you ever go to a dance with a pair of new shoes hurting you? And did you ever let that stop you when you were having a good time?"

Clay felt embarrassed to have her intimate that hop-picking with him could be named in the same day with such an out-and-out form of entertainment as a dance, but he refused to give back the shoe until he had fixed it so it wouldn't half-kill her. He carried it down to the harness-room at the farmhouse, borrowed a set of leather-needles, and whanged on an emergency sole with an old piece of collar-patching. It wasn't much for looks, but it kept the dirt out and it didn't hurt her to wear.

"It is better," she conceded, when it was on. "It ought to be, the time you've fooled away fixing it. I hope I'm here long enough to get some use out of it."

They worked late with the hops to make up for the time he had lost on her half-soling. It was dark when they filled their big shoulder-high basket for the last time. The weight-checkers had hung lanterns down by the road to finish adding up the day's weight-tickets with the owner of the yard.

"We'd better hurry this down before they quit," she said. Hops picked and left in the field overnight were liable to be mavericked and turned in at daylight by the first early riser who found them. "Grab hold of your side and let's get down there with it."

All during the day they had been carrying the filled baskets down the scales together. But it was a considerable distance and she sounded tired, and Clay felt a childish impulse to show her how much of a load he could walk away with alone. He got his back under the basket squaw-fashion and stood up with it.

"I can handle this one myself," he announced, modestly, trying not to stagger with it. "You go on to camp. Some of these tin-horns off work might lift something from us if they see there's no-body there."

She said she would have supper ready for him, and they separated. They made no ceremony of the parting, because both had a solid, common-sense feeling that it wasn't going to last long or mean much; the feeling of couples who have lived together long enough to get over their uncertainty about each other and to know that, no matter what comes up during the day, they will go on eating and sleeping together at the end of it. Nothing had happened between them to warrant such a feeling, but Clay felt it so strongly that he plugged between the dark rows with the basket without even hurrying. When he got a couple of rows distant from the weighing-stand, he set the basket down to rest and change holds, and saw that he was about to bump into visitors. There was a wagon at the gate with two men in it. They hadn't called out of neigh-borliness, for one of them showed a star on his suspender and then covered it with his coat. He was after somebody among the hop-pickers, because he handed down a paper with printing on it and the hop-yard owner read it and asked, indignantly, why the damna-tion he had come bothering a man's hired help right in the middle of the picking-season.

"You got the right place for this, I reckon, but you certainly played hell pickin' a time for it," he complained. "I can't have you wavin' your star and your papers around these camps. You'd scatter these pickers of mine like a bunch of quail, and I'd have this crop left on my hands till January. If you'll wait right here a few minutes, this criminal you're doggin' will be down to weigh up, and you can do your arrestin' and be on your way without stampedin' anybody. Damned if I don't believe this is a rannikaboo them Forty-Gallon church people down the valley has got up to rob my pickers away from me, anyhow. It's a wonder the blamed hymn-shoutin' robbers wouldn't hire somebody to put strychnine in my coffee and be done with it."

He was really outraged. Stampeding a man's hop-pickers in a big season was almost as mean as dogging his milk-cows. The offended clatter of his Adam's apple against his stand-up collar was distinctly audible. The sheriff's deputy said the hymn-shouters had nothing to do with his warrant, because it had come in from another county. He wouldn't mind waiting if it didn't take too long. In that hop-raising country, hindering a man's hop-harvest was serious trespass. He pulled his wagon in against the fence and asked how long it was likely to be.

"A few minutes at the outside," the owner said, unsociably. "You can see most of the hands has gone to camp already. They all fetch their hops down here the last thing, and this desperado you're drawin' the taxpayers' money for trailin' is almost the only one we've still got to hear from." He clacked his stiff collar and repeated the word desperado to make sure they got the sarcasm. "You certainly do hump down to work when it's some fool mail-order case that nobody gives a damn about, don't you? You all set around the office with your feet on the stove when that Wade Shiveley raises hell in another county, but when it's some measly family row or other, out you rip to fetch the mallyfactor to justice if it wears out every horse in the livery-stable. Are any of your men out helpin' to catch Shiveley? No, you're damn right they ain't!"

It had taken Clay very little time to decide that the warrant was for him. He was backing cautiously away when the mention of Wade Shiveley froze him in his tracks. If an out-of-the-way farmer in the far corner of another county was keeping tab on that case, it was more serious than he had thought. If Wade Shiveley had killed somebody since the jailbreak— For the first time, Clay cussed Uncle Preston to himself for not letting his blamed son stay in jail and be hung. But he was premature, for no more killings had been reported. The deputy remarked lightly that Wade Shiveley didn't amount to much these days, and they were sort of saving him for seed.

"They'll haul him in when they need him," he said. "With his nerve broke and all his hide-outs stopped on him, he'll be easy to head. He was layin' out on his old man's ranch in the mountains last week, we heard, and a sixteen-year-old girl on the place run him through the fence with a kittle of hot water and dared him to come back and fight. She hit him in the face with it, kittle and all, and scalded hell out of him. He took to the brush, but she like to burnt his eyes out and he ain't got any gun, so he won't git far. Your pickers' camps are over by them fires, ain't they?"

One reason Clay had not felt very uneasy about being caught before was that he had seen and sized up all the sheriff's men whose job it was to catch him. He couldn't see these men except as shadows in the lantern-light. They sounded most infernally like business, and that and the narrowness with which he had missed walking right into their laps scared him. If he had been three minutes earlier they would have caught him getting his hops weighed. If they had been ten minutes later they would have walked in on him in camp, with Luce standing by to watch them haul him away. Nothing had saved him but plain luck. His smartness, on which he had depended with such confidence, had failed him completely. He hesitated, wondering how he could ever trust it again and knowing that he could trust nothing else, and the hop-yard owner put the finisher to his scare by giving careful directions about where he was camped.

"Them fires is the main camp," he explained. "You have to go through that and past it till you strike that belt of big alders. Foller them up the branch, and it's the last camp this side of the wood-piles. If you let on to any of them other pickers that you've come to arrest anybody, you'll have 'em boilin' out of here like bees a-swarmin'. Damn, if I was sure that church outfit had started this to git my pickers away from me——"

Clay backed cautiously till he could no longer hear the owner's lament over his endangered livestock, and then ran. Nearing the

main camp, he swung wide and waded the spring branch to the
orchard where the horses were pasturing. For a piece of luck, no
couples were out in it so early, and for another the feed was poor
and unnourishing. He could never have caught the buckskin mare
in the dark if it had been a question of pulling her off decent grass
to go to work. But she was tired of weed stalks and choky dog-
fennel, and she nickered and came to him of her own accord on
the chance that he might be fixing to take her where the rations
were better. He strapped his belt around her nose to hold her,
sneaked back across the spring branch, and eased his saddle and
bridle down from the tree under the bank. His camp-ground was
about two feet from his head, and he could see the fire and hear
the woman putting wood on it. It was mean to slope without telling
her, but he knew that he looked scared and that she would be sure
to notice it and ask why, and he didn't want Luce to see him at all.
The wagon rattled across plowed ground, coming between the hop-
rows, and he backed away from that place and all thoughts about
it for good. He saddled and bridled the mare and got on at a trot,
took her over the rail fence at a jump, and racked out on the road
in the dark toward the low timbered ridge of the Coast Range
Mountains where the sun set and all the rainstorms came from.
The one thought in his head was that he must not let himself get
caught, and it was not entirely a selfish one. His arrest, he knew,
would humiliate the guitar-playing woman before the other hop-
pickers. He didn't much mind leaving her without notice, because
there was something wistful and desperate about the way she hung
on his company that made him feel embarrassed around her; but
she had been good to him and he didn't want her humiliated any
more than he wanted himself arrested.

Chapter XII

ALWAYS before he had taken to the road with some notion where he was going and what he was going to do when he got there, and usually there had been somebody along to travel with and talk to. Now his stock of companions was all traded out, he was alone and heading for a country where he didn't even know what people did for a living, and, though he stuck to side roads for the sake of inconspicuousness, the hop-farms kept his nerves edged because every one of them flagged him down and tried to haul him in to help pick hops. He tried explaining that he didn't want to pick hops, but that did no more good than if he had been a loose wagon-horse expressing a dislike for working in harness. For a while he got himself loose from them by telling them that he came from another hop-field and was going for a doctor for a couple of pickers who had got stabbed in a fight. Even that stopped working as he neared the mountains. The valley narrowed down and the hop-fields began to mix in with dairy country; silos, fields of red clover, and a profuse sprinkling of churches and meeting-houses alternated with tall hop-driers' and hop-pickers' tents, and the men who halted him got hard to convince. They looked too substantial and pious to be capable of lying themselves, but they were on full cock to catch anybody else doing it, and they drove holes through his stabbing-story with such unerringness that he stopped using it. The more information you offered those people, the more they found to ask questions about. He took to explaining simply that it was a case of sickness and that he was in a hurry.

That kept its efficacy pretty well until he got to the very last hop-yard on the road, where pickers were scarcest. There was a lantern out at the gate to stop travelers with, and the whole family was out to see that it got handled right. There was a rickety, domineering old man with a tremendous bass voice, a tall forty-year-old daughter with a scratchy voice and a red nose, and a solemn little runt of a son-in-law with a big bush of auburn whiskers and a pair of bib-overalls that had faded out white through being boiled with soft

167

soap to get them clean. He waggled a batch of butter in a fruit-jar,
churning it while he talked. All three of them came out in the road
and invited Clay to light down and climb onto the payroll. None
of them believed him when he explained why he couldn't.

"Who's sick?" the red-nosed daughter demanded in a voice so
near a squawk that it sounded intentional. "You looky here to me,
young man, there ain't any livin' mortal sick on this road or I'd
have heerd about it! Link down offen that horse this minute and
don't go tellin' falsehoods in front of Mr. Spaugh! We could have
you arrested for vagrancy, do you know that?"

"I ain't tellin' falsehoods," Clay said. He wanted to be cautious
and unassertive, and to avoid the mistakes he had made with One-
Armed Savage. He pulled the mare back politely, as a hint to the
rickety old man, who was inspecting her head with his lantern. "My
father has took sick in a deer-camp, and I got to git to him. Move
out of the way, grandpa. This horse of mine is restless, and she's
liable to step on you."

The old man hauled his eyebrows together and said, without
moving, that he had never heerd sech pusillanimous impertinence
in all his born days. He sounded as if he was trying to pick something to get mad about. The whiskered son-in-law dandled his
churning of butter nervously and inquired if Clay realized who he
was talking to. "Mr. Spaugh owns every foot of land between here
and the high timber, and plumb down the forks of the valley," he
volunteered. His function, it appeared, was to enlighten strangers
about the old man's power and accomplishments so they wouldn't
take offense at his bad manners. "Mr. Spaugh built that church
you passed down the road, right outen his own pocket. One of the
streets down at the county seat is named after Mr. Spaugh. It's
named Spaugh Avenue, right on all the telegraft-poles. Mr. Spaugh
is a director in one of the strongest banks in ——"

"Be done!" the old man put in, ungraciously. He had his hand
on the mare's rein. Clay could have set her on her hindquarters
and lifted him into the air like a kite tail, but he hesitated to do it.
The old man didn't look as if it would take much of a shock to
start him coming to pieces. He was plainly used to having his own
way, for he looked the mare over deliberately, felt down her

pasterns and blew into her nostril to test her nerves. "This horse ain't yours," he announced, very deep and loud. "You look mightily to me like a bound-boy runnin' away to keep from workin', and usin' another man's horse to do it on. You stole this horse, boy."

"A hell of a lot you know about it, don't you?" Clay said. The accusation didn't scare him any more. He knew it was guesswork, and it was becoming evident to him that the mare looked a little too expensive to match his clothes and appearance. But he didn't like to waste time arguing about it when the men in the wagon might already be started after him. "All right, she's stole, if you want to have it that way. Now stand out of my way or I'm liable to grab hold of you and steal you, too!"

The whiskered son-in-law jiggled his butter energetically and said the very idee of sech sass, and the woman called out that he hadn't better lay hands on Mr. Spaugh because it might bring on one of his spells. The old man ordered them both to shut up, and observed intrepidly that no pusillanimous little road-snipe could disabuse him on his own property. He held his ground by the mare's head, rumbling cavernously. He had been a good man when he was young, probably, and he hadn't been outside his own picket fence enough to discover that he wasn't one any longer. It would have been wicked to ride over him, and the only way Clay could think of to move him politely was to make a kind of joke of it. He remembered an old corral trick, and, backing the mare sideways, he reached out and grabbed the old man's shirt-tail and yanked it up over his head, sacking his arms and the lantern in it. The old man let out a tremendous lick of cussing for a philanthropist who built churches out of his own pocket, and then, being unable to see, fell down. His daughter and son-in-law both fell on him, clattering indignantly and trying to get the lantern away from him before he set himself afire with it. The mare laid back her ears inquiringly and hit up a trot. She went over a low hill covered with arrowwood and hazel and tarweed, and beyond that through a stretch of cut-over land where the moon came out and showed a clear road a long way ahead. There were no houses and no cultivated fields in sight, the old man's roaring faded in the noise of a wet wind scattering dew among the vines of white wild grapes, and that was the last

of the valley country and of the old men who lived in it and used
their strength and will, since neither was any longer needed for the
job of making a living out of new land in raw country, upon keeping their children from amounting to anything. It made Clay feel
better to get the whole district out of his sight. He hadn't liked
any of the people he found in it, and he couldn't recall a single
night that hadn't been hard to get through, either because nothing
happened or because too much did.

The change of road picked his spirits up so that even loneliness
seemed part of his good luck. Of course it wouldn't be an advantage
if he broke a leg or got bucked into a tree-limb, but he had run that
risk plenty of times traveling alone, and he wasn't afraid of it.
Having to look out for himself made him feel at home. If Luce
had been there he would have felt resentful and ill-humored because of her cold-shouldering. If it had been the guitar-playing
woman, she would have been over-eager about following him
around, and that would have bothered him. Drusilla would have
expected him to stew over the station buildings, and the Indian boy
always got disagreeable if you didn't act solemn about dreams,
portents, and omens. It was better not to have companions, to be
alone and unworried by what anybody else felt or thought or believed, to be free to enjoy the road and take an interest in the
scenery.

There were few houses along that mountain road. A frugal scattering of little log cabins, windowless, chinked with mud, mostly
with the roof-poles rotted through and fallen in. A few small clearings where somebody had raised oats or potatoes, with a close wall
of second-growth spruce and white fir doing duty as a fence and a
deep growth of dying bracken around the edge where the mower
hadn't reached. The fall of dew on that slope was as heavy as rain
in spite of the bright moon overhead. The mare was drenched with
it, and every bush she touched shed a couple of gallons more down
on top of her. The vegetation was heavy and, especially close to
the summit, without any of the restfulness that one ordinarily expects of an unpathed primitive forest on top of a wild range of

mountains. Every plant in it was in a tooth-and-claw fight to get sunlight. There were whole thickets of naked fir skeletons that had died stretching for it; trees that had been choked to death by wild honeysuckle climbing after it; vine-maples that had grown two hundred feet of right-angled joints to get one leaf into it for maybe half an hour a day. The only living trees were tremendous, because they had to be to live. There were cedars that had reached so high trying to keep ahead of sun-hogging trees around them that they had forgotten to put down roots, and the mere side-sway of the upper air had tipped them flat on the ground. Except in the road, green moss covered everything a foot deep, with bunches of sword-fern growing out of it as tall as a man. Thickets of salmon berries fringed the road because it was the one place open to the sun, and wherever water had collected there were pads of skunk cabbage with leaves two feet across and flower stalks as big as one's arm. You could have taken a double-fistful of moss off a log and wrung a big drink for a horse out of it. Dew moved and dripped off the sword-ferns and the dying saplings all night, and dawn came with a raw fog that dripped still louder and soaked the fir and spruce thickets till they bent sideways into the road. Afterwards a pale yellowing sun dried them off, and Clay came to a beaver-dam clearing where there was a store. It was a large building of weather-boarding, with curtains on the second-story windows and a spacious red mudhole in front, in the middle of which floated a man's felt hat.

Nothing in sight accounted for the hat, or, for that matter, for the store itself. The road showed no signs of travel, and the country looked as soggy and lonesome ahead as behind. Inside, the store appeared to be untended. It had several shelves of canned goods, two or three mowing-scythes, a stand of double-bitted axes, and some cheap single-barreled shotguns. There were also a rack of garden seeds, a display of spooled thread, several hanks of fish-line in assorted sizes, and an astonishing quantity of patent medicines. Mostly they were for ailments of women, but there were also blood-purifiers and stomach-tonics and kidney-strengtheners and system-builders, cough-remedies and rheumatism-cures, besides the specifics that were guaranteed to handle jaundice and lumbago and ague and melancholia and flatulence on a sort of blanket contract. On the floor behind the counter was a heap of loose fur pelts, mostly coon and bobcat, with a few mink and fisher scattered in for seasoning. Clay waited and thumped on the counter and heard somebody moving on the upper floor, but nobody appeared. He went outside and found the proprietor in a rocking-chair against the side of the building, waiting for him to come out and report what he wanted to buy.

The proprietor was a stolid man with a big face, a tousled stand of yellow beard, and no shoes. He had a batch of green mink-hides that he was making willow-rod stretchers for, and he opened the conversation by inquiring where Clay had got his horse.

"I found her in a bear-trap," Clay said, hoping to quench the subject by being flippant about it. "You sellin' anything that I could eat breakfast on?"

The storekeeper bent a green willow stick and peeled some bark with his teeth to tie it with. "Sardines to the right as you go in," he directed. "Crackers in a box under the back counter. Pay out here. They ain't anything in there worth stealin', so don't waste your time lookin'."

He couldn't have been used to seeing over one customer a week in such a place, and his statesman-like uncordiality made it look as if the sogginess of the climate might be infecting the inhabitants' manners. He had another stretching-frame started when Clay came out and asked for a feed of grain for his mare, and he said with considerable contempt that people in that neighborhood didn't feed grain to horses. Such expensive provender was reserved for poultry. The heavier classes of livestock subsisted on potatoes, which were cheaper and every bit as nourishing. Clay declined to be guided by neighborhood advances in the science of horse-feeding, so he brought a pile of rolled barley in a rusty shovel and announced that the bill would be a dollar and a half, payable entirely in cash. Clay said it was three times too much, and he agreed that for the groceries it probably was. His main charge, he said, was for Clay's knowing it all and refusing to take advice.

"People that travels this road at all hours of the night with high-priced horses can't afford to kick on an overcharge," he stated, working a mink-pelt onto a stretcher. "If they cave around about price, it's li'ble to start questions bein' asked about where they come from, and so on. You ain't pulled no wool over my eyes. I ain't fool enough to believe you found that horse in any bear-trap, because how could she have clumb into it? You stoled that horse, boy."

Seeing that he was in for it again, Clay decided to have it out quick. "You certainly notice things, don't you?" he inquired. "Sharp as a steel trap, you are. Maybe you've noticed that when people shoot off their mouths about somebody else's business they lose money on it? I won't pay you any dollar and a half, and I won't pay you anything, and you can ask all the questions and raise all the hell about it you're a mind to. How does that strike you?"

The storekeeper got his mink-pelt fixed and set it in the shade. "It ain't the money I care about," he said. "You think because I live off here in the backwoods that I'm an easy one to fool, and you're mistaken. I can read men. I can set here and see a man comin' along the road, and I can tell you, from lookin' at him, what business he's in and all about him. I've trained myself to do that. This business of expectin' me to believe you found that horse in any bear-trap is ridicklous. Why don't you own up about it?"

He was almost pathetic, in spite of his short manners to start with. Probably the only thing he felt proud of was his ability to guess out his customers' business. It would have been inhumane to let him think he had guessed one wrong. Clay said he hadn't rustled the mare, exactly, but that he didn't object to admitting, strictly in confidence, that he had got possession of her in a transaction that wasn't quite up to red-tape standards of law. He pitched a long yarn about how, after his father died, he had been bound out to work on his uncle's ranch till he was twenty-one, but he took to attending turkey-shoots and barbecues and play-parties and candy-pulls after working hours and his uncle blacksnaked him for coming home late and waking up all the work-stock climbing in the window of the barn where he had to sleep. So he stood it as long as he could and then snatched out and left, taking the mare along with him because he had raised her from a colt and couldn't leave her to be mistreated. He made quite a recitation of it and gave his uncle considerable of a character, explaining how he always laid in bed till noon with a jug and then staggered out and blacksnaked the livestock all round to start the day off on. The storekeeper tried to keep his stolidity through it, but he was moved. He had never attended a play-party himself, he said, but he had seen pot-latches in the Indian village down the river, and he couldn't see that they ever hurt anybody. And a man who would object to having the stock waked up and then go out and flog them himself for nothing was certainly lost to redemption.

"The quicker you make it to the Coast, the better show you'll stand to dodge him," he said. "You'd better cross the river at that Indian village and take their trail down. It'll save you nearly five mile, and there's less apt to be people on it. You'll have to ferry the river in a canoe, but the Indians will tend to that for you."

Clay inquired how much the Indians charged for ferrying. In some sections of country it was the native custom to get a man embarked and then stop halfway across and threaten to throw his baggage overboard unless he anted up some extortionate fee for his passage.

"They don't charge anything," the storekeeper said. "Anybody that hails 'em they've got to ferry across for nothing. That's their religion. Only, after they've put you ashore and turned down your money, they're as li'ble as not to knock you in the head and steal it offen your carcass. It ain't ag'in' their religion to do that. Don't you have anything more to do with them Indians than you have to, that's what I'd advise you."

The brutal-uncle invention had certainly hit his tap. He forgot all about the disputed charge for provisions, and favored Clay with some cautionary scandal about local Indian manners and customs. They hung their dead people in trees so a man sauntering in the brush near their village could never be sure whether his top-hair was being bedewed with a refreshing rain or the disintegrating remnants of somebody's great-grandmother. They tattooed their faces with laundry-bluing in the belief that it improved their looks. All the women bore their children at the same time every year, and made a kind of sisterhood rally out of it. You would see them going around holding in and eyeing one another appraisingly for weeks, and then they would all cave down at once and have a baby apiece as unanimous as a housewives' donation-party to furnish the parsonage. They ate Indian olives, which were a kind of pickled acorn, flavorsome enough if you didn't know what they were pickled in, and they ate dog, and they ate fish and fish and fish and fish and fish.

Clay inquired if the women's habits of diet and childbearing was responsible for the store's stock of female remedies, and also whether there weren't other people on the Coast besides Indians. It sounded like a big stretch of ground. There were surely farms and settlements and post-offices somewhere along it. The storekeeper said most of those things were down on Coos Bay, where the ships came in to load cedar. The coastline to the north struggled along without them.

"There's people, if you want to go lookin' for 'em," he said. "Mostly they're thieves and jailbreakers and hide-outs, from what I hear. We don't git much news from 'em till one stabs another and lights out across the mountains. The sheriff's out after one now for that, or was. They're smarter than these Indians, but that don't make 'em any safer to monkey with, women or men. But it ain't the Indian women that buys them female remedies. It's the bucks, and they drink 'em, too. I've seen a big old canoe-chief named Spillets or something like that swaller five full-size bottles of Dr. Turnbull's Prescription for Expectant Mothers as fast as he could git the corks pulled. Afterwards he took his clothes off and et fire. Yes, sir, fire. He licked it right offen a chunk of pitch and snorted a big stream of it eight foot out into the air. The squaws mostly take Our Baby's Friend Tonic Vermifuge or Mother Porter's Wild Cherry and Pine Tar Expectorant. They eat it on fish, like it was pepper-sass. Them Indians is a low outfit. They ain't worth an intelligent man's bother."

They didn't sound like much of a social resource, though the medicine business proved nothing. If a man wanted to eat fire and a Prescription for Expectant Mothers would help him to do it, there seemed no reason why he should go without it simply because it was supposed to be for something else. "Can they understand jargon?" Clay asked.

Jargon was the country name for the old Hudson's Bay Company trade-lingo, the universal conversational vehicle for all Indian tribes along the Northwest Coast, where a forty-mile trip would run a man through six or seven changes of native language, each as different from the others as French is from Gaelic. The storekeeper said disdainfully that he didn't know what kind of palaver they understood. "I don't know jargon myself, and I wouldn't waste my time learnin' it to accommodate 'em. I've traded here with 'em for thirty years, and I ain't never needed to talk to 'em. Don't show 'em any money and don't act too polite. Their trail ain't over a couple of hours' ride from the beach."

He framed another mink-pelt and set it against the house absently, listening to something a long way off. Clay listened, too, thinking it might be somebody on the road. But it was only the ocean, which they could hear between the intervals of wind in the cedars. It was louder, the storekeeper said, when the winter storms were on, and he had listened to it so many years that he sometimes wondered what the blamed thing looked like. He had never seen it. In winter when trade was slack the roads weren't fit to be traveled. In summer he had to stay with the store because Indians were showing up at all kinds of hours to trade, and his wife refused to have anything to do with them. Also he was afraid to leave her alone because she had streaks when there was no telling what she might do, and the only time he had attempted to take her out for a day's vacation she got scared of a ferry-crossing and screeched herself black in the face, and while they were gone some Indians broke into the store and stole everything they could carry off. His wife hated Indians and she hated the sight of deep water. Clay remarked that it was a strange location for anybody with that set of prejudices to be settled in.

"It wasn't any of my doin'," the storekeeper said. "I didn't want to settle here, to start with, but she said this travelin' around huntin' for land made people think small of us, and she made me swear that when we struck a place with wood, grass, and water we'd climb down and stay and wait for the country to settle up around us. This was it."

He gestured at the landscape with his toe. Clay remarked that the subsequent settlers in the country hadn't had much trouble keeping out of each other's way. The storekeeper said there hadn't been any other settlers, and that he had never expected there would be. His trade was entirely with the Indians. "I've got used to the place, livin' in it so long," he apologized. "But my wife she's lived here so long she's took a plumb cold spite ag'in' it. Sometimes she'll spend a week locked upstairs with the blinds pulled down so she won't have to look at it. And then she'll take a notion I'm goin' to pack up and move with her, and she'll fly all to flinders because I won't do it. There ain't anything here for a body to keep interested in, she claims."

"There's as much for her as there is for you, ain't there?" Clay inquired.

The storekeeper said modestly that it wasn't the same thing. She had no talent to entertain herself with, and he had. When he had time and the road was open he enjoyed exercising his powers of divination on the characters of travelers. "I've trained myself to read a man's business as far off as I can see him," he mentioned again. "Take you, frinstance. I could tell when I sighted you that you was a runaway boy from, well, maybe from some relative that had mistreated you. And I could tell right off that horse didn't belong to you. You don't run into many men that could call the turn on that horse like I did, I reckon. Or else you'd never have got this far from home with her. Do you reckon that guardeen of yours will hunt this far after you?"

"He's liable to," Clay said. A man in a place like that needed something to look forward to. "Or he might git the sheriff down here to come out after me. He's vindictive."

"You don't need to tell me," the storekeeper said. "I can read that uncle of yours from what you've told me about him, as plain as if he was a-settin' here. You don't need to feel uneasy about the sheriff for a day or two. He's off across the mountains workin' on one of them stabbin'-cases from the Coast. He'll most likely pass here on his way back, so all you got to do is keep ahead of him. Don't let your horse step on that hat in the puddle yonder. It's mine."

"I'll bring it out for you," Clay offered. The storekeeper eyed it wistfully and shook his head. "Better not, I guess," he decided. "I waded in and fetched it out a couple of times, but my wife throwed it back ag'in. The last time she throwed my shoes in after it. Mad because I wouldn't give in and move with her. Nothing dangerous about her, but sence that woman down on the Coast poked a fish-

splitter into her man I've been goin' kind of easy with her tempers.
The way women gits in this country when winter sets in, they're
li'ble to hack a chunk off of a man without realizin' what they're
doin'. You're lucky you ain't got a woman on your hands down
here."

Clay replied that he intended to stay lucky. He couldn't understand why the storekeeper's wife couldn't pick up and leave by
herself, if she hated the place as much as all that. Unless she was
crippled or in some manner incapacitated from traveling without
help. The storekeeper said no, there was nothing the matter with
her except that she was too allfired changeable, picking a place to
live in and then deciding she didn't like it.

"She couldn't leave alone, because we've lived together so long
we're both used to it," he said. "That's the reason she keeps after
me to move, and that's the reason I don't want her to. If I had to
stay here without her I'd git homesick as hell. It ain't that I admire
her character or like to have my shoes throwed into a mudhole.
But it's easier to git new shoes than to git used to livin' with somebody else, at my age. You ain't old enough to know about a thing
like that. If your uncle shows up here I'll steer him onto some road
into the brush so you'll have a good long lead on him."

He went back to making pelt-stretchers, and refused to take any
money for his sardines and barley and crackers. It was hard to
think how long he would go on sitting outside listening to the ocean
he had never seen, with his wife locked upstairs with the blinds
down, hating the country about which neither of them had ever
really learned anything, and how all the good their fidelity to one
another had done was to keep both of them from doing what they
wanted to. It seemed an unjust piece of punishment against two
people who had never done anything except love and stay faithful
and need each other. If that was all a couple got for practicing what
was commonly looked upon as a virtue, a man was a lot better off
going it alone.

The road beyond the store led through a big swale, with the
sound of the ocean getting louder beyond it. The country was even
waterier than at the summit of the mountains. Rivers of black

water foamed on either side of the road, and in places ran into it. The cedar timber was scant because the ground was too sour and weak for it to grow in, and only a few dwarf trees grew between great black-mud marshes full of cat-tails and dwarf elder-bushes heavy with bunches of scarlet berries. The wind had a rank sea smell to it, flocks of black wild ducks cruised low over the mud, and pale-blue herons stood one-legged, peering into the swamp water for eatables and, as far as could be noticed, not finding any. A few sluggish garter snakes fell off logs into the wire-grass as Clay passed, and once a herd of long-snouted wild hogs erupted out of a mudhole and ripped off into the swale, churning roily water behind them like a grounded tugboat. Some settler's old barnyard flock gone wild, probably. They looked fat and blocky on account of the myrtle-nuts and wapato-root of the damp mud-flats, and Clay marked their trail through the wire-grass with interest because they might mean meat to live through the winter on.

He struck an even better meat prospect at the turn of the road. There was a rise over a little knoll covered with fallen spruce logs and dwarf myrtle-bush and madroña. Beyond it, a cow elk stood alongside a log with her back turned to him. She was as big as a young steer and a good deal more awkward-looking. Elk of the Pacific Slope have their sterns and hams patched with a cheap dust-yellow color, which looks, from behind, like a new pair of garage-hand's overalls that got hung there by mistake. When the elk runs, the overalls jerk back and forth so stiff and idiotic-looking that it is almost impossible to look at them without laughing. It may have been for comedy-interest that they were put there, for there is nothing idiotic about an elk's ability to cover ground. The cow took one squint at Clay over her shoulder, and, without any backing for a start or preparation of any kind, jumped over the log sideways, came down facing him, and high-tailed it off into the brush with her overall-colored hindquarters working like windmill paddles in a gale. That looked encouraging. A man would have to be badly crippled to starve in a country where there were elk and ducks and wild hogs, no matter how bad the climate and inhabitants were.

The river where Clay struck it was not a mountain stream any more, but a big tide-reach nearly half a mile wide. The Indian

village was across it—a couple of dozen plank houses, quite large
and solid-looking, set on top of a swell of ground, and several
dozen buck Indians, mostly pot-bellied and indolent-looking, snooz-
ing in the sunlight in front of them. Clay signaled, and they
semaphored and yelled fragments of Chinook jargon back to explain that ferry service was suspended until the tide went out, and
that he would have to wait. None of them looked as if the notion
of work had entered their minds since the creation of the world.
But they were working right at that moment. Each of them was
watching a separate little mud-spit as the tide drew out. Every few
minutes a great crowd of sea gulls would cluster down on one,
squawking and quarreling over a big salmon that had run himself
aground and got left. Then the watcher would loaf down, knock
the sea gulls out of his way with a club, and lug the salmon back
to the village. The salmon, at a guess, would have scaled between
thirty and fifty pounds apiece, and they came in at the rate of about
one every ten minutes. None of the Indians acted excited over
them. It was no wonder that game was so plentiful, when a whole
village could collect its food by picking it up off the ground at the
rate of a quarter-ton an hour.

Clay watched while they lugged in close to two dozen large
salmon without relaxing from their attitude of bored apathy, and
then signaled that he would be back. He felt as well pleased that
they didn't want to ferry him immediately. His mare was going to
have to swim behind the canoe, and she was too tired to tackle it
without a rest and something to eat. He led her back through the
brush on an old pack-road, looking for grass that she could get to
without miring to her belly, and found a deserted clearing where
enough sun had got through to raise and ripen a half-acre patch
of timothy. It was fenced, and there was a board lean-to in one
fence-corner with dry ground underneath. He turned the mare
loose, hauled his saddle under shelter, and lay down to catch up
with his sleep.

He had wanted to sleep badly on the road and hadn't dared to.
Now he couldn't. His mind kept running over the details of his
escape; its narrowness, the shock it had given him, the two
women he had left, what they must be thinking of him. Not that
he cared enough about that to lose sleep over it, but he was so close

to the sea now that its booming jarred the ground under his head, and he wasn't used to it. It sounded like a herd of horses coming on a dead gallop, and as often as he started to doze it roused him with a scared feeling that he was about to be run over by them. It was much more restful not to go to sleep at all, so he lay awake and considered his situation. It was not an especially profitable line of study, for it worked out to the rather stale conclusion that society in general didn't have much sense. But he did work through to it by a different series of steps. Here, he thought, was the very last land on the continent, a place so rank and wild that even the United States hadn't been able to spare enough people to cultivate it and live in it. Beyond was the Pacific Ocean, seven thousand miles of it, and then China, where people were so abundant that they worked for ten cents a month and killed their children to get rid of them. That was how much people were worth in some countries. Probably it was wrong to hold them so low; but here, for some fool reason, they were so extravagantly high that he was being dogged out of every place he lit for unintentionally helping the killer of two to break jail. And it wasn't as if either of the dead men had been of any use to anybody. Wade Shiveley's brother had been merely a community nuisance, and old Howell nothing but a crooked backwoods tinhorn. It wasn't as if Wade Shiveley constituted any great menace to the public peace and dignity, either, if Drusilla had been able to chase him off the premises with a teakettle of boiling water. But, because nobody had thought the matter out sensibly, Clay had to go sneaking his way around a strange wilderness, harassed, hunted, friendless, alone. It was an outrageous piece of blamed foolishness, and he totally forgot, thinking about it, that he had spent the preceding several hours telling himself how particularly lucky he was to be alone. Having figured it out that he had a right to feel injured, he fell into a deep sleep that ended in an alarmed start of wakefulness because he heard a wagon rattling somewhere along the road. He told himself that there was nothing to be scared of yet, and turned over to listen which direction it was traveling in. A girl was leading a saddled horse through a dropped place in the fence, and she was Luce.

She put the fence rails up again and came leading her horse through the tall yellow timothy toward him. He wanted to get up, but the shock, partly fright, of seeing her took his strength so he couldn't. He sat helpless, and she sat down beside him and turned her pony loose to graze. She didn't look in the least out of temper. Her face was always alert and swift—strong, but changing so readily with her changes of thought that a man who was used to her could tell what was in her mind even when she wanted to conceal it. "I saw your mare down the road through the trees," she said. "Father's bringing the wagon up. We heard of you from a couple of places on the road, and the barefooted man at the store said you were going to take this old wood-trail into the swamps. I'm glad we caught you before you did. We traveled nearly all night after you."

She seemed to have forgotten that she had ever asked him to leave and that she had been angry with him for doing it. Maybe it was that she had had time to reconsider, or maybe it was because she felt pleased at his deserting the guitar-playing woman so offhandedly, or maybe it was because she had seen the sheriff's men hunting for him and felt better to know that he had something behind him to be afraid of, too. But she was glad she had found him, and her face showed it. Clay asked how she had managed to get the horse-trader to break camp and come after him on what must have been extremely short notice. "I thought he intended to stay with the hop-yard till the whole season was over?"

"Everybody left, nearly," she said. "The sheriff came, and they don't like to have people getting arrested around a hop-camp. So they loaded up, with the owner jumping up and down and begging them not to quit, and then we discovered you were gone, so we decided to leave, too." She studied him and shook her head as if there was some rather painful joke about it that he needed sympathy for. "You poor kid! I told you not to have anything to do with that woman."

"What's that woman got to do with it?" he asked, touchily. "She didn't know anything about what was up. I walked into them sheriff's men down by the weighin'-stand in the dark, and I got out ahead of 'em. That was all there was to it. What do you lay it onto her for?"

She sat back, studying him slowly. "You got out ahead of them?" she repeated. "And you traveled all this distance without knowing who they'd come for? Didn't you know they came to arrest that woman?"

"To arrest who?" Clay sat up. "Is that the truth? Do you mean they come for that woman with the guitar that ——"

Luce said it was so. "They had a warrant for her, and a printed blank with her description, and they took her. When the other pickers asked her where she was going, she said to jail, and so they all started packing up and moving out. Nothing stampedes those people like having somebody arrested in camp. They're not afraid, exactly, but it makes it look as if the place wasn't respectable. The women don't like it."

"I've heard something about that," Clay said. He didn't think to inquire if it was the reason the horse-trader had moved. He didn't think of anything except that deserting the woman on account of his own trouble had seemed rather gallant, and that deserting her in the midst of hers made him look like a good deal of a skunk. "Where did they take her?" he asked. "Did she say anything else before she left? Did she leave any word, or anything?"

No word had been left. "All she said to the men was that she wanted to get away from there quick," Luce said. "She wanted to be gone before you got there, I guess. They took her down to the county seat, but they're to bring her on down to the Coast here somewhere. She stabbed a fish-splitting knife into the man she was living with, and he may die."

"I know," Clay said. The horse-trader's wagon was climbing the hill. He focused his eyes on it and watched it slip away from them. "I didn't care anything about her," he said, haggling over his own exact shades of feeling as Luce had done over hers. "Not anything at all, except that she was alone and needed somebody, and where else was there for me to go? And now I wish I had. She must have been expectin' this all the time we worked together. She never let on a word, not even that she was uneasy about it. Only that she didn't have much time left, and she wanted to git all she could out of it. If I'd cared anything about her I'd have stayed, and I wish I had. Was that all you found out about her?"

It wasn't all. The hop-yard weighers had got most of the details of the stabbing and had told them around, trying to persuade the pickers that the arrest couldn't possibly affect their social standing.

The woman had come into Coos Bay on a dredger from California, living, it was said, with the mate. When the dredge tied up for the autumnal storms, the men, having nothing else to do, got to fighting over her and three or four of them got hurt. So the captain ordered her ashore, and she came up the Coast and lived in a deserted cabin for a month or two, and then she took in a helpless sort of man who had strayed down to the Coast dodging a warrant somewhere and was almost starved because he didn't know how to take care of himself in the woods. After they had lived together for several months he got over his helplessness and started in to run things to suit himself. Deer were plentiful and not hard to kill, but some old bush-rat in the neighborhood showed him how to make it still easier by imitating the blat of a young fawn in trouble. A man didn't have to do it more than three times before some anxious old doe would come running to see what it was and fetch up smack against the end of his gun. She didn't want him to get meat by any such trick and he stuck to it that he would, and, since they were already on one another's nerves, they had a fist-and-heel fight about it. She ended it by grabbing a knife off the table and hacking him with it, and she almost cut him in two. And it would have been no loss, but the Indians in that section had been complaining that they couldn't carve even their own relations without being hung for it, while the white people whittled on each other to suit themselves and never got punished at all. So, to shut them up, the sheriff went out after the woman and tagged her down. It was hard, of course, that they should have picked her to make an example of, but it was not Clay's fault, and he had no call to feel contrite about it.

"You didn't owe her anything, Clay. Do you think she was honest, not telling you about this?"

He said it didn't matter whether she was honest or not. If she had lied herself black in the face he would still feel sneaking about having run out without telling her. "She told me she might have to leave in a hurry," he said. "What more did she need to tell me? There's plenty about me that I didn't promenade out in front of her, too, and I don't see anything dishonest about that."

Naturally she asked what was against him. "Is it something you haven't told me about? Will you tell me now?"

The horse-trader had stopped the wagon on the slope to blow the horses. He waved his arm and Clay waved back, thinking, not whether he ought to tell her the truth about himself, but what make of yarn he could pitch her that would sound credible without scaring her. Telling her the truth he never for one moment considered, for fear of bringing back the coldness that had come so near separating them in the hop-yards. He thought of telling her the bound-boy-and-cruel-uncle story, but decided against it as being overcolored and biased. "It ain't anything much," he said, carefully, stalling in the hope that an idea would strike him. "It's a lawsuit over a piece of ground—a homestead contest, that's what it is. And they wanted me to testify about it, so they got out some papers for me. So I didn't want to testify, because some people of mine was mixed into it, and I'd have to testify against 'em. That's all I can tell you. I'll tell you the rest of it, though, if you'll tell me what you was afraid of down at the hop-yards."

That was well thought of. She looked worried. "I can't," she said. "If it was only about myself, I'd—No, I can't. I can't tell you anything, and I won't ask you any more about yours. Promise that if anybody does come after you, you won't leave without telling me. Or no, don't promise. It doesn't make any difference. If it's only a homestead, they wouldn't come this far after you, would they?"

He promised, anyway, because he was still ashamed of his cowardice in sneaking away from the hop-yards, and explained apologetically that it was a pretty valuable homestead. He had known, all the time that he was riding across the mountains and feeling content to be alone again, that this was going to happen to him. The knowledge that his loneliness wasn't going to last was what had made him enjoy it so much. But he had never imagined that he would have this kind of place to remember its having come to an end in; the black wall of spruce behind the rain-whitened fence rails, the long heads of white timothy jarring and shedding seed with the boom of the sea, the wind sticky with salt; or that he would feel, sitting with her in the one clearing that had held against the choking scramble of vegetation, as if he had landed in the middle of a city that boiled and roared with a different kind of life than his, that fought and destroyed itself in a million different

forms and paid no more attention to him than people in the heart
of traffic do to a shade-tree on an accidentally vacant lot. "I'll
always tell you," he said, too shaken to think of a better way to
put it. "I'll never duck out again the way I did from the hop-yards.
It was because I'd had a scare from them men, and I thought ——"

She put her spread fingers over his mouth so his words turned
into a kind of confused whaw-whaw-whawing. "You're a kid," she
said. "Nobody but a kid would run away from anything as silly as
a homestead contest. Sensible people would say we ought to wait a
few years to see if we change our minds about each other. But we
won't, because we might, and then we'd have lost ——"

She didn't exactly know what they would have lost. They sat
without saying anything, and, this time, without feeling ashamed of
it, while the wagon and horse-herd climbed the hill to them. The
horse-trader backed his stallion and chased loose horses around the
brush in embarrassment, seeing from their faces that they had
reached their understanding and were half proud and half scared
of it. His wife was more sensible about it, though not a great
sight more encouraging.

"Well, you patched up your quarrel, so that's one brand of
foolishness you're over," she remarked. "And now you're in for
another one. I don't suppose it would be any use telling you to wait
till you're older, and I always have had my doubts whether it
helped any. My father made me hold back till I was old enough to
know my own mind, and look what kind of a draw I made! At
least you've got a man that'll work."

Clay got up and unhitched her horses so they could pasture.
Since it saved her getting down and doing it herself, it made her
feel better. She observed that the old-fashioned idea of early
marriages was a sound one because it steadied young people down.
She wouldn't be surprised, she added, if early parental repression
wasn't to blame for her own spells of feeling moody and having
everything look black, and for her inability to cut loose and enjoy
herself like other people. Of course she struggled to conceal her
affliction, but it gave her a lot of trouble all the same. The horse-
trader said, low and hurried, that she struggled pretty successfully
when there were strange men around. Then he took Clay aside and
advised him, since he was lined up to become a member of the

family, that he ought to do something about the brand on the buckskin mare. "I got no doubt she's yours and that you come by her honest," he explained, diplomatically. "But we got word along the road you picked another fight about her and like to killed a prominent landowner. Drug him along the road for three mile on his face, or some such matter. That's bad business. You'd better have that brand run over into something else, and then you won't be so touchy about it."

It sounded like a good notion. Clay said that as soon as he got where there was a running-iron and a branding-chute to run the mare into, he would.

"No iron needed," the trader said. "You couldn't burn on a brand to match the old one, anyhow. You need acid to do that with, and I got some here with me. Fix up a brand that'll work on over them marks, and I'll lay it on for you as natural as if it had growed there. The materials and so on will come to two dollars, but it'll save you ten times that much trouble, and if this is goin' to be permanent ——"

Clay said that it was going to be permanent. Watching the horse-trader at work with his medicine-chest, he added that a man who traveled around the country with a full layout of materials for blotting brands so they wouldn't look blotted was in danger of being seriously misunderstood. The horse-trader said he didn't much mind being misunderstood, because he was used to it, and though the acid worked all right as a brand-rectifier, that wasn't what he carried it for. "It's to put harness-galls on that chestnut stallion with," he explained. "We git that horse out into the horse-Indian country, and git the Indians to thinkin' he's come off of a plow lately, and they'll bet every horse they own on some grass-tailed skate of theirs to outrun him. We been gittin' most of our tradin'-stock that way the last few years. One thing I wisht I could figure out is how he can run off from them Indian horses so easy and then let these valley plugs kick dust all over him."

The reason, Clay remarked, was that the valley plugs were trained racing-stock, owned and managed by men who never entered them in a race that wasn't a sure thing. The Indians, on the contrary, were gamblers, and their horses were Indian horses, trained on alkali water and grass. "Who rides your stallion when you race him?"

"I rode him myself the last time he raced," the horse-trader said, gloomily. "When I can git even weights I generly ride him. But some of these Indian races where they put up a kid for their jockey, I been lettin' the girl ride him. She gits half what she wins, and she enjoys it. I don't know how I'd git along in them Indian races if she was to quit me."

His wife had strolled over to watch the brand alterations. She glanced back at Luce, who was putting the bridle on her pony, and said, very low and positive, what Clay had wished somebody would say.

"You'll get along by running your business yourself, like everybody else does," she told the horse-trader. "You're not to go crying around that girl about how bad you need her and how it's her duty to go dragging around the country helping you make money when you're too big a fool to keep what you've already made. If she wants to come with you, all right. If she don't, you let her alone!"

"It's a funny note if a man can't say what he pleases to his own daughter," the horse-trader observed, with bitterness.

"All right, it's a funny note," his wife said. "You heard me, did you? I can do some talking myself, if I take a notion to. You let that girl alone, or I will."

"I'm lettin' her alone, ain't I?" demanded the horse-trader. "I ain't goin' to bother her, so quit jumpin' on me when I'm workin'."

Chapter XIII

THEY emptied the horse-trader's wagon and cached it in a deep patch of alder-brush where the wheels could soak in mud, and they informed the Indians that if any of the iron was missing from it when they came back for it they would cut down all the trees that had dead people stuck up in them and infect the water of the river with a medicine so much more powerful than Dr. Turnbull's Prescription for Expectant Mothers that no fish would ever dare enter it again. The Indians promised to touch nothing—it turned out that they got all the iron they needed from old driftwood on the beach—and ferried their baggage across, swimming the horses behind in bunches of five with their heads roped to the stern. Having crossed the whole herd, they ganged around in silence to watch the packing. They were dark for Indians, their complexions running to brown rather than red. All were fat, and their faces had the same combination of stupidity and covetousness that one sees among the peasants of Normandy. Only the older squaws were tattooed, and they only on the lower lip with a streak of bright blue that looked as if they had all just got in from an afternoon tea where the refreshments consisted of fountain-pen ink. They spoke Chinook jargon, didn't know what tribe they belonged to, and called themselves Tunné, which meant that they were of the same strain as the Navajo-Apache race a thousand miles to the southeast—a bunch of footsores, probably, that had straggled from some great prehistoric migration.

For money among themselves they used strings of mussel shells ground down into cylindrical beads, but they had no prejudice against outside mediums of exchange, and they were willing to sell fifty-pound salmon at a quarter apiece and directions about the trail down to the surf thrown in. Their houses were cedar, which they had split up into planks, and the interiors were windowless and extremely smelly, partly from lack of ventilation and partly because of the material they used for lighting. It was the bodies of little black smelt which, dried and hung up by the tail, burned with a very clear white light and an extremely loud odor. They worked every bit as well as any store-bought candle, particularly if the user was fond of marine life or had a bad cold in his head. There were few guns in the village, and no great sight of use for any because the people lived mostly on fish and killed their trapped game with bow and arrow at a range of from two to five feet. They trapped wild ducks by setting decoys on a brush-covered hole in the marshes, hiding under it till a flock lit, and grabbing their legs and pulling them under water to drown.

They seemed never to have been bothered by white invasions or civilized refinements, and except for clothes, flour, cartridges, and patent medicines, they depended on their own ingenuity and elbow grease for everything they used. Not many people in the world managed to live so easily and so entirely to suit themselves. But there was a stinger in that. Nobody who ever saw them would have wanted to trade places with them. There was a kind of hopelessness about that lost tag-end of a great people, stuck off in such a place without anything to use their brains on if any of them ever developed any, with nothing that they could ever amount to except to become chief of a shack-town containing maybe six dozen human beings, with strange people and strange languages all around them so that there could be no chance of ever getting away.

Not that there was anything mournful about it. They didn't want to get away, and they had stayed where they were for pretty close to a thousand years without the slightest suspicion that any place in the world could be finer or more interesting than their own twenty acres of it. They knew the point on the Coast where their trail ended, but they knew nothing about the country five miles away from it except that people lived there who didn't behave very well and that a woman had recently cut up her man and was going to be put in jail for it.

As the storekeeper had alleged, it was close to a two-hour ride before they turned out onto the hard sand and looked up at the sea towering into the sky as if it was stacked higher than their heads. Against it stood the continent, represented by a wall of low brushed-over hills, cut into shallow canyons where creeks ran. In a few places there were trees standing, but mostly the force of the wind uprooted them before they got any size. The creek bottoms were thickets of black alder, still green at this season because, though all the leaves were dead and drying up, there was not enough strength in the sun and not enough difference between summer and autumn to make them shed or color. The fireweed in those alder bottoms was gigantic; tall droopy-armed stalks topped with bluish tufts of cotton as ghostly as smoke, so that a man walking into it disappeared as if he had witched himself into mist. Most of the fireweed meadows had cabins, and the horse-trader and his wife stopped at one of them, less because it was a good place to winter than because the horse feed was good. The cabin had part of the roof gone, but they patched that with their tent until they could get time to split shakes for it. Clay and Luce went on and left them, intending to explore farther back in the canyons for something better. They had to be choosier because they had no tent to patch breaks with, and they didn't mind looking.

The country was pleasanter to ride in than it had looked. There was no marshy ground except close to the streams, and though all the slopes were one solid thatch of stiff salal and deer-brush and balm-bush and mountain-laurel, the wild game and half-wild cattle had made trails through it everywhere. With a horse that had been trained to jump logs, a man could ride anywhere at a gallop without danger of being thrown except on a few of the steepest slides. Even being thrown was not so bad as in open country. There was no place to light except on the brush, and once you had learned not to come down face first, the shock was not much different from jumping on a haystack or a stiff set of bedsprings.

It was a bee country all through those mountains. Outside of the fireweed there were few flowers, but none were needed. All the leaves of the alders were sticky with a clear honey, very white and heavy, and in places where the bees hadn't ranged it was crystallized on the dead foliage in flakes as big as a twobit-piece. The balm-leaves carried it, too, and the bees were still out working in them. One cabin that Luce and Clay looked into had been preëmpted by an old swarm to store honey in. All the space between the inner and outer walls and between roof and ceiling was one solid comb, so old in places that it was turned black, and the workers were carry-

ing their new stock down through a knothole in the floor. None of
their honey had ever been disturbed, which proved that there were
no bears in the country. Not enough small game for them to thrive
on, probably, and no berries except the worthless salal. The only
useful fruit in sight was wild crabapples. Thickets of them grew
up every canyon, loaded with sour little seedlings not much bigger
than garden peas. They cooked well if one had the patience to
gather them, and when Luce found a cabin close to a grove of them
she refused to look farther, though there was the carcass of a dead
deer twenty feet from the front door, half-eaten by timber-wolves.

"We can burn it," she said. "The roof sheds water, and there's
benches and a table and a fireplace and no rats. When you've been
wintering on what you can find as long as I have you'll learn not
to expect much more than that. Get some wood, and we'll boil some
water to scrub things up with."

Her housekeeping fever was surprising. Clay had supposed
women interested themselves in such matters mostly because they
were too timid or too puny to do anything else. But she could
herd, harness, and skin a team and ride as well as he could, and
here she was talking about scrubbing and cooking and fruit-canning
as whole-heartedly as if she had never ventured foot outside the
scullery. She was downright exultant about discovering a case of
empty fruit-jars on an overhead shelf.

"This beats any place we'd ever have found with father along,"
she said, scouring the table with hot water and an old piece of
brick. "People must have lived here not very long ago. I hope they
won't come trailing back on us after we've got everything moved in."

"They won't come back," Clay said. His voice was that of a man
who has been horse-kicked and is ashamed to show how bad it
hurts. He had raked among the old trash in the woodbox, and he
showed her what he had found. It was the broken D-string of a
guitar. He said nothing, but she was quick enough to understand
what his mind was on.

"It needn't have been hers," she pointed out. "Other people have
guitars around here, I suppose."

Clay dug again in the woodbox. "They might," he agreed. He
couldn't have told why he went to any trouble to prove the guitar

string's ownership, but he wanted to. He held out a broken satin slipper from the trash. Though old, the arch was high and the foot long, slim, and not spread with wear. "Other people don't wear that size shoe. She did, because I half-soled one for her and I remember it. This was hers. She lived here."

He looked around the cabin again, at the hand-split table and benches, the shelf of tin dishes gone half-rusty, the round-stone fireplace with loose rocks in the ashes to rest cooking-pots on. As a place to live during the winter with Luce, it had seemed a lucky find. When he thought of the woman who had lived in it before him, its poverty and lonely nakedness hit him and filled him with pity and shame. She would not have wanted him to know that she had stood all this, that she had sat on a home-made board bench and eaten from a pan-lid and slept on a bed-tick stuffed with old grass. It was like prying on her to be here, like sneaking around behind her to find out things about her that she would not have wanted known. Luce couldn't tell all that was working on his mind, but she saw that something was. She gave up her scouring and kicked the logs apart in the fireplace so they would stop burning.

"We don't need to stay here," she reminded him. "But I can't see why you feel so glum about this. Why shouldn't you have left her? She had no business making a set at you when she must have known how close after her the sheriff was. And if she'd thought of anybody else but herself she'd have left you when she heard their wagon coming. That's what I'd have done."

She wasn't merely talking to make him feel better. She meant it.

"Is that what you'd do?" he asked, to make sure. "You'd leave me any time you thought anybody was after you?"

"That's good and well what I'd do," she repeated. "Wherever I am, as long as I'm able to crawl, I'll leave if there's anything threatening me that might make you trouble. There won't be, up here in the woods, but if you don't want to keep this house we'll look for another one."

"No use of that," he said. If he hadn't been cowardly to run away, living in the woman's cabin couldn't hurt him. If he had, it wouldn't improve his courage to run away again. "There's no danger that she'll be back, I guess, and if she did I'd sooner be where she

could find me. I'll bring some wood for the fire, and then I'll go
down for the pack-horses."

The woman didn't ever come back while they lived there, which
was from late September until the alder-buds began to crack open
about the middle of May. There were a few weeks in October
when the days were warm and still, when leaves browned and
grass ripened in the sun and the reflection of light from the sea
lasted until long after nightfall, as if the sun from some distant
stand was shining back at them through the transparent curve of
water. Afterwards the sky blackened and snow fell, and from that
time until spring the rain never totally stopped and the light never
entirely started. Except on the line of surf, the sea itself was like
ink, and the tremendous winds that blew out of it carried fierce
twisters of rain that turned everything pitchy as they passed.

That was the time that wore people's nerves the hardest. Old
squatters from the creek canyons bucked mud and wet brush and
risked rheumatism for the sake of somebody to talk to, when all
the good they got out of their visits was to pick quarrels and flounce
back home to their heart-eating loneliness again. Even the Indians
in the river village turned short-tempered, though they had had
around forty generations of continuous residence to get accustomed
to the climate in. The horse-trader and his wife lost flesh and color,
squabbled incessantly, and split the blankets and whacked up the
cooking-utensils to separate permanently at least once a week. No
play-parties or dances went on, because the people who had lived
that season out before knew there was no use trying to improve
or lighten it. To Clay, it was the best time of all. He liked it so
deeply that he deliberately avoided the company-hungry settlers
for fear they would notice it on him and feel insulted about it. The
raining-in of all the roads meant only that nobody would come
across the mountains after him. Darkness and the storms jarring
the ground and flattening trees made life pleasanter by showing
how powerless all that strength was to hurt or disturb him. It
was the same with Luce, and during all those days when they had
to burn candles at noon to read by, he remembered how she had
looked riding back from the beach with him ahead of a storm. They

were hurrying to get home before it struck, and mounting the hill they looked back and saw the black center of it coming in from the sea and churning the flat water into a wall of foam ten feet high as horses churn a ford crossing it at a trot. Clay spurred to keep it from overtaking him, but Luce reined in and sat still. "Let's try letting it catch us," she dared him. "We know it can't hurt us, don't we? Let's see what it does?"

That was the storm in which twenty-odd head of cattle, pasturing the steep slopes over the surf, got blown off their feet and fell into the sea where the waves beat them to pulp. Cattle were lost that way every winter, but in waiting the storm out on the trail there was only the fun of danger without any of the agonies. The wind hit so hard the horses staggered with it, and water plastered them in a solid sheet. Through it Clay saw in a kind of blur that Luce was trying to pull her horse round to head into it and laughing because he wouldn't budge, and that when she opened her mouth to talk the water beat on it and stopped it so she couldn't. The rain slackened and passed on, and they galloped up the trail after it, trying to overtake it and face it down again, but it outran them.

One thing explained why people were willing to live on that coast in spite of the dismal climate. Food could be got literally for the picking up. A man with a sharp stick could dig more clams in half a day than a horse could carry. Every storm stranded big salmon in the freshwater inlets, sea-perch and rock-bass could be snagged from the rocks when the weather was calm, and shoals of little black candle-smelt ran some days into the creek-mouths so thick that they could be thrown ashore with a shovel. The little creeks were good fishing if one took it as a sport, and, when treated with a few bushels of hemlock bark, they would float up stupefied speckled trout by the cartload. Vegetable products were scarcer, but besides wild crabapple the women of the country picked a copperytinged wild sorrel which, when cooked, had a good deal the flavor of rhubarb. Mallard ducks settled wherever there was swampy ground, and Clay managed to bushwhack a few with his pistol. He also worked considerable on the deer, which were plentiful, though small—the Coast Range blacktails never get over a hundred and fifty-odd pounds, and a buck is well-grown that will dress

out a hundred and twenty—but his pistol lacked range, and though
he tried sneak-hunting and bushwhacking and night-lighting, he
could never get close enough to make sure of one with it. The first
shade of uneasiness happened between him and Luce on that account. He came in from an all-day hunt during which he had
sneaked up on four different deer without getting within pistol-
range of any, and said he wasn't going to fool away any more
time on the brutes until he could go after them with a rifle. Then
he tried to switch the conversation to something else, realizing what
subject he had reopened, and she surprised him by observing calmly
that they would manage that for him, all right. He stared, wondering if the missing wagon rifle was at last to be restored to the
light, but she wasn't talking about any such thing. What she had in
mind was to buy him a new one. "We ought to have one, anyhow,"
she said, "what with these timber-wolves around and our horses
running loose all the time. We'll send word down and have the
mail-carrier buy one down at the Bay for you when he can get
through. What kind do you want?"

It was plain that she didn't intend to break anything new about
the wagon rifle, which proved either that she had told the truth to
start with or that she intended to go on lying about it. It stirred up
a faint distrust, but he said, trying to beat it down, that the kind
of rifle he wanted was one that he wasn't likely to get. It was one
like Wade Shiveley's, with a peep-sight for running shots and a
box-magazine to keep the weight back in the stock, and it would
cost over twice as much money as he had. Sixty or seventy dollars, maybe, he added, expecting the amount to horrify her. But
she said they could handle that, and was so confident and business-
like about it that his distrust got out of control. He inquired what
she intended to handle it with. "I thought your father lost all your
money on a horse-race?"

Probably he showed too plainly that he was trying to catch her.
"We've made money since that horse-race," she said. "Things like
selling that black gelding to the sawmill man, and things."

"Yes, and things," he took her up impatiently. "Your father
got that money in a crooked horse-deal with a blamed simpleton, and
I don't want anything to do with it. Or with him, either, as far as

that's concerned. If that's the kind of money you intend to buy a
rifle with, we'll do without one."

"I didn't say I intended to use that money," she said. "We got
wages for our hop-picking, didn't we? You left all your weight-
tickets in the wagon with your pistol, and we cashed them with
ours. Have you got any objection to using that?"

He said he guessed not, trying to remember whether he really
had left his weight-tickets in the wagon or not. He had a clear
recollection that he had taken them all with him when he moved.
The trouble was that he remembered with equal positiveness that he
had taken his pistol along, too, and it had turned out that he hadn't
moved it from the jockey-box on the wagon. It was his memory
against her word, and his memory had let him down once, so he
didn't dare trust it. "Them weight-tickets of mine wasn't enough to
buy that kind of rifle with," he pointed out. "Nor half of one. I've
got a few dollars besides, but it wouldn't be near enough to make
up the difference."

"With what I made it'll be enough," she said. "Your tickets came
to around thirty-five dollars and mine to over forty. I'll take it
down to the mail-carrier tomorrow morning and we'll have your
rifle before the end of the week. . . . Why do you look like that?
Do you think I didn't get this money honestly? Do you think I
stole it? What do you think?"

He thought that his hop-picking earnings hadn't amounted to
one side of thirty-five dollars, and that it was funny she hadn't
mentioned them before. But he couldn't say anything, because she
would be certain to ask what they had amounted to, and he hadn't
the faintest recollection. He said to go ahead with the ordering if
there was money enough. Afterwards he wished he hadn't, because
the next shadow of distrust fell after the rifle came and as a direct
consequence of it. It was a beautiful shooting-iron, with sights that
fell into line like school-kids in a fire drill, and a hang that suited
his hand exactly. But the week it came was the stormiest of the
entire winter; gales and falling timber and whipping rain kept
all the deer bedded in the brush, and he was too hell-bent on shooting it to stay in until the weather let up. He went bulling out with
it every day and most of every night, tracked and shadowed and
bushwhacked and jack-lighted until he was too tired to see straight,

and merely succeeded in getting the deer stirred up so they were leery of him. It was over a week before he saw anything even to shoot at, and by then he was so foggy and fidgety that he couldn't have hit the side of a shovel with a hatful of gravel. What he saw was a middle-sized buck deer walking through a grove of firs as he was coming home—a close shot, though not an easy one, because it was late and the light was bad. He missed five shots at the deer running, resisted the impulse to throw the rifle after him, and went on to the cabin where Luce, having heard the shooting, was expecting him to fetch home game.

"Missed, and I'm done tryin'," he announced, and hung the gun on a peg without noticing whether the new stock could get scratched against the wall or not. "I can't find deer and I can't hit 'em when I do. You wasted your money buyin' that gun for me."

She said quickly that it hadn't been all her money, and then fed and put him to bed. That was the first clear night after the storm. There was almost a full moon through the window, though he slept too sound to notice it. She had made up her mind not to wake him till he was rested, but going to sleep with the moonlight on the floor took it out of her thoughts, and she woke to a tremendous crashing and breaking and splitting of brush in the creek-bottom below the house. It came closer and got louder. She could hear big animals panting, and men yelling faintly from the head of the canyon, and she yanked Clay's shoulder, looked out the window into the half-dark of morning, and shook him again exultantly. "Wake up quick! There's a big elk-drive coming down the creek right past us! Your gun, Clay! Hurry up!"

He turned over and stared at her, and she got the gun down and put it into his hands. He pushed it away, remembering the kind of work he had been doing with it. "I can't hit anything with it," he said. "Let me sleep. Go on away. There ain't light enough to see into that brush by anyway."

She picked the gun off the bed and went to the door with it. The light was bad, and the elk, being about the same color as the naked brush, looked not much plainer than one column of smoke seen through another. They had got packed into the canyon by men driving them from the creek headwaters, and they stuck to the brush with the idea that they were safer there than in the open.

Singly, of course, they would have been. Packed as they were, it had been possible for the driving-party to slaughter several tons of them by merely shooting at the loudest brush-cracking and picking up what dropped. Now, having outdistanced the drive, the elk were beginning to string out and spread. A tall old cow ventured out of the brush and trotted across the clearing. Luce rested the rifle against the door-jamb and shot at her. The cow set back on her hind-legs with surprise, and Luce shot again, swore under her breath, and shot a third time as the cow laid back her head to re-enter the brush. That bullet caught her square between the ears, and she went down with a sliding motion, spraddling her legs out on all four corners as if she was trying to be a starfish. Below her a young bull came into sight, jumping logs in the dead fire-weed. Luce threw two shots at him, worked the lever angrily because the gun had run empty, and saw that Clay had got up to watch. "Cartridges!" she ordered, pointing at the box over the fireplace. "Damn these sights, I don't see how you can hit anything with 'em! Where do you load?"

He showed her how to open the breech-block and crowd the loads down through it. "Don't you think you've killed about enough?" he suggested. "That cow you've got down will weigh around seven hundred pounds, and we'll be all winter eatin' her. What's the sense killin' more than we can use?"

A cartridge got crossed in the breech, and she ripped it loose and hurt her finger doing it. "We've got to have something for father, haven't we?"

"No, we ain't," Clay said. "Let that damned old hustler git his own meat. Give that gun here."

"Let go of it or I'll bite you!" she threatened, and yanked it loose and threw down on the young bull in the fireweed. She wasted two more shots on him and drove him up the sidehill into the open, and then hit him in the backbone between the shoulders. He fell, slid, and rolled down the steep slope into the creek-bottom. They could feel the ground jar when he landed. The rest of the herd dropped back into the brush again, and she emptied two magazines snapshooting without hitting anything. Her last shot was a long one. A tremendous old bull came into an opening where a fallen tree had beaten down the brush. He reared for a jump, and she got him square through the heart as he took off. She watched him come down head first, and then she handed the gun to Clay and went and sat on the bed. It was a brisk morning for a night-gown and bare feet, and now that the action was over she felt it. "Build up a fire," she said, chafing her ankles under the covers. "We'll have to bring those elk in before the men from the drive get down here, or they'll lay claim to them."

He got the fire going. "That was the best three minutes' work with a gun that I ever saw," he said. "I didn't have any notion you could shoot like that, or I'd have been about halfway afraid of you."

She sat up sharply. "Afraid of me?" she began, and then decided he hadn't meant anything. "Twenty shots to kill three elk, if you call that good work. I don't know anything about shooting."

That wasn't easy to agree to. One of those shots in a quarter-light through brush at a moving target might have been laid to luck. But to disclaim credit for three of them couldn't be anything but an overgrown case of false modesty. He told her that, whether she knew it or not, she had done an exhibition grade of shooting, and she said defiantly that she hadn't. "Because I couldn't. I don't know anything about guns, I tell you."

"Well, all right," he said. There seemed no reason why she should be so fierce about it. "Maybe you've got a natural gift for it. It don't make all that difference to you, does it?"

She cooled down. Part of it was probably the tail-end of the nervous tension from her rifle-work. "I haven't got any natural gift, though," she said. "And it doesn't make any difference except that I don't like for you to say what isn't so."

They dropped it and dressed, talking about the job of bringing the three elk in; but neither of them forgot it. A little more blunder-ingness on his part, a little more over-anxiety and fierceness on hers, and the thing could have gone to out-and-out hostility and hatred. Such things seemed to come up oftener the longer they lived in one place without any change of weather or landscape to keep them from brooding over small breaks and misunderstood inflections of voice. There had never been any such dangerous foolishness when they were on the road. They both knew that they would be better off traveling again, and that, oddly, led to another threat of a flare-up that started from almost nothing and ended only when they were getting ready to leave the Coast country for good. While they were working their horses down through the brush to bring out the elk, some men who had been on the elk-drive came down the canyon, going after horses to drag out theirs, and stopped to look over Luce's kill. It was a layout worth looking at. The bull she had tumbled down the side-hill was so big that it took both horses to roll him over so they could skin him. It was impossible to pack such a weight of meat out except in installments, so he had to be cut up where he was; and the men, always willing to neglect their own business to tend to somebody else's buckled down to help.

There were half a dozen of them, mostly small cattle-raisers from back in the mountains, and they explained that the elk-drive was an annual ceremony with them. The elk always yarded for the winter in some high meadow where a creek headed, because it was the one kind of country open enough so they could look out for wolves. On the first night that there was moon enough to shoot by, the ranchers always clubbed together and made a surround on them. The moon didn't have to be strong, because fine marksmanship wasn't usually necessary. Nobody except Luce had ever tried shooting individual elk on such occasions, and she wouldn't have had to except that she caught the herd when it was beginning to break and scatter. The settlers, by merely cutting loose at the bunch generally, had killed twenty-eight elk, the smallest weighing nearly five hundred pounds and the biggest not far from a thousand. That, divided among the six hunters who had come after horses and the three who had stayed with the game, added up to over half a ton of meat apiece. It was certainly not bad pay for a night's work, but they all agreed, working over Luce's three carcasses, that they were sick of the blamed country and tired of living in it. A man got enough to eat easily enough, but it was impossible for him to get anything else. Cattle-raising had promised well, but it had never amounted to anything. The herds never increased, because so many got blown off the cliffs every winter, and so many got lost in the brush and shot by hunters for deer, and so many more got killed by cougars and timber-wolves, that the normal supply of calves wasn't much more than enough to make up the year's shrinkage. The ones that were hardy enough to stand storms and fast enough to outrun varmints were so wild and fightable that their own owners couldn't get within rifle-range of them. There was no sense, in a country with so much free land as the United States, of hanging onto a section that had been created only to support hoboes and hide-outs and Indians. So, in the spring, they were all planning to round up what cattle they could overhaul, sell them for enough to buy wagons and harness, and load up for eastern Oregon, where there was open country and a dry climate. Luce put in, seeing that they were sociable and friendly, that she had come from eastern Oregon and that she and Clay intended to go there in the spring, too.

"If we can corner any money to stake a trip with," Clay reminded her. "We'll have to have a wagon and harness and a camp outfit, unless you want to go on taggin' around the country after your old man. I don't."

She said they wouldn't have to do that, as if it were old-maidish of him to bring up such a possibility. "A wagon and harness and camp outfit aren't much. We'll manage them easy enough."

Suspicion of her had been coming up in him so frequently that it didn't take much to raise it again. "How?" he demanded. "How are you goin' to raise any money around here? Either you don't know, or else you're afraid to tell me, and which is it?"

For a considerable time she looked at him without answering, almost as if she were taking a last look at him before telling him and his questions a general good-by. It frightened him. He realized that he had taken her up too quickly and that he might already have estranged her beyond any possibility of making up for. Not that his suspicions had any special harm in them. He was afraid that she might be thinking of buying their outfit out of money that her father had swindled on one of his crooked horse-deals. A little too much afraid, for it was unfair to tax her with it before she did it. He muttered something about being wound up too tight from lack of sleep. Lavran Baker, a big red-cheeked man with a bald head and a loud colorless voice, said that came from the Coast winters. "I used to rip my wife up like that, and she took her foot in her hand and quit me on account of it," he volunteered. How he knew it was on account of that rather than something else he didn't mention. "She walked across the mountains all by herself and hunted

her another man to live with. It's bad business to take your meanness out on women in this country. If they don't skip the ranch
on you, they're liable to haul off and poke a rat-tail file into you,
or some such knickknack. A woman off a dredger done that down on
the Coast last year. She's in jail now."

Clay said he would bear the warning in mind, and that according
to his information the woman off the dredger had used a fish-
splitter.

"That was another time," Lavran Baker said. "The rat-tail file
was first. She used it on a kind of half-hobo she picked up off the
beach because he looked uncared for. After she'd fed him up he
got domineerish and claimed she didn't have any right to leave
him. So they scuffled and she picked up an ax-file and wrote her
autograph on him with the sharp end of it. After that she picked
up another scarecrow and fixed him with a fish-knife tryin' to git
rid of him, and then she went across the mountains and they caught
her. You need to look out for women in this climate."

He stared, because Clay swallowed loudly and Luce laughed.
"Nothing's the matter," she explained, and dropped her hand on
Clay's shoulder. "Nothing except that he's been worrying all winter about something he needn't have. Here's one woman he won't
need to look out for, no matter what climate we're in. But we'll
be ready to leave for eastern Oregon when you do, and don't pay
any attention to what he says. He's always letting things worry
him more than there's any use in."

Chapter XIV

DURING the rest of the winter the cattle-raising settlers took to visiting Clay's cabin frequently. Sometimes they came with a hunk of venison or a churning of hard-won butter from a wild cow, sometimes to borrow something or ask advice about tanning elk-hide so it wouldn't smell, sometimes merely to sit around and talk. By disposition they were sociable and talkative, though suspicious of strangers whose business methods they disapproved of. The horse-trader and his wife they never got round to treating with more than a distant politeness. But Clay and Luce they accepted as voting stockholders in the community's intended migration, so they spent considerable time explaining about themselves by way of further-ing the acquaintance. It was much for them, in such a place, to strike neighbors with whom they felt intimate enough to talk freely without knowing quite well enough to quarrel.

Changing locations had been a regular thing with the settlers. None of them had been on the Coast any great stretch of time; seven or eight years was about their average term of residence, and they didn't seem to have stayed much longer than that anywhere. They all had come from different places, and only about a third of them were married. Most had been, but through desertion and incompatibility and flirtatious traveling-men and such causes, were so no longer. Some had worked with cattle before they came there, but most of them had worked at jobs that hadn't allowed them so much as a pet pig in the back yard. Lavran Baker, whose wife had hoofed it across the mountains to get away from his conversa-tion, had been an overhead-rigger in a Seattle ironworks, and ac-cording to the signs a good one. He had papers from the foundry superintendent certifying that at any time within three years from date he was welcome to come back to work as foreman, with full rank, pay, and allowances, and no questions asked.

He hadn't ever gone back. The work hadn't been bad, he said, but he had quit to stay because the foundry's system of avoiding industrial casualties didn't look good to him. Part of his work had been to report, regularly every week, all the men under him who showed the smallest symptoms of age or stiff-jointedness or faulty coördination, so that the company, humanely eager to prevent any of its men from falling off an overhead beam and hurting themselves, could discharge them to starve to death. Baker turned in his weekly boneyard-list for close to six years before the realization began to work into him that some sub-superintendent would undoubtedly slip him the same paternal kind of deal the minute he began to drag his feet and dodder. The prospect scared him, for he hadn't managed to save money. What his job amounted to was that he spent his pay to keep up his strength so he could earn more pay on which to keep his strength up to earn more pay to, etc., around and around. So he quit, took what money he had, and came down to the Coast, where a man didn't need wages to keep up his strength on or for. He couldn't justly complain that the country had fallen short of his expectations, but two things made him willing to leave. One was the loss of his wife, which worked on his mind so that he couldn't talk for three minutes at a stretch without referring to it. The other was that the damp and cold had started him on a case of rheumatism, which he was afraid might finally cripple him so he couldn't scratch out food and fuel for himself. If that happened, he wouldn't be any better off than if he had gone on working for the iron foundry. Nature was generous enough to a man in ordinary good health, but so was the economic system; and they were both totally cold and merciless to a man who had lost his ability to get around.

Most of Baker's stories about the iron foundry tended to get mixed up with reminiscences of his wife before she quit him, but he did tell one about a man who was detailed to watch a three-ton vat of molten iron alone, and when they went to call him at the end of his shift he was nowhere to be found. Failing to locate him around town, the company called in an assayer to analyze the vat of iron. The analysis showed a trace of gold that could have been his watch and his teeth-fillings, and a trace of brass that was probably his belt buckle and his pants buttons. So it was decided that he had been overcome by the fumes of the iron and had fallen into it and burned up; and the company, by way of showing its sense of bereavement, had the whole three-ton ingot carted out to the

cemetery and interred with appropriate ceremonies, several large
floral pieces from officials and fellow workmen, and a full set of
honorary pall-bearers assisted by two donkey-engines. Afterwards
the man's widow claimed five thousand dollars in damages because
there had been no guard-railing around the melting-vat, but the
company fought the case in court and strung it out so long she
settled for fifty.

Baker's state of feeling about his departed wife was hopelessly
old-fashioned, but he had reasoned it out so it sounded logical.
She was well within her rights, he conceded, in leaving him, because a person's happiness was more important than any obligation imposed by law. But her living with other men was making
him unhappy, so, on the same principle, he thought he would be
entirely justified in shooting her if he ever got a good chance. Not
as a matter of vengeance or personal spite. It was merely that he
knew her well enough to feel sure she was talking about him, and
he hated to have a lot of strange men get such a one-sided idea of
what he was like.

Women had also been a good deal of a bellyache to Given Bushnell, who owned over a third of all the cattle in the community and
was a master blacksmith and farrier and a very fair hand at manu-
facturing gouge-eye whisky for his personal use. Once he had run
a blacksmith-shop and refreshment-stand on a big logging operation
in the Pass Creek Mountains, with his forge in the front room of
his house and a whisky-barrel and tin cup on a string in the back.
Both rooms took in money so fast he had to stay drunk almost all
the time to celebrate his prosperity, and finally, not to be selfish
about it, he got married to a hard-working young widow who
washed dishes for the logging-camp cooks. She admitted owning
a couple of children who were farmed out on some relative because the logging-camp men had been unable to stand them, but
she agreed to leave them there so she could devote all her time to
what she had come to realize was the great love of her life. They
lived as happy as pay day at an army post for some months, and
then he began to notice that his business wasn't making anywhere
near as much since he had been keeping sober as it did when he
stayed drunk; and, digging a pit in the yard to shrink wagon-tires
in, he struck a whisky-keg buried close to the fence with around

six hundred dollars in cash in it. The keg was new and his own. So was the money, for there were a couple of rough gold slugs in the collection that he had got from the Bohemia Mining Company and marked with his initials. So he took it and twitted his wife about it, and she raised hob and ordered him to give it back to her because it was a fund she was saving for her children's future. She broke down under pressure of evidence and admitted that she had accumulated it by knocking down on the till, but she declined to see that there was any moral turpitude about it. She pointed out that it was her sacred duty as a mother to see that her children got a decent start in life, and that if she hadn't taken the money he would have wasted it on dissipation and foolishness. He agreed that it was right for her, as a woman with normal instincts, to want her children to have the best, but he didn't feel like blacksmithing the best years of his life away to get it for them. So he deeded the shop over to her, advised her to learn horse-shoeing and be careful about getting sparks in her eye from welding-jobs, and pulled out. It wasn't a particularly extravagant thing to do, because he was tired of the blamed place, anyway; and now, after six years of rousting savage cattle around the Coast underbrush, he was tired of that, too. He was undersized for a professional blacksmith, but he must have been a good one. When he saw Clay's new rifle on his first visit, he went down on the floor with it, took it to pieces, took measurements of the finger pressure that Clay was used to shooting with, and honed down the trigger-sear with an oilstone to such a perfect fit that Clay could shoot it merely by thinking the hummer off cock, without any voluntary muscular action at all.

Another woman-sent member of the settlement was Mace Hosford, though he was hardly entitled to hold any grudge against the sex for his being there. He had been a professional axman, made good money falling trees for a lumber outfit and shaping bridge timbers for the railroad, and made a habit every year of blowing in his year's savings on street carnivals. When he struck one that suited him, he followed it around the country until his money ran out, playing all the games and attending all the shows and riding merry-go-rounds and Ferris-wheels and bump-coasters wherever it stopped. He couldn't tell why he did it. The monotony, he said, used to almost kill him, and it must have affected the carnival people the same way because one day a woman game-tender locked up her game, led him to a justice of the peace, and married him, explaining that she was tired of watching him make a fool of himself. To break him of it, she decided to take him out of reach of temptation, and she picked out the Coast mountains as being the last place on earth where a street carnival would be likely to get to. Her reform was a success, but about the time it began to take hold she ran across a hide-out bank-cashier on the beach who had tried to play a stick-and-moccasin gambling game with the Indians and had got cleaned at it. Not only his money, but his clothes, gun, and fishing-tackle had all gone out on the tide. He was living on clams, enveloping his nakedness in a piece of old sail, and trapping a few mink-pelts to buck the stick-and-moccasin tantalizer some more. His foolishness made Hosford's wife indignant, and she decided to take him out of reach of temptation to break him of it. So she went away with him and joined a street carnival as being the last place on earth where stick-and-moccasin was ever likely to flourish. That, at least, was the story Hosford told about her, and though it seemed a little too well-rounded for exact truth, there was nothing improbable about it. He hadn't much minded losing her, because she wasn't a woman that one could ever feel really acquainted with. She meant so blamed well that she seemed to be putting a lot of it on, and it was impossible to catch her at it. He hadn't found the Coast a bad place to live in, but he was willing to leave it because all his neighbors were going to, and he liked them better than the country.

The rest of the settlers had avoided this brand of widowership, either by remaining unmarried or by hanging on to their wives harder. Some of them could hardly have been blamed for letting their hold slip, considering how matrimony had worked out with them. Tunis Evans was a long-built man with a sort of delayed-action cast of features, like one of those tormenting dreams in which things refuse to fall until ten minutes after they have been dropped, and a fine-looking strap of a wife who was always blaming her unhappiness on whatever country she happened to be living in. He never refused to move when she wanted to, but he did usually take a long time making up his mind to consent; and once his slowness had enraged her so she ordered him off the place, and then, because he went without giving her the satisfaction of arguing about it, she turned loose at him with a shotgun as he was climbing through the fence. The result, she used to relate, had made her practically an invalid for life. She had supposed light shot at such long range would merely scare him and make him move fast for a change. Instead, it knocked him flat, speckled his back with shot-holes from shoulder to crotch, and would probably have severed his spine if the center of the pattern hadn't been stopped by the leather cross-patch of his suspenders. On account of the shock the incident had given her, she had to be kept from all excitement and nerve-strain, and it was because the Coast winters wore so hard on her that they were intending to move.

Another of the married men was a big elderly Swede, very imposing-looking and not overloaded with brains, named Knut Lund, which he made to sound even more outlandish than it looked by pronouncing it K-noot Loont, like a man trying to talk with his mouth full. He was good-hearted when he thought of it, which was seldom, because thinking didn't come natural to him, and he was badly over-ridden with a hatching of big beef-countenanced sons who divided their time between stealing fur from the Indians' trap-lines and sitting on his front steps, waiting for him to bring home something to eat. His wife was also big and handsome. You could see that she must at one time have been very beautiful and maybe even intelligent, and her marriage to Lund had been, by their account of it, a real romance. He had been some kind of gamekeeper or herd boss on a big farm in the old country, working for a Swedish count. Mrs. Lund, who had been the count's only daughter, had married him because she was tired of the empty artificiality of aristocratic surroundings and hankered for something real. She had certainly got it. Her husband's table manners had enough rugged earthiness to last an ordinary hankerer after reality several years, and he was supposed to have a spider's nest somewhere in the fastnesses of his whiskers on which no human eye had ever gazed since it was first built. He worked hard keeping track of cattle, trapping, hunting, tanning hides, and raising a small patch of garden, and he spent a great deal of his time cussing about his sons, who were provocation enough to make anybody cuss. His wife, with as much reason, spent hers regretting her defaulted membership in the hollow artificialities of the old-country nobility and cussing about him.

Besides the sons, who were useless, they had a daughter about fifteen who was entertaining because she had a cleft palate and liked to recite poetry. The best one she did was a piece by Ella Wheeler Wilcox about a woman who was so infatuated over some man that she declared herself willing to toss off her chances of going to heaven in the event, which she considered likely, that he was not allowed to come along. The last line was—"And sink with thee down to sweet hell!"—and that somewhat startling sentiment, strained first through a heavy Scandinavian accent and then through a cleft palate, came out with an effect at once so deformed and so dignified that a man couldn't decide whether to blush or snicker. The daughter's name was Christina, by way of advertising her ancestral quarterings, which didn't need it. The sons' names were Isaac, Olaf, and Oscar, and it scarcely seemed possible to mispronounce such a simple concord of sounds. But the old man made it. "Mine Eesock he's purty gude boy," he would affirm, hopefully. "But mine damn mean Oo-*lof* and Oo-*scar!*" The truth was that none of them was worth his feed, and everybody else knew it, including their mother. She was anxious to move because she imagined a change of environment might make them amount to something, which was banking heavier on the regenerating influence of scenery and climate than most people who knew the situation would have done on a visit from the Angel Gabriel in person.

The rest of the men in the settlement had stayed single, or claimed they had. There was a tall white-mustached old man named Sheldon who had been a Congressional Librarian in Washington during Grant's administration. From reading, he had acquired an expert knowledge of all the geologic ages of North American rock-strata, and he had not learned in several years of close observation and experience when potato-vines ought to be pulled or what was the normal period of gestation for a cow. A middle-sized man with a poetical spread of whiskers and a stoop had been born in India, where his father was a non-com. in the British army. He was a cobbler by trade, owned a set of the collected works of Coke and Blackstone which he read of evenings for entertainment, and was called Shoe-Peg Pringle. There was a man named Rube Cutlack, small, dark-skinned, with scared-looking eyes, who was very fond of conversation and unable to take any part in it because in his boyhood he had been captured off an emigrant-train by a bunch of Piegan raiders who first tried unsuccessfully to break his spirit and make a chore-boy of him, and then cut his tongue out at the roots and turned him loose. It was a little unnerving, right at first, to have him drop in for a visit and sit for four hours without saying a word, but it could be got used to. He was a punctiliously friendly old runt, and a fine tracker and marksman. The clerical arm of society was represented in the outfit by Foscoe Leonard, a burly old bottle-knocker with a round oratorical voice who had been educated for the ministry and had taken up bush-ranching while waiting for some congregation to put in a call for his services. He had a fine pulpit presence, raised bear-hounds for recreation, and was in perpetual trouble about them because they got loose at night and kept all the settlers awake baying game through the brush. By way of contrast to him there was Clark Burdon, who represented the profession of arms. He had been a company gunman in the gold-mines around Wallace, Idaho, until a squad of labor organizers ganged on him and shot him up so badly he had to retire. He kept a good deal to himself, talked with an illiterate seen-that-thar accent when he was sober, and ascended when he got drunk into a stiff-legged elegance of speech that would have had an English society-novel licked without a laydown.

Different though all these people's histories were, there was one thing to be noticed about them. None of them told stories about things they had heard or read about other people having done. They considered nothing worth telling unless they had seen and performed in it themselves. It was true that they preferred telling about what they had done to getting out and preparing for what they intended to do. Winter, for instance, was the time to have rounded up their cattle, which were then pasturing the low brush close to the sea where they were easy to get at. But the men refused to disturb them till spring, when they had drifted back into the deep timber following the new grass. The fresh-foliaged brush made them hard to find, the good feed made them hard to catch, and the settlers

had over a month of extra work rounding up enough of them to
pay for the wagons needed to move in.

None of the settlers owned wagons. In the Coast country there
had been no use for any, because there were no roads to run them
on. There were children on some of those hill ranches who had
never laid eyes on a wheeled vehicle in their lives, and were rearing
to leave comfortable homes and dive blind into unknown country
for the sake of riding something that ran on wheels instead of
shanks; and their parents, from having lived away from a road
for so long, were almost as anxious. They worked their cattle down
from the timber by twos and threes, using as many as five well-
mounted men to drive two old cows because they were so wild,
and built their herd together on the open beach. Then, spacing their
drive between tides, they hurried them down the hard sand along
the line of surf to Coos Bay to load on the boat for San Francisco. Driving them was work, and Clay, riding with the point-
herders, came in for the worst of it and was glad he was along.
Surf broke white foam over the hoofs, a hard sunlit rain flogged
out of the sea and dripped off their horns and beat them sideways,
multitudes of sea gulls rose from in front of them and followed
them, flapping at their eyes and threatening to light on them until
the herd went down the tide-line in a kind of crazy seesaw, bawling
and trying to break with terror. The point-men tried whipping the
gulls with their ropes, and then Clark Burdon pulled his gun and
shot one a few feet from his head. The herd raised from a trot
to a gallop, and Clay headed them out of the driftwood by taking
a couple of shots into the air himself. The cattle galloped faster, and
all the men started shooting to keep them at it. There was no see-
sawing or breaking after that. The herd laid down to a run along
the dark sand, ripping through corners of the surf and jumping
creeks and drift-stumps, and they went into Coos Bay in the rain
at a clip that almost took the town a mile down the beach with them.
It was fast and desperate, and it was worth it. A man would have
something to tell about when he could say that he had taken a
shotgunning herd of cattle down a chute between the United States
and the Pacific Ocean, herding them with a pistol fast enough to

outrun several thousand sea gulls. The hardest work is pleasant if it is something that a man can brag afterwards about having done. The men rode back from Coos Bay in a fierce equinoctial hurricane that almost knocked their horses flat, and they didn't mind in the least.

The hurricane, it seemed, was nature's final attempt to break them down. When it was over, luck began to turn in their favor. A coastwise freight-ship went on the sand below the mouth of Metunné River in the storm, the crew hauled off in boats to another ship and left, and the final winds beat her on inshore until, when the seas went down and the weather cleared, she lay so high that a man at low tide could almost wade out to her. She was loaded with sacked flour, which wasn't likely to last long when another storm came along. But nobody came back to claim her and nobody seemed to be bothering about her, so the settlers clubbed together, hired a big dugout from the Indians, and went out to see how much of her cargo they could float to shore for their own use.

Floating, of course, was not the best kind of treatment for flour in sacks. But as a general thing the water soaked only a few inches of the outside, which could be lifted off in a cake, leaving the core dry and usable. The sacks that came ashore in the surf, of course, usually got burst or soaked through from pounding, but the little bays and creeks caught enough of them to pay for the work required to set them afloat. The men stocked up with axes all round, and paraded out between tides to cut through to the hold.

They could work only during low tide, which that week came about ten in the morning and latened half-an-hour every day. Counting the pull out and back, they could count on a bare two hours to get things done before the tide swung and cut them off from shore. Axe-work was hard because the ship was teetered over at an angle. The deck, which was easiest to cut through, stuck so high out of the water that cutting it would do no good. They had to coon up the tilted hull and cut down through that, and the first two days they worked themselves to a frazzle without even loosening a plank. The third day went better. They made openings in two places, got a couple of cross-cut saws going on the ribs, and not only opened a hole big enough to throw flour out through, but had a great twenty-foot section of hull ready to stave in when the tide compelled them to knock off. They tossed out a couple of dozen sacks for luck, and dragged back ashore to see if the high water would bring them in.

It had been the working agreement, as always in such wrecking-syndicates, that each member was entitled to all the cargo that he could find and catch when it washed in. Most of the men stuck to the big dugout and patrolled the mouth of the river. Clay and Clark Burdon caught up an old fish-spearing raft and worked it back through the cat-tail marshes to catch whatever drift should get past the swift water unseen. They knew that if any flour got within reach of the Indian village it was as good as gone. Flour was the one civilized article of diet that those Siwashes were genuine enthusiasts about. They didn't merely like it and wait for somebody to give it to them, as they did with whisky and chewing-tobacco. They bought it, regularly and in quantities, paying three or four prices to have it packed up from Coos Bay along the beach. Some of their recipes for cooking it would have knocked a hotel chef flat on his own cook-stove. They ate it with everything, and they even ate it alone and raw, claiming that, for a trained palate, cooking destroyed the delicate flavor. Since they drew a liberal yearly allowance from the government to spend on their flour, it seemed a shame to let them get hold of any for nothing. Clay and Clark Burdon patrolled the marshes carefully, raking in sacks at the rate of one about every three-quarters of an hour, and Luce, tired of keeping dinner warm, saddled up and rode down to the beach to see why nobody had turned up to eat it.

It was the first completely good day of that year. A warm squaw-wind eased in from the direction of China, and the high tide built glossy ridges of green water into draft-horse waves that smoked spray into the sun and collapsed booming among the dozing sea gulls on the hard sand. The beach at high tide was not a good place to ride, because every inch of sand above the high-water line was piled with mountains of driftwood—stumps as big as houses, dead trees sprawling dead roots and branches overhead and underfoot, beams and old timbers and broken lumber from wrecked ships, trimmed logs from timber-rafts that had gone loose from their tow-line in some storm, box-ends and fruit-crates and broken bundles of shingles and battered piles of wreckage in all sizes from a telephone pole to a toothpick, all littered from ten to thirty feet deep all the way along that Coast from California to Alaska. Even a man on foot would have had hard work navigating the tangle. For a horse it was impossible until the tide drew clear of the hard sand below it. Luce rode into the outer fringe of water and looked out at the ship. It was a long way out, but she could tell, studying it, that there was nobody on it. She turned back, and rode weaving among the stumps till she found tracks in the sand where the men had tied their horses. The horses were gone, which reassured her. There would have been nobody to untie them if the working-party had been drowned or cut off from land by the rising water. She thought next that maybe one man of the party might have fallen in and that the others were scattered, watching to catch the corpse when it washed ashore, so she tied her horse to a stump and walked out on the piled logs, hoping to run across somebody. She shut her eyes against the sun, felt the surf shaking the logs under her, and wished they could be lining out on the road for eastern Oregon, away from the dangerous sea and the dark winters for good. A big wave knocked water on her, and she opened her eyes again and saw, riding the big combers behind the surf, what looked like a great flight of white birds driving straight for her.

They weren't birds. The comber broke and they fell with it and drew back into the surf and came in again. They were sacks of flour. The sea had staved in the loosened planking of the ship, and the whole cargo was floating loose in it. More sacks floated close as Luce stared, and several burst, powdering lumps of wet flour in the water that lapped on the piled logs. She measured her height against the water where they were, took off her shoes, stockings and skirt, and waded in. At waist-deep, the sacks floated a good three feet beyond her reach, so she came out, stripped off everything except her knickers, and, with a flip of her hand to the interested throng of sea gulls, tried it again. To reach the nearest sacks she had to wade in to her armpits, with the surf sometimes breaking completely over her.

The water was colder than whaley. Half an hour of towing fifty-pound flour-sacks through it to the driftwood line chilled her to one solid ache. She decided to take fifteen minutes to thaw out in the sun, but she took little more than five. It was really almost as cold out of the water as in it, and flour came piling into the surf so fast that she forgot about being half-frozen in her anxiety not to lose it. The sun lowered and faded into a mist-haze. The sand chilled and darkened, and there was no place left to get warm if she had wanted to. She worked on, taking it easier because the tide was on the ebb and she could hold the flour-sacks by tossing them onto the sand instead of carrying them to the driftwood. Instead of her bringing Clay home to dinner at last, it was he who came to bring her. He was none too pleased at having to do it, for he and Clark Burdon had paddled the marshes till almost dark and had got in almost worn out, with a total of fourteen sacks for their afternoon's plunder. He found her sitting on the sand in the half-twilight, trying to warm her fingers enough so she could put her clothes on. Sacked flour was piled in the driftwood behind her and clear down the sand into the surf. At a rough count, there were three hundred and sixty sacks, all unburst and mostly soaked only on the outside, that she had dragged out and saved. Clay dropped his bridle-reins and came stumbling through them, and she laughed and called to him.

"Come here and help me dress," she ordered. "Then build a fire so I can thaw out, and then take my horse back to the cabin and get one of the pack saddles. We'll have to get this flour out of here before the Indians find it, or they'll start stealing it. Do you know what this flour is?"

He said that some of it seemed to be dough, but that most of it was flour, he guessed. "Hold still till I put this skirt around you. Do you want to give yourself pneumonia, and what for? All the men in this settlement couldn't use all this flour in twenty years. Don't you know that?"

She laughed, yanked at him as he stooped over her, and kicked sand on him with her bare foot. "They won't get a chance to," she said. "This flour is to sell to the Indians. I can get a dollar a sack for it, and do you know what that will mean?"

"Around three hundred and fifty dollars, I suppose," he said, hauling her stockings on. Her legs were so cold that touching them was like touching the sand under them.

"To buy a wagon," she said, as if she didn't at all mind being half-frozen. "To buy a wagon and a tent, and harness and an extra horse, and whatever we're going to need to start for eastern Oregon with. And didn't I tell you we'd manage the money for it, away last winter? And you mumbled and acted suspicious about it, and you didn't believe I'd do it, did you?"

Piling sticks for a fire, he admitted that he had felt some misgivings. He didn't spoil her triumph by reminding her that she had felt them, too, but he knew she had. He had learned to know her well enough during the winter so that he could tell, merely by the way she sat when he touched her, whether anything was bothering her or making her apprehensive. At such times a curious rigidity of conscience took hold of her and forced her, in a kind of atonement for whatever it was that she felt afraid of, to hold herself back from him as if merely touching him casually was something she must not allow herself. Sometimes she would try to avoid showing it, and he would discover it by feeling her flinch when he kissed her. It was nothing that she could help. Only, her nature was to understand love not as a last hope which you could turn to when everything else had gone out from under you, but as a kind of reward for good management, something you had a right to only when you had managed to keep everything else solid and in place around you. She might not have the right way of looking at it, but she was at least just with it, for she held herself to it as strictly as others. He had noticed it in her more and more during the winter since the elk-drive. He had surmised that it was about managing money for the wagon to move to eastern Oregon in, and that it was not because she was worried about where to get it. She had known where to get it. What had worried her was that she didn't want him to know, and now a whole string of wild luck had made whatever she intended to do unnecessary. Her coldness was over, trouble between them was avoided again, and he couldn't decide whether to be glad of that or sorry because a grain of the truth about her had slipped out of his fingers. He built up the fire with heavy driftwood and lit it, running over his suspicions again at the very moment when she twitted him for ever having had them. If she had intended getting the money from the horse-trader? But where could he have got that much, after losing every cent on a horse-race? "We're fixed to move," he agreed. "One thing about it, though. Your old man can't go. These men around here don't like him, and they won't have him along."

He got nowhere with that, and he didn't deserve to, for it was tactless and clumsy. "Certainly not," she said, stretching her legs to the fire. "He doesn't like them, either, and he's got other things to do than go trailing around after them. The only reason we'll need a wagon is because we won't be able to use his."

One miss was enough. He didn't try any more. It was tantalizing to have been so close to something about her and then to miss it, even though it had been something he had wanted to avoid knowing. He rode up the trail with the two horses in the dark, and at the place where they had stopped to let the storm overtake them, he looked back and saw her sitting by the fire among the driftwood. He decided it was a good thing he had avoided knowing it. If there had been anything bad about her, he would have found it out in a winter of living with her. The only thing he had found was that she was a little too considerate of the horse-trader, who wasn't worth it. That was nothing against her.

Chapter XV

It was nothing to her discredit, either, that she should feel badly because the trip to eastern Oregon made it necessary to part from her father. She had never appeared to take any special pleasure in having him around, and during the winter she had scarcely gone near him. But he was the only kin she had, she had never been separated from him, and his combined feeling of drama and sentimentality were strong enough so that he made the leave-taking a great deal more of an event than there was any sense in. He shed tears, demanded to be informed how he was going to get along in his business without her, and announced in a broken tone of voice that he was being abandoned forever by the one human being that he had lavished his care and affection on and that he would undoubtedly be dead before she ever saw him again. His wife interrupted his spirit of prophecy just when he was getting well warmed up to it, by taking him firmly by the shoulder and ordering him either to shut up and let the girl alone, or else pack up his wagon and go along with her. That he didn't want to do, because there were reasons of both business and sentiment in the way. None of the settlers liked him or wanted him along with them, and to drag a bunch of unsold horses back to the bunch-grass country in the spring would have been like going to a brass-band concert with a cornstalk fiddle. His wife led him inside his cabin, shut the door on him and held it, and remarked cheerfully that he was putting most of it on to exercise his higher vocal registers, and that she had often thought of renting him out as a shill for some tent-show evangelist, so he could not only do all the weeping and emotionalizing he wanted to, but actually get paid for it.

She was used to him, so his displays of ruptured feelings didn't bother her. Luce had been with him longer, but she was still too young to have outlived her horror of seeing a grown man cry. The dark sunless winter had bleached all the tan from her face, and she sat her pony, looking pale and helpless, while his weeping was going on, and anxious and remorseful after he had been led indoors. If it would make him feel any better about it, she offered, they could stay over a day or two before starting. His wife said positively that it wouldn't, and set her heel against the door to keep him from breaking out and arguing about it.

"If you let this man blubber you out of doing what you want to, you'll never do anything," she cautioned. "He'll keep you tagging around after him till you're sixty if you let him. Don't you know that? Go on and don't pay any attention to him. I'll tend to him."

She seemed well able to do it, and she was determined that Luce should not waste even an hour coddling him into good spirits, because she didn't want him to get it into his head that his staginess had impressed anybody. They told her good-by, lining their new wagon down the sand at a trot to get into Coos Bay ahead of the tide and catch the rest of the train before it got too far ahead of them. That night they stayed at the Coos Bay hotel, where the night clerk and the hostler took them for a pair of country honeymooners and winked over it with such relish as almost to ruin the set of their faces for food. The next morning there was a restaurant breakfast which, because the natural products of that country were beef, elk, venison, honey, wild-fowl and two hundred species of edible fish, consisted of ham, eggs, pancakes, and maple syrup. That was the town where the guitar-playing woman was in jail, but Clay made no attempt to renew acquaintance with her. He still felt sorry for her, but he had taken an aversion against the sight of her since hearing that he was only one of the numerous men she had rescued from loneliness, and that the others had all been half-starved bums and beach-rats. Possibly a good deal of her trouble had come, not from lavishing charity on the wrong men, but from failing to make them understand, to begin with, that it was charity and not something else. A man may be so totally lost to hope that he will refuse to believe he can ever do or be anything, but mighty few of them ever get so far down that they can't imagine a woman might be in love with them.

Having no packing or horse-feeding to do, they moved their wagon out well before sunup, and made it to the summit of the Coast Range by dark. It was a pretty place they found to camp in, alongside of a little gravel-bottom waterhole where dozens of little six-inch trout crowded to nibble their fingers when they dipped the water-bucket. White trilliums and wild-strawberry blossoms covered the ground, and the tall cream-colored wild lilies known in that country as lamb-tongues clustered in the undergrowth like grass-heads in a hay-field. Through those lamb-tongues they traveled all the way down the reverse slope of the mountain, sometimes along grades so steep and crooked that it was necessary to lift the hind wheels off the ground and put in drag-poles so the wagon wouldn't break loose and run down the team. They didn't get down to the hop-country again, but swung north, following the divide of the Pass Creek mountains, and went into the Cascade foothills by the road past the old quicksilver mines that had once been worked by several hundred Chinamen and were now not worked at all. Not that the quicksilver had run out, but the Chinamen had, and there were still old skeletons littered around the wild-strawberry patches below the pit-head where the mine's shotgun-pickets had managed to kill some of them when they dived for the brush. The wild strawberries grew so thick in that section that it was impossible to walk in the grass without being soaked ankle-high with the juice. Beyond that was an old gold-mining camp called Bohemia, no longer worked, with an elaborately-appointed dance-hall where some Indians, camping to hunt, had built a fire in the middle of the waxed floor and punched a hole in the roof to let the smoke out. From there the road steepened and got rough and full of stumps. Even with their light load, they could scarcely have pulled it if the settlers' train ahead of them hadn't cleared and widened it. With the rise of altitude the fir timber gave way to enormous cedars, and they in turn to tall, clean-trunked white pines, each as round and straight as a cannon, and each with a little tuft of foliage at the very tiptop.

Beyond the white-pine belt the mountain broke down into the ash-white bed of an old glacier, stony and grassless, with no trees except the white-barked quaken-asp. Streams foamed through the rocks, and their water was also white with excess of oxygen, and so infernally cold it had to be warmed before the horses could drink it. Nothing was in bloom here. Drifts of snow still lay in the shady places ten feet deep, sometimes squarely across the road, so that the train ahead had been obliged to halt and shovel it clear. Spring came to these summits about mid-July, and left again early in September. Summer didn't usually ever get to them at all. Deer never got so high, but there were chipmunks and big snow-rabbits and black foxes and bear, and there was a mark in the light earth where a mountain goat had sat up on his haunches behind a rock, probably to act as a lookout while the settlers' train passed. They made camp in a grove of glacier-pine, and suffered from the cold and from the knowledge that the horses were without anything to eat. The next day's trip was all downhill, first through quaken-asp and then white pine and then red-trunked fir. The only new thing was that, instead of white lamb-tongues there were blue lupins— the tall two-foot stalks of bloom that crowd every open acre of the plateau country, and, in places where water is scarce, poison sheep. When the fir timber ended they came to something new—a stand of yellow pine, not brushed close underneath, but open and sunlit because the turpentine in the fallen needles keeps down all small vegetation. A creek ran through a clearing in the pines, and there was good grass and the ground was warm and dry. But they didn't stop. For the first time they could see ahead to open country, and they saw that they were overtaking the settlers' train at last. Below them was the Looking Glass Valley, all open grassland among old orchards and caved-in houses and blackened remnants of haystacks. They could see the road clear across it, and the settlers' wagons making long pale-blue shadows in the grass as they wheeled out of the road to camp.

It was not a massive-looking manœuvre, because the settlers had spaced their wagons out in groups of three and four, with a couple of miles between each group so as not to overcrowd the pasture in any one place. While daylight lasted they looked merely like a bunch of country people winding home from a Saturday's shopping in town. It was different after it got dark. Clay and Luce got closer, and the camp fires lighting up across the valley looked like more of a crowd. There was an ungodly lot of them, though not so many as they seemed, because the wild grass of that valley had the power of reflecting light exactly like a body of water. Looking carefully, it could be seen that half the camp fires were burning upside down, and when the moon came up another moon

immediately appeared underneath and went moving along through
fences and farms and haystacks like the reflection of a sail following a ship.

Even by moonlight, the farms in the valley looked badly shot
up and dilapidated. They were all empty. Once Looking Glass had
been a rich locality, with six big heavy-set ranches running cattle
on the open grass, each making its proprietor ten times as big an
income as he needed to live on. The cinch was too good to last. The
valley, along in 1890, had attracted some three hundred industrious
colonists, who divided the open grass-country between them and
set out to make it pay as big for them as it had for the original
exploiters. Since it was only good for pasture, it went right on
paying the same as usual, with the difference that, instead of giving
six ranchers ten times too much apiece, it gave three hundred
ranches about one-fifth enough. The colonists lived for a few years
by borrowing, and when they could borrow no more they all got
up and left, and the mortgagors took their land and offered it
for sale for the amount of their loans, with accrued interest. That
was more than anybody could afford to pay, and more than it
could ever be made to pay off. So, as a demonstration of the way
capital operated in developing agriculture, the valley remained tied
up tight, without any colonists and also without the six ranches it
had supported to start with.

The removal of the colonists had meant also the abandonment
of their town, which in the big days appeared to have been a quite
ambitious sort of *pueblo*. Now all the buildings in it were deserted
and falling down, and it was among those crumbling monuments
of misplaced mercantile enterprise that Clay struck the Coast settlers' rearguard. It consisted of Clark Burdon, Given Bushnell, and
Rube Cutlack. They had stabled their teams behind the counter
of the bank building, with a lantern swung overhead to point up
the pleasantry. A big roan draft-horse stuck his nose through the
wicket marked "Notes and Collections" as Clay peered in, and he
nickered pleadingly, much as the original occupant might have done
about the time the depositors began to lose confidence. Burdon and
Cutlack and Bushnell were across the street in what had been the
saloon. They were raking through the trash-dump for bottles that
still had something to drink in them, and they had been doing well

at it, because all three of them were about half-drunk. Clay knocked on the glass and waved, not intending to interrupt them, but Burdon signaled to him to wait, and came out. He was so full his eyes wouldn't focus, and his diction was as precise and careful as a doctor lecturing a ladies' club on sexology.

"A number of new people have attached themselves to our, uh, cavalcade," he said, waving his hand gracefully and almost falling down. "A frugal year out in the big world, it would seem, and everybody that can get anything to move in is on the move. Which reminds me. Perhaps, when you've stabled your team and refreshed yourself, you'll drop back here for a few minutes' talk? It's, uh, it might be to your advantage."

He bowed his head and let on to listen attentively while Clay explained that he couldn't very conveniently drop back. He would be busy making camp and tending the horses, he didn't like to leave Luce alone, with strange travelers roving around loose, and he didn't care to sit around a gone-to-hell saloon swigging decayed heel-tap liquor, anyhow.

"That's where your prejudices mislead you," said Burdon. "You do the cheer a grave injustice, young man. We've located a keg down in the cellar that's over half full, and strong enough to lift you right through the crown of your hat. It won't hurt you a particle, and it might do you an enormous amount of good. But that isn't it. What I want to see you about has nothing to do with our rude shifts at conviviality. It's personal, and it might save you, uh, embarrassment and trouble. Put your horses up across from the lodge-hall and come on back. As a favor to—hurrup!" He had almost gestured himself down the steps on his face. "You'll run back for a minute or two? Good. Some beautiful roses in bloom across from your camp-site, if the damned pilgrims' horses haven't eaten them all. I'll be looking for you."

The roses had not been spoiled. A great shower of white ones covered the side fences around the lodge-hall. Under them were the slower-growing old-fashioned moss-roses and tearoses and butter-roses and cabbage-roses, sweet and strong, although the colonists' women who had planted them were no longer near to tend to them or care whether they lived or died. A quince-tree blossomed over them, and the grass in the shadows was starred with daffodils and jonquils and hyacinths. Across the road was an open side hill, matted deep with grass, and there was a spring branch crossing it along which some early colonist had planted a jungle of honey-locust trees, probably as a means of laying claim to the water-hole under the old timber-culture law. The locusts were all in bloom, too, and the wind went back and forth between them and the roses, carrying perfume from one to the other. There was grass, there were fence rails and porch posts for wood, there was the spring branch for water. Clay pitched the tent and unpacked, and hobbled the horses so they could graze.

It was spring in that country and no mistake. During supper they heard a flock of quail whistling themselves to roost in the locust thicket; a pair of swallows in the quince-tree knocked down a bushel of petals, settling for the night; a rain-crow a long way off in the fields sang like clanking a little copper bell. Clay and Luce sat listening for new sounds and watching the camp fires far up the road toward the mouth of the valley. This was better than the Coast, where the only birds after dark were sea gulls that screamed like a bunch of drunk washerwomen, and where the only sound of water was the tides of the ocean falling on the beach like a brick tower tipping over. It was a better country inland, better to live and work in even if it returned less. Luce said so, and they watched three new wagons pull up at the saloon, exchange words with Clark Burdon, and drive past to some assigned camp-ing-place ahead.

"It's a bad time to make a start in, though," Clay said. "Banks shut, and people throwed out of work and usin' clearin'-house cer-tificates in place of money, and all the land locked up with mortgages so nobody can farm it. Half the people in this country will be on the move like us before harvest. Some of these new outfits have been shipped out from Seattle and clear up from San Francisco."

He dwelt on the fact almost proudly, as a man during a spell of cold weather does on the announcement that it is the coldest in eighty years. The line of fires down the valley, the strange wagons pulling in and being directed to their places in the line, the knowl-edge that this was no longer merely a head-of-the-creek community on the move through restlessness, but an entire people, a whole division of society, gathering to tackle a new country rather than

live as peons in an old one, gave him a feeling of dignity and
strength that, though miles beyond his own reach, was his because
he belonged to these people. This was one of the great things that
happened as often as the men who financed the country financed
it too much and then, instead of admitting it, undertook to squeeze
their money back out of the men who worked it. Whenever that
happened, which it did about every ten years, the settlers picked
up and cleared out somewhere else to open new land and make
themselves a new country in which, maybe, they could become the
ones who did the squeezing instead of the ones who got squeezed.
It was not altogether a virtuously-purposed movement, but it was
a great one. It was happening now, and Clay felt glad he was in it.

"We've got nothing to be afraid of," Luce said. "Bad year or
not, it's better than mildewing on the Coast. All I wish is that we
hadn't had to leave father there. He's too old to be left alone like
that. Something might happen to him any time, at his age."

Her father, at a guess, was around fifty years old, and the only
thing that seemed in any danger of happening to him was that
somebody might shoot him over a fast-handled horse-trade. But
Luce seemed unable to get him out of her mind. Whenever the trip
let up enough so she had a few moments to think in, back she went
and fastened on him with that stiff-necked instinct that made her
feel, because he wasn't having a good time, that she mustn't allow
herself to have one, either. Clay reminded her that she hadn't beaten
a track to his threshold during the winter on the Coast, and she
said that had been different. She had been within reach in case
anything did go wrong with him. Now she wouldn't know whether
he made out well or ill, and he was alone.

"Alone with a wife," Clay said, sharply. These spells of unreasonable fretfulness wore his patience. "She looks out for him,
don't she? How many supervisors does he need?"

"That's another thing I'm afraid of," Luce said, stubbornly.
"She's only stayed with him this long because she liked me. Now
she's likely to leave him any time she gets mad at him. If she does,
it will kill him. He's had plenty of humiliating things happen to
him, but never that. If it happened, it would kill him. He can't
stand those things like—like ——"

"Like I can," Clay offered, unsympathetically. Her father sounded like a hard case, a man who could neither survive a particular form of calamity nor prevent it from happening. Such a combination of sensitiveness and helplessness was almost too impractical to belong in anything so coarse and selfish as a world. "Maybe your father ought to go live up a tree somewhere, so people couldn't reach him. He could come down at night for exercise after they was all in bed, and they couldn't wound his feelings if they didn't know he was around."

"You needn't make fun," she rebuked him. "You can stand things better than he can, I know that. And I know he's ridiculous sometimes, and that a lot of his trouble is his own fault. But when I get to remembering about him, I feel afraid about him. With hard times on the country, too."

"He's in a better place for hard times than we are," Clay pointed out. "No rent to pay, and plenty to eat. If he's got sense enough to stay there . . ."

She shook her head. Anything that depended on her father's soundness of judgment was not to be depended upon. "He'll leave because he'll want to see me," she said. "I know how he'll feel about it, and you don't. People you've lived with for years and years don't mean as much to you as they do to him, because you can find friends anywhere. People like you. Do you know that you've never once told me about the people you lived with before you met me? You've never seemed to miss them at all. My father would, and that's the reason I worry about him."

That innocent observation came so unexpectedly that it left him at a stand for anything to say. He let the argument trail off into nothing, and, after she had gone into the tent to sleep, he went back to keep his promise to Clark Burdon. A couple more wagons were halted in front of the saloon, with people from some crossroads trading-post who had seen the train coming into the valley and had hurried to tie on. There was one thing about all the new people who came to join the train. They were willing to stand discipline. Burdon directed the two wagons to keep going another five miles and make camp under an old wooden-paddled windmill, and they whipped up and wheeled away without a word. Gazing after them, Burdon remarked that it actually looked as if they intended to go where they were sent, and sat down beside Clay on the steps. He was still pretty well oiled up, and he had drawn off a quart or so of whisky out of the old barrel into a wicker-covered canteen, which he tapped as often as he thought of it. "There have been a lot of them the past day or two that stop and inquire very politely where they're to camp, and then go on and camp wherever they please," he explained. "And a considerable number of them that I'd much rather not have camping with our outfit at all, though I don't know how the devil I can prevent them. The road's free. I've tried to scare off the worst-looking specimens, but the worse they are the harder they are to scare, so the Lord knows how many jail-sweepings we'll have dragging around after us before we're through."

"I don't see what you need to worry about 'em for," Clay said. "You're not responsible for every blamed bill-dodger that travels this road with you."

"Not legally," Burdon said. "But as a matter of keeping on the good side of public opinion, we try to keep up a kind of pretense at supervision. If one of these plug-uglies steals anything or shoots anybody, it'll be blamed on the train, and people will conclude that we're all potential thieves and shooters. Out here it doesn't make so much difference, but we've got settled country to cross yet, and then it will. And there's one or two of these new acquisitions that I wouldn't want to camp too close to on a dark night myself. Which reminds me that I had something to tell you. . . ." He took a shot from his bottle, and tendered it to Clay absently. "A man joined on today about noon, when we were getting down into the pine timber, and if he wasn't a trouble-maker by trade I'm a bad guesser and so is he. Rube and Bushnell were both somewhere else at the time. They usually are when there's any chance to put this ushering job off on me. So I had to handle him alone, and I'm not sure I did very well at it. Have another drink out of that flask, and pass it along."

"I don't need any more," Clay said, and offered it. He had told no lie about the stuff being potent. It was almost fractious. A second shot so soon might do things to him that he didn't want to risk, but Burdon pushed the flask back at him and insisted.

"Take one, take one. You might need it later, and if you take it now it'll save interrupting me. . . . Well, this trouble-maker I was telling you about. He was a big oaf with a kind of peeled face and a gray pony-express hat, and he was riding an old swaybacked plow-mare without any saddle. He had a pistol stuck out all over the place, and that was all the outfit he had. Not what you'd call a winning personality. I explained to him that we were a quiet little private expedition, that the entry-book was closed, and that maybe he'd better seek companionship elsewhere. So he said he was looking for a man who had swindled and robbed him, and that all he wanted was to hang around a day or so and make sure he wasn't in this train. I told him that if he went clear up the line and camped with the lead-wagons it would give him a chance to look everybody over, so he said he would, and he left. But he didn't go there. He's camped about a quarter of a mile down the road. Didn't pay any more attention to me than if I'd been a book agent trying to sell him a twenty-volume set of Great Loves of History."

Clay expressed sympathy, without being able to see much in the story to be sympathetic about. "If he ain't botherin' anybody, you don't need to bother about him, do you?"

Burdon took another swig from his flask, and passed it over. "There was no excuse for his acting like that with me," he pronounced severely. "It was a deliberate slight, and I get mad whenever I think about it. If he didn't intend to camp where I sent him, he should have said so and had it out with me. But, no, he wouldn't do that. He went ahead and camped where he pleased, and I can't order him off. I've got no legal authority to tell people what part of the public road they can use. He played me for a slab-sided old cross-roads farmer, and what can I do about it?"

The best plan, Clay thought, was to do nothing. He said so, and felt, because the whisky was getting hold of him, that it was clever of him to suggest it. Burdon was not quite so much impressed.

"Maybe I'll think of something when I get sober," he said, hopefully. "Now, along in the course of his blustering, this punk stated that the man he was looking for was about your age and build, and that the property he'd been robbed of included a rifle and some money, a saddle, and a buckskin mare a good deal like the one you've got leading behind your wagon. I don't want you to think I'm trying to scare you or extort confidences from you, but I thought I'd better tell you. Help yourself to the flask and hand it here a minute."

This time Clay helped himself to the flask without protesting. He didn't feel scared so much as outraged. Was it possible, in a country where he had had to dodge and stall and bluff and lie like a pickpocket because he had accidentally let Shiveley out of jail, that Shiveley himself could dare to go blowing and complaining to strangers about having been robbed of a horse and gun? The reason, of course, was that Shiveley was used to living as an outlaw, and had learned when it was safe to shoot off his mouth and when it was advisable not to. Also, Burdon mentioned, he had been moderately drunk. "Not as drunk as I am, but it showed on him more because he hasn't got a meditative cast of mind. He looked to be slightly afflicted with vanity, too, and I expect he felt that the poverty of his rig-out deserved some kind of explanation. So he gave one, along with a fairly exact description of you and a lot of bluster about what he intended to do to you if he ever got his hands on you. He had you worked into some kind of conspiracy with some Siwash kid from those acorn-eating Indians down Elk Creek, but I didn't listen to him close enough to get that part of it clear in my mind."

"I can clear it up for you," Clay said. After all, if the showdown was this close to him, there was no use keeping it to himself any longer. The whisky made him feel like opening up, and Burdon was as good a man as any to open up to. Better, maybe. Some of his stories from the time when he had been a gunman in the Idaho mines were about exigencies in which good and well-meaning men hadn't been able to behave strictly according to the letter of the revised statutes. He had already been friendly; he was pretty likely to be at least understanding and tolerant. Clay decided to try him. "I want to tell you all about this. Are you sober enough to pay attention?"

"I don't have to be sober to do that," Burdon said, amiably. "Let's have a look at that flask to start off with. Take a snort yourself, and go ahead."

The flask passed, and Clay went ahead. He told about his childhood and about the Shiveleys and the toll-bridge station, about Wade's two killings and Uncle Preston and Drusilla, the doctored

pistol and the jailbreak and how he had taken Wade Shiveley's
horse on the sheriff's say-so; about looting Wade's cache because
it contained a rifle he needed and some things of his mother's that
he was entitled to; about meeting Luce and refusing to leave her
to go with the Indian boy; how he hadn't told her about himself
at first because it hadn't seemed important, and how he had been
afraid to tell her later because it did. All his acts had been performed without any intention of wrong-doing. A lot of them had
turned wrong afterwards in spite of him.

"Practically all of them have, I should judge," Burdon agreed.
"You seem to have made it a principle to give in to people's advice
when it's bad, and to hold out against it when it's good. If you'd
crossed the mountains when that Indian kid wanted you to, you'd
have had a clear road and nobody to bother you. Now you're in
for it, and you've gone and made it worse by saddling yourself
with a woman to look out for." He reached thoughtfully for the
flask. "The best I can see for you to do is to haul out of here before
he catches you. Leave this outfit as soon as your horses are fit to
travel, and go somewhere else. How would that strike you?"

"I won't do it," Clay said. "I've done all the dodgin' I intend to.
All it's ever done was to make me ashamed of myself." He reached
the flask back and took a nip out of it. The whisky tasted weaker,
and his spirit felt stronger. "I could hunt him up and pick a fight
with him. Maybe if I got the jump on him I could down him, and
then I'd be rid of him for good."

"And if you didn't you'd be plumb dead," Burdon pointed out.
"And likely you wouldn't, because he's had practice shooting men,
and you haven't. And if you did pick a fight and down him, what
would happen? You'd get hauled down to the head of the train,
and old Sheldon and Foscoe Leonard and Lavran Baker would
stand you up and try you for homicide. And they've got their
heads so full of keeping this train orderly and law-abiding that it's
about ten to one they'd cinch you."

The possibility, in Clay's high state of spirits, seemed fantastic.
"For killin' an escaped murderer?" he demanded. "You talk like
them three men was fools. I know better than that."

Burdon conceded that they weren't quite fools. It wasn't that
they were so touchy about a shooting themselves, but they were

afraid it would outrage people in the country they had to pass through. It was only natural for a man who had to consider other people's moral standards to be ten times touchier about them than the people themselves were.

"This escaped murderer story wouldn't help much, either. If he was on trial for shooting somebody else and you brought it up as evidence against his character, they'd probably take your word for it. But if you shot him and offered it as a defense, they'd certainly expect you to prove it. And how would you do it without landing yourself on that jailbreak charge?"

He reached for the flask again. The exercise of thinking was sobering him up, and he was speaking less correctly and reasoning more shrewdly. Clay agreed that the alternative possibilities he presented, of getting either shot, hung by a settlers' court, or imprisoned on a jailbreaking charge, weren't enticing. "It's all I can think of," he said, helplessly. "I won't run, and I don't want to set like a blamed rabbit in front of a weasel till he tags me. Ain't there anything else?"

"I can't think of anything," Burdon admitted. "It isn't altogether certain that he will tag you, of course. Several things might happen to prevent. If you caught him prowling around your camp after hours, you could shoot him and come as clear as a whistle for it, because there's been a few cases of that already and we're trying to discourage it. But it isn't likely that he'll try that, because I warned him that if he did I'd shoot him myself. The safest thing would be to pick up and go somewhere else for a while. Nobody ever accused me of being a coward, but if I had a girl on my hands that's what I'd do."

It was the plainly sensible thing to do, but Clay couldn't bring himself to agree. To switch off and wait until that stampede had ended would be to miss a sight that might never hit that country again. And not only to see it, but to belong to it and be in it. He didn't intend to miss that for a trainload of Wade Shiveleys.

"I'll hang on," he said, and, feeling that his tone lacked power, he put a little more into it from the flask. "I'm mindin' my own business, and I won't let any punk like him stop me from goin' where I please. I'll keep on the tail end of the line, and maybe in a day or two he'll drop loose and bother some other outfit."

Burdon was neither surprised nor impressed. "That's what I'd have done when I was your age," he commented. "You might make it through, if you have any kind of luck. Keep that buckskin mare out of sight as much as you can, and let me know if you need any help. Give that bottle another lift before you leave. Do you know how long we've talked?"

They had talked all night. There was not yet enough daylight to see by, and only a streak of it in the sky; but a dull sort of radiance rose out of the plain of grass, a flight of blackbirds went overhead, and the lantern inside the saloon burned without shedding any light outside. Under it, Rube Cutlack and Given Bushnell were both asleep on the floor under a pile of broken furniture. They looked light-hearted and peaceful, and Burdon remarked regretfully that he had spoiled his own seven-dollar jag to hatch out advice that couldn't be worth over eighteen cents.

"Get some sleep, anyway," he advised. "Don't try to start when the wagons ahead do. All you'll get out of that's a lot of dust. Wait and start when I do, and you'll have a better time and see more country."

It had not been a very heartening conference, but Clay left it feeling strong, rash, and resolute. Part of that, he realized, uneasily, was Burdon's whisky, which was likely to wear off and drop him farther than it had hoisted him. But a little of it was solider and more consoling. Merely telling somebody about the Wade Shiveley case made him feel better about it, and there was even a dash of comfort about knowing that Wade was with the train. It was easier to avoid a man when you knew in which direction to look for him, so that, strategically, the night's conversation had given Clay a distinct advantage. He was not too full to walk straight, but the road showed a tendency to get out from under his feet and run him against unfamiliar landmarks. In front of the lodge-hall he halted and looked over his camp for several minutes before he realized that it was his. The tent looked startlingly white in the quarter-light; but the new wagon was mud-smeared and the new wagon-canvas dusty and weather-stained already. The buckskin mare grazing close to the tent convinced him that he belonged there, and he remembered that hereafter she would have to be staked out of sight. She raised her head and stared inquiringly at the back-

end of the wagon. Clay stared, too, and the fly in the wagon-canvas
opened. A man climbed down over the end-gate, reached back inside, and hauled out a saddle—the saddle that Clay had adopted
along with the buckskin mare. He was a big man, heavy-built, and
his silhouette against the canvas showed that he had on a gray
pony-express hat.

Councils to decide one's future conduct did very little good in
a pressing emergency. Clay, who had talked all night trying to
decide what he should do about Wade Shiveley, ripped loose his
pistol and drew a bead without even thinking it over. The light
was too bad and Burdon's whisky too conquering for any close
marksmanship. His first shot plowed dirt under the man's feet,
his second glanced off the wagon-wheel and went howling off over
the hill. The man dropped the saddle and ran in the same direction,
heading for the locust thicket. Clay gave up trying to hit him, but
banged a third shot after him by way of helping him along. To
judge by the lick he traveled, the hop-yard story about his nerve
being broken was well founded. The thicket was a good three hundred yards away, and he got to it while Clay was settling and
cocking the pistol for a fourth try at him. He didn't look back on
the way, either, and Clay sheathed the pistol and went to camp with
an exultant feeling that this was not going to be so hard to settle,
after all. The first round was his so easily that he doubted if there
would even be any more to it, and he decided not to tell Luce
anything about it until he saw. He hurried the saddle back where
it belonged before she came out. She was barefooted, and she had
the rifle ready.

"Nothing but a stray dog," he told her, easily. "I smoked him
up a little to scare him."

He imagined that he looked urbane and reassuring. The expression he actually achieved was a half-shot smirk, which she sized
up disapprovingly.

"You did a good job of it," she said. "You scared me half to
death, and you must have stampeded the new wagon-horse clear
out of the county. I don't see her anywhere."

The new wagon-horse was nowhere in sight, but the dew on
the long grass held tracks, and a dark continuous line of them
headed up the slope to the locust thicket. Two dark lines, if one

looked close, but Clay didn't call attention to the more widely-spaced one. He pointed out that a hobbled horse couldn't stampede, and that she must have strayed up the hill before the shooting started. "Went up to water, probably," he said. "She won't be far. I'll go up after breakfast and chase her down. We don't start today till late, on account of the dust and one thing and another, so there's no hurry about her."

She took him by the shoulders, jiggled him back and forth until he was dizzy, and then turned his face to the light part of the sky and inspected it carefully. "You're drunk," she pronounced. "I knew you would be if that old ape of a Clark Burdon got hold of you. You can go up and bring that horse down right now. It'll help you walk off your jag."

It didn't seem quite bright, after putting in the night getting a jag, to turn around and put in the morning getting rid of it. But she was set in the notion, and Clay, after puttering around for close to an hour to give the camp-prowler plenty of time to get out of the thicket and be on his way, took a halter and dragged up the hill with it. The strayed horse was pasturing on the far side of the thicket, and, being fore-hobbled, should have been easy to overhaul. But she was used to hobbles, had learned a kind of crow-hop gait in them that was almost a lope, and used the clump of locusts as a kind of manœuvring-point to exercise her play-fulness on. When Clay approached on one side, she dodged to the other. When he headed her off from the thicket she took to open country, and when he went after her she circled him and came back to it. She kept that up until Clay had worked off all of his jag and most of his patience. Finally, cornering her among some bushes, he made a grab for her, and she whirled and charged into the middle of the thicket and hung up in a tangle of thorny sap-lings, snorting and pretending to be panic-stricken when Clay squeezed through and haltered her. It was not all put on, that panic. Leading her out, he came to a deep little gully full of black mud, and in it there was a man lying face down. A pony-express hat was jammed crooked on his head with the mud soaking the gray felt, there was a dark wet patch on the back of his shirt, and flies were buzzing over it peacefully. He was dead.

The shock of the discovery contracted Clay's heart so violently that he had to sit down. It was less fright than surprise. He couldn't comprehend how the thing could have happened so quietly; how Wade Shiveley, who had always been so loud and big-acting about the triflingest things, should have managed this one so modestly and secretly. There should have been noise, argument, yelling, blustering, arm-swinging, a long rigmarole of accusation and scolding beforehand and a long one of explanation and denial afterward. This had happened so simply that there seemed something wrong about it. Still, it was death and it was here in plain sight. Clay tied his horse to a tree and climbed down to investigate. He avoided looking at the body until he was a couple of feet from it. Then he knelt down so he could see the face without having to lift it from the mud, and turned his eyes on it. The man was not Wade Shiveley. It was one of old Lund's worthless sons. He didn't stop to ascertain which one, but climbed out of the gully, unhobbled the horse and mounted bareback, and rode for the saloon to get Clark Burdon.

The edge that Burdon had honed onto himself during the night was not yet worn off. He was out in front of the bank, currying his team, with his wicker flask sticking out of his shirt-bosom, and singing "Good-by, My Bluebell." He greeted Clay in a ringing voice and said he was singing in the hope that it would disturb old Bushnell and Rube Cutlack, who were still asleep. He didn't notice the solemnity of Clay's face until Clay explained hurriedly what it was about. Then he climbed on his horse, spanked him with the currycomb, and lit out for the grove at a trot. When Clay caught up he had hauled the dead man out of the mud and was standing over him. "You busted his heart all to smash," he said. "The bullet went in under his left shoulder-blade, and it's stuck between a couple of his front ribs. You can feel it."

Clay said he didn't need to feel it. "I must have hit him with the last shot I took," he said. "He traveled upward of two hundred and fifty yards after that. I figured I'd missed him a mile."

He sat down, feeling weakish, and Burdon looked from him to the dead man.

"This would be easy if it was any ordinary harness thief," he said. "We could roll him into a hole and forget about him, and nobody would miss him. We can't do that with this fool. Them old

Swedes are good people. He's theirs, and they've got a right to him." He rolled the body sideways with his foot, thinking. Even through its smear of mud the inert face was still half-handsome with the father's peasant stupidity and not his honesty, with the mother's inbred petulance and not her sharpness. The frenzy of a long-drawn-out death had put no new thing into him and had taken no old one away. "It's Isaac," Burdon commented. "That makes it worse. Old Lund might take this sensibly if it was either of the other boys, but he's always had it in his head that Isaac was a spear of sanctified hyssop. The old lady knows better than that, but she'll raise hell about losing any of them. They'll want somebody's neck for this. What do you think you'd better do?"

"My God! I don't know," Clay said, helplessly. He had expected Burdon to tell him, not ask him. To have the Lunds after him, to land in some sagebrush jail where people, even if they believed him innocent, would want to know who he was and where he came from and could he prove it. He stared at the dead man and felt so sorry and apologetic he wanted to cry. "It was that damned hat. When I saw that I thought it was Wade Shiveley come back to hell me around, and it made me so mad ———"

"Don't bawl now," Burdon warned him. "We've got to counsel this out sensibly. You could leave him here and pretend not to know anything about him. I wouldn't advise you to, because the old people are going to look for him when he don't show up for meals, and with Foscoe Leonard's tracking-dogs they'll find him sure. Then they'll know that he was in your camp last, and it will be ten times worse for you than if you'd come out with the whole thing to start with. If you shot him thieving your wagon, how did he travel all this distance with a bullet through his heart? He did travel it, you say, but nobody will believe it. And then, they'll ask, why were you afraid to come out and own up to it? You can see what kind of fix you'd land yourself in."

It was no trouble to see. People would find out that there had been shooting in his camp. Luce might tell them. If he cautioned her not to, she would wonder what he was trying to dodge. Then the dogs would find the dead man, and she would think he had murdered him. "I won't leave him here," Clay said. "I took him for somebody else, or I wouldn't have shot to hit him. But he was stealin', and I had a right to. If they don't believe the truth they wouldn't believe a lie. Let's pack him out of this, and I'll go down for the wagon."

Burdon said he was being sensible, and that he would be a man yet. "They might be induced to believe a lie at that," he added, thoughtfully. "If we could find the Lunds somebody to hang that wouldn't be missed—" He pulled a spray of locust-bloom, twirled it, and tossed it into the mud. "This Wade Shiveley might be an idea, if he was handled properly. He wouldn't camp where I told him to, and he had all that list of things fixed up that he was going to do to you. You say he's killed two men already."

"Two men," Clay confirmed. He didn't think it necessary to mention that Wade laid claim to only one and had a fairly good plea of self-defence in that. "His brother in a fight, and an old horse-race gambler that he waylaid and robbed. He got eight hundred dollars out of that."

"I used to get a thousand when the mining business was good," Burdon said. "That was less than it was worth. Anybody that will shoot a fellow creature for less needs hanging. If you're willing to swear to these two killings of his, we'll break him of sucking eggs for the rest of his natural life. You know the names and dates and places, and all that truck?"

Clay hung back. He began to see what emotional strain had hitherto kept him from noticing. Burdon was still pretty well ginned, and the vehemence of his grudge against Wade Shiveley brought it out on him. He was actually willing to hang Wade Shiveley for refusing to camp where he had been told to—so willing that he lost sight of everything except that one object. And there might be other consequences. "If I testify against him, he'll bust loose and testify back against me. And then the court will hold me and look up my record across the mountains, and where will I be? And people know I shot this morning. Luce knows it."

"She knows you shot from camp, too," Burdon pointed out. "This man wasn't killed within pistol-range of your camp. The court won't hold you, because there won't be any court. Nobody is going to ride a hundred and forty miles to the county seat to take in a man that's got two murders on him already. We can handle a case like that right out here, and if he don't like it what did he stick himself onto this train for? He certainly wasn't invited. He won't accuse you of anything, either. I'll fix that with Lavran Baker before the trial starts. Have you got papers on that buckskin mare?"

"I told you she belonged to him," Clay said. "I have got a bill of sale on her, though. Come to think, I had her brand smeared, too. Look here, we can't make a thing like this work. How can we prove anything on him?"

"We'll prove all we need to," Burdon promised. He took out his flask, squinted appraisingly through the wicker, and emptied the contents into the mud to show that he meant business. "If it don't work, you can tell 'em the truth about it, and I'll take the blame for putting you up to this. Go saddle your mare and wait for me. Tell your girl there's been a murder up in the pasture and you're deputized to help run in the man that did it. We'll teach that bushwhacking son of a bitch that he can't go killing people around this train whenever he feels like it."

When Clay got to camp, Luce had the wagon-seat dismounted and breakfast spread on it. To his relief, she took the news of the killing very calmly.

"That worthless Lund ox," she said, with scorn. "I shouldn't think they'd need to arrest anybody for getting rid of him. You're sure you didn't hit him with a wild shot when you were celebrating this morning?"

"No pistol could shoot clear through a man three hundred yards off," Clay said, and wondered thankfully that a simple statement of irrelevant fact could make such a fool of the truth. "We know who shot him, and I've got to help grab him before he breaks camp. We'll have to take him down to the head of the train, so I may not be back till late."

She straightened up from arranging plates on the wagon-seat. "You've got to help?" she repeated. "Why? Who is it you're going to arrest? Clay, is this some trouble you're in that you're afraid to tell me about? Look at me. Is it?"

For a moment he was afraid she had guessed something from

his looks. Then he understood. She remembered that he had left the hop-yards ahead of trouble, and she was afraid he might be planning to do that again. Her guess was so far short of the awful reality that he laughed. "I won't go over the hill on you," he assured her. "This really is an arrest I've got to help with. You might remember who the man is. The day I first saw you, there'd been an old horse-race gambler killed and robbed up Shoestring. This is the man that done it, and he's—we think he's the man that killed Isaac Lund. You can come along and watch us take him, if you want to."

That quieted her. Her voice went down almost to a whisper. "That man again? And now he's killed another man, and they'll hang him. Is that what they'll do?"

"That's what they'll do," Clay said, hoping fervently that he was forecasting correctly. "I'll saddle your horse for you if you want to come along."

She sat down beside him on the ground and touched her cheek against his shoulder. "I don't. Only for a minute I was afraid. Take hold of my wrist." She put it out, and he tightened his fingers on it. She never asked him to do that except when there was a horror of loneliness on her. When it struck her, she was like a little girl afraid of the dark. "Sometimes I see how little you need me," she said. "How independent you are and how you can have a good time whether I'm with you or not. Then I get nervous for fear you'll see it, too, and leave. Without telling me. But now it's all right. Let go, and try to take some interest in the breakfast I've fixed for you."

The delegation of justice-doers didn't keep him waiting long. They had Burdon's wagon, and Burdon saluted him from the front seat, looking very fresh and picnicky, with Rube Cutlack and old Bushnell standing behind, holding on. They were both wet from the shoulders up from being dipped in the watering-trough, and they looked injured about the bumping of the wagon and mad about everything. Bushnell had a hickory ax-handle stuck down the front of his shirt, and it kept whacking his chin whenever the wagon hit a rock. Clay turned in to ride with them, and Burdon waved

him back and told him to give them a few minutes' lead and then
come on at a trot. When the wagon went out of sight around the
turn, he spurred up and racked after it, and Luce stood beside
their new wagon and waved good-by to him before he went out
of sight too.

Wade Shiveley was camped alongside an old branding-corral
partly overgrown with wild yellow roses. He didn't look much
changed except that some dropped petals were stuck in his hair
and on his shoulders, and that the red of his face was patched with
paler areas where Drusilla had scalded him. His voice was as
bawly and as hell-roaring as usual. Not understanding that Burdon
wanted a fight, he showed a good deal of anxiety to start one,
braying that if they didn't get out and let him alone he would
fence-rail the whole damned boiling of them. He saw Clay coming,
and stopped short. For a moment the whole group stood in a silence
so complete that it seemed religious. Burdon keyed his voice low
and spoke without moving. "We'll have to put you under arrest
for murder," he said. "That young man in the road is a witness
against you. I warn you that anything you say will ——"

Shiveley paid no attention. His eyes were fixed on the road.
"It's him, by God!" he yelled, and jumped back out of Burdon's
reach and drew his gun. He shot twice, fast. The buckskin mare
squatted like a dog, and Clay keeled back and felt both bullets
whip wind close to his hat. He grabbed out his pistol, Shiveley
cut down again, and Burdon shot through the folds of his coat at
a range of about five feet and broke Shiveley's elbow. He watched
Shiveley's gun drop, and kicked it across the grass and picked
it up. "That'll be all for him, I expect," he told Rube and old
Bushnell. "Let him alone a few minutes."

The mare got back on her legs, but nothing else moved. Wade
Shiveley held his arm straightened as if still sighting a pistol,
and watched it sag down from the joint like a broken fence-picket.
It drooped slowly, a couple of inches at a time. After a little,
blood ran off his fingers and dripped into the yellow roses, and he
let the whole arm drop and stared around at the men.

"God! boys," he said. His voice trembled. "God! she's shot off!
I can't move it, and there ain't a particle of feeling in it! God!
if I'm crippled for life ——"

He gave way at the knees and sat down. Burdon got a rope out of the wagon. "There'll be feeling enough in a minute or two," he promised. The effect of being shot with a heavy bullet is to numb one's nerves, much like a local anæsthetic. When they revive, they yell a great deal louder than if they had stayed awake all the way through. Burdon tossed the loop of his rope over Shiveley's feet, and sailed a couple of half-hitches on after it. "A man that's as fond of shooting other people as you are ought to find out how it feels, anyway. And you resisted arrest."

"You're a damned liar!" Shiveley said, automatically. Then he thought the rumpus over, and sweat broke out on his upper lip. He didn't see the beauty of Burdon's timing, but he did see its danger.

"Look here, boys, that wasn't anything but a misunderstanding. This damned kid robbed me and lied to me and played it low down on me, and when I seen him there in the road I got so mad——"

"You got so mad you tried to murder him, didn't you?" Burdon prompted him, coldly. The fact that his man was wounded didn't chill his enmity a particle. His eye was as pitiless as a hawk's. "You didn't want him to testify about them two men you killed across the mountains, did you? One murder today wasn't enough for a bad man like you, was it? What did you camp here for, when I told you to go on down to the head of the train? You took me for some damned old side-hill apple-knocker that you could run over to suit yourself, didn't you? Shut up, or I'll whale you over the head. Let's see if that arm of yours needs doctoring before we load you in the wagon."

They tied up his arm above the wound and loaded him, and rolled down the road toward the head of the train. He sat on one side of the wagon-bed, holding his wounded arm tenderly and staring at Burdon's back as if he couldn't understand how there could be such a man. Rube Cutlack and old Bushnell stood behind the seat, watching him. On the floor-boards was stretched Isaac Lund, his dead face turned up to the clear dark-blue sky and jolting reproachfully sideways whenever the wagon hit a rock. Clay followed behind on the mare. So far the plan had been a success, but he felt no sense of triumph. It was not his game or his grudge any longer. It was Clark Burdon's, and he felt sorry for Wade

Shiveley in spite of everything for having ignorantly got a man like Clark Burdon set against him.

One thing that happened on the road interested him because it showed how blind and aimless the movement of people in that bad year was. A train of about fifteen wagons came plugging along the grassed-over road, heading west against them, and they turned out to let it pass. All the wagons were sun-shrunk and gaping at the joints, with paint bleached by strong light and covered with white dust. The horses were little and long-haired and ribby and shod only on the hind feet. It was a sagebrush line-up, both in looks and in temperament, for the wagons, instead of pulling past, hauled up in a bunch and stopped. Men and women and kids stood up and gawked out at the dead man and at Wade Shiveley roped into the back of the wagon with his arm dripping blood. An elderly couple in the front of the column explained that they were five separate families, though they were all inter-related. Their name, with a few insignificant exceptions, like sons-in-law and accidental children, was Carstairs. They had been holding down hay-land and pasture south of the Burnt River Mountains, and they were giving it up because they had run out of seed and feed and money and credit. Since the Coast country was a region they knew nothing about, they thought it would be better to live in, so they were moving to it. It would have been a first-class chance for them to have collected information about it, but all they wanted to know about was the dead man in the wagon. What his name was and where he was from, did he have any folks, how many and what ages they were, how he had got killed and by whom.

"Him," Burdon said, and motioned behind. "We're taking him down to the head of the train for a trial. You're blocking the road."

The elderly man said he knew it. He drew his finger around his neck and pointed skyward inquiringly. Burdon nodded, and said, intending to be discouraging, that it would probably be another week before that happened. First they would have to hold a funeral for the murdered man, and then they would have to wait till his relatives felt able to interest themselves in retaliatory ceremonies. People began climbing down from the rear wagons and ganging around the elderly man, and the elderly woman said, wistfully, that she hadn't seen a real funeral with mourners since the lawsy knew when. Then they all started arguing and muttering among themselves, and took so long at it that Burdon invited them to either move on or clear the road so he could. "Are you going or coming, or don't you know?" he inquired.

"That's what we're a-tryin' to decide," the elderly man explained. "Where-at are you people all strikin' for, mister?"

Burdon said they had no particular locality in mind. Anywhere that there was open land, with earth and grass and wood and water. The Carstairses conferred further.

"The Burnt River Mountains is your country," said the elderly man. "You couldn't have described it closer if you stood lookin' at it. And with people that knows the ground like we do, you could have your whole outfit located in a month better than they could do it alone in a year. There ain't a better feedin'-country this side of the mountains, and I'll guarantee it. You reckon you could induce your outfit to go there?"

"It sounds possible, all except the locating," Burdon said. "You can't help much with that if you're going to the Coast."

The elderly man let off his brake and picked up his whip. "We ain't," he said. "We'll go back there with you. Hell! we got homesick for the damned country talkin' about it, and I wouldn't miss that trial and hangin' for forty Coasts."

Chapter XVI

THERE was a social ordinance, of which everybody knew the existence if not the precise terms, against burying a man in ground that wasn't a regularly-constituted graveyard. Looking Glass Flat had none, so they pulled away from it with Isaac Lund's body in one wagon and Wade Shiveley roped and under guard in another. They passed several families of settlers wandering around looking for land that they had paid a couple of hundred dollars apiece to a location agent to pick out for them, and they passed a herd of eighty-odd scrub steers being driven to market by forty-odd mounted Indians, all with dark complexions and exhausted expressions, as if each was trying to look the tiredest. The cattle-driving job did not require any such crew of men. A couple of good hands could have managed it easily. But there were no two men whom the Indians felt able to trust to sell the cattle and get back with all the money, so they all came along to make sure. The women followed behind in buckboards with camp equipment, and though they were dark, too, a good many of the younger ones were extremely pretty.

It was these Indians who claimed Looking Glass Flat as part of their ancestral territory. Once they had been a powerful set of people, who had managed to maintain a distinct language, religion, culture, and set of taboos and traditions against surrounding tribes for a good many hundred years. But that had all gone to pieces, a few light waves of casual philanthropy from the white race having proved more destructive in sixty-odd years than outright hostility from the red had in centuries. The Indians were of an amiable disposition, easy to get acquainted with when treated courteously, and first their country had been traversed by French-Canadian fur-traders, who liked them and intermarried with them to have a place on their trap-line to sleep. Later came the American missionaries, who, though not in favor of intermarriage themselves, imported retinues of Kanaka flunkies from the Hawaiian Islands to prove that they really could convert somebody, and the

Kanakas intermarried busily and hatched mobs of children. Still later several crews of Chinese tie-cutters, imported by the railroad, stirred themselves into the mixture, along with a few caravans of horse-trading gipsies, some Mexican sheep-herders, and two or three early-day negroes who, to judge by the general pigmentation of the tribe, must have been miraculously powerful and persistent. All was accomplished in the name of peace, friendship, religion, and racial understanding, and the result was these cattle-drivers, of whom the men were all thieves and the women all prostitutes.

The morals of the women may have been Nature's way of evening things up. There were few white youngsters around that country who hadn't been enticed to a two-dollar round of inter-racial dalliance at some period or other, and the ones who fell generally packed away a tangible memento of the occasion, which sometimes got cured and sometimes didn't. Several girls tossed coquettish challenges at the settlers' wagons, and some of the men wanted to pitch camp and get up a horserace; but they found no customers. The wagons left them and dropped out of the well-watered mountain foothills into the scant grass and granite bluffs of the Deschutes River.

Close to the water it was beautiful; the dark blue camas patches in bloom and the mock-orange and wild cherry flowering over the swift black water. Over it stood tall straight-up-and-down bluffs where hawks nested to catch fish from the rapids, and one with a two-foot salmon still wiggling in his claws flew so close over Clay's head that he stood up in the wagon and tried to kill it with the lash of his whip. The best he could manage was to cut loose a tail-feather and scare his horses, and he sat down and sawed them to a walk, wondering at himself. In one wagon ahead was the unburied body of a man he had killed. In another was a wounded man against whom he was scheduled to give evidence so the other settlers would be induced to hang him. Yet he had had fun deviling the hawk. He felt sneaking about it and humble in the presence of Luce, who could not have shed her conscience so off-handedly. When anything bothered her, she showed it.

Nothing was bothering her now. Whatever had been on her conscience all winter was letting go of her. She stared after the hawk, holding the wagon-seat with both hands so the jouncing

wouldn't pitch her out, and she looked as if she would like to jump
and grab the salmon out of its claws.

"You could have made him drop that fish," she accused. "It
would have been fun to have it for supper. Next time you let me
handle that whip, if that's the best you can do."

The surest sign of her carefreeness was that she was solemn
about it. People playing some game to keep from thinking about
more serious matters are inclined to be loud and rip-roarishly
mirthful in a spirit of defiance. But those who play entirely for the
fun of it usually go at it as gravely as a board of church elders
breeding a sixty-dollar sow. Children at play are the longest-faced
of all, the most passionately serious, because they have nothing but
the play to worry them. Clay handed her the whip and remarked
that her spirits seemed to have improved. She looked startled, as
if she had been caught doing something she shouldn't, and then admitted it. "This is new country, and I like it," she said. "And we
know you didn't kill Isaac Lund with that wild shot of yours,
and you got back safe from arresting that man. Always before I've
had to wonder how things were coming out. Now I know, and it's
better."

They were nearing the river where there was a toll bridge. The
road under the horses' feet was black shellrock, speckled in places
with yellow-and-black snapdragons, jarring and dripping spray
from the cold wind off the big rapids. Water glittered in the air
and settled on the harness and the coats of the horses. Another hawk
went overhead, and though he was twenty feet up, she threw the
whiplash at him, laughing when it popped close enough to make
him flop and dodge sideways. The horses jumped, and she almost
fell out. "What would you have done if I hadn't got back safe?"
Clay inquired, when she got settled again. "From that arrest, I
mean?"

What he wanted to know was whether she would go back to
her father if anything happened to him, but she misunderstood.
"That would have depended on how badly you got hurt," she said,
too intent on the hawk to follow shades of meaning. "I'd have held
Clark Burdon responsible for you, and if it was serious I'd have
hurt him. I'd have had a right to, because he had no right to make

you go. Look, the hawk's going down to his nest. Drive slow, and
maybe he'll fly back over us."

"He'll be in a lot of danger if he does," Clay said. "You couldn't
reach him with that whip if you waited here a month. You imagine
things are easy to do because you've never done 'em. How would
you have handled Clark Burdon if I'd have got killed? You don't
know, do you?"

He was trying to make her see, without saying it straight out,
that his going to help with that arrest was nobody's responsibility
but his own, and that she was too ignorant of such business to
mix herself into it. But she took her eyes from the hawk and
looked at him, and she did not seem ignorant at all. Her face
looked as it had the morning she shot the elk from the door of
their cabin on the coast.

"Of course I know," she said. "Do you think I'd be afraid to
kill him if he had got you killed?" She took a deep breath, and
shook the whiplash out again. "Here comes the hawk. Hold back
on the reins, and I'll make him drop that salmon yet. I'll bet you
anything you dare on it."

She tilted back, waiting. He studied her, trying to guess what
she would be like now that nothing troubled her, and feeling too
bashful of her strange gaiety to try and see.

"It's a bet," he said. "You'll lose, and if you do I'm liable to collect right here."

She tossed the whiplash and missed, and said she expected him
to collect. "But not here, not with that dead man ahead and those
old people blubbering and that man you arrested waiting for whatever you're going to do with him. You wouldn't want all those
things behind you? We'll only need to wait till tomorrow, maybe,
and they'll all be settled and you'll be rid of them."

It was precisely because the settlement was so near that he didn't
want to wait. How could he tell whether he might get caught in
it? If Shiveley blurted out something, if the men happened to be in
a humor for investigation, he could get caught.

"We could leave the train right here," he said. "We could drop
out and leave 'em to settle their rumpuses without botherin' us.
What do we need to bother about 'em for, anyway?"

She put the whip away and said no, that wouldn't do at all.

"That's what I've been doing all my life, getting to know people and then having to drop away from them and never see them again. Lots of times I've ridden past places where people were being buried, and wondered who they were and what their families were like, and you don't know how it feels to be here with people I know well enough to feel sorry for. We're not going to leave them."

They kept on in the road, and struck the river at mid-rapids. There was a salmon-run on, with a bunch of Chinook Indians camped in the rocks to snag the salmon when they jumped the falls. The toll bridge was closed with a big wooden bar, chained and padlocked, and since the bridge-tender's house was empty, they got out to watch the fishing until he showed up. It was a long-winded, got-three-years-to-do-this-in kind of process, with most of the action being provided by the salmon unassisted. Below the falls was a box canyon, with spray booming up into the sun like a heavy thundershower walking across plowed ground. All the men of the camp were hung down over the cliff on ropes, close enough to the water so they could almost dabble their moccasins in it. Each man held a gaff-pole about twelve feet long with a big eight-inch sturgeon-hook on the end of it. When the spray didn't cloud the water too heavy, one could see the salmon lying in it, noses upstream, as thick as shingles on the roof of a barn. The Indians paid no attention to them. They watched the spray under the falls, and from that, every eight or ten minutes, a salmon would throw himself straight into the air some eight feet and fall back with a helpless smack. There was neither grace nor intelligence about the effort. Not half of the salmon ever got halfway up the fall, and most of them didn't come anywhere near where it was. Falling, the heavy body would hit the water sideways and float for a second dazed and helpless, and the Indians would get to work on it with their gaff-poles, chopping one another out of the way like children in a game of shinny, and twirling on their ropes at a rate that ought to have brought the whole mob down with seasickness. The pole that snagged the fish would be passed up to a squaw on top of the cliff, and the men would stop twirling and glare at the water again without paying the slightest attention to one another. None of them ever looked up to see which squaw grabbed the gaff-pole when it was passed up. Evidently the right one was always on deck, for there was never any trouble among them.

Once taken in charge, the salmon was either beheaded and cut into strips to dry or else lugged to camp whole to trade with visiting mountain Indians for watermelons, patent medicine, or tanned deer-hides. These river Indians were a good deal uglier and smellier than the Looking Glass cross-breeds, and far less intelligent and sociable. Their manners didn't lack much of being downright insulting, which had probably preserved them from being crossed out into French-Canadian, Chinese, Kanaka, Ethiopian, horse-thief, venereal diseases, and racial degeneracy.

There was nothing specially interesting about watching them, once one got the swing of it, but it was the kind of thing that a man goes on watching after it has palled on him completely. Clay started the team twice and let them stop again for fear he might miss something, and there were half a dozen wagons stalled at the bridge with people waiting for the bridge-tender to come, who looked sneakingly disappointed when he did. He had been up the river, planting out a young peach-orchard in ground that, as he pointed it out, looked to be a mixture of conglomerate and red clay. He was a large, bright-faced old gentleman with a kind of babyish expression and a ten-cent straw hat yanked down so tight that it wiggled up and down when he talked, and he agreed cheerfully that a peach-sprout set out in that ground was liable to have a tough childhood.

"That ain't no never-minds to me, though," he said. "I ain't plantin' 'em to eat, I'm plantin' 'em to sell, on account of this old railroad that's fixin' to build up here. Old E. H. Harriman is a-buildin' her, and it ain't been two months sence I talked to him right here at this old bridge. Face to face, just like I'm a-talkin' to you. Well, what would he be doin' out in this shirt-tail end of nothing unless it was to build a railroad? And when he does, where else can he build her but right up this canyon? That peach-orchard of mine will lay right on his right of way, and he'll have to buy her all or he won't git a foot of her. You know how much orchard land sells for on the market? A thousand dollars an acre. Twenty acres in that patch, boys, and when I git the cash for it, I'm leavin'. This country's due for a boom, sure as hell. You ought to pick you out a patch of ground and wait for her. The canyon's all took up, but them hills is just a-bulgin' with fertility. Raise anything, and the more people they is here the surer that old railroad is to come here. And then you can sell out and hunt you up a decent place to live."

The hills had a fair stand of bunch grass on them, which meant nothing. Bunch grass grows anywhere in the spring if stock will let it alone. Clay remarked that the ground looked shallow, and that he hoped to find a place so much to his liking that he wouldn't want to sell it. The bridge-tender laughed at his simplicity.

"Then you better turn around and go back where you come from," he advised. "People don't come to this country to live, they come here to make money. The ones that don't make it, they stay because they got to. She's settled up close now, but you wait till old E. H. Harriman gits down the stakes for his railroad, and you'll ride a horse around these hills for a month and never see a soul except these Indians. Let 'em have the damn place. They like it, I reckon."

He unlocked the bridge, and collected fifty cents per horse from the settlers, receiving the money in a cigar-box to show that there was nothing personal about it. Only one outfit could cross at a time because the stringers were shaky, and the man who owned it was in Congress and therefore under such heavy expenses that he couldn't afford repairs. The reason he was in Congress was that the county kept threatening to build a competitive public bridge and let people cross free, and he had to keep hold of a good deal of political influence to prevent them doing it. His system for holding his constituency together was sweeping and simple. He owned all the wool warehouses around the upper country, and when anybody started to electioneer against him, all his superintendents got orders not to handle the sonofagun's wool any more. If he hired a freighter to haul it to the railroad for him, orders went out to the warehouses that the freighter was to do no more hauling for them. Under such management, things stayed pretty well in line, and the bridge, in slack times when there were a good many people on the road, took in on an average of four hundred dollars a week, counting sheep at a nickel a head and cattle at a dime. A man with brains enough to keep up a business like that was a good man to have in Congress. His ability to take care of his own interests proved that he was qualified to look out for other people's. The public issues which he had dedicated himself to were to acquaint the provincial East with the ravishing beauties of Western scenery and climate, and to levy an import tariff of two or three hundred per cent on foreign wool. He also believed that the United States had done perfectly right to separate from Great Britain, and he wasn't afraid to come right out and say so. He was a smart man and a profound statesman.

"You can see that the country don't need to worry, with a man like that at the head of it," Clark Burdon said. He had caught up while they were waiting, and, since he couldn't have been elected anything, he always went out of his way to take digs at people who could. "This bridge must have cost him almost as much to build as he makes out of it in a whole day and a half."

"He's careful," the bridge-tender agreed. "He's got to be, with times what they are. Right now, he's had to shut down all his warehouses till he sees which way wool's a-goin', and it's tied things up some. But a man's got to deal for himself around here, or he'll be stuck here for life. Look at them Indians. No guile about them, hey? Do they look like they had any prospects of movin' to any place that's fit to live in?"

He proceeded, on small encouragement, to tell them about the Indians. Racially, they were a fringe of the species that held down most of the Columbia River and a good deal of the coastline, and they practiced, or at least had practiced within his memory, the ceremony of the potlatch. It was a species of performance that might very well have been adopted by more substantial white families in cities, for it was nothing more than a sort of showing-off bee in which each Indian undertook to demonstrate how much wealthier he was than anybody else in camp. They would hang ornaments on themselves till they jangled like a dray-team, they would throw presents at everybody in sight except, perhaps, members of their own wickyup circle, and they would stagger around wobble-kneed as a dramatic presentation of the fact that their excess of wealth was almost too much to carry. Big kettles of food would be cooked up and given away till everybody had guzzled themselves pop-eyed, and the rest would be dumped on the ground or thrown in the river. In old days they had run to even greater ostentation. It was the custom then for a man to marry all the women who would have him, and they were something of an asset because they helped with salmon-drying and produced children to join the line of fish-snaggers. So a couple of chiefs got to bragging against one another, and one of them, to show what a spendthrift he was, pulled a pistol and shot one of his wives dead. The other chief, a little put out because he hadn't thought of it first, shot two of his wives, and the first chief shot three of his, and so on till they ran out of ammunition. That, he ended, was the kind of people they were, and plenty good enough for the country, too.

It was a fact that the Indians looked incapable of such a flow of spirits, and Luce remarked that surely some of the wives must have raised some objection while the shooting was going on.

"Shucks, no," the bridge-tender said. "The dead ones couldn't, and the live ones was tickled to git 'em thinned out. But there ain't any of that polygamy business any more. Let one of the men git to lallygaggin' another woman, and what happens? His squaw waits till he's swung down into that canyon, and she hacks his rope off on him. They're afraid to be immoral, and they ain't got brains enough to be dishonest, so there ain't a better-behaved set of people outside of a Christian Endeavor meetin'. And what does it git 'em?"

It seemed much the same order of morality to go around bragging about wealth that had been snagged out of a river as to brag about what was exapected to be swindled out of E. H. Harriman's railroad with a right of way through a fraudulent peach-orchard. But the bridge-tender wasn't bothered about ethics. Somebody was going to hand him a fortune, and he didn't perturb himself over whether he had earned it or not, because he felt entirely confident that he deserved it. He scarcely showed interest when one of the Carstairses mentioned, with considerable pleasure over giving out the news, that the train was packing a man who had to be tried for murder, and could he advise them what authorities they ought to apply to about it?

"There's a deppity sheriff over at Dead Dog," he said, indifferently. "He might take the case off your hands if he ain't too busy snortin' wind into his worthless real-estate boom. If you're sure you don't want to locate here, I'll git back to plantin' peaches."

None of the people from the Coast stopped, and none of them felt entirely cheerful going on. Something was wrong with a country where the white population had settled not to live, but to get rich, and where they were expecting to do it by means of a swindle. Not that there was anything wrong with the ambition. Nobody would have picked that canyon as a pleasant place to live at any time of year; the cliffs reflected all the heat in summer and shut out all the sun in winter; and nobody could blame a man for wanting to raise money, even by fraud, to get out on. The trouble was that the fraud sounded impractical and weakminded. It sounded like a little boy digging out a coyote-hole and gabbling confidently about how he would spend the bounty on the coyotes before he knew for sure how far the hole went or whether there was anything in it.

But for really high hopes and a genuinely finished contempt for probabilities, the river canyon wasn't a circumstance alongside of Dead Dog. It was on a high, handsomely situated plateau, as windy as politicians' alley in hell, covered with a deep stand of grass run through with great patches of wild flowers. There were blue lobelias and red wild pansies, portulacas and snapdragons, orange-colored wild hollyhocks and delicate pink-white rock-roses, bird-bills and lupin and wild sunflowers, white-blue wild iris and spreads of intense blue foxgloves so vast and blinding with color that a man could hardly hold his eyes level to see across them. They shook and shadowed magnificently in the wind, which was strong and intensely cold. Sometimes a dark cloud would drag across a high point on the horizon and dump a sprinkling of rain off into the long grass, chilling the air still more. The reason for the low temperature was that it was sheep-shearing time. In that country it scarcely ever failed to turn off scorching hot about the last of April, so the sheep started sloughing their winter's wool before the shearers could harvest it. As a consequence, everybody would rush crews in to get it clipped and stored, whereupon the weather would switch back to freezing and chill a large number of naked sheep to death. Big flocks drifted around in the billowing grass, which did them no good because they had to bunch against the cold, and their newly-exposed whiteness and solemnity of expression made them look a good deal like a bunch of pot-bellied old women caught out with nothing on but their union suits and trying to remember where they had put their corsets. Few herders were in sight. You could tell where their night camps were by the white flags stuck up on sticks to keep coyotes from wandering off with lambs after dark, but the herders themselves were mostly gone down to the shearing-corral outside of Dead Dog to make a social afternoon of it.

The herders didn't exhibit any enthusiasm for real estate, but they did show the kind of spirit the boom had found in that country to work on. There were about thirty of them assembled in the corral, and the meeting could be heard quite a distance. Due to their being accustomed to loneliness, all of them talked at once in a kind of monotonous bawl like deaf people, and nobody paid the slightest attention to anybody else. They sat around in a circle, passing a three-gallon jug from hand to hand, and their sole form of entertainment, outside of talking, seemed to consist in getting odd couples of men drunk enough to quarrel, then sobering them up so they could fight, and then liquoring them again so they would shake hands and swap complimentary speeches and apologies. A couple of them would rise from the circle, stalk over to the watering-trough, and slosh their heads, a good deal like a couple of old hens drinking. Then they would post off and clout one another till both fell over exhausted, and, having been dosed with more strychnine-whisky, they would sit up and start swapping compliments. "So you're this-yer Ep Carter I've heerd all the talk about. Well, sir, I didn't ketch the name at first and I'm powerful pleased I didn't. I'd never have tied into you if I'd had any idee who it was, and this'll certainly furnish me somethin' to tell around, all how I stood up to Ep Carter for a solid forty-two minutes."—"Standin' up as long as you done? Well, shuckins, mister, ef you'd stood up ary longer you'd had me broke plumb in two! I laid I could lick ary man around here that acted ungentlemanly—and I kin, too, if he'll stand up and declare hisself and let me git this thumb of mine pulled back into joint—but you had me a-reachin' for a hold on the dirt from the first lick! I'm mighty glad this fight happened, because it's got me acquainted with a man I can respect. The way she feels,

I believe you busted one of my ribs, what did you say your name
was?"—"Collins, sir, Hardee Collins, and I wouldn't be surprised
if that last kick of yourn hadn't busted my nose. She's a-swellin' to
beat hell, but she's worth it if it draws you and me closeter together.
Put 'er there, Mr. Carter, and be keerful of that middle knuckle,
because I can feel a loose bone grindin' in it."—And so on, very
bellery and sloppy, while a couple more candidates were getting
themselves rubbed up to hit for the watering-trough and start a
new fight.

Mostly the fights lasted around three-quarters of an hour apiece,
without rounds and usually without any decision, because the men
were too drunk to be knocked out. They did it all out of pure high
spirits, and they were all American sheep-herders. Foreigners
worked at the trade in that country, too, mostly Scotch Highland-
ers in the north and Spanish Basques in the south, but such people
were never capable of such courtliness, or, for that matter, of such
foolishness. You have to know a country intimately to have lost all
fear of it and all doubt about your ability to survive in it, before
you can whole-heartedly make a jackass of yourself in it. That
may be one reason why a man does badly if he stays all his life in
the place he was born, and tolerably well if he picks up and moves
to one altogether strange to him.

The sheep-herders were only a temporary lapse from the spirit
of temporal enterprise that was working through the country like
a fever. Dead Dog Station was nothing much for a town, its principal attractions as a coming center of population seeming to be a
windmill watering-trough, a feed-yard for freight-teams, and a
combination hotel, barroom, and restaurant in which a skinny
woman with a hard black eye and several bawling children served a
fifty-cent dinner of tough mutton-steaks, fried potatoes, and
canned corn, topped off by a dessert of canned pears. Such a diet
for a week would have colicked a bitch wolf, but none of the diners
complained about it. Even the freighters ate it uncomplainingly,
though they kicked freely about everything else—scant work, star-
vation wages, bad climate, foul weather, monotonous scenery, and
horse feed that was one-third dirt and two-thirds weeds. Afterwards they explained that she was Gentle Annie, a forthright spirit
of the district with a considerable name for disciplining exacting

patrons. Once, when a traveling-man had requested a glass of milk, they related, she had opened the bosom of her dress and drawn him a brimming beaker of her own personal lacteal fluid, and then stood over him with a cleaver while he downed it, and they also told that during the balance of his stay he quenched his thirst with nothing but whisky because he didn't want to risk having her draw him a glass of water.

That was the kind of management the hotel-saloon-restaurant had—rough, old-fashioned, a little forbidding, maybe, but efficient and anxious to accommodate. Outside things were different. White survey-stakes were specked out fifty feet apart across the sunflower and sagebrush and lupin, and at more economical intervals were neat white posts flaunting such street names as Pringle Avenue and Railroad Street and Orchard Boulevard. A billboard which had been faced the wrong way to the wind and was threatening to blow down announced the development to be Pringleville, the Gateway to Eastern Oregon, Home sites on Easy Terms, Industrial Locations Free. Parties interested were invited to lay their cases before the J. B. Pringle Real Estate Company, whose offices adjoined the hotel dining-room.

It turned out that Mr. Pringle was the husband of the hard-eyed woman who threatened drummers with a cleaver, and that she had sited his office so she could keep an eye on him. He was large and fleshy, and he wore a boiled shirt and a set of finger-nail marks on the left-hand side of his face which there was no need to explain. He also wore a deputy sheriff's star with a spot of fried egg hardened into the "E," and he was a man of enterprise and imagination. With little encouragement and no reason that anybody could see, he was spreading the new Pringleville around over enough country to accommodate a population of around thirty thousand people. Where they were to come from, or why, he hadn't bothered to figure out, but he was not going to subject them to the discomfort of sleeping two on a lot when they got there. Even Pringleville didn't represent the end of his vision. Beyond it, up the side hill, was another billboard announcing the release for public sale of the Pringle Home Garden and Orchard Tracts, five acres per tract, which were destined to supply the seething thousands down in Pringleville with fruits, vegetables, and dairy products, and the

J. B. Pringle Real Estate Company with revenue at the rate of eight hundred dollars per tract, payable either in cash or on time.

The whole project was so stately that some of the settlers hesitated to disturb Mr. Pringle's reflections with so simple a thing as handing him a murderer to take care of. He could be seen through the dusty window, making marks on a big blueprint with a piece of lumber-chalk so he wouldn't make a mistake and sell the same lot twice or peddle off an industrial site for a residence. Clark Burdon would have pulled out without bothering him, but the Carstairs outfit didn't intend to leave anybody in ignorance of the interesting load they were packing. They pulled up, blocking the road, and told everybody about it from the hotel porch to the front entrance of the feed-yard. The Carstairs elder did the talking, with his wife chipping in remarks when she thought his narrative gift was falling short.

"Dead man in the wagon up yon," he explained, as if it was something he wouldn't like to tell everybody. "Shot. And the feller roped up behind, that's the man that killed him. We want to know wher'bouts around here we ort to deliver him. We got witnesses, and it looks mighty black for him."

"Witnesses!" Mrs. Carstairs fetched in good and loud. "Why don't you explain to these people how it happened, in place of all this doodaddle about witnesses? Why don't you tell 'em this man is a desperate outlaw that's already killed a half a dozen men around what was the name of the place? Jere Carstairs, what was the name of that place?"

Her husband mumbled, trying to discourage her, that he couldn't see what difference it made, and Mrs. Carstairs remembered, missing the correct location not much over a hundred miles, that it was Coos Bay. "And now he's killed one of the finest young men in the whole train, hard-workin' and well behaved, with aged parents dependent on him, and you ort to heard the carryin'-on they done when he was brought in. He was their oldest, and they'd banked all their expectations on him. What was their names? Jere Carstairs, you know what them people's names is. What makes you set there like a dummy?"

She knew well enough the type of minutely detailed information that townspeople around those water-trough stations expected trav-

elers to volunteer about any sensational case. The men stared at
Wade Shiveley, who said it was all a damned lie, and at Clark
Burdon, who hated to be stared at, and inquired if there was any
reward out. They weren't townspeople at all, it seemed, but itinerant
sheep-shearers, lambers, freighters waiting to haul out wool, and a
couple or three traveling-peddlers who had camped there to swap
merchandise with the Indians. Finding there was no reward, they
advised the Carstairses to apply to Mr. Pringle, and everybody
glanced across at the office where he was. He bridled, stuffed his
shirt-bosom into his pants, and labeled eight lots on Pringle Avenue
as withdrawn from sale to be used for a public auditorium, opera-
house, and social center while the Carstairs men were climbing
down from their wagons to go and tell him about it. Clark Burdon
kicked off his brake to go on without them, giving it as his opinion
that Mr. Pringle didn't look capable of taking care of himself, let
alone of a criminal with a shooting record.

The freighters agreed that he might be right about that, but they
advised him to hold on. Mr. Pringle might be this and he might be
that, but if they left without giving him a chance at their murderer
he would probably feel slighted in his dignity, and then there was
no telling what he might do. Possibly he would telephone to the
county seat and swear out a complaint against the settlers for
illegally detaining a man without a warrant, or for vagrancy, or
anything that came into his head. It could do no harm to see him,
because it wasn't likely that he would do anything, they agreed.
Then they all strung out in the direction of the Indian camp to
watch the squaws trade wool with the peddlers. There was nothing
especially interesting about it; the squaws always failed in their
attempts to cheat and the peddlers always succeeded in theirs; but
it was the first tribe of Indians east of the mountains in which the
women tended to all the business. Female domination seemed to be
a kind of tradition in that sagebrush country, and maybe the country
itself was to blame. Being compelled to set up housekeeping in a
region where the climate is hard, the land arid, and the scenery
lonely and monotonous gives a woman an instinctive feeling of sacri-
fice, and she is apt to make up for it by telling the old man where
to head in at. The Indian women did, and the men lounged along
the fence and took it. Mr. Pringle watched them disapprovingly,

shook his head at the Carstairses and Clark Burdon and Lavran Baker, and said things couldn't go on like that much longer.

"I been leenient with them Siwashes," he said. "When I first took up my homestid here I'd let 'em come every spring and dig camas the same as usual, and I didn't charge 'em a cent. And afterwards when I took up my swamp-land claim and my desert-land entry and a quarter-section for a timber-culture and my preëmption hundred and twenty acres and the section I bought up on railroad scrip I'd let 'em come and camp on it like they'd always been doin', and I didn't say a word to 'em. But now, by George, it's about time to call a halt. You can't develop a city with them do-nothings lollin' around fightin' and nussin' kids in the middle of the business district. They've got their blamed lodges pitched on ground that's goin' to be the railroad roundhouse and union stock yards, and they're a-peddlin' their blamed wool square on top of the site for the city hall. It gives people a bad impression, and I got to put a stop to it. You lookin' for a location around here?"

"You make it sound interesting," Clark Burdon said, and told no lie. There was an odd sort of feeling about looking at the long thread of white road and the great stretches of open grass clouding in the wind, and thinking that the patch on which the wool-trading Indians had their rumps was liable, maybe any minute, to rise majestically into the air and leave them sitting, wool-sacks, kids, and all, on top of an expensive new city hall. One could see from the blueprint that the entire landscape was loaded with similar possibilities. A patch of blue lobelia in a dried-up mud-flat was only a temporary drapery which veiled a municipal auditorium, a big sweep of blue lupin and white everlasting strained back and forth, not with the wind, but with the exertion of holding down the subterranean birth-pangs of a four-caisson grain-elevator and eight or nine warehouses for the packing and storage of fruit and vegetables yet to be planted. The lupin-and-everlasting lots were priced, in consideration of their commercial importance, at two hundred dollars for a fifty-foot front. Several were marked sold. People in Portland and Seattle and such places had bought them for investment, though city-dwelling investors as a general thing hit straight for the Pringleville Home Garden and Orchard Tracts. A bearing orchard to retire to in the fullness of years seemed to appeal to them more, the difference between such property and a gold-mine being that the orchard didn't require any expensive machinery to operate. Apples of the finest quality retailed in cities at around ten cents apiece. The great thing about raising apples of that class was to have lots of potash in the soil, and the soil of the Pringle Orchards contained enough potash to inebriate and saturate all the apples in the known world.

It would hardly be accurate to say that Mr. Pringle spoke of his development with enthusiasm. His was not a character that allowed itself to cut loose before strangers, but he did have a dignified confidence. Pringleville was bound to be a big thing for him; but, he added, he had certainly put work into making a go of it. What kind of work he didn't mention. Probably the toil of standing in the land office to file on his homestead and his desert-land entry and his swamp-land claim and his timber-culture had taken a lot of the youth out of him. Burdon remarked that, if he understood right, the future of Pringleville depended mostly on the possibility that a railroad might be built through it. To judge from the lay of the country, it would take considerable of a grade to fetch a line up from the river canyon for no purpose except to bring a well-merited success to Mr. Pringle's real-estate holdings.

"It'll be built," Mr. Pringle averred, calmly. "I ain't a man to go off half-cocked on a deal the size of this one, and I got the word of somebody that ought to know something about it. There ain't no secret to it; the man that said so was nobody but old E. H. Harriman hisself. Or as good as. He stopped here and et dinner, and my wife heard him say to the feller that drove his automobile that he guessed before long all these people would be ridin' around on trains, or something like that. So she come right out and asked him if he was goin' to build here, and he set back and looked wise. If it hadn't been so he'd have spoke up and said so, I reckon."

"It sounds good," Clark Burdon said. He was sober, and feeling mean. "I'll certainly order a couple of train-loads of that potash of yours if I can ever git hold of an apple-tree. Right now the only part of your development we're interested in is your jail. We've got a man out here that's committed murder in this county, and we want to turn him over for trial. He's mean, so you'll need to watch him close."

Mr. Pringle looked as if he couldn't believe it, so they showed him the wagon with Wade Shiveley tied in the back of it. He inquired if there were any witnesses, and when they pointed out Clay he wanted to know if there was any reward out. They told him no, and he got more sociable.

"Mostly I serve papers," he said. "Criminal business takes up a man's time, and I've lost money on it. Like last winter, one of them freighters shot a man and I put him under arrest and boarded him here a week and finally had to hire another freighter to haul him down to the county seat before he et me out of business. I put in a bill for my expenses, and it ain't paid yet. The county allowed it, but they ain't got any money to pay it with. If you want this man jailed, why not take him to the county seat yourselves?"

"Too far out of our way," Burdon said. He inspected the Carstairses out of the edge of his eye. They looked perfectly satisfied, not having really cared whether the prisoner got turned in or not. All they wanted was to let everybody know they had him.

"We'll try to find somebody else to farm him off on. There's other deputy sheriffs down the road, I guess?"

"None that'll help you any," Mr. Pringle said, kindly. "Old Ten Per Cent Finley down at Sorefoot that thinks he's startin' a town on that alkali flat of his. A town in that hole, and what do you think he's fixed to name it? Belvista! Yes, sir, that old fool a-tryin' to induce the public to call that cheap gut-dump Belvista, when everybody knows blamed well she's been Sorefoot for fifty years! Well, he's old and kind of childish. You're missin' your big opportunity right here, but I ain't the arguin' kind. I can make more out of these lots holdin' 'em than sellin' 'em."

They thanked him for his counsel. Leaving, one of the Carstairses remembered another important item of news. He mentioned that they had a dead man in one of the wagons, and that they were looking for a graveyard to bury him in. The request took Mr. Pringle a little off his feet, and he explained, laughing at his own forgetfulness, that a graveyard was one thing he had neglected to include in his town-site plans. The salubrity of the climate was such that they had never required one, and probably wouldn't until Pringleville grew to be a shipping metropolis, when, of course, industrial accidents would make one necessary. There was a sort of burying-ground at Sorefoot, though. It was only about fifteen miles along the road, a nice quiet spot, and likely, in spite of Ten Per Cent Finley's ambitious preparations, to remain so. Lavran Baker remarked that the Lunds would feel cheated if they didn't have their funeral in a genuine tried-and-tested graveyard with tombstones, and Clark Burdon put in with his last and meanest gouge.

"You'd better make arrangements for a graveyard here before them people you've sold lots to start movin' in," he remarked. "When they take a look at this layout, they'll start fallin' dead all around you, and where are you goin' to put 'em?"

"You're blockin' the street with your wagons," Mr. Pringle replied, with dignity, indicating the road. Several horses had taken the advantage of the halt that horses usually do take, and, those orisons being attended to, were unfurling their understructures to the refreshing sunlight. The panorama was not in the least sexy, but it looked it, and Mr. Pringle regarded it with disapproval. "A thing like that in the main business avenue of a town," he commented, "and my wife a-workin' in the dinin'-room where she's got to listen to men titterin' about it. That's disorderly conduct. I could put you under arrest for that. I got the authority and I got a legal right to do it."

They were leaving, anyhow, so there was nothing about the threat worth paying attention to, but something about the cold wind and bright sunshine brought out their combativeness. The youngest Carstairs said they would pull their wagons out when they got damn good and ready. Lavran Baker said anybody who called owning horses disorderly conduct was a liar and a pissant, and Clay said the sooner he started putting them under arrest the sooner his abrasions would get healed up afterwards. Mr. Pringle retreated behind his map-table and took up a position between his projected railroad-yards and his grain-elevator, and Clark Burdon, who had started the row, broke it up by pointing out that Mrs. Pringle could see them from the dining-room. She could easily reach them through the window with a platter, so they left Mr. Pringle to count up how much he had won by not selling them anything, and went back to their wagons. The run-in made them all feel tolerably good, foolish though it was, because, without thinking or consulting at all, they had stood in with one another in it.

When they came out, the women leaned out from the wagons to find out what had happened, but Wade Shiveley, who should have felt the most concern about it, sat lolled over in his ropes, asleep. Pain had kept him awake all night, and the jolting of the wagon all day, and his curiosity was not strong enough to hold out against the necessities of his body. He had not been crying, but his face was red and swollen like the face of a half-grown child who has been flogged for a fit of contrariness and cried himself to sleep hating everybody.

The Carstairs women sat in their wagons, looking dusty and sun-faded, and so plain and usual that they seemed comical, like an old horse who unconsciously does something that everybody has expected him to do. Homeliness always seems to make a woman easy to understand, because it seems always to have been produced by the spirit underneath it. But beauty in woman is never easy to understand; she is all the more a mystery on account of it, because you know very well that her spirit has nothing to do with it and may be altogether its opposite. Homeliness may imply all sorts of virtues and weaknesses; beauty implies nothing; the woman it belongs to has had no more part in forming herself so than a square mile of prairie has in getting itself illuminated by a flash of lightning. The Carstairs women were easy to understand, and Luce was not.

She sat in the wagon, as they did, holding the horses and leaning out to hear what was up. Curiosity was all that was in her thoughts, but her beauty made it seem as if she was about to make something exalted and miraculous out of it. Of course she was not, and she didn't even know that it seemed so. Clay climbed in over the wheel, and she passed him the reins and looked inquiringly ahead at the wagon where Wade Shiveley slept.

"They won't have him," he said. "The nearest graveyard is fifteen miles on. We go on tonight, and the funeral tomorrow. They don't know whether they'll turn this shooter over to somebody there or

not. Maybe we'll have to lug him around the country with us the
rest of our lives."

She saw that he was thinking of their bet and of her putting
him off about it. "The Lunds wouldn't let them do that," she said,
confidently. "Maybe it's better this man refused to take him. You
might have had to stay here as a witness against him. Maybe they'll
tend to him themselves, after all, and we won't have to lose time
waiting in some freight station for his trial. I want to get that
settled, so you won't have anything left to worry about."

It didn't sound right to hear her talk so eagerly about hanging
a man. He said they would see, and shook out the reins. For traveling, they had it lucky. The roads were hard and unworn, and the
grass deep and full of seed. Ordinarily there would have been
hundreds of freight-wagons busy hauling out wool, kicking up dust,
occupying all the water-holes, rooting up the best pasture, and
wearing the roadbed into chuck-holes and ruts. The Congressman-
toll-bridge-owner's organizing genius had stalled all that. He had
fixed it so nobody in the country could buy wool except him, and
then he had stopped buying it. The only people who escaped his
benevolent management were the Indians, whose business was too
trifling to monkey with. They picked cull wool off sheep that they
found winter-killed in the hills, and the peddlers bought it less
because they wanted it than because they had to keep hold of the
Indians' business or lose it completely.

Mr. Pringle at Dead Dog had been a lion's whelp, honing his tusks
for the killing that was to crown a long career of far-sighted effort
and deep thinking. Old Ten Per Cent Finley at Sorefoot was a
strong ass kneeled down between two burdens. One burden was
that a railroad actually was being projected to hit the country
somewhere, and that if he didn't cobble up some kind of town site
on his holdings somebody with more faith and enterprise was liable
to start one close to him and draw a lot of settlers' money out of
his lap. The other was that cobbling one ran into a lot of cash, and
nobody knew for certain if he would ever get it back. He was like
a man betting a pair of kings into a lone ace in a stud poker game,
and wishing to thunder he had never paired at all so he could lay

down without looking like a fool. He hated his town-site development, and every nickel he spent preparing to cash in on the railroad boom hurt him almost as intensely as it would have to see
somebody else do the town-siting and cash in on it in his place.

He had all the money he needed, and he had worked hard for it,
starting back in the times when there were still military posts in the
country. He had run a trading-station in the pine foothills, swapping whisky to the soldiers for government rifle cartridges at a
cent apiece, and turning the cartridges over to the Indians at five
dollars a dozen. While the Indians remained hostile, the business
returned a fair margin of profit. Afterwards all the garrisons were
ordered withdrawn, the land had peace, and old Finley began worrying about what he was to keep his establishment running on. But
that was not a country where a hard-working young man with
industrious habits was ever likely to starve. An army captain in
charge of a logging detail had been living with a Paiute squaw,
and, being ordered out, he hated to hurt her feelings by telling
her to consider herself ditched. He hunted up old Finley and offered
to give him the logging machinery and portable sawmill if he would
take the squaw along with them. It was true that the machinery
had been paid for by the War Department, but that was no problem to a man who had been trained in modern strategy. The captain
lumped it in his report with a couple of dead mules and a car-load
of cartridges as expended in service, and the War Department
charged off the whole works and billed him with a shortage in his
subsistence accounts of eighty-two cents. Old Finley started sawing
lumber on contract for Indian reservations, and sawed so diligently
that he not only made good money out of it, but neglected the
squaw till she got tired and went away.

Afterwards the reservation contracts got filled up, the sawmill
wore out, and he opened a freighting-station at Sorefoot and began
lending money to sheep-ranches and settlers. From that practice he
got his name of Ten Per Cent Finley and built up a really hefty
fortune for himself, though he was always modest about it. Anybody, he claimed, who was willing to work as hard and live as
temperately and frugally as he had could do as well.

He was a small-faced man with a woebegone expression and a
complaining voice, tighter in his business dealings than the back

end of a bull in the fly season, but he was enough used to handling money to know how to be generous with what hadn't cost him anything. He paid no attention to the Indians who were camped in his meadow to dig camas. They were out working at it, their curved digging-bars flashing in the sun over the spread of lilies that were the exact deep blue of the ocean when a cloud passes over it. Old Finley was surprised at the notion that such an out-of-date spectacle might discourage progress in his town site, and said it would be time to tend to that when he caught any of them doing it. They had never bothered him any, except when one of the women had a baby. That was sometimes disturbing because, at whatever hour it happened, the father was expected to get up, dig a hole in the ground, fire off a gun, and ride a horse at a gallop. The noisiest cases, of course, where those in which the parentage of the infant had not been definitely established. Sometimes a whole platoon of riders would come ripping down past the house in the middle of the night, and bang loose a broadside that sounded like a cavalry charge. They were a pleasant-mannered class of people, who moved around a great deal—camas-digging and wool-picking in the sagebrush in spring, hunting and huckleberrying in the mountains through the summer, haying and branding cattle on their reservation in fall, and gambling and horse-trading around camp during the winter. Their name for themselves was Lema, which means people in the Nez Percé dialects, but they did enough traveling to know that there were other people in the world besides themselves, and they always identified their tribal subdivisions according to location— Meli Lema, Pakiut Lema, and four or five others, standing for grass-country people, canyon people, hill people. They worked harder and enjoyed themselves a great deal more than any of the fishing-village Indians, and they practiced the habit of spending their money as fast as they got it instead of saving it to show off to their neighbors. Wandering had kept them from getting dull and stupid, as the Coast Indians were, but it had made them a little flighty and light-minded.

Old Finley maintained that it was a good thing for them, nevertheless. It kept them from hanging around a settlement long enough to become nuisances and garbage-pickers, and a man got used to having them show up every spring. It was almost as if they were responsible for pleasant weather instead of the weather being responsible for them. It was somewhat the same feeling that one struck in school-reader poetry, in which grateful acknowledgments for the mild spell were paid to skylarks and thrushes and linnets and a lot of assorted poultry that actually had nothing to do with climate except to exploit it. Of course an Indian was not as poetical a subject as a bird, but if a man ever undertook to write poetry about the advent of the vernal season in Sorefoot he would have to put the camas-digging Indians into it or tell a lie about his feelings. And poetry was nothing but a kind of lining up of a man's true sentiments about a thing.

It was a good deal of analyzing for people to have to listen to, considering that it was afternoon and they had a dead man to find a graveyard for. But nobody ever came to see old Finley except to borrow money, and nobody ever borrowed money from him except as the next resort to suicide, so loneliness gave him plenty of time to figure things through to their fundamentals. By the time a visitor did pull in on him, he had usually accumulated several dozen, which he could only get rid of by telling somebody about. He was grateful for anybody who would listen to him without putting in a bill for it afterwards, and extra grateful when he found the settlers hadn't come to borrow money, which he had stopped lending on account of the hard times. If there hadn't been a graveyard at Sorefoot he would probably have invented one, out of pure benevolence. He did manage to keep enough hold on himself to explain that his graveyard wasn't much of a place. Most of it was some soldiers who had got bushwhacked during the Bannock uprising in 1877. There was also a Chinaman or two, he believed, and a Mormon missionary who had converted some sheep-herders' wives and got that far with them before the sheep-herders overhauled him. It was not much of an assortment.

"It'll do," Lavran Baker said. "If there's people buried in it, it's a graveyard, and that's all them Swedes want. Is there any tombstones?"

"There's headboards over the soldiers," old Finley said. "Government put 'em up, and they looked right fancy for a while. The paint's all wore off of 'em now, but if you gentlemen could raise some whitewash, I'd be willin' to furnish a brush and help you retouch 'em. It's a kind of a funny thing, come to think about it, these Swedes wantin' their son buried where other people is. This graveyard here, with five soldiers that got killed for gangin' on a lone squaw, and a Chinaman that tried to build a fire with a stick of dynamite, and that Brigham Younger that must have lived on raw eggs, to judge by the women he felt able to handle. Not but what you're welcome to it. It's a graveyard, and if the old folks will feel better havin' their son planted in it, let's plant him."

"He'll feel right at home," Lavran Baker said. "We'll tend to whitewashin' the headboards. You wouldn't have any loose lumber around that we could fix up a marker for him with?"

Plenty of boards were lying around, because old Finley had a couple of men with wagons hauling them in from the country. The town site of Belvista was being got ready for industrial activity, not merely by sprinkling stakes around the scenery, but by putting up actual houses for people to live in, the timber for the purpose being obtained by knocking down deserted homestead shacks and moving them down to roost on city lots. It was not the first time those boards had been put to work to constitute a town, and most likely not the last time they would occupy the middle of a quarter-section of sagebrush under the open, limitless sky, unpolluted by signs of any human presence except eight or nine tons of dust blown up from papa's plowing. Lumber in that country was expensive, and every boom, whether in farm property or town lots, meant a hurry call for it. Since the two types of boom occurred in fairly regular alternation, the lumber got dragged back and forth until it was as travel worn as a trained rodeo steer. The boards had initials cut in them, sentiments written and painted on them, layers of wallpaper hanging from them. Old Finley looked them over and said he didn't see how he could spare a single one of them.

"I'll tell you what I'll do, though, and maybe it'll do as well," he offered. "There's a slide down the creek a piece where there's a lot of squared rimrock layin' around loose, all blocked off as pretty as any stone-mason could do it. You could lay a coat of whitewash on one and have as good a tombstone as you'd pick out of a catalogue. Loan me a team and wagon, and I'll go down and fetch one up for you."

It didn't sound a bad idea, though they couldn't feel sure that he wasn't intending to charge for cartage afterwards.

"Tell us where the place is, and one of us can fetch it," Lavran Baker said, cautiously. "These old people are poor, and we want to save 'em all the expense we can."

"No expense at all," said old Finley. "Glad to be able to help out. Anything I can *do*"—he bore down on the word so they wouldn't think he had said disburse or donate—"anything I can *do*, name it, and you've got a man for it right here. Which wagon do you want me to take?"

They picked him one with the freshest-looking team, and he piled in and drove off, declining offers of assistance. He was an antique spirit, Ten Per Cent Finley was, with a view of the difference between work and property that was fast going out of date. He wouldn't give away a second-hand board because that was saleable, solid, permanent, and not subject to obsolescence or shrinkage, no matter how long he had to hang onto it before he cashed in on it. But he would willingly give away three dollars' worth of his work, because that was something that went away from him whether he did anything with it or not. He would sooner have sold it, but since he couldn't, there was no sense in standing around, letting it run to waste.

Chapter XVII

THE Lund funeral was merely a common side-hill burying, with a back-row audience of Indians who sat their ponies, trying to see over people's heads and swapping impressions of the ceremony in an undertone. Foscoe Leonard preached the sermon, and did fairly well with it. He avoided committing himself about the merits of the deceased, and stuck instead to the less disputable argument that the bereaved family felt mortally bad about losing him. Big purple-and-white clouds went trailing across the sky, sometimes dragging their shadows across the people at the grave; the Indian women in the camas meadow called across to one another at their work, and the crew of house-haulers fetched in and unloaded the makings of four suburban bungalows before the ceremony was over.

Nothing else went on worth noticing except the sympathetic demonstrativeness of the Carstairs women, who fell into one another's arms and wept piercingly when the men started filling in the grave, and the different expressions with which the various members of the Lund family took it. Olaf Lund tried to look solemn and succeeded in looking annoyed and sulky because people kept staring at him as if they expected him to do something and he couldn't think of anything to do. Oscar Lund also strove for solemnity, and the expression he achieved was a haunted sort of blankness, as if somebody had anæsthetized him before the ceremony by hitting him over the side of the head with an ax. Christina Lund, whose specialty was reciting Ella Wheeler Wilcox, looked pale and dramatic and pleasantly excited at being one of the main figures in a situation which heretofore she had been obliged to take Ella's word for. The old man Lund stared from the grave to the men around him, with much the expression of a hurt bull being creosoted for maggots, who cannot understand how anything that burns him so can be for his own good. When the men started filling the grave, he reached mechanically for a shovel to help. That was when the Carstairs women started squalling, and their noise scared him off. He ducked, dropped the shovel, and stumbled over it, and would have run away if a couple of men hadn't caught him and soothed

him down. Their gentleness apparently got it through his head that
he was an object not of retribution, but of sympathy, and that
broke him down. Standing between them, he turned his face to the
sky and cried, trying to hide behind them so people wouldn't look
at him.

A kind of lunatic logic sometimes comes out of the most frantic
extremes of grief. Mrs. Lund had it. She hated her husband, and
some women, Luce among them, had to hold her on the opposite
side of the grave to keep her from getting at him. Being naturally
quicker-minded than the rest of her family, she needed no long
course of collecting associations in her mind to understand what
this death meant. The realization tortured her, but she had got used
to it, and she was like a shot animal which, having finished kicking
in the first horror of pain, looks around for the hunter who caused
it. She put the blame not on the man who had killed her son, but
on her husband who had given her this son to be killed. The women
held her tight, but when the grave-filling began she strained forward
to look. They told her it was not her son that was being buried,
only his body, but that didn't have much weight with her. It was
his body that she had taken all her trouble with, and nothing else
about him—if there was anything else about him—meant anything
to her.

Afterwards people stood around, not having anything to stay for,
but hating to be the first to leave. The women led Mrs. Lund away
and the other Lunds trailed after her. The Carstairs women trailed
after them, talking low about the main points of the interment to
make sure they hadn't overlooked any narrative possibilities. One
of them thought Mrs. Lund's straining to look into the grave had
been an attempt to throw herself into it, so they elected that into
the story and made quite a colorful episode out of it. The Indians,
having ascertained that there was not going to be anything to eat,
rode back through the willows to their camp, and the Carstairs men
left with old Finley, talking about the pathos of the burying and
the loss Isaac Lund was going to be, as if they had been breathless
spectators of his unfolding merits from the hour he was hatched.
They told about the killing as if they had been there when it started,
and they talked up Wade Shiveley's murderousness and the plans
they had for turning him over to the law as if they owned stock in

him. Clark Burdon and Lavran Baker and Given Bushnell stayed to put up the headstone, and Clay walked down to the creek and sat down in the tall grass close to the water. It was a quiet place, cut between steep banks so nobody was able to see into it. After a while, Clark Burdon came down to wash the clay off his hands, and sat down too. He wanted to say something, but he was sober, and it took time for words to come to him.

"There's a good many things about that Carstairs outfit that I don't go much on," he began. "If they was to see a man goin' for the doctor in a life-and-death case, they'd ear him down and hold him till they'd told him about havin' a murderer tied up in the wagons, and where was an officer they could deliver him to? This must be the first thing worth tellin' that they ever got hold of in their lives."

Clay felt little interest in the Carstairs news-fever, and it hadn't helped his power of reflection any to watch a funeral for which he himself had provided the centerpiece. He couldn't make the Carstairses shut up, so he saw no use in ciphering out their motives and peculiarities. The creek water was so still and clear that it was impossible to see the break between it and the air over it except when a blue butterfly rippled the surface. Seeing that he was not going to say anything, Burdon went on.

"It ain't that I object to any harmless form of personal recreation," he said. "They enjoy havin' something to talk about to strangers, because it's new to 'em. But this is liable to be inconvenient to other people. Every time, they whoop it up about this man's criminal record from across the mountains and how you're a witness to 'em. That makes it sound as if there ought to be a reward out for him somewheres. You notice everybody so far has asked if there was one."

"There ain't," Clay said, without looking up from the water. "There was one, but it paid off when they caught him the first time."

"I understood so," Burdon agreed. "But these people are goin' to go on blabberin' this thing and askin' where for mercy's sake is a deputy sheriff till we find one that will start figurin' this thing out. He'll figure there ought to be a reward, and he'll hold this man till he can telegraph around and find out if there is one. And what's more, he'll hold you for a material witness. The first thing you know after that, here will come a sheriff's detail from that county where you helped with the jailbreak, and along back with 'em you'll go. That's what you can count on if something don't happen to shut these people up. And nothing will."

He was right about that. He was cutting close to the probabilities about everything. Clay memorized the shape of grass-stems in a foolish effort to start his mind working. "What do you think I'd better do? I thought they aimed to hang him out here?"

"They could have if the Carstairses hadn't opened up," Burdon said. "Among ourselves, we could have fixed up something to make it look legal. Now too many people know about it, and it would be lynchin'. They'd be afraid to risk trouble doin' it. And it looks like this was a case where the only thing you can do is something you'd sooner not. I think you'd better pull off the road till the wagons git past, and then go somewhere else. That's what I'd do."

When a man like Clark Burdon recommended ducking to avoid trouble, it meant that the trouble looked bad. It also meant that he was risking something. Without Clay's character testimony Shiveley might be turned loose. If that happened he could cinch Burdon for shooting him in the arm. He was willing to run that chance to get Clay out of danger, so the danger must be considerable. It would be better to leave. Luce would refuse to, and how could she be persuaded? "I'll try to go, but maybe I can't," Clay said. "They couldn't hold me for any witness. It's against the law to hold a man without layin' a charge against him."

Burdon said it was also against the law to sell whisky to an Indian, but he knew of several comfortable fortunes that had been founded by the traffic. "When there's money in it, the law means what these people want it to mean. You've got too much to lose to take any chances. You pick up and pull out, do you hear?"

"I hear," Clay said. Burdon's earnestness was impressive. And he was soberer than usual, which meant that he was more cautious; and it was going to be a long quarrelsome job inducing Luce to leave. He hated to think of it. "I'll do it if I can. Maybe we'll turn up some other way to handle it, if we think it over a little."

"Some other way hell!" Burdon said, losing patience. "You damned little idiot, do you think I'm tellin' you this to be sociable?

I've figured you out of one hole, and I'm tryin' to figure you out of another one, and, by God! you'd better let me do it! Are you goin' to pull out of this train, or ain't you? Are you goin' to do as I say, or not? Answer me!"

A shadow fell across them, and Luce stepped down the bank and stood in front of him. "So you're going to make him answer you, are you?" she said. Her voice had a tone that Clay had not heard in it before, a kind of muffled harshness like plucking a bass-fiddle string with one finger muting it. She had heard only the last few words of the conversation, which was something to be thankful for. But she was willing to make plenty out of them. "He's got to promise to do what you say, has he? Now you've taken to hauling him off into corners and telling him what he can do, have you? How did you get any right to do that? What is it you want him to promise?"

Burdon sat without moving until she had finished. "It wasn't anything," he said. "Nothing of any importance whatever. A little matter of—a little matter of— Well, it wasn't anything."

Possibly it was disappointment at his deciding not to tell that made her fiercer. "It wasn't anything, and you had it laid out to make trouble for him if he didn't promise to do it?" she said. She seemed not to notice Clay at all. He felt like some helpless village brat being rescued from a group of larger boys who have been trying all afternoon to make him go home and let them alone. He was not that helpless, and Burdon was not that brutal and overbearing.

"Look here, this ain't got anything to do with you," he protested. "It was nothing but an argument. We'd have it settled now if you hadn't come along, and you'd never have known anything about it."

She ignored him completely. "This isn't the first time," she told Burdon. "You took him with you after that murderer, and you almost got him killed. If you ever come near him again, Clark Burdon, I'll kill you. If he ever gets into any trouble in this train, I'll know you're back of it and I'll kill you for that. You'd better heed what I say. I'll do it."

Burdon got to his feet with his self-possession apparently restored. "I'm not in the least afraid of being killed," he said. It was probably true because of his face, which was something that had to be got used to. In the Idaho gold-mines he had undertaken to cramp a dynamite cap on a fuse with his teeth, and it had blown exactly half his face into a blank, shining scar, marked only by a hole that had been his eye. It was painful to him in cold weather, and it made him dislike strange people, who were apt to forget their manners and stare. "I believe you can kill me, of course, but I hope on your account that you won't. It's no fun killing people, you'll find that out if you ever try it. And I was merely advising the kid for what I thought was his own good. Maybe it wasn't my place to, but he needs it."

He climbed the bank and went away. Being a gentleman, he didn't look at Clay, whose stuttering and hesitation had let him in for such a currying. Luce watched him through the graveyard, in which during the funeral he had deported himself with so much reverence and solemnity. Now, because everybody was gone and the corpse covered with earth, he walked as casually as if he had been taking a short cut through a hog-pasture. When he had straddled over the fence on the far side, she sat down. She did not appear in the least out of temper with Clay, but rather pleased that she had happened around in time to take a difficult piece of management off his shoulders.

"What was he arguing with you about? Some crookedness that he's afraid to undertake himself?"

He had intended all the time to tell her, with, of course, a little doctoring up of details. "It wasn't anything except that he wanted to save me some trouble," he said, going slow so as not to tell anything that needed too much explaining. "He didn't browbeat me and he didn't threaten me, and it wasn't anything except a plain argument till you lit all over him. I don't know what you had to do that for. I don't need any help to keep people from runnin' over me. I ain't like your father."

"You talk like him," she said, shrewdly. "He used to start off exactly like that when I'd kept him from being egged into some foolishness. Why didn't Clark Burdon tell me what it was when I asked him?"

"It was something he thought we ought to talk over alone, I expect," Clay said. "He thought on account of things that might come up that we'd do better to pull away from this crowd for a while. Find somebody else to travel with, or maybe settle down around here, he thought. . . ."

She was silent for so long that he glanced sideways at her to see what was the matter. She sat staring at the still, colorless water with her eyes half shut, and he noticed the secrecy about her face as if she had seen too much of a good many things and its childish willfulness that showed how completely they had failed to break her. He noticed also that the strong reflected light from the water made her eyelids look half transparent, as if she had lowered them not to shut off sight, but to see through. "So he wanted you to leave this train. That was what he was trying to persuade you to do? I don't wonder he didn't want to tell me."

"That was it," Clay said. He knew she was angry, but there was no use letting on until he had something more to go on than her tone of voice. "It wasn't that he stood to gain anything by it. Only, some things have changed since we hit this country, and he thinks if we pull off into another road—" She continued to look at the water through her lowered eyelids, and he explained about the Carstairs' new-found liberality with news, the impossibility of shutting them up, and the probability that some cross-roads constable would see money in Wade Shiveley and hold Clay himself for a witness. "They could float up some excuse to do it. Title to some of the horses, or something. Then we'd be stuck here till their court term—two months, maybe more. These people wouldn't wait around for us that long, so we'd lose 'em anyway."

A long way off they could hear the Indian women talking across the camas-patch, and, nearer, the sound of Mrs. Lund crying, which distance made quite musical. There were wild doves in the willows expressing their happiness in the most dismally doleful voices that are to be found in all nature.

"For two months," Luce said. "And what after that?"

"A trial for murder, I suppose," Clay said. He wondered irritably why she needed any more to look forward to than two months' detention around some side-hill freight-station in the heat. "Court, and juries, and lawyers askin' questions and tryin' to make me out a liar, and if they can't they git tired and call me a lot of names, and if they can I git arrested for perjury."

She refused to let that contingency upset her. "And then they will hang him and you can go where you please?" she said. "That's all that would happen, isn't it? What's that to be afraid of? They wouldn't even keep you in jail; you could camp around where they could watch you."

He said he wasn't afraid of it. Only, it would be a blamed nuisance, and he was anxious to put in his time doing something more useful. There was, for instance, a possibility that the jury might turn Shiveley loose; nobody could feel sure how a trial in one of these tail-end-of-nothing counties would turn out. If they did, he would come after Clay for having given unfavorable evidence. It would be necessary to do some shooting, and if he got Shiveley he would be jailed for manslaughter. If he didn't, he would be dead.

"But they won't turn him loose!" She acted as if there was something disloyal about the very notion. "We know he killed Isaac Lund. Why else would these men have arrested him? You can tell them that, can't you?"

"I didn't see him do it," Clay reminded her. "You can't tell anything in a court except what you've seen."

"Well, the two men he killed across the mountains, you can tell them about that, can't you? We're only guessing that they'll hold you for a witness at all, but if they do you can tell enough to make sure they won't turn him loose. He tried to kill you when you went to help arrest him, didn't he? He wasn't afraid to do that to you, but now you're afraid to do anything back at him. Something has changed you lately, since yesterday. You didn't use to be afraid."

"I'm not afraid," he said. "Nothing's changed me."

"Yes it has," she insisted. "Don't you think I can see? I came down here because I remembered that I'd made you a promise down at the Indian fishing-grounds on the river. I wanted to keep it with you. I hoped you'd remember it. All the time I was looking for you I kept thinking . . . Well, I'm not going to cry. That wouldn't do any good."

She had looked for a minute as if she were going to. It was a child's trick, this business of telling yourself about your hopes and expectations so they would contrast with some discouraging piece of reality. But she didn't do it as a stratagem. She had genuinely talked herself to the point of tears, and she held them back with a genuine effort. He pulled her head across his lap to console her, and she shut her eyes against the light of the sky so that a few tears did squeeze out on her lashes. He laid his own head between her breasts and told her, without meaning much of anything, that she must not mind, that he would fix it so everything would be all right.

"Then it will," she said, without opening her eyes. "I knew it would. I knew you wanted me enough not to hurt me. You didn't know it, but I did all the time. . . ."

She had moved so that her lips were close to his ear, and her voice was saying something altogether different from what she said in words. She turned half over him, her lips partly open, her skin damp so that a sprinkling of green-white pollen from the grass stuck to it. The grass walled them off from everything except themselves; the earth under his head, the sky over hers. He knew that this was going to bind him to something that was dangerous and dishonest, that it would have to be paid for by lying Wade Shiveley to death, that it would have to be paid for. But it would have been worse to leave. Being sure of him, she let go all holds on herself and lay waiting, short-breathed, unable to move or speak. Not to take her would mean setting up enmity between them, and it would be an enmity of her body, which couldn't understand such matters as moral responsibility and ethical scruples. He dared not risk that, no matter what it got him into.

Afterward, drowsing while the sun turned past over them, they heard a noise from the direction of the wagons that sounded new. It was not the wild doves, though it was solemn and mournful enough. It was like a woman's voice, and there was a kind of determination about it although it didn't seem to be saying anything.

"It's Mrs. Lund still crying," Luce said. "She's been going on all the time, only you didn't notice it. Isn't that what it is?"

Clay shook his head. "She'd have to feel a lot worse than she does to make that kind of a noise. That's a hound bayin'. One of Foscoe Leonard's, I guess. I didn't suppose there was any game in this sagebrush that hounds could run."

He got up and looked to see whether the hounds might have got loose after a jack rabbit. The baying came again, and he knew that they had not. It was not a running-cry. The hounds were making a cast for some trail that they had been laid on, and there was only one kind of game that they could be set to catch. It was either a youngster that had got lost, or it was Wade Shiveley loose again. Clay set no great store by the pack of little prattlers in the train, but he hoped with every inch of tissue in him that they were all safe where they belonged. If Wade Shiveley had been fool enough to pull his freight and get-up enough to go on pulling it, everything might come out right yet. Men were crowding around the wagons, and one of them climbed a wrangling-pony and went out toward the horse-herd at a run. Then Clark Burdon walked out in the clearing with his pistol and shot. Three shots meant somebody lost. He shot twice, waited, and shot twice more. Luce sat up, looking scared and wondering.

"He's callin' everybody in," Clay told her. He didn't dare tell her what he hoped it was, and she climbed out of the creek ahead of him without asking. He took no notice of the place on leaving it, but for a long time afterwards he was able to remember every detail of it, even things that, at the time, he hadn't even noticed. The long willow leaves that moved not because of air-currents, but because they were alive, the wire grass going to seed in powder-brown tufts, the slate-blue doves, the red-winged blackbirds that nested in little caves in the dirt bank, and the white-and-black magpies tending their basketwork nests in the middle of the thorn-bushes. Except for what had happened he would never have remembered them; but that fixed them in his mind so clearly that in course of time he found he was able to give much more precise account of them than of what had happened.

Chapter XVIII

WHAT fool notion had led Wade Shiveley to make his break at exactly the time when it was certain to do his case the most harm nobody ever undertook to figure out. Probably it was too entirely instinctive to respond to any kind of figuring. A captive coyote will break out of a cage though he is being well fed in it, though food outside is scant and uncertain, and though a pack of dogs are waiting to chew the giblets out of him the minute he emerges. Not because his reasoning is defective, but because on the subject of enforced confinement he doesn't reason at all.

During the funeral Wade Shiveley had been left roped in the wagon with only tongueless Rube Cutlack to stand guard over him, and the chance was too much for him to resist. As well as Rube could explain by his system of signs and grimaces, Shiveley had groaned a good deal over his inflamed arm, had talked incoherently, and had actually worked up what seemed to be a touch of fever; not especially hard to do, if a man knows how. It is possible to fake a temperature that would fool a pretty good doctor by rubbing fresh-chewed tobacco into a cut or a bad scratch. Rube Cutlack had been completely taken in, and when Shiveley begged to be helped down the road to the creek bridge for a necessary function, he unroped him and steadied his faltering steps with no more suspicion than he would have felt of a new-foaled colt. Shiveley retired under the bridge and he stood modestly above, and his first warning of anything wrong came when he suddenly had his legs yanked out from under him and took a dive head first down into the gravel. He was knocked half-senseless, and Shiveley finished the job by beating him over the head with a rock till his eyeballs walled backwards. When he came to, people were coming back from the funeral and Shiveley had gone. He had taken Rube's pistol and the pony which had been kept saddled at his wagon, and Rube had no idea which direction he had pointed or how much of a start he had. For all he knew, it might be a week or ten days.

"About an hour, more likely," Foscoe Leonard calculated, pleas-

urably. He was having a congenial day of it, first preaching a
funeral sermon and now exercising his hounds on live game with
everybody watching him. "It would take him that long to get out
of sight in this open country unless he stuck to the brush in the
creek. And we took the hounds there first, and they wouldn't find.
All we can do is get saddled up and wait."

The hounds were casting on an open rise beyond the horse-
herd. They moseyed in circles, first wide and then short, and now
and then a couple would meet, put their heads together, and discuss
the prospects before going at it again. Clay got his buckskin mare
saddled, and Burdon led over and stood watching with him. "I was
in hopes you'd come along," he remarked, cautiously. "Better if
he's got clean away, but people would notice if you didn't help tag
him. Take it easy now. The hounds may not find within a mile of
where they're workin'. The longer they take, the farther our man
will travel, and it'll be a blamed sight better for you if we don't
catch him at all."

Clay stopped twiddling his bridal reins. He was glad that Burdon
didn't refer to anything that had happened down the creek, and,
since wishing wasn't going to affect the pursuit one way or the
other, he wished the hounds would hurry up and do something.
"Why didn't they start 'em from where he took the horse?"

"They did," Burdon said. "How else do you think they'd know
which horse they're after? But we didn't start 'em till we'd found
Rube would live, and there'd been so much millin' around by then
that the trail was all cut to hell. And when they did pick it up, it
run into the horse-herd and got lost again. That first bayin' you
heard was when they picked it up here."

Clay said he had heard that, and fiddled his reins some more.
Once the hounds all bunched together, but then they scattered again.
Burdon stood close and took him by the arm.

"You're a good kid, son," he said. "I want you to keep up with
this run, if there is one, but I want you to hold back in it. Keep
behind the men, so if anything happens it won't look as if you'd
had anything to do with it. I hope we don't catch him, but if we
do and I can git half an excuse to, you won't need to feel uneasy
about him ever any more. I'm tired of— Well, that looks like
they'd done it."

A big bow-legged hound ran back and forth on the hill, trotted experimentally for about fifty yards, and lifted his head and said "Woo-woo-woo-woo!" loud and hollow-sounding. All the dogs looked up, and he dropped his head and went straight up the hill and over it with them strung out and yapping after him. Deliberately, all the men mounted, the horses surging and plunging and being reined back, and Burdon laid his hand on Clay's bridle.

"Now take it easy," he advised for the last time. "Them hounds can't keep that lick, and there's no use wearin' your horse out. They won't find him till he stops, and then you remember what I told you. I expected your girl would raise some objection to your comin' along."

Now that it was called to Clay's notice, it did seem curious that she hadn't. She had watched him saddle and get his rifle, all without uttering a word.

"Maybe she thinks it's safer where there's a lot of men," he suggested.

"If she does, she's wrong," Burdon said. "It ain't a damn bit safer. Maybe she wanted you to go because everybody else was goin'."

There was something in that, too. The party to arrest Wade Shiveley had been a sort of fence-corner expedition, with no credit attached to it because there was no weight of public approval behind it. But this was a thing that a man couldn't stay out of without being noticed and probably talked about. It was still harder to figure why any of the men cared whether Wade Shiveley was caught or not. None of them had known what to do with him when they had him. An impression seemed to have got round that his escape on the very afternoon of the funeral had for some reason made the Lunds' bereavement harder for them to stand, and that fetching him back would make them feel better. Nobody knew for sure that it would, but it was at least a way of showing them that people felt sorry for them and willing to go to any amount of trouble to see that the man who had bereaved them got what he deserved. It was not in vengeance and not out of any stern notions of justice that they were trailing Shiveley, leaving their own work to dog the daylights out of a wounded blow-hard who would have considered it a privilege never to see any of them again. They took after him out of a much more Christian set of sentiments—pity, sympathy, concern over an old couple's helpless grief, and anxiety to find some means of expressing what they felt. They donated their pursuit in the same spirit that makes people in more settled localities donate expensive floral pieces: not to make the stricken family feel better, but as a sign that they wish they could.

The dogs loped along fast because the trail in the grass was plain enough to follow by sight. On top of the hill all the grass petered out. There was a long, almost level plain, on which nature had originally laid down a good twelve-inch coating of earth. Lack of rain had converted that into dust, and winds had picked it up and rearranged it in a regularly-spaced series of hummocks shaped something like well-settled shocks of hay. On top of them sagebrush grew, holding them against blowing any more. The ground between was naked shellrock, so hard it held no tracks and so dry that scent was faint and spotty. The dogs, used to trailing on the moist ground of the Coast, overran their slot several times and had to cast back. This was called potato-hill country, and except for a two weeks' pasture every spring and fall it was totally worthless. Nobody had ever attempted even to map a town site on it.

It was almost sundown when the dogs got down out of it and crossed a shallow valley where there was water. Beyond was a pleasant spread of bunch grass, pale green and unbroken for miles except in places where small birds had built grass-tufts into little peak-shaped pedestals to build their nests on. Tracks held well in that, and the dogs cocked their tails and went whooping across it hellity-split.

None of the men tried to keep up with them. Foscoe Leonard reined back beside Clark Burdon, looking solemn and responsible. "Begins to look bad," he mentioned. "Goin' to be dark on us in a couple more hours. If we don't keep the dogs in earshot we'll lose 'em, and if we do we'll have to ride perilous fast, with this whole damn country loaded with badger-holes. I don't want to lose any of them dogs, but I'd hate to have men banged up or killed."

"We can't do anything else except go back," Burdon replied. "We'd all look like idiots doin' that. We can take it slow. There's bound to be sheep where there's all this pasture, and they'll slow up the dogs. And this open-country trailin' can't last forever. He'll pick up a horse-trail somewhere around here, and then we can pelt along as fast as we please."

Long after the sky had got dark enough to show stars, the great spread of grass held light enough to see by. The men rode easy and the horses kept their heads down, smelling for tripholes under the deep mat of grass. Then the grass got dark and only the men's faces held the light, and then they got dark. Sounds became noticeable that had been going on all the time without registering as long as there was anything to look at. Saddles squeaked, a bit-ring rattled, an interfering-gaited horse clacked the calk of his fore-shoe against his hind-shoe. Another horse kept snorting in an effort to blow something out of his nostrils, and a man kept scratching matches on his saddle-skirt and muttering when the heads came off. The open grass was silenter than any of the men were used to. They had lived in fir timber, where even on windless days there was always a faint rushing sound with the movement of upper air through the boughs. A couple of them mumbled together and giggled nervously, a man cursed his horse for stumbling, and somebody started humming a tune. Foscoe Leonard, to relieve his own nervousness, told them all to shut up. "Listen for the dogs, if you can't think of anything else to do," he ordered. "They could have cut back on us as easy as not, and we could ride plumb on into the Pacific Ocean before we found it out."

A long time passed. On good ground there is pleasure in riding a horse when it is too dark to see where he is; it gives you the illusion that the whole earth is swinging under you and that you can set it to any kind of rhythm you fancy. In badger-hole country it is about as much fun as blindfolding yourself on a roof and going for a long walk to see if you'll be lucky enough not to fall off. A man pulled his horse around suddenly, bumped several riders behind him, and stopped. "I can hear 'em," he said. It was Tunis Evans. He never talked until he had deliberated for ten minutes over what he was going to say, so they knew there could be no doubt about it. "Way to whaley and gone over to the right. They're still runnin'."

All the men pulled up. Clay could hear nothing, but Foscoe Leonard said he did, and that it was them. The dog who was baying was old Reverend Spurgeon, he said, and he rather believed that

Henry Ward Beecher and Dwight Moody were helping out. He reined his horse over, with all the men following. Clark Burdon dropped in beside Clay and remarked that it was like his luck to have Tunis Evans get an attack of intelligence at the wrong moment. "I've been workin' to run 'em off the line for the last hour. Now it's all spoiled again. Whatever happens, now, you remember to keep back."

Clay remarked that since the dogs were still running they might easily get lost again. But he was never good at offering consolation, and he felt privately certain that the dogs wouldn't be lost any more and that they would pin their game before the night was out. They would find him and he would be taken, and he would go to some watering-trough town for trial, with the Lunds all sitting on the front bench in court. Clay would sit up in a chair in front of a jury of bar bums and unemployed sheep-herders, and a strange lawyer would ask him questions. Be careful now, young man, do you know of your own knowledge that this man fired the shot and how do you know that? Do you know of your own knowledge that he broke out of jail, and how does it happen that you know so almighty much about it, anyhow?

That was what he was in for, but at least the feeling that he was in for it through some piece of injustice rankled in him scarcely at all any more. He had agreed to do it now, and he had already drawn his pay for doing it. Whatever came of it, he would have nothing to complain about. Riding in that darkness, a man could turn his thoughts over as freely as if he had been completely alone. Probably the other men were busy turning theirs over without thinking much of equestrianism, for when the horses topped the bunch-grass slope and stumbled down into a deep-worn pack-trail there was a good deal of surprised grunting and cussing and fumbling for lost stirrups by men who hadn't been expecting that the slope would ever end.

The pack-trail put an end to the contemplative life for the rest of the night. One of the men said damn this falling down holes in the dark; he was going to wait for daylight and then go home. There was a general dismounting and sitting down in the grass, with nobody opposing except Foscoe Leonard, who hated to abandon his dogs and didn't want to go after them alone. He got off, too, and after the horses had got through blowing and stretching everything fell quiet. In the silence, they heard the dogs yelling almost straight ahead. Not the long woo-woo-woo this time, but a short-spaced hubbub of yapping and yelping like coyotes after a rainstorm in summer. In the middle of that they heard a shot, and a long succession of echoes trading it back and forth like something falling downstairs. Old Leonard got up, and they could see his profile against the stars.

"My God! Come on!" he said, bellying himself onto his horse. "He's murderin' them dogs, and he'll have every last one dead before we can stop him! For the Lordamighty's sake, boys!"

So it was not to avenge innocent blood that the trail was finally run out, and it was not even for the charitable satisfaction of showing sympathy with the Lunds. It was solely to keep Wade Shiveley from shooting poor old Leonard's pack of hounds, which were the only living things he took any satisfaction in. All the men mounted, with the usual accompaniment of colliding horses and men missing the saddles and hopping around with one foot stirruped and the other on the ground. The trail was wide and well used, and they lit out at a gallop.

The horses knew that this was ground they could be sure of, and they made a regular homestretch drive out of it in the dark. Hoofs walloped the ground like hail on a tin roof, and the men moved up toward the chin-strap, sat high, and let them drive. It was no longer a hurry-up call to rescue old Leonard's hounds, it was the half-drunk breathlessness of being part of the rush, of belonging to and going with the speed and weight of the whole pack, it didn't matter where. Wind and pebbles stung them, trail-side bushes ripped at their legs with the sound of a saw going through slab-wood, legs and saddles were jammed so close that the whole charge moved like one body, without even room enough for a horse to fall down in.

Topping a swell of ground, they spread out a little and piled down into a patch of half-dried blue mud that balled on the horses' feet without cutting their speed. The darkness was still total, but they saw where they were going. It was to a camp fire not over a half-mile off. At intervals the flame disappeared and then winked into sight again, which meant that somebody had walked in front of it, and as they closed in they could see a dirty canvas wickyup behind it, and a haystack behind that. The wickyup looked small and flimsy, something on the Bannock style of architecture, and it didn't look like a place that would extend hospitality to a fugitive outlaw. But it had, for the dogs were running circles around it outside of gun-range, yelling with ecstasy at having treed their meat and with indignation because nobody showed up to tell them what to do with it.

None of the dogs had got shot, probably because their unpopularity with the neighbors on the Coast had taught them how to act under fire. They ran toward the horses eagerly, and then got out of the way for the rush to go past them. A shot came from the wickyup, and Clay, holding well back in the pack, heard a loud meaty smack a couple of feet from him. A voice said, solemnly and hollowly: "By God! by God! I believe he hit me, by God!" which seemed such a silly remark for a man to crown his last moments with that Clay couldn't believe it was so. Nobody else said anything, but as the light from the fire got closer, he noticed that the horse beside him was riderless. Then he felt Clark Burdon's hand on his elbow. "Somebody got it," Burdon said. "In the head, it sounded like. If he got killed, mark the place and come on in. This may make it easy for us; you can't tell."

The announcement fetched Clay back to the exercise of his senses, and it was about time. He had forgotten where they were going or what for, right along with the rest of them. He pulled the buckskin mare sideways, sawed her till she dropped behind, and got her turned around and headed back by pulling her head till her neck bent almost double. That took him away from the firelight again, and since it was no use trying to see anything, he eased her along at a walk, yoohooing every minute and looking back to see if anything happened when the men ramped down on the wickyup. Nothing did, and nobody answered him. He continued to call, because it didn't seem possible that the man beside him could have been shot from the fire. The whole column had been packed close, and Clay and the lost man were riding with at least a dozen men between them and the wickyup when the shot was fired. It would have had to hit one of the front men first, unless Shiveley had his gun trained to shoot a curve. The buckskin mare stopped, fluttering her nostrils inquiringly. Clay got off and lit a match, and found his man.

Not all of him. A man run down by a bunch of sharp-shod horses has a tendency to scatter around badly, and what Clay found to start with turned out, on close examination, to be a strung-out human entrail. He tossed his match away hurriedly to avoid looking at the thing, and then lit another to avoid stepping on it. It stretched along the trail for about ten feet, and on the end of it was Foscoe Leonard.

It required no medical examination to see that he was dead. Not only was he completely disembowelled, but a lick from a horse's shoe-calk had opened the top of his skull. The brain was visible through the gash, and it was still throbbing. Clay blew out his match again and backed away out into the sagebrush. He had intended to look the body over for gunshot wounds, but a sight like that took away all his zeal for research. Death was something he was fairly well used to and not especially afraid of, but death that did only half a job, that let a man get torn up and left alive that part of him that knew about it, was a refinement that was better left uninvestigated. He backed away, sliding his feet to make sure of not stepping in anything, and he led the mare well back up the trail before he built a signal-fire to mark the place. Then he rode for the wickyup, and he no longer felt nervous or afraid of what he was going to run into there. A man had only a certain amount of pressure to blow on being scared, and his was entirely blown.

After all, there was nothing to be nervous about. Wade Shiveley stood in front of the wickyup door, staring from one to another of the men as if waiting for them to start something; the men stared at one another as if in doubt what to start, and a scrawny little Basque sheep-herder hopped nervously on one leg in the shadows, trying to get the other leg into the sleeve of a woolen union suit and gabbling to himself in Spanish. Clark Burdon stood at one wing of the arc, gazing thoughtfully at the empty pistol which Shiveley, recognizing him, had tossed on the ground in front of him. Seeing Clay, he picked the gun up and stuck it into the front of his pants. "You didn't take long," he said. "It was old Leonard, was it?"

He spoke with noticeable clearness so everybody would pay attention, and he didn't take his eyes off Shiveley. "I found what was left of him," Clay said. "It was old Leonard. His insides pulled out and the top of his head ripped off. The horses done that, I guess."

Burdon told a couple of the Carstairses to go fetch him in. "We knew it must be him," he said. "We wanted him to call in his dogs, and we couldn't find him. Well, he never got to know whether his pack of hounds was all right or not. . . ." He drew a pathetic sigh, working to get the men's emotions all chafed up, and looked at Shiveley again. "You didn't shoot to hit anybody, eh?"

Everybody waited. The silence must have lasted over five minutes, and then the Carstairses came back. They had wrapped the body in a saddle blanket, and they unloaded it in front of the fire, unwrapped it, and stood back. Several of the men craned their necks over to look, and Lavran Baker spread the blanket over it again.

"I shot to scare the dogs," Shiveley said, as if he had been waiting for that. He was telling the truth; anybody with good sense could see that. The men were too shaken with horror at the dead body's disfigurement to see anything. Most likely he knew it, but he went on. "I shot in the air, and I can prove by this sheep-herder that I didn't aim anywhere near anybody. You men take me when I ain't done anything; you break my arm and tie me up and run me with dogs . . ."

He turned his back on them. The Basque herder, having got his underwear on wrong end up, sat down and started taking it off again, muttering *vergas* and *pendejos* and *chingalas* into his large mustache. Burdon spoke up again. "You tagged on with our wagons tellin' what a habitual shooter you was, and how all you had to do was yell at a sheriff to make him climb a tree. You tried to kill this kid, and now you talk about how harmless you've been, standin' with that dead man in front of you. . . ."

He was not talking for the men. He was trying to work on Shiveley's nerves, to scare him into making some break that would settle things quick. But the denunciation sounded imposing, and the men chipped in on it with a kind of amen-chorus. That was right, by God! and damned if they hadn't stood about enough of this, and how about Isaac Lund killed and Rube Cutlack hammered over the head with a boulder, and so on. Shiveley sat suddenly down in the dust and said they couldn't prove that he had ever

killed anybody, not at any mark of his career. He had fired in the
air, in the air, in the air. . . . Burdon pushed Clay forward into the
light, and he thought now for it.

"I know that's a lie," he said. "I know he killed his brother in a
fight, and I know he killed a man on the road and robbed him of
eight hundred dollars. I know he broke jail. He'll lie about it, but
he done it. Turn him loose and he'll do more."

His voice kept clear and steady and indifferent. This was easier
than testifying in court. He was getting through it luckier than
he had expected. Shiveley still made no break to get away, and he
didn't interrupt Clay or accuse him. He sat stubbornly in the
dust and said that this was the end. He was through trying. When
the kid he had raised and made a home for turned on him and robbed
him and lied about him, he was done. Done with everything, he
added, so they wouldn't think he contemplated running a prune-
orchard or something in his retirement. He knew, better even than
Burdon did, that the men were there to finish him, and that the
only thing they still balked at was the physical disagreeableness of
the job.

It was an oddly insignificant thing that brought them to the
point. A couple of birds twittered questioningly from the hay-field.
It was a sign that daylight was getting close. They all stirred restlessly, and Tunis Evans, the slow man, reached for a rope from his
saddle and walked over to Shiveley. "Well, git up off the ground,"
he said. "You're a grown man, and it ain't goin' to do you any good
to act childish."

Shiveley got up and stood while the rope was being fixed around
his neck. The before-dawn cold was like any other cold of that
hour, the sky like hundreds of others that he had seen, the men
no different from men he had traded and squabbled with all his life,
so he had difficulty in getting it into his head that these were all
final events in his life. For such an occasion there should have
been more to them. There should have been more to him, too, and
he could feel nothing unusual.

"I want to say something to you men," he said. "All the trouble
I've had with this outfit of yours has been on account of that kid.
When you hear about it, when you hear what I've got to tell you,
you'll wonder how I ever put up with half of it."

He had waited a little too long. The men were under way, and they were anxious, and possibly a little curious, to see it over with.

"You can say what you've got to say when you're on top of the haystack," Lavran Baker told him. "Come on, before you're tempted to kill somebody else without intendin' to."

They walked through a scurf of brittle grass to the haystack, feeling the stems break under their shoe soles. It was dry and the ground under it was dusty because no dew fell in that country so late in the year. As they crawled through the stack-yard fence, a pond of water where the sheep came to drink whitened slowly out of the dark, and the sky turned a clear faint gray like a suddenly blown-up bubble. In the dim light, everything they had looked at by the flicker of the fire seemed to have increased in size; the wick-yup, the shivering horses, the sheep-herder humped over the fire in a bed-quilt, themselves. No man felt that he himself had grown any overnight, but it seemed that all the others had, and there seemed a kind of obligation to do what they did because they looked so big and mysterious.

Nobody said anything. Three men climbed up the haystack ladder, caught Shiveley's lead-rope when it was thrown, and hauled in as he came up. Tunis Evans hove the free end over the derrick-tripod and bent the end to one of the poles. It was a rawhide riata, built for roping in timber, and therefore a good sixty feet long. Shiveley stared at it and at himself and at the sky, and they waited impatiently. They all had a fidgety feeling that it was important to get the thing done before daylight came.

"Well?" one of them said. "If you've got any talkin' to do, now's your time for it."

Nobody ever knew when or how the realization had got worked through to him that he was going to die there. It had worked through, and so had something else—something so wild and unexpected that Clay, who knew him best, was never able to think of it afterwards without feeling glad he had seen it. Of his own part in it he felt sick and ashamed. Shiveley's made it worth remembering.

"I know I did have something to say," Shiveley said. "But it don't make any difference now. Go ahead whenever you want to. I don't care."

"You'd better talk up," Lavran Baker warned him. "This is the last time around."

He had not made them understand. He had expected that he would be scared, he had discovered that he was not, and he felt proud about it. "I don't care, I tell you!" he said. "All you've got to say and all you're goin' to do don't make any difference to me! I don't care, I don't give a single good God-damn! That's plain enough, ain't it? I'm ready when you are!"

Daylight came almost as he dropped—at least it must have, for the first thing anybody noticed after he died was that the clouds overhead had turned pink and the colors of objects were visible, as well as their shapes. It was not as horrible as any of them had expected. There are a good many ignorant notions about what happens to a man when he is hung—convulsions, involuntary micturition, and such like—all based on the supposition that hanging means death by strangulation. Shiveley had dropped fifteen feet before the rope took him, and it broke his neck as instantly as turning off a switch. There was no pain or fright visible on his face, nothing but the half-amazed triumph of that last moment of finding himself not afraid, after all, and that lasted even against the slackening of his muscles when the nerves let them go.

The men wrapped him in a spare saddle blanket and buried him in stony ground outside the hay-field fence. None of them had eaten since the morning before, and nobody wanted to strike the Basque for a handout, because to feed all of them would have cleaned him out of a month's provisions. But when the burial was over he came out with a blown-up goat-skin of coarse red wine. He held it under his arm with his thumb on the nozzle, and every man knelt on the ground and had a good big slug of it pumped down him. He was a pleasant little man, that Vasco, after he got rid of the idea that they were going to swing him off the haystack, too, and he volunteered a good deal of information about himself by way of convincing them that they would be wasting their time if they did. His name was Pablo Urriagiarte, he was forty-two years old, unmarried, frugal, temperate, and afraid of nothing except snakes, bad horses, lizards, Indians, and carelessly-handled firearms. It looked as if he had picked a bad country to lavish his lion-heartedness on, considering that there was nothing much in it besides those particular things, but he had no intention of ever trying any place else. Precedent forbade. All the Vascos he had ever heard of went either to eastern Oregon to herd sheep or to Mexico to run bakeries, and he didn't know how to cook. So he stood it, and he thought in time that he might get used to rattlesnakes hanging their tails negligently down through holes in his roof and lizards getting marooned in the dishpan and having to be helped out. He had been there eighteen years, and it was already easier to stand than it had been at first.

"We ought to round up old Leonard's dogs, I guess," Lavran Baker said. "He'd want 'em to be around to see the last of him, and this little runt don't want 'em botherin' him."

The elder Carstairs stopped that wave of sentiment. "You'd better leave 'em alone," he advised. "They know they've done something they ortn't, and they'd be hard to run down. I don't want to bring up anything disagreeable, but anything that's got blood on it is meat to a hound, and that place out in the trail was— Of course we brung in all of the body we could find, but— I hate to talk about this, boys, but if I was you I'd let them hounds be."

They bequeathed the hounds to the Basque, and left him trying to decide whether to eat them or move out to get away from them. Riding back to Sorefoot was a long lug. The horses were stiff and jaded, and the men sleepy, hungry, and inclined to be snappish from a half-notion that they had done something that they might yet be called to law for. They talked little about the hanging, only mentioning, from time to time, their impression that somebody else had been responsible for it. Afterward, being fed, rested, and getting a grave ready to bury old Leonard in, they let out to old Finley what had happened. He was so hearty in his approval that they began to think it had been all right, after all, and that the country owed them considerable for having thought of it. The final effect was to bring them, whether as lynchers or public benefactors, into an instinctive feeling that they were a community among themselves and that people who entered it thereafter could never wholly belong to it. The dead they had buried could never be anybody else's now, and the blood they had taken for it stood only against them. No new man, however much they liked him, could ever vote himself into what they had seen and experienced together. No man who had not been there could be more than a visitor among them.

They buried old Leonard alongside Isaac Lund in the Sorefoot graveyard, and having contributed that much to the development of Belvista, they took old Finley's advice and shoved on to get across the county line before word of the interment got to the county seat. The reason was one that none of them had ever thought of. It had nothing to do with the killing of old Leonard and the hanging of Shiveley, only to their informal and inexpensive manner of disposing of them afterwards. In those regions the county coroner was always elected to office from the undertaking profession, which he continued to practice in connection with his political dignity. Being a coroner commonly paid no salary and not enough fees to amount to anything, so he depended for his profit upon handling the men who got shot or frozen to death or poisoned by bad whisky without leaving any relatives to claim the remains. It was his job to investigate such deaths and afterwards to see that the dead men got properly and decently buried, and he attended to it conscientiously, supplying coffin, hearse, cerements, graveside attendants, and all the trimmings that his professional training enabled him to think up. The expenses were borne by the deceased, if he was unlucky enough to have died with money still in his clothes. If not, the bill was paid by the county. In either case the coroner-undertaker managed to avoid losing on the deal, and the report that any corpses had been interred in his territory without the proper complement of funeral furniture would have made him red-eyed mad; not unlikely, old Finley thought, to the point of digging the bodies up, burying them all over again, and holding as suspects everybody who had taken any hand in burying them.

They pulled east out of the region of town sites and real-estate fortunes to come, and traveled an everlastingly long stretch of dry grass-country. Few people lived in it. Most of them were poor and either scared to death of the chances they had taken in settling there or too ignorant to realize that they had taken any. Time on that pull was measured not by the alternation of days and nights, but by the places where there was water. When they found a spring not too strong with alkali, they camped, though it might not be noon yet. When there was none they kept on, even after dark, with chil-

dren bawling and young colts pleading with mother to wait a minute
from one end of the parade to the other. There was no marker on
the road to show where the county line was, but they crowded distance enough behind them to give it plenty of leeway before they
allowed themselves any rest. It was good for all of them, for it
worked them too hard to let them think of the night hanging and
the two burials until they had got their consciences cooled off.

The first sign of restored balance was one of the younger Carstairses, who came for water to the warm mud-tank where Clay
and Clark Burdon were watering their teams with a bucket. "That
was the first man I ever laid out to be buried, that old Leonard,"
he explained. All the Carstairses were almost blindingly frank about
the limitations of their experience. There were times when it got
downright irritating. "Well, I thought, it ain't a thing I take much
relish out of, but I've got it to do and I'd hate to have people
ask me things about it afterwards that I'd been too jooberish to
notice. So I paid attention, and there was a funny thing. The calk
of that horse's shoe took the identical piece out of his head that
had got hit with the bullet. I felt glad I'd looked, because that
was a thing that wouldn't happen once in a million times. You never
knowed it to happen before, I'll bet?"

"Never in all my born days," Burdon said, and grinned his half-
grin when Carstairs went away with the rarity of his observations
confirmed. "Nor this time, either," he remarked to Clay. "I wondered if anybody else would notice that. A good thing nobody did
that had any sense, or you'd see some sicker-lookin' men around
here than there are now. Did you notice when you found him that
he hadn't been shot?"

Clay let his horse-bucket empty out onto his feet, and said not
particularly, no. "I heard him yell that he was shot, and then he
was on the ground. It didn't sound reasonable that he'd lie about
it."

"He did," Burdon said. "He thought he was shot, I expect,
hearin' the pistol right then, but it was more likely a hoofprint of
mud took him in the head. A horse's foot can pick up ten pounds
of that blue doby, and it was flyin' wild. He was bruised all the
way down to his chin, if you remember."

"I didn't notice," Clay said. "This ain't funny to me, did you know that? If it's a joke, say so, and if it ain't don't grin about it. How do you know he wasn't shot, too?"

"No place he could have been, except where the horse got him," Burdon said. "Carstairs had sense enough to figure that, but he didn't know what a man looks like that's got a bullet in the head. I do. It don't matter how dead they're killed or how quick, you'll always find the eyes rolled up tryin' to see where the slug got 'em. You notice the next chance you git."

"I'll remember," Clay said. After all, he told himself, it made no difference. The bullet could only have been accidental even if it had landed, and they had no more right to execute a man for an accidental shot than for none. Nevertheless, enough was plenty. "I don't expect ever to git any chance," he added. "I don't intend to look at a dead human being again as long as I live, and when I die I don't want anybody to look at me."

Burdon backed his team and picked up his bucket. "I said that once, a long time ago," he said. "Something a good deal like it, anyway. And now look at me."

He went away, and Clay looked at him. He had manœuvred the men into hanging Shiveley; it was his work as surely as if he had pulled the rope single-handed. He had disliked Shiveley, but not enough for that, so he could have done it only to help Clay. It was more help than Clay felt comfortable with; it was like being befriended by a tomcat who persists in bringing you donations of stinging-lizards and rattlesnakes from his hunt. But it was a favor, and he knew that when he had time to rest on it he would feel grateful. He tried to now, but it was too soon.

Chapter XIX

THE country through which they traveled grew nothing that could be observed from the road except six weeks' grass, a scrubby species of sagebrush, a few blue-green dwarf junipers so crooked that there wasn't a straight piece on them long enough to clean a pistol, and a few bunches of greasewood. The grass had once been superb. Mostly it was prairie bunch grass and *afilerilla*, which cures like hay and keeps through all changes of weather, so that the early pilgrims to the section had found a stand of it belly-deep to a horse and a mat of it on the ground that a man couldn't dig through with a pitchfork. Cattle wintered on pasture in those days, and fed themselves by pawing down through the snow to the grass that had been curing for just such an emergency for several hundred years. No better feed ever grew. Eastern Oregon cattle could trail faster, stand up longer, and grow better meat than any class of bovine that ever waved a horn.

Afterwards it got eaten up and destroyed, not by the introduction of sheep, as legend commonly makes out, but by the prevalence in the cattle-raising industry of hogs. Two-legged ones, who, judging that somebody else would get the grass if they didn't, hustled in every class of stock they could lay hands on to eat it clean, ending up with sheep to burrow down and eat out the roots. They made a good thorough job of it, and wound up with several hundred thousand head of livestock on their hands, nothing to feed them, and no place to sell them. They also filled the country with stock-trails which washed into barrancas down all the low ground so that the rain ran off as fast as it fell instead of soaking down to start more grass and furnish year-round water. Then they pulled out, firmly believing that the Lord's hand was against them, and the country had a chance to recuperate.

Not completely, for new families had come into it since. There was a bunch of them assembled in a pole corral alongside the main road, the men breaking some wild horses, and the women watching

them from the shade outside the fence. They were poor-looking
people, who lived by rousting a few head of calves to market every
spring, harvesting a back-yard patch of rye hay every fall for
winter feed, and subsisting principally on hog meat because hogs
could be fed on wild horse flesh and rattlesnakes. Their main object
in settling there appeared to have been to find a place where civilization hadn't cornered all the opportunities for wealth away from
them, and where a man could start fresh without being at a disad-
vantage on account of poverty and prejudice. As to the way it was
working out, there could be no grounds for complaint, for they were
all as even as a row of fence pickets around a court-house, with
not a feather of difference either in the length of their hair or the
brand of overalls they wore. But the fact that they had shrunk from
civilization didn't mean that they disliked it. They had only gone a
little piece up the road in hopes of heading it off instead of running after it. Now there was nothing to do but wait for it, and
they were beginning to wonder, as most all-or-nothing gamblers
sometimes will, whether they hadn't come a little too far, whether
they shouldn't have gone somewhere else, whether they might not
have been better off not coming anywhere. Mighty few prayers were
ever addressed to the Throne of Grace as fervently as theirs were
that old E. H. Harriman might be moved to build his railroad their
way so the country would settle up and put civilization back around
them again.

One thing about them was that their ambitions were reasonable
—or rather, modest. All they wanted was a near-by shipping-point,
a town where they could sell eggs and truck and do their small
marketing, and a decent increase in property values so they could
sell out, if they took a notion, for enough, at least, to pay up their
bills and take them somewhere else. If a fair-producing homestead
with water and buildings could be sold, say, for forty dollars an
acre, a man would feel that his work and hardships had not been
entirely wasted. The estimate was set by a stoop-shouldered old
gentleman with a feathery white mustache, a collar-band shirt with
no collar, and a pair of chaps busted out at the knees and mended
with binder twine.

"That would be sixty-four hundred dollars for a quarter-section,"
he added, after calculation. "Well, it ain't much, the way prices is,

but I could make it do. I ain't sayin' I'd let the place go for that, mind, if the railroad pointedly did build through here. Sixty-four hundred dollars for eight years of hard work, that's mighty small."

It seemed rather liberal, considering that there was nothing in sight that any of them could have put in eight years of hard work on unless they went around digging holes and filling them up again. Nevertheless, all of them claimed to have spent all their time at hard work, too, and they didn't consider forty dollars an acre any more than a fair return for it; and the women pointed out that *their* work had to be figured in, too, and began adding up the disagreeable chores they had performed till it sounded like an experience-meeting with everybody squabbling over who owned the blackest sin. The scroll of hard work ran up to something incredible. So much labor so long sustained ought to have been enough to cover the whole country with two feet of choice vegetable mold, spread and leveled from wheelbarrows and equipped with a complete sprinkler system to keep it damped down. The peak they ran their selling-prices up to sounded as if it had. They got to fifty, sixty, eighty dollars an acre, and maybe they wouldn't sell at all. The land, by some mysterious impulse to be communicated by the railroad, was going to raise ton lots of everything—cattle, hogs, sheep, chickens, turkeys, geese, silver foxes, strawberries, gooseberries, apples, peaches, plums, garden-truck, flax, cut flowers. The climate would cure asthma, tuberculosis, rickets, melancholia, goiter. It was going to be a remarkable region.

Taking that collective glimpse at the future made them all feel better. Not one of them, alone, would have dreamed of going for so dizzy a balloon-ride before strangers. But doing it in a bunch, each felt that he was only taking a short hop past the last speaker, and they ended at a ridiculous altitude without feeling that they were being ridiculous in the least. And there was something to their belief that the harder they worked the more certainly they could count on getting something out of it. It wasn't right, for often enough a man will throw away his work for nothing, get nothing out of it, never see it again, and never even know what the trouble with it was. But the rule these people knew was that they never got anything without getting in and digging for it, and the harder they dug the better the find was likely to be. So it was only natural for them to play the rule both ways, and conclude that if nothing came without work, everything must come with work. It helped their feelings to count up what a pile of toil they had accumulated that was still to be paid off on. It did not strike Clay, listening to them and feeling sorry for their simple-mindedness, that the same thing might still work out against himself. He had paid for Luce with the hanging. It had cost him scarcely anything; it had been easy when he expected it to be difficult, and yet it seemed to him that the account was squared and that he had at last got something without paying for it.

There was a low divide between two creeks, one flowing north into the Columbia drainage system, the other south into the alkali rain-tanks of the Great Basin. No main road came near it, but a sort of pack-trail struck through it from the alkali country to the breaks of the Burnt River mountains. Almost at the summit of the divide was a spring of water hemmed in by rimrock; and the flat below was brushed up with junipers and mountain mahogany and mock orange and clumps of wild cherry heavy with reddish-black clusters of fruit. Over the water was one single big cottonwood tree, with initials and comments cut in its bark, most of them dating from the period of the Civil War and expressing sentiments disrespectful to the Union, the President of the United States, and everybody who held a job under him. It was along this line that a part of the western Confederate armies had gone to pieces and deserted after the Union troops broke their hold on Missouri. The cottonwood was seeding, and a deep haze of blue-gray tree-cotton floated on the surface of the spring and had to be skimmed before water could be dipped out. Especially at morning, numbers of little birds came there to drink and bathe, and when you dipped water they flew up and settled on your hat and shoulders, watching nervously for fear you might be going to dip it dry.

Clay's tent was pitched among the junipers about fifty feet from the spring, and there was a little trail worn to it through the dry grass from his going there and coming back with water. It was a silent place, because he had let all the wagons pull past and go on ahead, rejecting the women's offers of help because he did not

realize at the time that they could be of any. The horses were hobbled and grazing loose in the brush. They stayed close on account
of the water, which was a lucky thing, because he had no time to
watch them. Even in the time it took him to bring wood or water,
he would hear Luce calling him, first low and indistinct, then rising
into shrill terror at the thought that he might have left her alone.
She was afraid to be alone even for the time it took him to travel
the fifty feet to the spring and back. Her own body was what frightened her. It had turned on her and set itself against her; it griped
her with such a building up of one agony on top of another that she
was afraid to trust herself with it alone, as if its system of torturing her was something secretive and intimate which the presence of
somebody else could hold back.

Her sickness started commonly enough. As their wagon passed
up the deep canyon over the divide, she caught clusters of wild red
gooseberries from the overhanging bushes, and though the berries
were barely colored, she insisted out of contrariness on eating them.
That evening she got on Wade Shiveley's mare bareback to ride
down on one of the other wagons. It was the first time she had ever
tried to ride the mare; before then she had always refused to. The
mare, for some reason, objected and threw her full length in the
short rabbit-brush. She didn't seem hurt, and even wanted to get
on and try it again, but Clay prevented.

That night she tossed a good deal, and in the morning she admitted to a case of abdominal cramps, which the jolting of the
wagon seemed to make worse. They pitched camp again to wait until
she felt better. It was that day that the wagons all pulled past,
and several women leaned out to inquire if there was anything
wrong. She was able to sit up outside the tent, and she told them
no, it was nothing but underripe gooseberries. But the next day
when the road was empty she gave up and stayed in bed. There was
nothing to give her for the pain except whisky and powdered ginger,
which was supposed to be good in cases of indigestion. He dosed
her with it, but by evening the pain was worse, and they tried cloths
dipped in boiling water. He sat up all night changing them for her,
and they helped her to get a couple of hours' sleep about daybreak.
Fright began to take hold of her when she woke up. It was not near
time for any such thing, but she was bleeding.

There was nothing that he could think of to do about that, but having him know of it made her feel better able to stand it. At least, she said, the pain was better; maybe the bleeding was getting rid of some congestion, and maybe when it went away she would be all right. She talked herself into so much courage that when he wanted to ride after the wagons and fetch back one of the women, she wouldn't let him.

"It might get worse while you're gone," she said. "I think if you stay and go on putting hot cloths on that it'll be all right by tomorrow. By tonight, maybe. And I'd sooner not have any of those women fumbling and clucking over me and trying to find out things about us."

He noticed that she seemed weak and that there was no color in her lips, but that could be accounted for by the pain she had been through. He brought hot cloths all that day and all the next night. The pain did not increase much, only hitting her in sudden blasts that stiffened her out rigid for two or three minutes and left her weak and whimpering that she had done nothing, and why was such a thing happening to her? The sun moved up and moved down the cottonwood onto the tent and burned hot through it. Toward evening the hemorrhage had let up a little, but the pain kept her from sleeping except in little three-minute naps. Both knew now that she was desperately sick, but they were so eager not to believe it that they took the slowing of her loss of blood as a sign that she was getting better, that she would be well maybe by morning. They talked through the night about going on and about the chances of finding some cross-country short cut by which they could overtake the other wagons and get there along with the rest of them. She blamed herself for having ignored his warning about green gooseberries, and was apologetic because her sickness was holding them back.

The fact that it took so little to build up her courage was not any sign that she felt better, merely that her nerves had got thin so they were easily worked on. She got no better, and the next morning something happened that made them realize what the trouble was and how dangerous a thing they had been trying to cure with ginger and hot water. The hemorrhage turned to something that even they in their ignorance could not mistake or be cheerful about any longer. She had been pregnant; the fall from Wade Shiveley's mare had hurt her inside, and she was going through a miscarriage.

That was when she gave up attempting to hold onto her courage. The discovery that it was a thing that he had been half responsible for seemed to release her from any obligation to stand it steadily, and she turned on him, crying and accusing him, striking at him when he tried to make her lie quiet, and taxing him with indifference and neglect when he backed off and let her alone. That lasted all that day. When he dozed she woke him up and cried fiercely about his selfishness, callousness, cowardice, clutching him desperately so he wouldn't leave her and talking out spite and hatred of him in a shrill voice that was all the harder to stand because it sounded perfectly natural and calculated. There was nothing that she wanted him to do, nothing that he could do. What seemed to hurt her most was the injustice of her having to suffer for what they had both done. She hated him when he ate and when he tilted over and dozed, because she could not. The right word possibly would have soothed her, but he didn't know what the right word would be. He got up and took down his rope and bridle. It was then about eleven in the morning.

"There's no use keepin' on with this," he said. "I can't do you any good stayin' here, and I may find somebody that can. A doctor, a woman, somebody. I'm goin' to look."

That was not quite honest, if there had been time to dig out exact motives. Without her accusations, he would have stayed and tried to help, no matter how much worse she got. She clutched him and said in a shaking voice that he must not leave her, that this was a sickness he had helped to bring on her and that he must stand it with her. He pulled away, and she fell back and lay watching him. "If you leave now, it's for good," she said. "You'll never see me again, I promise you. Look now, because this will be your last time."

He was ashamed to go. She could well be dying. People left alone and helpless in such country had been known to come out of it insane for life, merely from the loneliness. Yet he could do nothing by staying, he couldn't even calm her or keep her from being afraid. He told her so and pulled loose from her hand. Outside, he saddled the buckskin mare, and because Luce had been torturing him he cut the mare up with his spurs and flogged her with his quirt to see if it would make him feel better. To his surprise, it seemed to. The mare threw somersaults down the road for three miles, and he gouged her with his spurs when she didn't buck and peeled her with the quirt when she did. The job of staying on and keeping his backbone from being sprung out of joint brought him to a calmer frame of mind, and he could see that he was doing right and that he had been right not to let her frenzy dissuade him from it. He gave the mare a last tanning because it was her smartness in throwing Luce that had brought on the trouble, and rode north.

There were many birds throughout that country, because it lay on the ridge between the great nesting-grounds of the Bitter Lakes and the marshy tributaries of the Upper Snake River. Every little wire-grass mudhole had a bluish-feathered heron standing ankle-deep in it. Crimson-marked wood-ducks nested where there was fresh water, and one or two heavy pelicans from the timbered lakes to the west flapped awkwardly up from the fresh-water seeps at the edge of the tule-beds. Wild swans were nesting in the tules, and two or three lone ones went overhead, flying low with necks stretched and legs trailing, paying no attention to him. He paid none to them, because they were flying to their nests for the night. It was getting dark on him.

At sundown he followed the heaviest-marked of two roads, and rode down a long ridge over a half-dry swamp grown up with reeds and red willows. A herd of little pronghorn antelope drifted along even with him, trying to decide what he was and lifting their long shoulder-tufts of hair nervously to express suspicion of his intentions, and an eagle coasted along behind him, watching for jack rabbits that he scared up out of the road in front of him. The sky got red and then dark, the swans all settled for the night. He saw a fire on the horizon about twelve miles off, and headed for it without knowing whether he would strike anything when he got there or not.

It was not settlers' wagons and it was not a town, but it was the next best thing. Four round-topped huts of bent willow rods covered with dirty canvas were built in a square with the fire in the middle, half a dozen buck Indians lay in their blankets with the bare soles of their feet turned to the warmth, and eight or nine squaws of all ages sat on the ground barking young juniper-roots with their teeth for material to make baskets of. Inside one of the huts a very old man sat pitching and moaning and jabbering to himself, with nobody paying any attention to him, and outside on a pole was a willow cage in which a young bald eagle sat picking the eyes out of a jack-rabbit head. These were desert Indians. They were the Paiutes, the extreme northern raveling of the great Shoshonean race that ranged the backbone of the continent all the way from the Snake River to the Rio Grande in Texas. These were real wanderers; homelessness was one of their traditions; they had no feeling of belonging in any country and they lived in the desert as nature and the seasons drove them, following the muddy river downstream as frost locked the upper waters in winter, trailing it back up as the heat dried the lower reaches in summer. Religious prophecy was one of their addictions, and they looked upon communion with the Almighty by means of fits and swooning-spells as almost an everyday occurrence. The old gentleman in the wickyup was probably taking down a declaration from the Throne at that very moment. The caged eagle was another piece of theological furniture. Eventually he was to be turned loose to carry messages aloft to dead relatives.

The plateau Shoshoneans did not call themselves after any location, because they changed residence too often to have one, but after the pursuit in life that most bothered and interested them. Their name for themselves was Dika, which means eaters. They distinguished between tribal subdivisions according to what each ate the most of. There were Salmon Eaters, Sucker Eaters, Sheep Eaters, Digger-squirrel Eaters, Sunflower-seed Eaters, Dog Eaters, Chipmunk Eaters, Grasshopper Eaters. They were poor, hardworking, harmless, not extremely clean, and with a habit of sizing up present company by past contacts that didn't speak very well for their discernment. The Paiutes didn't know the Coast trade-jargon, and Clay tried them with what he knew of Plains sign-talk. He stuck one thumb between two fingers to indicate that he wanted to see one of the women. A wrinkled old hen grinned at him, motioned one of the girls into an empty hut, and held up two fingers, as a sign that her services would cost him two dollars, cash in advance.

"Oh, to hell with you, you low-minded old fool!" Clay said, almost crying with weariness and too much to think about. "Find me somebody that's got a little sense, can't you? I've got a sick girl, and I want somebody to come and help me tend to her."

The women all took counsel together. It took a long time, because a peculiarity of the Paiute language is that every speaker has to repeat word for word what the last speaker has said before answering. The girl who had gone into the hut said: "We are not doctors, but if there is anything sick with your girl that we know, one of us will go. It is not smallpox?"

Clay told them what it was, and they talked that over until they all got it straight. Then, irritatingly, they tittered. "But that is nothing very bad to be sick with," the young woman said, comfortingly. "All this woman have make that sickness much, not to have children. With hot rocks, with bumping against a camas-digger, they do that. And they do not die. Look, they are not dead?"

Obviously they weren't. "Come on, anyway," Clay said. "If you've been through it you ought to know something about it. Load up whatever you need and let's get started."

Another conference ensued, and the wrinkled squaw fetched a couple of bundles of dried weeds. The young squaw remarked diffidently that as her original idea of what he wanted had been quoted at two dollars, she thought this ought to be worth five, because it would take so much more of her work and time. He paid her and she put the money away, and one of the men got up, apparently out of a profound sleep, and caught her a horse. She remarked several times that she was not guaranteeing that she could help any. In her experience of such matters, no help was needed. You did it, and you either got over it by yourself or you didn't. But she would try. Clay urged her to come on and quit talking about it, and they started.

He had not realized, coming out, how much road he had laid between him and the spring on the divide, because the point he made for had always been merely the nearest horizon. Now all the horizons were points that he had to get over, they were all barriers between him and the place he had to hurry back to, and every one of them took hours to top. There was nothing to look at except the road, which gave him the impression of having stretched under him, and a few stray owls. The darkness held him back. He didn't want it, but he didn't want it to end, because it would mean that he had been away that much longer, that Luce would have been lying alone in the tent with nothing between her and the menace of her body for close to a whole day. A day, and she had been out of her head with terror at being left by herself for three minutes while he went to the spring for water.

Daylight came. Swans flapped overhead, rabbits got out of the way in the gray light, a flock of quail trotted across the road and flushed noisily, the sun moved its edge over the naked water-cut hills. He could see the cottonwood over the spring a long way off, so it seemed that he was almost there. But the sun moved faster than he could. It was a quarter of the way up the sky when the Indian woman turned her horse into the junipers ahead of him and got off. The mare was so tired that he dismounted and ran the last two hundred yards through the brush to the tent, and there was no tent there. There were nothing but the stakes, the worn place on the ground where it had been, the pile of ashes where he had heated water. She was gone, she had carried out her threat and left; she had told him it was the last time, and it had been.

It was not only that. Everything else was gone, too—the tent, the horses, the wagon, the bedding and cooking things. There was no sign to show when she had left. The fire was cold, but that meant nothing. She had been too weak to keep it built up when he left her.

He explained to the Indian woman what had happened, persuaded her that he had not lured her there on a pretext to assail her virtue, and cast around the junipers for more sign. Somebody had helped her move; that was a sure thing. She could not, even in twenty-four hours, have gained enough strength and spirit to strike a tent, load it and all the camp-rig into the wagon, and run in and harness a team of horses. But she had got better, for she had remembered to make a kind of division of the property. In the middle of the thickest junipers he found the part that she had left for him; a roll of blankets, a package of food, his rifle that she had helped pay for, some extra clothes. Nothing else, and no sign to show where she had gone or why. He carried the things back to the road, and the Yahandika woman had news for him. The tracks in the road, as well as she could read them, said that after Clay left one wagon had come with many horses behind it. All the horses had gone away, and two wagons had gone away. They had gone down the divide along the road that the settlers had taken.

"You can't tell how long ago?" Clay said. Of course that could only be the horse-trader. The helpless old bawly-ike had reached her at last, and at a time when she was ready for him. "Does anybody else ever travel this road? Or anybody with a house on it where I could ask whether they've seen her go past?"

The woman said a freighter traveled it, hauling ore and concentrates from some placer mines around Burnt River. He was on the road most of the time, going or coming. But, she mentioned doubtfully, he was not a good man. He didn't tell the truth, he let his horses steal pasture that belonged to other people, and he was a half-breed and refused to admit it. He was also a good deal of a blowhard, and it would not be possible to say which side of the divide he was on or which way he was going.

"Maybe I can trail 'em by the tracks," Clay said. "You might as well go on back home. I'm sorry I bothered you."

The woman said she was going, and lingered uneasily. One thing that bothered her was her inability to understand why he should want to follow a girl who had skipped out on him. Another was a thing that he had just finished learning, having the lesson and the moral beaten into him far more thoroughly than was necessary. A man paid for what he got, he paid all it was worth, and he was lucky if he didn't pay more and in a different coin than he had bargained for. She had learned it, too.

"It is the money you paid me," she said. "The five dollars you gave me in the camp. But now I have not done anything you paid me to do, but if you would still want me for anything . . ."

He told her to keep the money and never mind, and he felt, watching her ride away, that he had at least helped somebody to beat the blamed rule once. He was probably wrong even about that. The

Yahandika woman worried all the way back to her camp for fear she must be losing her looks.

There was little over the divide to measure distance by except the time it took to traverse it. He set his marks on a juniper in the distance and rode to it, and set them on another and rode to that. He shut his eyes and promised himself not to open them until he had pulled even with it, and opened them, feeling sure he must have passed it, to find that it was still as far away as ever. The mare was so tired when he started that her feet dragged, and by nightfall he was riding with most of his weight on his spurs to keep her from quitting on him. In that alkali-flat country curious things happened, which he might have put down as worth the trip if he had been fresh and had his mind clear. In the big stretches the alkali reflected the exact dark blue of the sky, and that parted to right and left as he rode into it, so that he rode with the sky rubbing either elbow and washing softly back from the mare's feet as she advanced. There were places where spots in the clear air expanded with heat and magnified distant sections of scenery so they seemed only a few feet away, and then they would go on expanding until they got gigantic, until a couple of sage-rats cutting grass would look as big as colts; and then they would vanish as if they had been dissolved in water. A herd of antelope would rise into the sky and move solemnly through it, every hair patterned clearly and naturally, only ten times as big as antelope ever grew, and upside down. All that was the effect of reflected sunlight from dazzling white ground against perfectly clear air. The final effect was that the glare beat against the under side of his eyeballs until it was agony to move them, until even the touch of his lids on them burned like live coals. Then the sun went down and blackbirds and yellowhammers flew in the salt-bush, and the mare did quit.

He camped that night at a mud spring in some scrub cottonwoods. The water was vile with alkali, and there was no grass except wild rye, which nothing will eat, but he fed the mare cottonwood bark and washed out her mouth and nostrils from his canteen. He spread out food and looked at it, hoping to tempt himself to eat, but at last he put it way again and lapsed into a sort of drowsiness that at times almost became sleep. It never got to be sleep entirely, for he had run himself to that nerve-wracking stage of being too hungry to sleep and too sleepy to eat. But he made out to rest, and at daylight he got up and hunted out his food again and ate. He peeled more bark for the mare and slept, this time soundly. It was about noon when the rattling of a wagon woke him. He could see it coming five miles off across the plain, with a great billow of white dust hoisting along behind it. He got up, pulled his packs together, and ate again while he waited for it to pull in.

It was a ragged-butted-looking outfit, the wagons all loose-wheeled and threatening to shed spokes and tires, the horses wash-boarded at the ribs and not much bigger than good-sized deer, and the harness nothing but collar and hames, patched with pieces of rope and old overall-cloth and uncured rawhide. In pleasant country such horses probably couldn't have scraped up strength to keep such a rig moving at all. But the layout around them was so unpleasant that they were willing to outdo themselves to get out of it. They dragged along by a series of convulsive efforts, and the freighter sat in his saddle on the near-wheeler and threw rocks at them when they threatened to collapse. He packed a jerk-line which he didn't need because there was only one road and no temptation to wander from it, and a brake-rope which he didn't use, because the outfit moved lethargically enough as it was. He yelled, "Hold up!" threw a rock at a horse that tried to lie down, and sat back in his saddle to snort some of the dust out of his gullet. The Indian woman had said he was a half-breed, but under that white coating of alkali he could have passed for anything—an albino, an eighty-year-old Pullman porter, any age or any color. Clay explained that he was looking for a girl who was probably traveling with a horse-trader's rig.

"They're supposed to have come along this road yesterday night or early this morning. Two wagons, a man and a woman, and a pretty girl that looks like she'd been sick. If you've passed 'em, how far along was they? I'm in a hurry."

The freighter ate a helping of tobacco, got it working well, and pulled out his shirt-tail to wipe his face on. He stared from Clay to the buckskin mare and back, and said he would be teetotally

snuggered if this country, hellhole though it was, didn't draw everybody in the world.

"Ever' damn thing a-goin'," he insisted. "Old E. H. Harriman
a-rangin' around eighty mile or so from here last month, a Nazarene
revival over at Chicken Springs last week, a flock of settlers day
before yesterday or so, and now this. Hell, I'd know that buckskin
mare if she swallered me in my sleep, and I'd know you if you was
stuck head first into a mudhole. That's Wade Shiveley's mare from
Shoestring, and you're that kid of his that let him out of jail.
Never mind your gun, now. Hell, I'm a married man with two
childern, and you couldn't raise a fight out of me with a fine-comb.
You beat me out of a pair of pants once, do you know that?"

Clay put the gun away. He knew the freighter now. It was the
big loud-mouthed boy from old Phin Cowan's half-breed ranch
who had helped him plant the empty pistol to take to Wade Shiveley
in jail. His name was Zack Wall.

"I remember the pants," Clay said. "I remember you helped with
that jailbreak when I didn't want you to. It wasn't supposed to
work, but it did."

"I don't know anything about helpin' with any jailbreak," Zack
Wall said, primly. "You can't prove that I did, and you got no
business sayin' things you can't prove. Ain't that right? I got a
wife and childern to look out for now, and I've straightened up
and got over all that rippin' around that I used to do. And helpin'
a man to break jail is bad business. Did you know there was a
reward out for the man that done that, not sayin' who he is? Yes,
sir, two hundred and fifty dollars cash, gold coin of the United
States. The sheriff hung that up, because he's afraid they'll beat
him in the election on that Shiveley business. They ort to, the mess
he made out of it. Turnin' an outlaw like that loose on the country
after all the trouble they'd had to catch him."

"Shiveley's dead," Clay said, "never mind how, and if you can
use any of that reward you can start earnin' it right now. If you
can't, I'm lookin' for a two-wagon outfit, a bunch of tradin'-horses,
a man and woman, and a sick girl. If you saw 'em, which way was
they headin'?"

Zack Wall shook his head. "She works out all right, except the
woman," he said. "No outfits been along with any woman in 'em.

A man and a bunch of horses and a sick girl. Well, she did look peaked. She was layin' on some quilts in the ——"

"Where, damn it, where?" Clay said. "Let that tobacco of yours alone for a minute!"

"Right on this freight line," Zack Wall said. "Headed right apast me, and said they wanted to go to the nearest settlement. That's Burnt River Station, where I run to, so I directed 'em and away they larruped. But there wasn't any woman there. There was a man and a girl, and they said they wanted to go to Burnt River and they might do some horse-racin' around there, and they said not to tell anybody I'd seen 'em on the road, come to think about it. I got a wife and childern at Burnt River Station, and I believe this horse-racin' business brings in an undesirable element."

"You've got a wife and family; now talk about something else for a change," Clay said. "Which one of 'em said they was goin' to do horse-racin'?"

Zack Wall didn't recollect. They had both talked kind of all at the same time, he thought. One thing he could swear to, though, was that there had been no woman along.

"If you're fixin' to stay around here very long, there's a spring of good water about eight miles down," he added. "Good water and wild hay. It ain't much of a country, but she's all right for a man to lay out in awhile. Election's this fall, and then you won't need to worry about that reward any more. The sheriff will draw back on it whether he gits beat or whether he gits elected. You could shack up there and nobody'd ever know it. I ain't a man to go around doin' any loose talkin', you can depend on that. I don't know a blamed thing about you. Never laid eyes on you before. It ain't any of my business, and I've got a wife and ——"

"I don't aim to stop here," Clay said. "Passin' through, that's all."

"Burnt River Station might suit you to lay over in," Zack Wall said. "There's a stage-hotel you could put up at, and there ain't much ever goes on there. About all the news they git is what I bring in with me, and I don't do any talkin' about what don't concern me. A man can't, in my position."

Clay said he didn't plan to stop there, either. He could see all too clearly what the prospects would be. With Zack Wall to start news and the Carstairses to spread it, Burnt River Station was no

place for him. And what was there to go there for now? She had
left him, she must have known that he would try to find her, she
was trying to fix it with people she passed on the road so he
wouldn't. It must be more than anger at his leaving her alone, it
must be that terror over her sickness had worked deep into her,
and that she wanted to go back to a kind of life where such things
didn't happen. And the risk was hers, so she had a right to say
whether she should run it or not. He shook hands with Zack Wall,
explained that he thought of dropping down into the tule country
for the rest of the summer, and pretended to be busy packing up
until the freight-wagons had pulled away into the glare of sunshine
behind their pillar of white dust. Then he pulled more cottonwood
bark for the mare and ate again.

His first decision had been to stay away from her because she
was in the right. After eating he felt steadier and more capable of
figuring, and he decided to stay away from her because she was in
the wrong. He had promised her once that he would never leave
her without first telling her. He had not asked her to promise,
because she hadn't seemed to think it possible that she could ever
want to leave him. She had gone into a bargain without knowing
enough about herself to know whether she could keep it. Of course
it was not the same as lying; it was simply that she had been too
ignorant of herself to know what she could stand, but it did the
same amount of harm. She had been wrong to do it, and if he went
near her she was liable to do it again.

Along in the afternoon, he thought of moving to the spring that
Zack Wall had recommended. But he did not do it. For some reason
the naked seep of bitter alkali that had seen the start of his determination to go it alone seemed to help harden him in it. He
divided the remaining water in his canteen between himself and
the mare, fed her more cottonwood bark, and slept there that night.
In the morning he got ready to move, and a heavy-set man with
gray hair came over the divide on foot, leading a pack-horse, and
helped him to decide where to go to.

For an ordinary crop-worker, the heavy-set man had the most
complete set of business-like ideas that Clay had ever run into. He

had a new clean shave and a clean shirt, a tight, self-satisfied expression about his mouth and eyes, and a camp outfit that weighed close to two hundred pounds and contained every essential of housekeeping except a cookstove and a carpet-sweeper. He had been working as a lambing-hand in the alkali lakes country, and, the season having ended, he was heading north for the wheat-fields to work in the harvest. He was an expert sack-sewer, and six dollars a day and board was the lowest wages he ever looked at. The way to get ahead of this short-stake labor game was to learn some kind of work that people were likeliest to be short of, and then instead of having to beg and kiss people's tails for a job, you made them beg you. The thing to do was to sell your work, not your complexion or politics or church membership or ability to do sleight-of-hand tricks for the girls after working-hours.

"You're up mighty late, for a young man that expects to live on the work he does," he remarked, critically, sitting down. "You'll never git anywhere that way, and you'll have to learn to do different if you're goin' to throw in with me."

Clay explained that he had been going it hard and that he would adopt more punctual habits when the time came to get any good out of them.

"It's time right now," the gray-haired man said, firmly. "Lookin' for work is exactly the same as workin'; it's got to be charged in against the wages you draw. That's business, and I'm a business man. I don't do this pitchforkin' and lambin' drudgery as a business."

His regular business, it developed, was running a laborers' flop-house, generally around the North End of Portland or the slave-market section of Seattle. Ten cents a night, a place to lock up your valuables where the other lodgers couldn't steal them, and a hot bath recommended before turning in. There was money in it, but it was a trade you had to know thoroughly or it would fizzle on you sure. Take such items as bad-smelling clothes, or bedbugs. Most new hands at the business tried to eliminate both, and eliminated all their steadiest customers in the operation. Flophouse lodgers didn't expect their quarters to smell like a boudoir and most of them had bedbugs or they wouldn't be there. The people who hadn't

were too few to bring in any money, so the business way was to
let them object and be damned. He always did that.

There were some things, of course, that you could afford to be
strict about, and some that you had to. Whisky in bed was abso-
lutely barred, because a drunk man annoyed people trying to sleep
and was liable to wreck furniture. Women were on the blacklist
because having them around was sure to start the men fighting
over them. It was like any other business, everything had to be
figured on the basis of what would pay and what wouldn't.

"But you quit it to come out here and work lambs?" Clay said.
"What was that for?"

The gray-haired man said with the greatest frankness that he
sometimes struck a run of hard luck and got his flophouse locked
up for non-payment of rent or some similar quibble. What he was
doing now was raking together a stake to start another one before
winter set in. Winter was the season when they paid best, though
it seemed that the last one had gone broke during the winter. He
was a little hard to find the right explanation for, his complacency
was so profound, his understanding of business precepts so strik-
ingly shrewd and farsighted, and it was so clear that every time he
undertook to get action on his accumulated wisdom he went busted.

It was the fact that he had gone busted that accounted for everything. All his precepts and principles had been got up, not to run
a business on, but to excuse himself for having failed to run one.
A man who is making a go of anything doesn't bother to draft a
table of maxims about it; he does what his common sense tells him
to do, and he may not do it the same way twice in succession. But
an insolvent banker before a grand jury, a busted merchant facing
a creditors' committee, will almost invariably be prepared to deliver a regular philosophic discourse upon the great precepts underlying the business of banking or merchandising, and it will usually
be a good one because it is a matter of pride to him to convince
everybody, including himself, that his hard luck was not his fault.
Nobody can discuss agriculture so learnedly as a farmer who hasn't
paid the interest on his mortgage for eight years, nobody can
describe a military campaign with so deep an understanding of the
principles controlling the art of war as the commander who got the
worst of it. At least, the gray-haired man didn't offer anything on

the fundamentals of sewing sacks for a threshing outfit, so it seemed possible that he got along at that pretty well.

"I can't sew sacks, but I can handle a team," Clay said.

"You'll probably jig sacks," the gray-haired man said. "I'll see that they put you to doin' something. Sack-sewers is scarce, so they'll hire you to git me. You'll have to take to gittin' up earlier than this, though."

Chapter XX

THE sky over the alkali desert and over the gray sagebrush that fell away from it to the north was so intensely dark blue that a man was likely to get the impression that it contained little light, and a few days of practicing that theory were sufficient to burn his eyes out so he couldn't see at all. Beyond in the wheat-fields the light was weaker, but it looked stronger because the sky was all a hot, blinding yellow from the dust and chaff particles that floated up from threshing. Sometimes in the shank end of harvest it got so heavy that the sun moved through it as through thick smoke— small, round, and blood crimson. In such times the air cooled and was easier to breathe. But work went no easier, because it got on the men's nerves to have such a sun over them. They kept staring at it and stalling through their work without keeping their minds on what they were doing.

The header-separator system of threshing was the one in use in that country. Farther north in the Palouse there were combined harvesters, working thirty horses on one drawbar and cutting a twenty-four-foot swath at one swipe, all threshed, sacked, and ready to deliver before the stubble it grew on had stopped wiggling. But combines were too heavy and cumbersome in those days for country that was rolling or broken. The separator stood still, the headers waded out cutting the grain, and the header-beds caught it and brought it in to be threshed.

The separator stood planted in a cleared space in the middle of the field; tall, angular, bright scarlet in color, and louder than forty tons of junk falling down a sheet-iron chute. The stationary engine that drove it was black and located well off to one side so sparks wouldn't get in the threshed straw. It looked greasy and hot and hellish, and it was connected to the thresher by an eighty-foot driving-belt, crossed in the middle so it wouldn't jump the wheel. The mobile section consisted of the headers, which were also red, with tall skeleton-fans to bend the grain into the sickle, and the header-beds which traveled with them to collect it when cut. The headers were red, too, and it was a pretty sight to watch them working up through the dark yellow stand of grain on a side hill, leaving a white track where they had cut over. One man drove the header, and one, called the header-puncher, guided the sickle so it cut all the grain an even distance down the stem. When enough grain had come out to fill one header-bed, another took its place and it drove to the separator to be unloaded, the grain being shoveled off onto a slotted belt arrangement which carried it in to be threshed. The men who did the unloading were spike-pitchers, the man who oversaw the process was the separator-tender. Clay was the sack-jig, and his station was beside a spout on one side where the threshed grain came out. He held a gunny sack to the spout, shaking it down as it filled, and when it was plumped clear to the top he set it in front of the gray-haired man to be sewed, and hung a new one on the spout.

The sacks, filled properly, weighed seventy pounds apiece. A strong man could rather easily have killed himself jigging a day's run if he went at it ignorantly. The trick of the business was to post one foot on the ground, bend your knee, and tip the sack over it. The worst part of the job was the noise, which was incessant and deafening, and the chaff and dust, which worked into throat and clothes and skin and eyes and hair and itched an unpracticed man half-crazy. The best part was to look up, when the headers were making their round in the heat of the afternoon, and watch them climb up through the hot yellow wheat into the hot yellow sky and move in it, tall and scarlet and steady, turning their fan-arms in its yellow light for a couple of minutes and then wheeling and coming down again as if that had been nothing.

In that time wheat-ranches did not own their own individual threshing-rigs. There was usually one to a community, and it threshed for everybody in turn, cleaning up each ranch as it went and charging for the number of acres handled. The proprietor was generally a man who was not able to make a living without that extra revenue, and in most cases he was afflicted by some handicap like a missing limb or twelve children or political ambitions or weak-mindedness. The handicap of Clay's employer was piety. It had kept him from getting anywhere all his life, but he hung onto it, and maybe he was justified, for it did at least make people feel that he needed to be looked out for. He had once owned a ranch of his own, but he neglected it to follow a series of revival-meetings around the country, and the bank took it away from him. Then the community clubbed in and bought him a spring wagon and team, and gave him the contract to haul their kids to school morning and evening. He stuck to that faithfully until a protracted meeting hit the country, and that tempted him beyond his strength. He passed it at ten in the morning on his way back from school, and tied his team to a stump and glanced in to see what was going on. At eight in the evening he was still there, testifying to his own miracle of redemption, and his team got scared at a passing load of hay, ran away, and smashed wagon, harness, and themselves all to pieces. The threshing outfit was the community's final throw at keeping him going. He couldn't tie it up to attend prayer-meeting, because the men's wages went on whether they worked or not, and he couldn't take it to prayer-meeting with him, because it took up too much room and the men sat around outside and said bad words.

He was a nice-looking man, a widower of around forty, very well-meaning and polite with everybody, and without any bad habits except his unbreakable addiction to religious conventicles. He had tried to break himself of them several times, but never with any success. One hallelujah was enough to start him off on a regular round of them, following wherever they went and stopping wherever they stopped until his money ran out. It was only in his more despondent moments that he would admit that the habit had harmed him. He neglected his job of separator-tending to explain to Clay and the sack-sewer that, taking one thing with another, it was a great satisfaction to him to have lived a godly life, and worth every cent it had cost. Once, he related, he had eaten a meal without saying grace over it, and it gave him a colic that he was a solid week recovering from. Since then he had never omitted to return thanks for every crumb he touched. He appeared to think that was a kind of recommendation of the practice, though it seemed much better not to start if it was apt to catch a man up so smartly for neglecting it afterwards.

The man who gave him the most trouble on the crew was his engine-operator, a sawed-off old ex-soldier with a beaky face, a felt hat with the top of the crown burnt out, and a hard, mean voice like picking a comb. He couldn't be fired, because the engine was his and the separator couldn't run without it, and he devoted all his ingenuity to taking digs at the separator-owner's piety.

"Come over here a minute, Reverend," he would call, having thought of another one. "I want to ask you something, and I want you to tell me the truth. How many women have you ever had intercourse with besides your wife?"

The owner never got it through his head that he was being joked with. He would assert, with rigid earnestness, none, and the engineer would flatten out on the coal-pile and let on to be scandalized.

"You a Christian, and lie like that!" he would murmur. "Why, there ain't man in this country that could make me believe a thing like that about himself. Come on, now, tell the truth," and more of the same until he had the poor votary of the Light on the verge of a fainting-fit trying to clear a charge of untruthfulness without stumbling into one of adultery.

Another of the engineer's favorites was Biblical commentary. He would lead off with some allusion to the liquor question, the miracle at Cana, or the wine-for-thy-stomach's-sake gag, and manœuver the reverend into asserting that the beverage referred to was non-alcoholic—according to revised readings, grape juice. Then he would snatch the debate back to another section of Scriptures, and come up with a challenge about that. "Grapejuice is a mocker, look not on the grapejuice when it is red, hey? Come on, now, explain that one!" Which, of course, the reverend couldn't do, except by offering feebly that when the Bible was against it, it was wine, and in other places it was grape juice. The engineer delighted in such pin-downs, and took merciless advantage of them. "Lot's daughters got him drunk on grape juice, did they?" he would sneer. "That explains considerable. I never did think that old scalawag was as drunk as they made him out to be."

The engineer had read and memorized nearly all of the poetry of Lord Byron, in which he seemed to have found the virtues for which he had ransacked humanity in vain. He had never met any man in whose acquaintance he took the smallest satisfaction, though he had been through the Civil War and seen Grant and Meade and Sheridan, Lee at the surrender, Longstreet when he was garrisoned in the South, and he didn't remember who all else. He thought nothing of any of them. Some had been too lazy to do anything, some had been fools and done too much. When you were young you went around thinking people in the world were arranged in layers according to merit, but afterwards you got over that and found the layers simply fell that way in the shuffle. Plenty of men got big names by not doing anything except concealing the fact that they didn't know enough to pour chamber lye out of a boot. As for the war itself, he had supposed it would teach him something that would be of use in later years, and it hadn't. It had merely taken a lot of his time, frittered away a lot of his energy that he might have spent on something useful, and had left him no recollection that was of any service to him except that men generally made fools of themselves in a crisis.

In illustration he told about the battle of Fredericksburg, in which his brigade had been sent to charge up a long bare hill against a stone wall which the rebels occupied. At least he had been told that it was a stone wall; he never got close enough to see it. The rebels shot the front of the brigade all to hell, and the men lay down and refused, sensibly, to take any more of it. So another brigade was sent up to charge over them and take the wall so they could get out of there alive, and a funny thing happened. His outfit wouldn't let the relief brigade go through. No, sir, they hadn't been able to take the wall, and they didn't want anybody else to. They caught hold of men's coat-tails and pants legs to keep them from going on; they grabbed and threw them, and when part of the brigade got through anyway they fired into the men's backs. So the charge went to pieces again, and they lay there and got picked off like gobblers in a turkey-shoot till nightfall, and then what was left of them retired.

"Them's your heroes for you," he said. "Them's the white-haired but gallant old ranks of veterans that march in the G. A. R. parades. Preservers of the Union, hey? I preserved as much of it as they did, and I know how it was done. Yes, and Gettysburg, too. I killed a man at Gettysburg. I bored him right through the heart, and then I went over to make sure I'd downed him good. He was the colonel of my regiment, and a stuck-up damned nincompoop, and I killed him to save somebody else the trouble. I didn't bother the rebels. What's the use shootin' a lot of men you've got nothing against when there's plenty on your own side that ought to be shot? Kill off the men you don't like, no matter which side they're on, that was the principle I always stuck to. I'll bet I had more fun out of a battle than anybody else in it. Come to that, I may have done more to put down the Rebellion, too. I killed a power of damn fools, I can tell you that."

Clay remarked that the war must have been of some benefit to him, by that showing.

"Not me," the engineer said. "Hadn't been for the war, I wouldn't have needed to kill 'em. It was only on account of the war that they bothered me."

The other men on the threshing-crew were pretty much ordinary livestock, mostly hoboes and home-town incorrigibles grown up, with the addition, almost indispensable to any threshing-crew, of one frightened-looking youth with fuzzy hair who was supposed to have written some poetry, and on that account not to know much about the great rollicking world. Largely for his benefit, they talked a good deal about past naughtiness that they had been guilty of, mostly when they were between twelve and fifteen years old. One old dodderer who drove header-bed for a while claimed to have fought Indians and narrated some powerful yarns about the performances of the boys in blue at the Black Kettle massacre.

Wheat cultivation on that plateau had been going on for over fifty years, and two different methods were practiced. There was a settlement of French-Canadians—pink-cheeked, shapeless people with bristly black hair and oxlike expressions—who stuck to one modest quarter-section apiece and farmed it so diligently that it fetched them from forty to fifty bushels an acre regularly. The other school of husbandry was Americans, who owned two thousand to three thousand acres apiece, scratched over it the best they could in the time they had, and raised around twenty bushels to the acre and yearned for more land. The threshing season ended, in their country, on a four-thousand-acre ranch that belonged to an old couple named Helm who had been there longer than anybody else. The old man was frail and delicate-looking, with a long frizzly white mustache like old lace and a loud bawly voice. His wife was half a head taller, with a hard countenance and a fixed notion that nobody around her was getting enough to eat. She had one talent of which she was extremely proud—that of being able to get a full hot meal, at any hour of the day or night, on five minutes' notice. A stranger would ride up to the gate to ask what time it was or which road went where, and her voice would salute him from the kitchen.

"Take your horse down to the barn and throw him a feed!" she would order. "Your dinner'll be ready against you git back!"

Sometimes a man would try to argue with her that he wasn't hungry, and sometimes one would hurry to catch her before she could get the table spread, but none of them ever succeeded. The dinner was always there on time; it was always hot and well-cooked, and people always ate rather than offend her. Usually there would be young beef or bull veal, a dish of string beans with ham, fried cabbage with bacon, a dish of corn in milk, boiled potatoes with cream gravy, red gooseberry preserves, and either pie or a bread pudding with raisins.

She disliked harvest-hands, and worked from four in the morning till ten at night cockering up grub for them that they wouldn't get tired of. She disliked horses, and wouldn't allow a man on the place who sat down to her table without first stabling and feeding his nag; she had it in for all of her neighbors, and kept a calendar of their gestation periods and would ride miles through a blizzard to be on hand with help when one of them was having a baby. About the main purpose of the ranch, which was wheat-raising, she appeared to care nothing whatever. It took her exactly as much work when the yield was five bushels an acre as when it was thirty-five, and she did it with exactly the same energy and drive. She squabbled with her husband incessantly, and because their two children had gone away and dropped out of sight years before, she watched him and fretted constantly for fear he would overdo at some job of work and damage himself. It was on that account that she asked Clay to stay on after the harvesters were through work, so that, in case the old man should undertake to bust a two-year-old colt or tail a full-grown bull, there would be somebody around to pull him off before he got killed.

Clay did not think much of the job, being afraid old Helm would fall apart from constitutional ricketiness and that he would be blamed for it, but it was two dollars a day and board, and the sack-sewer told him to take it.

"It ain't business to turn down an offer like that, I don't care if you would sooner come with me," he said. He was pointing for Montana for the late harvests there. "It's for your own good, and if you turn it down you can't travel with me, anyhow. I won't travel with no man that's fool enough to refuse a good business offer. If you're around Portland any time this winter, I'll see you. I've give you your start, now take advantage of it."

It was quiet on the naked plateau with all the harvesters gone and all the wheat headed; quiet and hot, with nothing much to do except a little fence-mending and a little horse-breaking which didn't get along very fast because old Helm insisted on helping and getting in the way. Winds came and blew the dust out of the sky, though it still hung around the horizon in a red-yellow ring that cooled the sun early in the afternoon and kept it dark gold and feeble until late in the morning. Quail and prairie chickens hatched out in the stubble late in July, and the first rains came early in August. Rain did not change the appearance of the landscape much. It was all wheat, and the dead white stubble stayed as dead after the rain as before it. But it did catch Mrs. Helm riding back from one of her confinement cases, and it fetched her down with a lung congestion that sounded so bad Clay wanted to go for a doctor. She had a curious old-fashioned bashfulness about doctors, and she had some mystic belief that nothing would ever go seriously wrong with her until her husband was dead.

"You go look out for Mr. Helm and let me be," she ordered him. "I'll bet he's out there right now doin' something that'll over-tax his strength. Go out and see what he's up to. I'll make out all right."

That evening supper came on the table late for the first time in her married existence, and she had fever and could only talk in a hoarse metallic croak. The next morning there was no breakfast at all until Clay got it, and Mr. Helm complained thunderously at having to start his day off with a miserable spread of eggs and sowbelly and cold bread. Clay wanted to ride for the doctor again, but they were both against him and he did not insist. He had ridden for help once against a patient's wishes, and once was more than plenty. He slept in the house that night instead of in the hired men's bunkhouse, and along past midnight he heard the old lady moving and went in to see whether she was worse. She had got up and dressed, and she was sitting on the edge of the bed fumbling with her shoestrings. She broke one and went "tst!" to herself so naturally that he had a wild notion she must suddenly have got well. Her voice was also entirely casual and natural. It was only when the moonlight through the window caught her face that he saw how far gone she was.

"You're the boy we've got workin' for us," she said, without troubling to remember his name. "Go out to the barn and throw a saddle on my horse—the gray one. Hurry up. I thought I could do this in the daytime, but I won't have time. It's got to be now, and we've got to hurry."

He tried to make her lie down, but she pushed him away and repeated her orders about the horse. He could either saddle for her or she would go do it herself. She meant it, so he saddled her stiff old gray mare and helped her on in the moonlight at the gate. Then he saddled his own horse and followed her, and it was a ghostly ride. She was out to look over the land that she had spent her life on and to count up all that her fifty years of work had got her. This was the first time she had stopped long enough to think of it.

Clay had intended to hold well behind her and not show himself unless she fainted or started to get weak. But she had trouble opening the gate into the home wheat-field, so he caught up and helped her with it, and she waited for him and rode along, talking to him as if his being there was entirely natural.

"This was the land we took first," she said. "A donation land claim, this was. Twelve hundred-odd acres of it, all in sagebrush when we come here. We grubbed it and worked it over with a drag. The two children was born while we was clearin' this land. We fixed a seat between the plow-handles for the biggest one, and I packed the little one on my back. Once the Indians burnt us out, and I laid here in the green wheat with the two of 'em and watched."

It was a mile and a half to the end of the home wheat-field. The ground beyond sloped to a half-meadow and the wreck of an old cabin near some little springs. "We bought this," she said. "Five years we took payin' for it. It wasn't high for the kind of land it is, but money was scarce and there wasn't many markets for wheat then. There was a grove of cottonwoods around the springs, and we cut 'em and pulled the stumps. Five years for this piece of land, and we got it cheap. I didn't see a woman or have a new dress till we got it paid for."

They crossed that and climbed the slope to the ridge. Harvesting had been good there because the wheat ran so heavy. "A pack of Indians claimed this section," she said. Her breath was coming short and heavy, but she paid no attention when Clay ventured that they had better postpone the rest of it till some other time. "They claimed it and wouldn't move off. We got some men together and come up here in the night. The men set fire to their house and shot 'em when they run out into the light. One woman had been goin' to have a baby, but they shot her, too. Afterwards there was some lawsuits about it, one lawsuit after another with the gover'ment. But they never proved anything, and Mr. Helm bought the land from the men and paid for it honest. It was high then, but we had to have it. And yonder across the fence ——"

Her voice sounded as if her mouth was being muffled in a heavy shawl. She took almost a full breath to every two words, and if Clay had not grabbed her she would have pitched head first into the stubble. "Hang onto the saddlehorn," he told her. "I'll git your horse turned around and we'll go back."

"I'll go back when the time comes," she said. "I can tell better when that is than you can, and I want to finish this now. Here across the fence was a piece that a young couple starved out on back in—back in—" She couldn't get the year. "I remember lookin' up here and wonderin' how much longer they'd stand it before they give in and sold to us. If we'd give 'em anything to eat, they wouldn't have sold. She left first, and he sold to us and struck out to try to find her. And that strip across the top of the hill was—that was land we got from a man in the Land Office. A lot of 'em went to jail for sellin' land that belonged to the gover'ment and he went to jail finally. I don't remember what we paid him, but I remember sendin' the children up here to plow summer fallow when they was nine and eleven years old. Little towheaded tykes workin' at their cultivatin' and cussin' their teams as big as men. But it was too hard work for 'em, and afterward they run away from home and never come back. We don't know what become of 'em. . . . That land down this slope— Hold me on, I want to go down there."

He held her on obediently, but she had misguessed the amount of time she had left. It had run out, and what drudgery and crime and cruelty and torture of women and slavery of children had gone into acquiring the rest of their land she never got to tell. The fight to get her lungs open was so long and desperate that he felt sure she was going to die on his hands. When she did succeed in driving breath back into them she could not move, and he turned back, holding her in the saddle all the way home, and rode for a doctor.

She died the following afternoon, holding to the end the conviction that the doctor had been brought to prescribe for Mr. Helm, and Clay stayed on the ranch another two weeks, helping the old man over the shock of the bereavement and with the funeral and rearranging the house afterwards. Then, the time being nearly autumn and the county-fair season in swing along the river, he left, and he heard only in short installments from hay-balers and wheat-haulers what happened from then on. Early in September he heard that Mr. Helm was getting married again, to a young widow whom he had picked up through a matrimonial agency. Late in the same month the word went around that the widow was installed and doing fine, Mr. Helm not thriving noticeably; and well along into the winter he heard that Mr. Helm had died and the widow was completing arrangements to marry again. The new object of her adoration was the piously-given man who owned the threshing outfit Clay had worked on, and they planned to build him a church to preach in when he could get anybody to preach to.

Such was the history of one four-thousand-acre wheat-ranch through one cycle of usefulness—its origin, how it was acquired, what the acquirers paid for it, what good it did them.

Chapter XXI

TIMES were livening up in the Columbia River towns that fall, because the upper country was getting not one railroad, but two, and old E. H. Harriman and James J. Hill were out letting contracts, buying rights of way, and banging court injunctions back and forth with a fury that showed neither of them had meant business, that both of them would sooner build the blamed railroad than back down and admit it, and that they were both mad at being caught windying. Men were already piling into the middle river ports to be on hand when work opened, every side-hill freight station in the upper country was petitioning to be the county seat of a new county, and windows of real-estate offices were loaded with maps of Jonesville and Wilkinsburg and Petersonville, Cherry Vale and Apple Heights and Gooseberry Villas and Sweet Pea Home Sites, all right in the path of future development, and all requiring only the investment of a little small change to make a man a capitalist for life. There was a carnival on all over the streets, and deckhands and cowboys and shovel-stiffs and real-estate promoters elbowed their way around under the arc-lights with mobs of street-show pitchmen and girls on the prowl picking at their flanks. Steamboats snorted and boomed their whistles from the river, a merry-go-round tooted and wiggled its varnished ponies, and Indian squaws, who spent fifty weeks out of every fifty-two riding horseback to pick up a living, eased themselves over their vacation period by straddling the imitation horses and jiggering around and around and around, beginning at eight in the morning when the merry-go-round opened, and knocking off when it locked up for the night.

Snake-shows squalled against freak-shows, pavilions presented exhibits of prize agricultural products—apples, peaches, prunes, grapes, bundles of wheat and clouts of wool and glass jars of assorted truck—and people crowded restlessly to see them and then didn't look at them. A light drizzle of rain fell, there was a smell in the wind of dead leaves and of apricots trodden into the ground, of things changing and moving and not going anywhere, and Clay felt hollow and lonesome.

It was an old enough feeling, that of realizing that whatever you touched changed to something else under your hand, but so is cancer an old disease, and yet people still die of it. Earth changed, it grew and shed grass, filled up old gullies and cut new ones; rivers changed, a flood in one season, low water in the next. Old people died; young people lived and got old. You tied to a tree, and it grew and broke the tie-rope; to a house, and it rotted and fell down; to a woman, and she got frightened of what her own body could do to her and went away.

What hurt him so much was not that everything moved, but that it was moving when he was not. The best antidote against a sense of life's restlessness is to get showered with a dose of it. There was a street-corner pitch on a saloon corner where some old home-remedy expert had set up a display of bottles of rattlesnake oil, which he offered as a specific for rheumatism. To prove that his product was the pure quill, he also exhibited as a side-attraction a row of half-gallon fruit-jars, each containing one large live rattler, coiled and torpid with the cold. A big stoop-shouldered man came past, arguing heavily with a loud-looking woman, and she hauled off and slapped his face. He backed involuntarily, fell off the sidewalk, and knocked a couple of jars down from the snake-table. The jars smashed, the rattlers crawled sluggishly out, and the proprietor grabbed one and shoved its head wrathfully into the stoop-shouldered man's face and invited it to take a big nab out of him. "Bite him, damn his soul to hell!" he exhorted. "Come on, now, bite, or I'll pinch your tail off!"

It was lucky he didn't, for he would have given himself a rousing surprise. Pinching a rattler's tail sets up some reflex that fetches its head right back at the pincher's hand. There was plenty of room around the stand, for the uncaught snake had scared everybody away. It tried feebly to climb the curb out of the wet, and Clay picked up a stick and flipped the creature at the proprietor's ankles. The proprietor yelled, dashed snake number one violently to the ground, and backed away, yelling urgently for the police. The stoop-shouldered man got up and took Clay by the arm and walked him away.

"Damn me, a couple more inches and that reptile would have had me by the nose," he said. He had a kind of blurty way of getting his words out, as if it mattered less what he said than how far he made it carry. "And what in the hell would I have done then, for God-sakes? A man can't take a toornekey around his nose, hey, by God? Well, sir, by the blue lights of I don't give a damn where, I got to buy you a drink on that! No excuses. Pour her in the spittoon if you want to, but I'll buy her in spite of hell! Come on in here and wood up!—Stand up, you damned cheap dock-rats!" he added in a yell, pushing open a saloon door. "Stand up, damn you. Captain Waller is a-comin' in!"

The grogshop was one that specialized in waterfront trade. All the customers stood up, and Captain Waller explained to Clay that it was steamboat etiquette to remain standing until a captain was seated. He planked into a chair at a table, and a great many of the men greeted him loudly, invited him to poison himself at their expense, and inquired whether Brighteyes was keeping in training or not. The captain replied shortly that Brighteyes and he were not speaking any more, and that as far as he was concerned she could go do this, that, and the other thing with herself. He then turned his back on them and glared when the bartender mentioned that Clay looked a little young to be taking up ardent refreshments.

"When they're big enough they're old enough," the captain stated, as if it was something from the Revised Statutes. "Load 'em up and lay 'em down, and what becomes of 'em afterwards ain't any of your damned business. Tell them hogs over at the bar to kill one another and git it over with, so we can visit."

A dispute had started between a couple of deckhands, or was about to. One of them stood hauled back with a broken bottle, and the other rummaged a razor out of his sock and laid the blade back between his thumb and forefinger. A razor is a fearfully dirty thing in a fight, and a broken bottle is not much tidier. Clay remarked uneasily that they would bleed all over the place.

"I wish to God they would," Captain Waller replied, heartily. "Maybe it would clean some of the punks out of here so decent people could talk business in it. But they won't do anything. Stand around and peck straws for a while like a couple of cheap barnyard roosters, that's about their size. Where do you come from? Where do you figure to go to?"

Clay explained that he had been harvesting up Round Prairie. He didn't know where he was going, and wished he did.

"Easy settled," the captain said, downing the second drink without noticing that it wasn't his. He kicked the stove for the bartender to rustle up a couple more. "Easy took care of. My boat is laid up off the wood-yards, and there's plenty of room on her. I drift her down to Cook's Landing and sail her upriver with cordwood. You do your own cookin' if you don't like mine, and you can help steer if you want to. But it don't matter a damn. By God! a man that rides with me does as he damn pleases. That's the only way to develop the human race, ain't it? Do you know what all these laws and etiquettes and not eatin' with your knife businesses are intended for?"

"I never thought about that," Clay said. He saw that the captain had been pretty well ginned to begin with, and that he was improving his start fast. "What do you want me to work at on your boat? I've never been on one, and if there's anything to learn——"

The captain came down from his philosophic heights, and explained there wasn't anything to do, and therefore nothing to learn.

"All I want is somebody for company, like. A man alone is liable to git hurt or take sick or something, and then where is he? Rippin' down the damned river to the Pacific Ocean, by the blue lights of what d'ye call it, and I don't want to go there. I'm afraid I might lose something and have to go back for it. How much wages you been drawin'?"

Clay told him, and added that for work at which he was a greenhorn he would not expect so much. The captain repelled the notion of small economies, and commanded two more drinks to be driven up and moored within easy reach. "You'll have to kind of stand watch on the boat when I'm away on business," he explained. "Nothing to it, but it's quiet for a boy of your age, and you ought to git paid for it. Two dollars a day and board. You can do your own washin', or you can leave it here at the laundry. We won't run much past fall, I ought to tell you. Ice starts runnin' in the river then, and we tie up for the winter. Then you're out of a job."

"That'll be all right," Clay said. It would save him the trouble of quitting. He had stayed too long on the wheat-ranch, that was mainly what was the matter with him now. "I'll go bring my clothes and hunt up a place to board my horse."

"I'll help you," Captain Waller said, amiably. "You got a horse? Well, by God! One of the troubles with this damn country is that the people in it is horse-crazy. What the hell use is a horse, except to git into jams with? If you've got one, you go wallerin' around from here to yonder, never a week in the same place, more trouble wherever you land, dodge it and ramble away again. If you stay put there's only one kind of trouble at a time, and it lasts long enough so you git used to it. Ain't that a fact?" He raised his voice without waiting for an answer. "Stand up and shut up, you damned mud-dobbers! Captain Waller is goin' out!"

There had seemed a mournfulness about the river in the dark and the rain, as if it had something to do with the wistful crowds walking under the lights and having a good time looking for something to have a good time at. But it must have been the town itself, for driving the scow downriver was not mournful at all, but gay and restful, and the river itself cracked with entertainment from morning till night. Wild geese were already beginning to wheel down from the north, big flocks of honkers to the winter wheat-fields, long files of teal and mallard ducks to the swamps of Arizona and New Mexico, and, highest of all, the great white and black Canada snow-geese driving for the lakes of Mexico. There were little shanty-camps built down onto the beach in places where the stern-wheelers could nose in close, and a family or two at each bringing cordwood down from the hills for engine-room fuel. There were fish-wheels built on scows close to the shore to dip salmon when the muddy flood-waters drove them to the bank to find out where they were going. The big Chinook run ended when spring did, but a few wheels turned on, grabbing for the small bluebacks that came moseying along almost any time of year, and there were seines hung out to dry on sand-spits against spring when the big run would start again. Steamboats went past with the passengers leaning over and yelling. Once there was a gang of Indians who had hooked a big sturgeon on a set-line and were trying to land him with a team of horses. They didn't do very well at it, for when the scow passed again on its up-trip the sturgeon had drowned himself and the horses were still working to get him out. He was as long as both horses put together, and the Indians thought he would weigh close to nine hundred pounds.

There was nothing to do on the scow except ease along, fiddle the steering-sweep when the current took her too close in, and watch things happen. Nothing happened close enough to bother, and yet there was no feeling that anything was outrunning you, because the scow was going somewhere, too. Clay spread out on the roof of the cabin in the sun, and the captain set his back on the steering-sweep and obliged with a repertory of songs that must have been the work of a lifetime to get together. They were of all periods and all degrees of moral elevation—"The Gray-haired Judge" and "Queen Lil," "Booker Burns" and "Nigger Lost John," "Brady, Brady," "The Arkansaw Run," and "Snappoo," "Bang Away, My Lulu" and "High-Low Timber," "My Father Was Hanged for Sheep Stealing" and "Three Girls from Sitka," "Root Hog or Die," and "Cooney Up a Gum Stump," and hundreds of less note. He would sing and be reminded of a story; tell it, and be reminded of another song. He would charge into the cabin to make sure the beans weren't burning, and emerge all loaded with more anecdote and melody that he had thought of while stirring them. He never played the same piece twice, and he kept it up as long as Clay would listen to him. He had run the Columbia River steady for forty years, and he knew no more what the country looked like five miles from the high-water mark than he did about the interior of Thibet. He had worked as chief engineer on one of the big boats when they raced one another for passenger business, and he remembered running soldiers on the Upper River to head off a bunch of hostile Bannocks that were reported to be swimming their horses across to get away from an infantry column behind them. The soldiers had a Gatling machine-gun mounted on the forward deck, and they gave it a lively workout, killing no hostiles that anybody knew of, but shooting the daylights out of several families of friendly Yakimas who had been ordered back to their reservation and were trying to go there.

And about steamboats exploding their boilers, which happened in roily water when the boiler feed-pipe caught a stick or a dead leaf, and stories about the long war for the trade of the gold-mines in upper Montana, when San Francisco merchants fought with boats up the Snake River and St. Louis fought back with a line up the upper Missouri, and how St. Louis won and went millions in the hole doing it. Of races for the passenger trade when the *Telephone* and the *Harvest Queen* would come neck-and-neck at a channel wide enough for only one, and neither would give way, so they would take it locked together, banging their hulls and cracking posts and ripping hunks out of each other, with the passengers all screaming bloody murder and the engine-room men firing like fiends and throwing cordwood and loose freight in an effort to knock some opposing fireman out. The captain sighed when he thought of it.

"She's a river, boy," he said. "They may make better ones, but this one suits me. I wouldn't trade a bucketful of her for any damned stream on this earth."

He knew every turn and every ripple in it, and he even claimed to be able to tell, from the quality of rubbish that came floating down, exactly what sort of industrial activity was going on upstream and in what neighborhood. But he didn't get to do much with that talent, for the river was low and quiet on their upstream trip, and there was no rubbish to show off on. The water was clear and light green, though winter was already beginning to darken in it. The air had a bluish cast, and though the frost held off, there was already yellow in the miles of willow scrub along the low-water line. They tied into the river-port wood-yard at twilight, and Captain Waller said vaguely that he would be around town for a while, and went ashore.

There was always something about a beach at a steamboat port that was interesting to look at. This time it was a bunch of Indians who were being kept under guard as a sort of end-product of the carnival for which there wasn't room in the jail. As near as any of them could recall, they had all got drunk and started playing games, some of which were a little bit rough. When they came to, three of their men were dead, and it looked a good deal as if they had been beaten over the head with a big sharp-cornered rock. Nobody could remember that any such thing had happened, so the authorities were holding the entire bunch to let them talk the thing over and decide who they wanted cinched for it. The fun had run so lively that the women's clothes were torn all to gun-wadding, and as the red-light houses of the town overhung the sand-flat where they were detained, some of the girls had sent down cast-off clothes to keep them from freezing to death while they invoked the Muse of Memory and got their testimony fixed up to jibe.

The effect was odd, to put the very lowest quotation on it, and the squaws' uneasiness and misery and bad-whisky headaches made it all the more startling. Their costumes had been designed to put power and conviction into an evening of free-hearted, unmitigated entertainment, and the job that they were up against was to decide which of themselves had better be handed over to be hung. Clay studied them through the dusk, and a steamboat turned in for the wood-yards, blared its light on the scow, and backed, with the usual quantity of jangling bells and cussing.

"You're in the way," the mate said from the lower deck. "Take a line, and we'll pull you out. We want to load wood."

The line came over, and Clay let it slip back. "I can't," he said. "This ain't my boat. Captain Waller's uptown."

The boat jangled more bells, and there was conversation and some quiet snickering. "Hunt him up," the mate said. "We'll ship our freight first and be back in two hours. Have him here by then; he'll be easy to find. Go to Mercedes' place, the tall house yonder where you hear the piano. If he ain't there he'll be there, so all you'll need to do is wait."

The reception-room of Mercedes' place looked about like the parlor of any well-to-do small-town business man. There was a nice carpet, nice furniture placed very precisely around the walls, and some nice pictures, mostly landscapes and coy French mezzotints. The landlady was a gentle-looking grandmotherly old woman with snow-white hair and a very placid, plump face without an atom of expression in it. She was dressed in black and wore a long woolen shawl, explained that Captain Waller was a little overdue, and installed herself in a rocking-chair with a fat female fox-terrier in her lap to entertain Clay until he showed up.

She was an interesting old lady when she got warmed up to her material, and she had been almost everywhere—in the gold-camps at Orofino and Canyon City and up the Prickly Pear; in Astoria when nobody lived there except Italians, fishermen from Genoa, and lumber-hands from the Piedmont, and afterwards Finlanders came and they moved out; in San Francisco when it was little and in the Reese River mining-towns when they were big; in Spain, where she had been born; in Greece, where her father had lived when she was a girl; and in Mexico, which she had liked best of all but couldn't remember much about.

Her reminiscences were mostly rambling and disconnected, and all the pleasant ones were hooked up in some way with a friend of hers who was named Maud, a beautiful blond girl who had been, the old lady recalled delightedly, tough. Not in point of morals. In the old lady's business, a low and mercenary scale of sexual ethics was included in every beginner's kit, and Maud had been no more finicky than her unfortunate sisters. But she had had a temper, she was wild and reckless and as touchy as gunpowder, and she had done some very funny things, such as throwing a Swede out of a third-story window for wanting to climb into bed with his shoes on. For a wind-up, Maud had played some Portland sport for his money and told him so in a fit of rage, so he shot her. The old lady had admired her enormously, possibly because of the very temper that had made her hard to get along with. It was an admiration, maybe, of passion in another because she lacked it herself. She had no passion, and it was doubtful if she ever had had, but she could still tell stories about Maud and giggle over them to herself.

"It was a shame she got killed," Clay said. He thought that the dead Maud must have been patterned a good like the dead Wade Shiveley, in whom he had never seen anything to giggle reminiscently over, and it made him uneasy.

"No, that was all right," the old lady said, calmly. "I would not want to be young again without Maud, but I am old now and if Maud was alive she would be old, too. I would not want to see Maud as old as I am. For me it is better to be old, but Maud would not like it. You will let me call a girl for you?"

She was quite cordial and over-the-counterish about it, like a

bartender inquiring whether he hadn't better fix something for
that cough. Clay said no, because such things reminded him violently of the tent on the divide below Burnt River Station. "I'd
sooner wait till old Waller shows up," he explained, being polite
about it.

They sat and talked some more, and the two hours were almost
gone when Captain Waller came in. He paid no attention to Clay.
"Where is she?" he said to the old lady. "Bring her out here.
I want to see her."

The old lady said, trying to ease him into a better humor, that
she believed the object of his attentions was asleep.

"Bring her on out!" the captain said, rocking on his heels. "By
the blue lights of hell, I'll have her out here if I have to roll her
bed out with her in it!"

The old lady sized him up fleetingly, saw that he meant business,
and retired, tucking her fat dog under one arm. He still didn't
look at Clay. After a minute he seemed to recollect something, and
he fed some money into the electric piano, which growled for a
minute or two and sailed into a ditty of the period called "I Don't
Like Your Family." As if it had been a grand march in her honor,
the lady he had summoned parted the curtains and entered. It was
the girl who had slapped him the night of his meeting with Clay.
She was large-framed, with big shoulders and a voice that vibrated
the floor like a locomotive whistle. She was dressed very modestly
in black, and she went over and tried to turn the piano off, and,
failing, kicked it and talked through the noise it made.

"So you're back, you big itch!" she welcomed the homing swain.
"What do you come bulling in here waking me up for? Keep your
hands off of me or I'll cut you in two!"

The piano ran the scale twice and played—

"On your way, bum, on your way!"

"I'll touch you, all right!" the captain yelled over it. "Where is
that dress I give you for a present? Where is it, damn your heart?"

The girl vociferated that it was around, she didn't know where,
and what difference did it make? "Do you want to wear it down
to the scow?"

"Wear hell!" the captain squalled, and kicked the piano himself.
It heaped coals of fire by jingling right onward—

> "I don't believe your Uncle John
> Ever had a collar on . . ."

He hoisted his voice higher. "I'll tell you where that dress is, and
then I'll wring your blamed neck for you! One of them squaws
down on the beach is wearin' it, that's where it is, and by the blue
lights of, of, of ——"
He stuttered. The piano did not. It sang—

> "I don't want to bother
> Lending money to your father! . . ."

"Well what if it is?" the girl said. "Keep back, now, or I'll poke
this knife clear through you and clinch it where it comes out. The
dress is doing more good down there than it ever did up here.
Shut your big mouth about it. Go sober up."
She turned her back on him, intending to make a lion-tamer's
exit, and he kicked the piano stool after her and took her in the
back of the knees. She grabbed the curtain and pulled it down, and
plucked a buckhorn-handled knife from her dress and threw it at
him. Idiotically, he whirled and caught it in his back point first.
It dangled down like a Christmas-tree ornament, and he turned
back and cut loose at her with a pistol. She squalled like a scalded
cat and turned to run. He drew a more careful bead and let her
have it again, and she yelled and fell. Girls yelled and came running
from all over the place, a couple of male visitors jumped out of a
back window into the mud-flat fifteen feet below, the piano caroled
along blithely, and the captain laid his pistol carefully on a taboret
and sat down. Clay got up to pull the knife out of his back, but he
insisted on having it left there until the old lady got back with
the police. He explained learnedly that it was always important in a
case of this kind to leave everything exactly as it was, because you
could never tell how prominently small things might figure in the
evidence. The point of the knife had hit one of his ribs, so it
wasn't endangering his life much. He sighed and said he was glad
it was all over with.
"I've knowed for a year that I was goin' to have to do this," he

said. "Now it's all off my hands. Or no, come to think of it, there
was one other thing." He picked his pistol up and shot carefully
into the piano until it was empty. Two or three strings twanged
horribly, but the rest of them jingled grimly on. "I turned it on
because it's always easier to git mad when it's runnin'," he explained. "Let it go. Just for curiosity, what am I in for? Did I
kill her?"

He had not killed her; he had been shooting wide to the right.
His first shot, as near as Clay could see over the girls' heads, had
opened her arm lengthways below the elbow, and his second had
cut a deep slash in her right buttock. An inch more and it would
have missed her cold. He reported, and the captain sighed con-
tentedly. "It'll ruin her commercial value for a while, anyhow," he
said. "By God! her hangin' a present of mine on a low-down
Indian squaw for everybody in town to laugh at! It makes me mad
to think of it!"

"She's wore it, though, ain't she?" Clay said. "How long has
she had it?"

"Oh, damn, I don't remember exactly," the captain said. "Let's
see, I give it to her long about last February, I guess. What the
hell, though, a dress don't wear out in six months! I've wore this
suit of clothes for five years, and there ain't a break in it! You
might as well stay around and see the rest of this now. Company
and so on. What the hell!"

"I can't," Clay said. "There's somebody here that I don't want
to see me."

Partly it was that he didn't want to be pulled in as a witness, but
there was somebody there, in the mob of girls hanging over the
wounded lavisher of good-as-new frocks on Indians. It was the
woman who had been the horse-trader's wife. He could scarcely
have told why he was anxious to avoid her; possibly because he
was ashamed to be recognized in such a place, possibly because she
might be ashamed to be seen there. He left, got his clothes from
the cabin of the scow, and explained to the steamboat men that
Captain Waller was unavoidably detained and that they had better
pull the scow clear without waiting for him. Then he went up into
town.

What he intended to do next he didn't know. Nothing, maybe,

for he had money enough to take it easy on. Several men along the boarding-house and farmers'-hotel section of town braced him to sign up with them for railroad construction work when there was any. That was one of the smaller money-making enterprises of the time. A man who was a little louder-mouthed than average would get a gang of laborers together and hire them out in a lump, with himself as foreman. Once hired, he would knock a few dollars out of their wages for an employment fee, set up a dining-car concession and overcharge them for board, and pick some extra small change out of his employers by running dead names into the payroll and drawing wages for them himself. It worked best with foreigners, and it was for that reason and not because Americans were any choosier about what they worked at that most big construction jobs were done by immigrant labor.

There was also a strike called in the railroad shops, and some farmerish-looking wipers and engine-hostlers were staying away from home late to tell each other about that. They convinced themselves beyond question that a labor delegate from Kansas City knew more about their usefulness and chances of victory than they did, and that it would only be a matter of weeks before the Union Pacific System would be scratching on the door trying to get them all back at their own price, though sometimes that didn't happen. Horse-traders dickered for work-stock on the sidewalk, a family hotel advertised a fifty-cent chicken dinner with all white help, tinhorn gamblers idled around the saloons, waiting for somebody to bring in some out-of-town money, and a boy on a bicycle poked smeary two-page newspapers around the doorways and hurried away as if somebody was going to hold him responsible for what was in them.

He would not have been overloaded if they had. Presidential-campaign news had a headline: Bryan speaks against administration; Taft supporters rally. Court dissolves injunction against proposed Harriman construction and issues restraining order against Hill lines, another court sets aside injunction against Hill and pastes one on Harriman. Developments are awaited with breathless interest. Miss Erma Belle Judson announced her betrothal at a delightful announcement party to Mr. Grover C. Hudson, both popular members of younger set, the young lady's father in agri-

cultural machinery, the young man employed in his pa's drygoods
store. No date yet fixed for the nuptials, which are awaited with
breathless interest. Candidate for mayor pledges himself to close
disorderly houses if elected, stating you can't have such things
around a coming commercial center, and announcements of opposing
candidates are being awaited with breathless uhuh.

There was something unreal about such truck. A man had to
live down over half the interest he had been born with before he
could get breathless over whether Hudson espoused Judson or
whether the red-light district became a commercial center or whether
the whole works blew away in the next high wind. Nobody would
be out anything if it did, nobody, outside the place itself, would
ever know the difference. They passed groceries along to the people
in the upper country, and they passed wheat and wool and lambs
along to be shipped back out. Out of what they passed back and
forth they dipped a little for themselves and lived on it. They
dipped, and married their Hudsons to their Judsons, and that was
all they ever did. It was better to be like Captain Waller and lug
wood up the river on a scow and know the river inside out and
upside down. Even the life he led made him childish and unable to
look out for himself. He hadn't even known that a woman couldn't
be expected to wear the same dress for six months at a stretch or
that a girl on Mercedes' payroll was not worth shooting. About the
most that could be said for his business was that it was better than
the town. Clay liked that town less every time he saw it.

At the feed-yard where he had left his mare he ran into a bashful-
looking man with a red mustache trying to find hands to work in
the grass country near the Nevada line. Early rains had brought
out a heavy stand of bunch grass on the open land, and it was
curing, and he wanted men to cut it for hay. They would not be
working for him exactly, because the grassland was no more his
than anybody else's. But he would furnish teams and machinery,
and whatever hay they cut he would buy from them at ten dollars
a ton dry and haul it himself.

"It ain't a bad deal at all, if you want to try it," he stated,
modestly. "I got a bunch of Indians workin' at it, and they're
knockin' off seven and eight dollars a day apiece. You know how
Indians work."

"It sounds lonesome," Clay said.

"It is," the red-mustached man agreed, frankly. "Not as much as it may sound, though. People come through, there's dances and shows, sometimes some speculator happens along and organizes a horse-race meet for the Indians to bet on. There's several of 'em that usually comes rollin' around about this time of year. There ain't anything to compare with this place, of course, but things go on."

"I'll try it," Clay said. "Show me about the roads, and who do I report to when I git there?"

He knew that he was going to see her. He had known it since the morning by the alkali spring when he decided not to follow her. He would have followed her then if he had felt the least doubt of it. He lay awake all that night thinking how she had looked at different times and how close he was to seeing her again.

It was not going to cut any more figure to the world at large than what went on in the town, than the Hudson-Judson union, but he did not think of that. He awaited it with breathless interest.

Chapter XXII

THE grass country was quiet, because there were only service berry and scrub juniper bushes to catch the wind and the bunch grass cushioned the earth against sound. A horse galloping could not be heard a hundred yards off, and people who lived there long got used to dropping things and not expecting any noise when they hit. But it was not as uneventful as the red-mustached man had represented, on account of the other mowers who were working it and the etiquette in use among them.

There were no boundaries in the grass, no signs of ownership or prior claims. A cutter could mow on any ground that nobody else had marked off first, and he marked off his selected area by mowing a swath all the way around it. Once that was done, the grass inside it was his, and nobody bothered him. But if he poked along too leisurely at finishing it, or if he tried to gobble too big an area and got caught with his enclosure unfinished, there was liable to be trouble, for as long as there was an opening in it any opposition cutter could drive through and whirl off a second enclosure inside it, which then belonged to him, the only restriction being that he had to get it closed before the big-area man finished mowing around him. The rule was entirely fair, and everybody stuck to it strictly, never fighting over pirated territory with anything more dangerous than an ash neckyoke, and never continuing to race mowing-machines with a competitor after one horse had dropped dead and the other had refused to drag him.

The white hay-cutters were generally the hardest to beat. They didn't drive as recklessly as the Indians, but they never started a race unless they stood a fair chance of winning it, and, once started, they didn't quit until they were run completely into the ground. A man who had picked a good lower slope where the grass was tall and the ground unbroken could count on racing at least four mowers before he got it hemmed in, and on coming out with about half as much acreage as he had planned on, and that rule held no matter what color the competition. White men bluffed the hardest, but they were camped mostly along the road, where there was fresh water and company and where they could keep an eye on the man they had contracted to cut for. The Indians had little two- and three-lodge camps strung out all over the landscape, and a man couldn't drag his sickle anywhere without some of them seeing him and making a run to fudge in ahead of him.

Racially the Indians were all of the Shoshonean fringe, though of different tribes and locations—Walpapi Snakes from the Malheur desert, scrawny Diggers from the Four Corners country, and Paiutes from the jack-rabbit pastures across in Nevada. They got on well together, and they seemed mild-spirited and unaggressive, but there were people among them who were able to put liveliness into the husbandman's lowly trade. Clay had his hottest race with one of them one morning when he struck a two-mile spread of deep grass on both sides of a shallow arroyo, and, seeing nobody around, started in to mow around it all. He had his circle about one-third drawn when another mower turned down the slope, dropped the sickle about two feet from where he had started, and began driving a long, pear-shaped hunk out of the middle of his patch, hogging the best grass and leaving him a ridiculous crescent around the edges that would be more trouble to reap and rake than it was worth. He whipped up and shortened his circle to get it closed first. The opposing driver whipped and shortened his, and they both sat high and laid down to the job of getting back to taw in a hurry.

A mowing-machine is springless, all iron, and too hard a load with the sickle in gear for horses to gallop with. The Indian did manage to tease his rig to a high half-lope, and Clay, with considerable expenditure of leather and much jouncing and back-snapping that almost threw him into his own cutting-gear, induced his to shamble along at the same clip. He had better horses than the Indian, but he was nowhere near as good a driver. The one advantage he did have was that both machines had their sickles pointed at the inside of the circle—his on the side toward the Indian, the Indian's on the side away from him. It was a mean trick to use in a fair race, but he hadn't asked the Indian to race with him, and he used it. He wheeled his team sharp across, as hard as they would go, and laid his mower so the sickle hung ahead of the Indian's horses. The Indian pulled in to go around him, and Clay pulled in with him, crowding him steadily to the center. They raced at that for a while, and then the Indian saw what he was being made to do—he was drawing not a circle, but a spiral, and the farther he went the less chance he would stand of ever getting it to close. Clay had learned the trick watching a coyote herd a sheep away from the herders' tents by constantly hanging beside her and tempting her to try to go around him.

The Indian tried exactly the stratagems that the sheep had. He pulled his team off at an angle, and Clay pulled off and headed him again; he slowed up and tried to fall behind, and Clay slowed up with him. Then he spun his team to turn around, and Clay laid the sickle exactly across the track he was turning in and stopped him entirely. He turned around to see how his challenger liked that, and it was somebody he knew. It was the Indian boy with the crippled hands who had lived with Uncle Preston, who had ridden up the mountain to warn him about the jailbreak, who had parted from him in anger afterwards and stolen his rifle.

The Indian boy had grown a good deal, and he had lost much of his sullen consecration to the red man's life and ways, probably because he was following them for a living instead of merely to show off. He had his hands wrapped in buckskin bandages as they had been when he was a baby, to keep people from looking at them. He was glad to see Clay, and he leaned out and greeted him as if there had never been a minute's dissension between them in their lives.

"*Klahowyam*, boy, how you stackin' up, hay?" he said, grinning and using all the stale forms of greeting he could remember because they reminded him of old times. "You travelin' or goin' some place? When you come pullin' that sickle into me I sayin' to myself you must be somebody I know, and sure enough. What you doin' up here, huh?"

"Cuttin' hay, and if you poke yourself into my ground again I'll mow your team off at the knees," Clay said. It had been so long since he had met anybody that he could talk to without introductions that he forgot all about the stolen rifle. "So this is where you lit, is it? Have you been here all the time since I saw you last?"

The Indian boy said no. He had crawled in with the Warmsprings his first winter, but he hadn't liked them because they were citified and all balled up about points of dance ritual, which they kept on practicing long after they had forgotten why. Also, the reservation police had pestered him with questions, where did he get his horse, how much did he pay for it, where did he inherit his saddle, who was his legal guardian and what reservation was he registered on. So then he ranged down into the Klamath-Modoc country where there were rivers and fine timber and plenty of everything to eat; but they hadn't liked him and he couldn't get used to the snakes. The place was alive with them; mostly harmless, people claimed. You would see barefooted children walking logs in the brush where snakes were sunning themselves in a layer a foot deep, and the kids would amble along, boosting a path through them with one toe. So then he had come on to this country, and he liked it better. When you saw a snake here, you weren't bothered by people hastening mirthfully to assure you that he was harmless, and what had you jumped so high for? You know that all the bunch-grass snakes meant business, so there was nothing embarrassing about grabbing a club when you saw one and going after him. The Indians were mostly pretty worthless, with childishly vague ideas about religion that they could neither be pinned down to nor shaken loose from. But they made the time pass. Sometimes several camps would get together and they would gamble on the stick-game, half of them singing and beating drums and *moraches*, while the other half tried to guess it out; and sometimes, when anybody came along who was willing to speculate, they got up horse-races between his horses and theirs.

"It ain't any place you likin' to live, but you come over for a visit," he said. "Maybe we git up that stick-game. Everybody likin' that stick-game, I winnin' lots of money on that."

He took a buckskin sack out of his shirt-bosom and clanked it, and then pointed out where the trail to his camp was. Clay promised that when he got a little time ahead he would come and see what it looked like.

"So there's horse-racin' people along this way sometimes?" he said. "Look here, you send word over to me the next time one pulls in, will you? You can stick some kid on a pony, and I'll pay him well."

The Indian boy said he would do that, certainly. Then he asked about a good many things—what Clay had been doing, about Wade Shiveley and how he had died and what for, and about the new bulge of homesteaders up in the north, and so, easy and careful, to the question that was really in his mind. "Some horse-tradin' people that you went travelin' with that time," he said. "A man and a woman and a girl. You ain't travelin' with them people any more?"

"Not since spring," Clay said, falling into the exact tone of casualness that the Indian boy was playing to keep the conversation down to. "She wanted to go somewhere else for a while, and maybe it's for good. I don't know."

"That's all right," the Indian boy said. "For good, that's all right. Because, look. I makin' a dream once, I askin' how's it comin' for me and that boy. My dream say, for you and that boy, good. But for you and that boy and that girl—" He spread his hands and made a noise in his throat, arrrrrrrrkh, as if he had choked on something bitter.

"Well, she ain't botherin' me any now," Clay said. "And if she ever does, it don't need to bother you. Remember now, if any horse-race outfit comes along I want to hear of it. I'll ride over your way one of these days."

He thought he had played the thing carefully, but he hadn't done it well enough to take the Indian boy in. No man can get up a more convincing falsehood than it takes to fool himself, and the Indian boy was not easy to fool. He knew why Clay was anxious to keep posted on horse-racing visitors, and he knew that if the right ones showed up his dream wouldn't be heeded for a minute. He gave his promise faithfully to send word lickety-split whenever a racing-string hove into sight, and he broke it all to smash. Luce and the horse-trader came to the Indians' main camp three days afterwards, and he knew them immediately and sent no word whatever.

Strictly speaking, his omission was not a direct going back on his word. He had promised to report horse-racers, and Luce's father explained, when they drove in, that he wanted only to trade for work-horses, anything from a thousand pounds up that wasn't crippled, gray-headed, or an outlaw. But dickering for horses with an Indian camp always slipped so naturally and offhandedly into gambling that it was never possible to tell where one order of commerce stopped and the other started. A dispute would blow up over some trade, neither side would budge, and, merely as a device for expediting business, somebody would propose to arbitrate the dispute by means of a fast quarter-mile workout between a couple of the horses in question. The Indians liked racing better than trading, so in the next deal they would stiffen their terms on purpose to have a race to settle them, and by the end of the day the legitimate trading would be laid completely in the shade and every deal would call for a horse-race right from the start.

When it got down to real business-like racing the Indians mostly lost, for the horse-trader's big chestnut stallion had speed, and Luce, who rode him, knew how to get every link of it out of him. He had been trained to start with a pistol-shot, he knew exactly how she was going to sit every stride he took, and there was scarcely a race in which he had to extend himself to win. Sometimes, to let him rest and keep the Indians from getting despondent, they would change to another horse and lose a couple. One thing about the stallion was that, being racing-stock, he wanted to win everything he ran in, and Luce was not strong enough to hold him in. But she enjoyed winning. She was merciless about it, like a child who goes over and over something he likes with such intense enjoyment that he fails to notice that the spectators may be finding it monotonous.

Neither she nor the horse-trader recognized the Indian boy among the spectators. They had seen him only once, and then for only a few minutes, and he had grown since. He didn't join in the betting, and he didn't say anything until the second day, when most of the Indians had got tired of losing and the racing had come to a halt. Luce had gone over to her tent a quarter of a mile off by a spring, and the horse-trader was walking the stallion around to cool him out. Three vaqueros who had stopped in to pile their small change on the less hopeless-looking events were limbering up a jug in the shade of their horses. For genuine cares and trials, the homely, slighted shepherd's trade is not in the same forty-acre lot with the labor of working cattle. Every calf has to be branded, ear-hacked, and the male ones have to be castrated in a dirty corral with a pocket knife. Every cow in season has to be presented to the bull, and the bull has to be watched so he will not overwork himself from an exaggerated sense of *noblesse oblige*. All cattle have to be watched for cuts and treated with medicine against blow-flies; they have to be driven to the mountains in spring and personally conducted to grass, not having sense enough to find it themselves, and they have to be hunted down like thieves in the fall and brought home again so the snow won't bury them. The cows have to be watched against freezing winds in spring so they won't slough their calves dead; the ones who do slough have to be helped and doctored, and of the ones who don't all the first-year heifers require the services of the vaquero as a midwife. People who lead such lives can scarcely be reproached for oiling themselves up with squirrel whisky. The three vaqueros oiled up thoroughly, and gave the horse-trader a slug to grow on every time he passed them. After he had shipped eight or nine and started perceptibly to grow, the Indian boy spoke up.

"That horse he's runnin' good, for a work-horse," he said. The stallion still had harness galls burnt on him with acid. "He makes fast workin', too, huh?"

The vaqueros snickered at his innocence, and the horse-trader said firmly that he was one of the fastest working horses that ever laid shoulder to singletree. "That's the reason I brung him out here, to see if I could locate some work that was up to his speed. But it don't look like I was goin' to find any."

As a tribute to his ready-wittedness, the vaqueros passed him the jug again, and he winked at them. The Indian boy studied the stallion thoughtfully, and said he knew a kind of work that it might be interesting to try him at. "Only maybe you'd be afraid to do it," he said. "It's a kind of racin' and workin'. This people bet and lose their money on the kind of racin' you know, now maybe you'd be afraid to bet your money on the kind of racin' they know."

The horse-trader went down the chute before it was scarcely ready for him. "Godamighty, I ain't afraid to race anything or bet anything!" he said. "Call your race and lay down your money, bub. I'll accommodate you for any money you've got and any kind of racin' you know!"

The Indian boy produced his buckskin sack. Twenty-dollar gold pieces were in use then, and he had a sizable double-handful of them. The horse-trader told him to hand it to one of the vaqueros to hold, and bring out his blamed horse and name his race, and the vaqueros kept him from making too big a fool of himself by pointing out that he had no business putting the chestnut stallion into a trick race against a fresh horse until he was rested.

"It ain't no trick race," the Indian boy said. "He's sayin' this horse is fast-workin'. All right, we race with mowin'-machines. He hitchin' his horse to mowin'-machine, I hitchin' my horse to mowin'-machine, we cut grass a mile and back. You pick what mowin'-machine you please. That ain't no trick for a workin'-horse."

The horse-trader said nobody but a blamed Siwash would think up such an idea, but that he was game, and why not get up and get at it? The vaqueros held him back again, and announced that the stallion would either be allowed to rest up or there would be no race, and gameness be damned, and finally they brought the horse-trader to agree that it might be better to wait till evening. "There's one thing, boys," he said. "I'm out to win this race, and I'll win it. Hell, I've handled more horses than this tad ever heard of. But that girl of mine is set against big stakes on a race, and she'd shoot this horse right through the head if she thought I was backin' him heavy. Partly my own fault, on account of raisin' her strict, but it gits in the way sometimes. Don't mention what the purse is when we call this race. Make it a team, or twenty-five dollars, or something."

They promised, and he led the chestnut stallion weavily across to camp. It was a good thing he had made the stipulation, for Luce came over while they were still talking about it. She started with the three vaqueros.

"You men got my father drunk," she said. "That wasn't your fault, probably. He can't carry very much and you couldn't know that. But there's one thing I want you to tell me. Has he bet any big amount of money on any horse-race? If he has, who with?"

The Indian boy kept still and let the vaqueros do it. They were shallow young scrubs, a good deal in awe of her and full enough to feel tickled over a chance to mislead her. They told her that there had been a kind of comedy race matched up, but the stakes were something measly—a horse, a handful of chicken feed, something like that. "It couldn't have run much higher, because here's the kid he bet with," one of them said. "Take a look at him, and you can see that he wouldn't be holdin' much to bet."

She looked at the Indian boy, and he said the race was mostly to see if the chestnut stallion was really a work-horse or merely doctored up to look like one. And he had bet some money, but his people didn't allow him to have much. He thought for a minute that she was going to remember him, but she turned to the vaqueros again. "He hasn't bet with anybody else?" she insisted. "You'd better tell me; it'll save trouble. People take advantage of him when he's drunk. He can't look out for himself and they take his money away from him. If anybody's done that I have to know about it now, while there's time to call things off. Do you know of anybody?"

They were quite sure there was nobody, and they felt secretly overjoyed at their smartness in deceiving her with the truth. "Nobody but this *tenas* buck here, and he's told you what his bet amounted to."

"And you won't talk him into betting with you, if he takes a notion to bet high?" she asked. "It won't do you any good if you do, because you won't get to keep it."

They exhibited their collective funds, which amounted to one dollar and forty cents. She went back to the tent and lay down, for she still got tired more easily than she once had. She intended to be awake in time for the trick race, but the horse-trader got out without disturbing her, and it came off while she was still asleep.

It was really a first-class race, though not an easy one to watch because the chestnut stallion came so near killing himself trying to win it. He had everything against him; he had never worked in harness before in his life, he knew nothing about putting drive into a trot, and when he tried to gallop with the mowing-machine the gears clogged and braked the wheels on him till they dragged. He put all his strength into his legs instead of his shoulders, trying to pull standing up, and the harness chafed his acid-scars till they bled all down his knees. It was a fight for him to get through the race at all. An ordinary cold-blood plug would have laid down a dozen times and waited for somebody to bring a gun. He did not lie down till the end of it, and the horse-trader got down from the mowing-machine seat and kicked him ceremoniously in the ribs.

"This is what I been feedin' you grain three times a day for, is it?" he said. "You'll win a forty-dollar race standin' on your head, but when it comes to something with money in it . . . " He kicked again, and the Indian boy got down and knelt at the stallion's head, sprayed water into his mouth and nostrils, and talked to him quietly. He repeated some phrase in his language over and over. In a minute or two the stallion got up.

"He's goin' to be all right now," the boy said. "Don't you go kickin' that horse no more. Give him to me if you don't like him. You lose, huh?"

It was the custom in races with Indians to lay the stakes out prominently on a blanket at the start. That had not been done because the horse-trader was afraid that Luce might come over before she was supposed to. But he was always punctual about paying off when these things went against him. Most poor gamblers are good losers, contrary to a widespread belief. "I lose," the horse-trader said, as steady as a rock. "I may not git around to payin' you till later in the evening. As soon as—as things is clear, I'll fetch it over to your camp."

The Indian boy said any time would be all right. The horse-trader had no more money to race with, so he would quit racing and go somewhere else out of people's way. "Any time before mornin', that's all right. I leavin' early in the mornin' to work, before my boss finds out I been gone."

He left early in the morning with his winnings safely pocketed. The morning after that, Clay rode over to visit him in his camp and found him lying dead in the trail with buzzards flying around over him.

The Indian boy had been bushwhacked, that was easy to make out. The bullet had gone in back of his left shoulder, ranged forward through his heart, and torn a big hole in the front of his chest coming out, evidently having gone to pieces when it hit. It had been fired from a hiding-place about fifty yards away in the grass, which was pressed down in a sort of deer-bed, with deep elbow-marks in it. It had happened the day before, because the pressed-down grass still held dew that had fallen on it in the night, and in standing grass the wind always dried it off an hour after sunrise. Horse-tracks led from the hiding-place to the trail, but where they came from and where they went it was impossible to tell because they mixed with other tracks and the crust of dew on the dust made them all look alike. The Indian boy's team was grazing along about a mile away, still hitched to the mowing-machine.

That was all the sign and that was all there was to it except that there seemed something contemptuous and insulting about death in such a place. Among people and among animals, there is an instinctive feeling that the place to die is in some kind of shelter, or at least in a place that has something to distinguish it from the surrounding two hundred square miles of landscape. A mortally wounded coyote will always keep alive long enough to drag himself to the nearest deep gully or patch of trees. If there is only one finger-sized sapling in sight he will get to that and die under it. Here there was nothing but a horse-track in the grass; in front and behind and on both sides there was grass and nothing else. A man wouldn't even have stopped in such a place to take down his trousers. Dying in it had a nakedness and offhandedness about it that didn't seem right.

Clay loaded the body on the mowing-machine and took it on to the Indians' camp. There was nobody there except a few women, and they had heard nothing of the horse-racing yet, so the explanation that seemed likeliest was that the Indian boy had practiced some of his high-speed mowing against some new hand who hadn't taken it in the right spirit. Some men came in the afternoon, and they talked among themselves while they were getting ready for the burial, but Clay couldn't understand anything they said. He helped them dig the grave in the middle of some junipers, and helped them wrap the body in its blankets.

Looking for the last time at the wound, something went lightly through his brain, a vague speculation about the kind of rifle that could wreck its bullet so badly, but it was too vague to be worth telling, and the Indians needed help with the funeral arrangements. They knew nothing about the burial customs in use among the Tunné. Their notion of a proper funeral was to make the thing last, to bury with the dead man only a few sample mementoes from his estate, and save the rest to be sacrificed at their spring dance in commemoration of all their dead if somebody else wasn't using it by then. The Indian boy belonged to people who believed that death was something contagious, that a dead man's property got infected with it, and that you had better hand it along into eternity with him if you didn't want to catch it.

The hay-cutters saw no sense in such a conception, but they were tolerant enough to agree that if the Indian boy had believed it they ought to follow it. They brought his bone flute and the old straight-fork saddle that he had stolen from Uncle Preston, and Wade Shiveley's rifle that he had stolen from Clay, and put them all into the grave, and they held his red colt ready to kill over him when it was filled in. But instead of filling it they looked inquiringly at Clay as if some contribution was coming from him.

"His money," one of them said, as if he didn't think much of the idea but was willing to string along with the crowd. "He used to got money, we ought to put that in too. You don't find no money on him?"

"There wasn't anything in his pockets when I found him," Clay said. "Whoever shot him would have rolled him afterwards, I suppose. Did he have much with him?"

The Indian nodded and picked up a shovel. The knowledge that somebody was going to get some use out of the money made him more cheerful. "Some," he said. "He winnin' money yisterday in hoss-race. Four hunderd, five hunderd dollars he winnin'. Maybe six hunderd. I don't know."

Clay put out his hand for them to wait. "What kind of a horse?" he asked. They told him, and vague things that had been drifting through his mind began to fall into place and form something that he had been trying to avoid seeing, it seemed, longer than he could remember. It was horrible, but he couldn't keep them mixed up and shuffled out of place any longer. "Leave that rifle out a minute," he said. "Lead the colt up close. I'll shoot him, because there's some-

thing about this gun I want to find out. Then we'll put it back and
fill in, and you can drag the horse across it afterwards."

A man always feels like a sneak killing a horse. Even when the
brute is mean and worthless there seems a kind of treachery about
it, as if you ought either to tackle him barehanded or else give him
a gun, too. The red colt came close to the grave, and, smelling it,
lifted his head and blew loudly. Clay waited till he started to pull
back, and let him have it behind the eyes, and he broke at the knees,
lay down, and stiffened out awkwardly in the grass. Clay pitched
the rifle into the grave and nodded to the Indians to go ahead. He
didn't know what he had proved, but it was proved and done with.
He stood watching until the Indians had filled in the grave and
dragged the dead colt across it. They came, one by one, and shook
hands with him and went to their horses. Buzzards, drawn by the
dead colt, began to drift downward till there were a dozen of them
wheeling a patient circle overhead. The sight of the skinned-headed
carrion-guzzlers always made Clay sick, and he went to look at the
colt so he could leave before they came close.

He found out what he wanted to know, and it was what he had
known without looking. Wade Shiveley's rifle had not split its bullet.
The colt was drilled on each side with a clean hole, a little bigger
where it came out than where it went in. The bullet had hung together, or it would have ripped the whole side of the colt's skull
out. There was nothing more to do there.

He caught his mare and mounted and pointed for his own camp.
Behind him, the buzzards came down and settled on the red colt,
the wind blowing their dullish-black feathers backwards and rocking them off balance as they picked and dug to rip open the broad
exposed belly. It was easy to see, after they got well settled to their
work, why nature had given them naked red heads. A nice sprouting of feathers would have made a decenter looking ensemble, but
only until their first mealtime. Red blended perfectly with what
they dived into and smeared themselves with.

They fed on, going deeper, and when one of them got too full
he staggered heavily to one side, vomited, and came back to fill up
again. A buzzard does not eat out of any desire to satisfy hunger,
seemingly. He consumes food for the simple pleasure of getting it
down, with possibly the extra pleasure of knowing that when he

has got through with it nothing else will be able to use it. There are only two divisions of North American animals that can stand in the same light with the buzzard for plain, dull, senseless gluttony. The Canadian wolverene can; he will tear up and befoul with urine any food that he hasn't got room for himself. The other division is a little too tony to bother with spoiling mere food, and that is the one people belong to. Clay had shown signs of it, lying a hanging onto Wade Shiveley; Luce had, in wanting him to. The horse-trader was plastered with tokens of membership, and the Indian boy had been sprouting them.

The hay-cutters had left Clay so he could do his mourning by the grave alone. The shock of the death and burial and buzzards wore off, and there did not seem to be any great sight of material to mourn about. The Indian boy had never felt deeply concerned about anything except his own people, and they were all dead before him. The people he lived with he had despised, and his entertainment had mostly been swindling and slickering them. Now his own people had him, and it was all right.

Clay caught up with the hay-cutters, and they had a different opinion about his future arrangements.

"That hoss-trader, he gone," one of them volunteered. "One of the boys seen him pullin' his outfit for the Mormon Flats early. You wantin' to catch him, you better gittin' started pretty soon, I guess. The boys think he killin' that kid."

It was plain enough what they expected of him. Reason told him that there had been no particular harm done and that the horse-trader and Luce would be too badly scared and conscience-struck to be worth bothering with yet. But people in that country didn't usually act according to reason. There were things that people expected of a man, and reason had nothing to do with them. What the hay-cutters felt Clay ought to do was what everybody would expect him to do once the news got spread. He made one small stab at being judicial before giving in to them.

"You don't know the horse-trader shot him," he said. "It could have been some Indian, or somebody in the hay-camp. One of the women in the horse-tradin' outfit might have done it."

They shook their heads solemnly. No Indian could have shot so straight on a moving target. There had been only one woman with the horse-trader's outfit, and he hadn't let her know what was going on. That, in fact, was one of the main points against him. "He scared of that woman. All the time he sayin' not to tell her anything about the bet. So he shoot the kid and steal his money back, so when she sayin' to him how he losin' their money he can say back, no sir! No sir, he say, I don't losin' no money, because here she is! That's what the boys think."

They rode silently, waiting to hear from him. Not as to what he thought of their hypothesis, but to hear what he intended to do about it. It didn't strike them that the shooting might not make any special difference to him. They would merely have thought him white-livered if he had explained that to them, and he didn't explain it. He began to think about it as they did, and to feel that he had been outrageously bereaved of a valued friend. "I'll go after him," he told them. "He's done plenty to me already, and if he's done this I'll see him cinched for it. Now you keep your mouths shut about it till you know for sure what you're talkin' about. I talked too quick about a shootin' once, and they hung a man on my say-so that never had anything to do with it."

The next morning he got ready to leave the grass country. He drew his money for hay-cutting, packed up, and took the Indian boy's mowing-rig back to the contractor's camp where it belonged. Hay-baling was going on at the contractor's camp when he got there, with the power being furnished by an old-fashioned horsepower rig which worked better for such jobs than a gearless engine because it was easier to start and stop. The power was produced by means of a long beam with one end bolted to a worm-drive arrangement. The horses pulled the other end around and around and around, and the driver stood on top of the worm-drive housing and applied the leather to them when they flagged, which they did most of the time. It took a man of strong stomach to drive horsepower, because he had to stand being twirled in a circle ten hours a day steady, without ever letting himself get too dizzy to flog the right horse. The youth of the country generally regarded a horsepower-driver with awe because of the tests he was supposed to have gone through in qualifying for the job. One of the best drivers was supposed to have got his start by chewing a man's ear off in a fight and swallowing it.

The hay-balers were middle-aged men, with a family and a quarter-section of land apiece, and with too high a sense of their position in the community to get out and hack hay with common Indians. They had homesteaded water-holes mostly, and they got a little rent out of stockmen for them and a little bounty-money out of coyotes and a few dollars by catching and breaking wild horses and a little out of odd-jobbing around when there was anything to do. They were not in the least lazy. The amount of work they did to keep going was almost inhuman, and what seemed to hold them back most was that they were too proud or too bashful to get out and hunt up a kind of work that would get them anywhere. It was impossible to feel very sorry for them on account of their hard life, because they didn't know that it was hard. The subject of their conversation was how a man could get through the winter most comfortably, and a tall man with a flat chest, high shoulders, and a mean black mustache maintained that the boss formula was to kill a deer out of season and get put in jail for it. It was only a county-jail offense, you got fed and taken care of, and the county, by removing you from the ranks of productive toil, assumed the responsibility of taking care of your family till you got out.

There was pretty good stock in those men, if there had been anything in the country to use it on. A man could leave a saddle on a fence in their territory and come back and find it undisturbed a month afterward. But they were narrow-minded, hard, bad fighters with the knife—which all of them used to settle disputes with—and ignorant beyond the fondest dreams of a traveling exhorter. One of them gave his comrades a brief and quite accurate account of the principal events of J. Fenimore Cooper's *Deerslayer*, which one of his kids had read to him, and he had the sublimest confidence that it was all a chronicle of things that had actually happened, probably year before last, which the county grand jury might still get around to doing something about. All of them had always worked like coon dogs and it had never done them any good, but they were not embittered about it, because they hadn't expected it to. Clay drove past them to hunt up the contractor, who was behind the bale-stack, weighing up bales and noting the number of pounds on pieces of shingle. He was down on all fours, squinting at the steelyards, and Clay tossed the lines on the ground and told him not to get up.

"One of your men got killed over by New York Springs, a day or so ago," he said. "An Indian kid with crippled hands. I'm on the move, so I brought his rig in for you. He's got no folks, so if there's any money comin' to him you'd better turn it over to the Indians out there for buryin' him."

The contractor said much obliged, made a note in his pay-book, and got up. It was Clark Burdon.

He was glad to see Clay, and he sat down on a hay-bale and talked about how the settlers had made out over the summer. For a start, they had done pretty well. The country laid well, it was open and required no clearing, and though the creeks all went dry about May, they had got some wells down that actually ran water right out onto the ground, so everybody was sinking them. The ground itself was rather shallow and certainly not hurt with fertility, but they had plowed it and got in a crop of winter wheat that, with the help of the unusually early rains, might do well.

"And it had better," he added. "When a man sells wheat to the warehouse, it's six bits a bushel, but when he's buyin' it for seed it's around a dollar ninety. They'll have some cattle to sell in the spring, and that'll pull 'em through till harvest, I guess. But if there ain't anything to harvest— And how in thunder can a man tell, in a country that's never been planted to wheat before? There might be forty different things wrong with it. Nobody knows till they've tried."

"How did it happen you left?" Clay said.

Burdon said vaguely that when a man started traveling it was hard to stop, and that it looked better to put his money into haying-machinery that would pay out instead of into wheat that might. Neither reason was the real one. Burdon had streaks of bashfulness sometimes. "The outfit was all right and the people was all friends of mine," he said. "But after you people left it got a little bit flat and slow, and I couldn't keep interested in it. You mentioned being on the move. I might give 'em another try if you decided to hook up with 'em again. You could find something to do here till our baling is over, and your girl ———"

"There ain't any girl," Clay said. "She's travelin' with her father again. It suits her better."

Burdon said, oh. He seemed disappointed. "I wish you could have kept on together. I don't know, if that's the way it is I don't know that I'd want to go back there with you."

"That's the way it is," Clay said. It was annoying to have Burdon act regretful when he had convinced himself that there was nothing about it to regret. "She's gone, and she'd better not let me catch her again, either. She let me into something that I've just found out about, and I'm after her for it. Or that old man of hers. It's the same thing."

He explained what she had let him into, and Burdon sat back and laughed. His laugh looked ironical, because it was all on one side of his face. "Three killings we hung on that poor Shiveley punk, and it turns out he didn't do any of them," he said. "Her old man killed the Indian kid, of course. Scared to own up he'd been speculating with the family funds, so he went out and committed a murder to save himself embarrassment. A weak-backed man will do the damndest things to avoid doing the simplest ones sometimes. It's a shame he broke you up with the girl. There was something about the two of you together that I used to like to look at. Why don't you get the sheriff out after the old wart, and maybe she'd come back to you?"

"She wouldn't," Clay said. "She'd stick to him harder than ever if he was in any kind of trouble. She likes this camp-and-run hoboin'; let her enjoy it while she can. It won't last, I'll guarantee you that. Let me ever catch her old man showin' a rifle that's reamed out bigger than the bullet, and I'll haul him to jail myself. But I don't want to see that girl any more, and I'm through accusin' people of murder on guesswork."

He untied his mare from the mower. "I wouldn't take in after the old buck too promptly, if I was you," Burdon said. "You'll never find any rifle on him till his scare wears off, so why run yourself to death trying? You'd do a good deal better to pick some quiet section and wait for him to show up in it. He plays this country regularly, and he's bound to come your way if you wait long enough. And then come down on him quick, when he's feeling large and expansive."

"I might do that," Clay said, and held out his hand. He liked Burdon, but he wished he hadn't seen him. It had made him feel lonely and bereaved. What Burdon had liked about him was seeing him with Luce, and that was done with. They shook hands, and Burdon stepped back so only the good side of his face showed. He did that usually with casual acquaintances.

"Any place where it's quiet, and where he's never worked this bushwhacking trick," he said. "You'll get him, and if you don't, why, it's time you were settling down somewhere, anyway. You've been at this camp-and-run hoboing around the country long enough."

The place Clay had kept in mind to go to when he got ready to settle down was Uncle Preston's toll-bridge. He could go there, not only in safety, but in a kind of triumph. Without thinking that the things he had promised to do for Uncle Preston and Drusilla were more than childishness, he had done them. She had wanted him to find out where the Howell money was hidden, and he could come as close to telling her as she would need. He had promised Uncle Preston to help with Wade Shiveley's death, and he had certainly kept his word on that.

He sat loose in the saddle, considering whether to go there, after all, and the mare, understanding his irresolution, eased her course around and walked fast and purposefully, as she always did when she wanted to go somewhere and didn't know whether she would be allowed to or not. He couldn't go back to the toll-bridge if he intended to nail the horse-trader, because old Howell had been bushwhacked there. He couldn't count on much of a triumph if he did go, because once he had saved all of Uncle Preston's sheep from drowning, and when he came in and told them about it they said yes and got him ready to go to town with Orlando Geary. And he wouldn't find out anything new by going there, because he could tell what the people were doing without moving from his tracks. They always did the same thing, year in and year out. But the place that he felt curious about, and the place he could find out about only by going to, and the place to lay for the horse-trader, was Burnt River.

He gave up Shoestring and the toll-bridge; and the mare, understanding that now she was safe in the course she had picked, slowed her gait and walked toward Burnt River confidently. She didn't know what a tussle it was to him to let her shove. Shoestring had been the one place he had wanted hard to live in. Luce had taken him away from it and spoiled him for it.

Chapter XXIII

THERE was no triumph about being with the settlers, but they were glad to see him without one, and that was better. They had spread themselves around a sort of shallow basin with mountains to the north; not all together like a colony, but spotted around in places where the land looked best. For the time they had had to work in they had got a lot done—houses and a school up, wild hay cut and stacked for their animals, land plowed and fenced and seeded and the wheat well along in the boot, wells drilled and water running for stock and to irrigate gardens when the growing season came.

It was true that most of their improvements did nothing to enhance the beauty of the landscape, which was nothing extra to start with. What was the original reason for the invention of the homestead style of architecture it would be hard to say. It couldn't have been comfort, for the half-inch board walls leaked heat in winter and were furnaces in summer. It certainly wasn't looks, for they were the ugliest objects in sight, so much uglier even than the naked plowed ground that they stood out on it like pimples. It wasn't availability of material, for the country around had tons of stone and adobe, either of which could have been organized into a fairly sightly scattering of residences. The homestead houses were built of undressed lumber, which had to be shipped first by railroad from the timber belt and then hauled south a hundred and thirty miles across the mountains by wagon, the trip taking, as a general thing, from eight to ten days. Bad roads accounted for the slow time, and they were unavoidable. If they had been good the land wouldn't have been found open for entry.

Old Carstairs and his wife, with whom Clay stayed while he looked around the land that was left open, had been there longer than anybody else, but their house was no better. It was rough cull-lumber with the cracks slatted up, rooms a religious eight feet square with one small window apiece, and the floor set up four feet off the ground because it had been too much trouble to scrape it level and build down on it. It also furnished a place to store articles of value such as old harness, broken mowing-machine parts, barrels that had come apart, unused lengths of rope and wire, an assorted collection of rusty nails and staples and old gunny sacks, and a couple of washtubs that were going to be mended as good as new when anybody could remember to buy solder in town.

The ceilings were built low for warmth, though it would have been twice as effective to bank earth up under the floor so drafts couldn't blow through the knotholes. The water-supply was a spring with the wash-house built around it. Old Carstairs had put down an artesian well and it spouted profusely, but he used its water only for stock, and mostly it ran wild on the ground and made several acres of mud which were of no use for anything. Inside, the house was finished with a kind of cheesecloth called house-lining, and on that was stuck ornamental wallpaper with patterns of gigantic liver-colored nasturtiums. Old Carstairs was not such a fool as to imagine the place was anything to go into a fit about, or that he couldn't have put up a better one if he had spent more time and thought planning it. But he was used to it, and as a caution against building a class of house you were not used to he told about his father, who had sold a right of way to some railroad company and built himself a three-story dwelling with the proceeds. His very first night in it, the dogs started barking and there was some rumpus in the horse-corral, so the old gentleman grabbed his gun and stepped out the window to see what the trouble was. He fell three stories, lit on his head, and broke his neck, and that was the kind of thing that happened when a man moved into a stylish place after accustoming himself to an humble one.

The Carstairs furniture was on a little more elaborate scale than the house. There were several rocking-chairs carved with flurri-diddles and adorned with quantities of brass tacks and headrests made out of varicolored ribbons; a center table of which the legs represented birds' claws, each grasping a yellow glass cue-ball; and a porcelain lamp with a globe painted with a marine landscape so the light would shine through it. There was a stereopticon rig with views of an apple-orchard in bloom in Michigan, Niagara Falls in winter, Santiago Bay at sunset, hauling artillery on the walls of Peking, and the Meeting of the Waters at Killarney. There were two books, one called the *Royal Path of Life,* and the other *The*

San Francisco Horror of Earthquake, Fire and Famine, and there
was a faint but piercing smell of stale food about the whole place
because the kitchen was so arranged that drafts carried through it
to the rest of the house. The diet was corn-meal mush, pancakes, and
fat bacon for breakfast, baking-powder biscuits, fat bacon, potatoes,
and beans the rest of the time except when the neighbors got together and went whackers on killing a beef.

No family ever butchered a whole beef for itself, because too
much of the meat would have spoiled before they could use it. It
would have been about as well that year if they had. Late in No-
vember an east wind brought in a blizzard and zero weather when
all the cattle except milk-stock were still being kept on pasture to
save hay. They had not been herded because the range was short
and they had to scatter to get any nourishment out of it. The blizzard lasted three days, during which nobody dared to go out after
them for fear of being snowed in and frozen to death. When it let
up everybody saddled and struck out to see what it had left of them,
and it had left nothing but cold-storage meat. There had not been
time for the cattle to yard together for warmth, and they were
littered around in little *manadas,* three and four in a bunch, frozen
as hard as iron. Some of them had even frozen standing up.

That was the first toll they paid for taking the country on trust,
though the Carstairses, who should have known something about
it, swore that bad weather had never hit so early before in history
and that nobody could have foreseen such a thing. They saved as
much as they could of the beef, worked at hauling wood from the
mountain canyons which were three days off by wagon, and spent
the rest of their time staring out of the window at the snow drifting and stacking over their green wheat. Wheat was one thing that
the snow helped. As long as it stayed, there was no danger of the
crop freezing out. But also as long as it stayed their horses and
milk-cows had to live on what hay they had, and it ran so short
that some of the men put runners on their wagon-beds and struck
out to buck the road through to Eight Dollar Valley to see if they
could trade for more. They didn't trade, for about two-thirds of
the way down they met men bucking wagon-sleds up from Eight
Dollar Valley on a chance of getting hay from them. There was
a week or two when the stock lived on potatoes, and not very liberal

rations at that, and then February came and made things look better. A Chinook wind hit in the night, and by morning it had cleaned the whole basin of snow except for a few sickly-looking patches where an east slope kept the wind off. That was an event. Men hooked up and took their families around visiting one another merely to stand out in their shirt sleeves and yell when the last patches pindled down and disappeared.

They turned their stock out on the last-year's grass for the rest of the spring, and they even began talking about putting in gardens, pointing out to one another that the basin was sheltered and the grass beginning to sprout, and that if grass didn't know what kind of weather to count on, who did? The Carstairses planted no gardens, and luckily nobody else got round to doing it, for February was not through with them yet. Late in the month it rained, and then a freezing wind set from the east, laid a sheet of ice around the roots of their wheat, and killed it as if somebody had turned a blowtorch on it. Every spear froze stiff, and then dropped and turned brown in the fierce dry winds that blew in over it. That seemed the last card, but there was still one left to help them make up their minds. In the middle of the dry-wind spell, all the artesian wells stopped running and dropped the water-table so low that it was impossible even to draw it.

It was pure unfounded faith in the benevolence of nature that had led the settlers to depend on those wells to start with. They could come only from drainage water, the drainage area was relatively small, and a good deal of its supply wasted out into creeks that dribbled down into the lake in Eight Dollar Valley. There had been an abundance to start with, because it had been storing up underground since the dawn of creation, but now they had drained it all out, and it would require another 5,912 years for it to fill up again. Other localities got hit by their wastefulness, for Eight Dollar Lake dried up into a mud-flat, all the fields in that direction froze out and caked for lack of moisture, and the plowed ground, being light volcanic ash instead of the heavy black valley soil, scattered on the wind ten miles high and a hundred miles away, with the dead wheat-sprouts riding along with it. Dust whined against the windows unendingly, food got filled with it, clothes weighed heavy and smelled choking, and there was a grittiness about people's skins and hair and mouths that no amount of washing could get rid of.

They called a meeting in the school-house to decide what they had better do, and had their minds made up for them by a packed wagon that drove past from Eight Dollar Valley while they were ganged around the school-yard explaining how they felt about it in case the meeting got too formal for a free exchange of unpolished impressions. The wagon pulled up, the horses leaned against one another to rest, and a man leaned out and grinned.

"Havin' your meetin' to decide about leavin'," he remarked, not in the form of a question. "We got a little beforehand with ours. Held it five days ago. Sorry we didn't think to send word to you; we could have made one do for all of us."

"Where do you people think you're goin'?" Lavran Baker said. "This is no weather to camp out in. You can't pitch a tent against a wind like that, and if you could it would rip to pieces."

"It's as good for travelin' as it is for stayin'," the man said. "The way I figure her is this. I've been through a good many starve-outs in my time, I've seen 'em with smut and rust and wire-worms and drouths, and I've even seen a wheat crop choked to death by them damned blue bachelor-button flowers. But this is the Godliest-damnedliest one I ever did see, and I want to git out of it alive so I can brag to people that I went through it. We're headin' down to hunt work on these new railroad jobs that's openin' up, and we want to get there before they're all took."

"By God! you've converted a member," Lavran Baker said. Having no wife to consult, he could make his decisions on the fly. "If any of your outfit want a place to stop overnight, foller along after me and help yourselves to anything you find loose. I'll be packed up to leave with you by tomorrow morning."

Mrs. Lund registered the second vote. She was old and tottery and slow to understand things since the funeral, but she knew that a country didn't increase in value according to what you put into it. She had put more into it, all told, than most of them, and she hated it. She climbed into her wagon and said something in Swedish to her husband. He climbed in with her, and they drove away to pack up. Given Bushnell and Mace Hosford had come in one wagon, and they rode away together in it, contorting their faces with the effort of yelling their reasons for leaving at one another against the wind. Tunis Evans' wife got into their wagon and waited for him to catch up with what was going on, and, getting tired of that, she drove up the road alone, with him trotting behind, calling for her to wait, and trying earnestly to figure it all out. There was a scramble of untying teams and turning wagons and mounting saddle-horses, and Clay and old Carstairs and the Eight Dollar Valley man had the school-yard to themselves.

"Well, by God," old Carstairs said, dejectedly, "I thought I'd gone through this the last time I ever would. Now just when I git my house fixed over fit to live in, it goes and happens again."

He was under no obligation to leave. But there was still the feeling among all those people, not clear, but strong, that held them in a pack and made it seem necessary that if most left, none should stay. The Eight Dollar man knew that feeling himself, for he didn't question the necessity, only old Carstairs' regret over it.

"Hell fire, feller, you're a child," he said. "Wait till you've had eight or nine different countries go to pieces on you, and you won't think any more of bunchin' the deck on one and lookin' for another than you would of changin' your shirt. We'll find us some land. That's what the country's made out of, ain't it? You gentlemen got your horses? I can give you a lift if you need one."

They said no and went to their horses. That night they spent loading things in the wagon and helping Mrs. Carstairs pack valuables—the globe lamp, the center table, the rocking-chairs, her dishes, the stereopticon outfit. She even remembered to load in what food they had. They finished by lamplight the next morning, and wagons were already rattling along the road going toward the mountains.

This was different from the move they had made from the Coast. Then they had mapped the trip and stocked up for it and got their horses in condition before they started. They had undertaken it at a season when grass was plentiful and they had taken their time and picked roads where the feed was good. Now there was only one road they could take, there was no grass except winter broom straw, and people and teams were gaunt and lank when they started. But it was better to go than stay, and better to go early while the railroads still needed construction hands, if they intended to go at all.

There was likely to be competition for railroad work, for the starve-out that year was general, and people emptied out from dozens of new settlements, hurrying to change their status from landholders to payroll hands. Nobody ever counted up how many dry wells got left for cattle to fall into, how much good grass got plowed up and left as worthless stubble, or how much lumber was abandoned for town-site promoters to haul off and make suburban residences of. The Eight Dollar Valley man said it had anything licked that he had ever seen. Not even the winter of 1888 could touch it.

"You and me are luckier than most of 'em," he said to Clay. "How would a man feel cartin' a woman through a place like this?"

It was a bad place to cart through. Where their road hit the summit of the mountains, a whole striping of other roads branched into it from canyons to the east. There were wagons on all of them, and there was a tie-up ahead, so they all had to fall into column and wait. Looking at the roads separately, the travel didn't appear extra heavy. There would be a couple of wagons and some loose stock maybe every mile, with sometimes a man between driving some loose mules or a sounder of brood sows. But there were a good many roads, and wagons moved on all of them without break or let-up. Ahead, they stood lined in the road as far as a man could see, so many that the Burnt River and Eight Dollar levees were lost in the swarm. There were wagons from localities that nobody had ever heard of before, places like North Pole and Hardscrabble, Wagon-tire and Blue Joint and Axehandle and Hooligan Flat, places so remote and new that the people who came from them had never got round to naming them.

The tie-up was where the road pitched down over the north slope of the mountains. It had been a sort of graded-out pack-trail, with many switchbacks to make an easy lug up the steep scarp. But the spring thaw had made it slide off, and all the trail was gone, wiped down as slick as the roof of a barn. There was no way for wagons to get down except by a two-mile open drop so steep that a man couldn't navigate it without using both hands to hold on. Down that the wagons had to be taken one at a time, with a picked team to point the wheels, a picked driver to steer them, and a crew of men holding the wagon back with a rope so it wouldn't break loose and run wild.

The work went slowly, though everybody helped at it. Men

tended to split into work-crews according to the communities they came from, though the work was for all of them and their communities stood little chance of ever existing again. People from Eight Dollar Valley graded a kind of toe-hold out of the worst of the slide, and regraded it as often as a wagon destroyed it by crossing it. A gang from Currant Creek helped lighten and repack the wagons before they started down, and ex-settlers from the High Desert repacked the teams at the bottom. The Burnt River people worked on the cordeling-line that held back the wagons, with Olaf Lund and Given Bushnell and Mace Hosford and old Sheldon packing a side-line up the slope to hold it from tipping over. There was no out-and-out competition between localities over the various divisions of labor. A man merely fell in where there were people he knew, and worked along with them.

The one piece of work that had style to it was the job of driving the wagons down the slide. That took nerve and management, for a fool horse or a weak harness-strap or a rickety-wheeled wagon could easily mean the finish of the whole outfit—driver, team, load, and all. The man elected to handle it was a youngish ex-freighter from Cherry Creek, with a wife and two children who stood at the top of the pitch and prayed him clear to the bottom every trip. When he landed safely they all looked as proud of him as if they had taught him how. He did know how to handle wagons, for he could lay every wheel on a quarter-inch chalk line and make it roll there; but the horses were strange to him, and his self-consciousness with so many people watching him made him crowd the reins more than he needed to. He fiddled with the horses so they got nervous, and finally, taking down an old-fashioned mud-rig with high springs, he let the front wheels cramp so the load overbalanced. Olaf Lund and the side-line crew got dragged through a patch of rocks trying to hold it from upsetting, but a wheel broke and it went over and started to roll. The driver fell off, but the horses went dragging and floundering along with it for two hundred yards before the tongue split out and left them lying tangled in the harness.

One of them was dead when the men got to them. Its neck was broken. The other, a big chestnut stallion, had a piece of the broken wagon-tongue driven into his lungs, and he lay snorting blood and trying to kick the harness loose and get up. There was nothing to

do for him except shoot him. It was not the custom to turn the job
of shooting a wounded horse over to any sympathetic bystander. No
matter how urgent such a case was, it had to be tended to by the
horse's owner. Some men went back to the wagons with the news,
some others went down to salvage what they could from the wrecked
wagon, and Clay sat down beside the dying horse to wait.

He knew who the owner would be; he had seen that old chestnut
too many times. It was unlucky that his meeting with the horse-trader
should happen when there was so much else going on, when all the
communities were too busy getting themselves out of there to be-
stow much attention on private grudges. He almost decided not to
bother with it after all. Then Luce came down the rocks, walking
gingerly because of the steep slope. She had done her hair in two
big braids so the wind wouldn't blow it loose, and she carried an old-
model rifle under her arm. Wind had burned the blood into her face
so she looked sharp and eager and excited.

Luce had wintered what was left of her father's horse-herd at a deserted mining-camp in the Strawberry Mountains. She had broken
camp and started north as soon as the roads were dry enough to
travel, without suspecting what a well-patronized peregrination she
was falling into line with. There had been no settlements in range
of her wintering-camp except an oldish wheat-raising colony down
in the lowlands, and she had not kept close enough track of its
people to know what they were lighting out about the same time
she did.

They were not the kind of people that one got acquainted with
easily. A couple of times, when the loneliness of her naked mountain canyon got too much for her, she traveled down to their settlement to inquire about boarding with one of them till spring. Mostly
they declined to consider such a thing at all. A few did agree reluc-
tantly to take her in, but the price they set for her and her horses
would have cost her everything she had, horses included, in two
months. They felt obliged to make it high because they didn't know
anything about her. None of them could understand why she didn't
have a place of her own to stay, and anything they couldn't understand was, in their scale of ethics, wrongful.

She stayed it out in the mining-camp. It was the first winter she had ever gone through entirely alone and it wore hard on her. The dry winds of spring, which brought starve-out and failure to the settlers below her, lifted her spirits and made her eager to be out in it and going somewhere. She tied her loose horses head and tail to the hind axle and left without looking back, because she didn't want to remember what the mining-camp looked like.

Starting so early in the year, she had thought, would give her all the road to herself; but the settlers had got out ahead of her. At first she passed them all moving south against her, heading to hit the railroads on the Humboldt River. That drift of travel held up until she got clear of the rock plains and the juniper foothills beyond, and then it turned and moved north with her. Both directions were bad, especially when she made camp for the night. Water was scarce and grass scarcer, and she could pick no camping-place that looked halfway decent without the certainty of being crowded off it before morning. A community string of wagons would pull in and unload bedding, women and children would start housekeeping right in the middle of her baggage, and men would drive off her horses so theirs could eat what feed there was. By the time she got into the high country of the north she was as anxious to get off the road as she had ever been to get on it. She had known how to manage with a camp-rig when travel was scarce, but she had never before had to stand up and keep going when all the people in the country were doing the same thing in neighborhood lots. She hung on, promising herself that she would rest and feed up her horses at Burnt River. When she got there, all the houses were empty and the fields blown off clear below the grass roots.

Beyond Burnt River several of her horses went down from lack of feed. She had to leave them, and that, coming at the end of everything else, frightened her. Once, after she had left Clay and was getting well of her sickness, she had been glad to leave Burnt River, because it was monotonous and ugly and full of people who had no use for her father. But now she was alone, and she had counted on it as a place she could always go if the road got too hard to stand. She gave way to fright without even being ashamed of it, and cried, driving her horses along the road for the mountains with the cold wind burning the tears into her face and the dust sticking where they smeared. On the summit, she got packed into the column of waiting wagons a couple of miles behind the slide, in the midst of some people from Cherry Creek.

Wagons from Burnt River were scattered in the bunch ahead, but they were too far away for any of the people to notice her, and they had other business on hand than looking around for old acquaintances. The first greeting she got was from the wagons nearer. A committee of Cherry Creek dignitaries—the speech-making, know-it-all stripe of men that always float to the top of an American crowd when any sudden emergency hits—informed her that their driver couldn't do himself justice without the loan of her chestnut stallion, and that she would have to hand him over in the public interest. The stallion meant considerable to her, and she didn't think much of their driver's looks, but there was nobody to back her up if she refused. She cut the stallion loose and let them have him, and it made her feel lonelier and more deserted than ever.

It was not the Cherry Creek spokesmen for the public interest who brought the news that the stallion had been hurt. They were above such a trifling errand, and they were also anxious to avoid seeming responsible for borrowing the stallion, to start with. The word was brought her by a slow-spoken man whom she had known at Burnt River and on the Coast. His name was Tunis Evans.

"You oughtn't to loaned out that horse of yours," he informed her, breaking it easy. "That's too valuable an animal to hand over to a bunch of ignoramuses like them Cherry Creek people. You ought to told 'em no. That young feller of yours is along with us, so we'd have backed you up. Now you've lost him."

"Lost?" she said, and got down over the wheel at a leap. Evans backed, fearing that she was after him, and went into details.

"He's all broke up in the rocks, and you'll have to shoot him," he explained, luminously. "I looked him over careful, and he's plumb done for. You better come. Bring your gun to finish him with. The horse, I mean."

Relief that it was only the horse showed on her when she went down the rocks with her rifle. If Clay was here and if Burnt River claimed him, it might claim her, too. Maybe her days of fighting all communities and belonging to none were about done with. She hurried down, and he got up and opened on her before she could speak.

"That's the rifle you didn't want anybody to know you had," he accused her, glaring at it. "That's the gun you lied about, and you got one man hung with your lyin'. Give it here to me."

She looked at him and at the rifle, trying to understand what was so awful about it. The end of lone traveling had seemed so close that she had been thinking of that and not of anything behind her. "This is our rifle," she said. "We've had it in a bracket underneath the wagon-bed, and I did lie to you about it, but it doesn't matter any more. What do you want with it?"

"I want it to settle something with your old man," he said. "He bushwhacked two men with it, and all I need is his gun to prove it. It's got a swelled bore, and the bullets come apart in it. Hand it here or I'll take it away from you."

She tossed it to her shoulder and shot. The chestnut stallion laid his neck heavily flat on the ground and died. The size of the wound showed that the bullet had dumdummed when it hit. She looked at what she had done, and tossed the rifle at Clay's feet. "There it is, and there's how it shoots," she said. She was a little defiant, but not frightened or conscience-stricken. "Is that any proof against my father, and what good is it going to do you if it is? My father is dead. Did you know that?"

He stirred the rifle with his foot, staring. For the horse-trader to have dodged retribution by dying seemed a piece of deliberate meanness. Still, if he was dead, that was all people could expect of him. She must have hated losing the chestnut stallion; her father had thought a lot of the old plug. "Was he sick, or was it something— some trouble he got himself into?"

"It was trouble," she said. She kept her voice flat and rather loud so it would not sound emotional. She had been raised to feel responsible for the horse-trader, and the more she knew of his help-lessness the more responsible she felt, even now. His death had come through her refusing to help him, and she was sorry for it. But she didn't sound oppressed and fearful as she had been over her cares of conscience when he was alive. Her father had bought a shipment of horses from a Basque squatter in the Goose Creek country. They had come cheap because the Basque had no feed to keep them over the winter. When the deal was closed a stinger appeared in it, for the horse-trader could not get feed, either, and bad weather was so close that it was dangerous to try to move them anywhere else. It was not even possible to get vaqueros to help trail them; everybody was afraid of being caught out with them in a storm. So he confessed to Luce what he had got himself into, hoping that she might go to the Basque and prevail on him to trade back.

She refused to do it. Always before, when he had made a foolish bargain and got his fingers pinched in it, she had helped him to get out. Now, she told him, he must tend to this one himself, and maybe it would teach him to be more careful. Instead of trying to deal over with the Basque, he undertook to avoid unpleasantness and embarrassment by trailing the horses out himself, and a blizzard caught him when he was too far out to find shelter. Some vaqueros found him after it let up, frozen, with the horses packed close to him. Nearly all of them were dead, too. He had not looked as if dying had been any trouble to him, merely as if he had stopped holding out and had found it less disagreeable than he expected. That was her attempt to teach him self-reliance, and that was how it had ended.

"I don't see that you've got anything to blame yourself for," Clay said. He kept his voice carefully impersonal. He had been raised to consider all people as apt to hurt him if he gave them the least chance to. She had got to him deep once, and he didn't intend that it should happen again. "He got into it himself, and he'd have got caught up for some of his other performances if it hadn't happened. I'd have tended to him for that killin' in the grass country if I'd caught him. Now I ought to go up and help our men."

"You can leave me," she said. "I left you, so it would make us even. But first there's some things you don't know, and I want to tell you about them. I want you to know that my father didn't kill anybody. I did."

She half-shut her eyes to keep out the glare from the gray rocks and the frost-white dead grass, and talked, leaving out nothing, but hurrying to get it over with as she had done their first day together at the mountain homestead in the snow. She began with the horse-trader's wife, who had been good to her but hadn't bothered much about preserving high moral standards with male acquaintances. When the horse-trader owned that he had got cleaned out in a match-race with old Howell, she broke out in a rage. Nobody knew what dealings there had been between old Howell and her, but he had promised her solemnly that he would let the horse-trader alone. She swore that she would get the money back from the forsworn old pup, or else she would go on the street and tell people that he had put her there. She and Luce got on their horses and rode through the rain to head him off, and they waited in a patch of scrub-oak with dark coming on until he passed. The horse-trader's wife stepped out on him, and he spurred his horse and made a pass at her with his quirt to make her get out of the way. She fell down, and called to Luce to stop him, and Luce shot. She stopped him. Then she lay in the sour-smelling oak brush and trembled while the horse-trader's wife collected his money, and then they went back and moved their camp hurriedly, so the rain would wash out all their tracks.

Nothing happened to them for that, but what kept worrying them was that they had not only the money her father had gambled, but also the money that old Howell had put up against him. They dared not send it back for fear it would be traced to them; she dared not take it with her for fear Clay would find it and want to know where it came from. She left it with the horse-trader, and his wife promised to see that it was sent back as soon as it was safe to send it. But afterward she left, too, as she had often threatened to. The horse-trader was alone when he found Luce sick in the tent on the Burnt River divide.

"So you went along with him to watch it," Clay said. "You got up and left me because you felt afraid he'd spend the money you'd stole?"

It was his old habit of quarrelsomeness that made him throw that at her, and he felt sorry the minute it was out. But her leaving him was something he had to find out about. "Tell me something I wasn't afraid of on that divide," she said. "I was afraid to stay there any longer alone. I was afraid of what had happened to me. I was afraid I might get out of my head and say something that would drive you away for good. I didn't know what I'd said, and I was afraid I'd already blurted something and that was why you were leaving. Something about what I'd done or about that Lund shooting of yours, I thought, because I'd caught myself starting to talk about that several times. You'd left one woman because you got scared over a thing like that. How did I know you weren't

leaving me? There were all those things I was afraid of. I left on
account of all of them."

He said that she hadn't let out anything; the Lund business had
been a pure accident, and she oughtn't to have attached importance
to it.

"I did," she said. "I was standing in the tent door when it happened, and I heard your bullet hit him when he ran. When you
wouldn't tell me about it I knew it must be dangerous. I didn't get
over that for a long time, not till they ran that outlaw down and
lynched him for it. I hated that Clark Burdon because he knew
about it and I wasn't supposed to. . . . Well, my father found me
in the tent and took me along with him, and for a while it was better. You see so much outside when you're traveling that you don't
notice what's happening inside you. Then we traveled down into
the grass country, and this last thing struck me. That was the worst.
I almost went out of my mind trying to think what to do. The only
thing I felt glad of was that you weren't there, and now it turns
out you were."

She had put off sending old Howell's money back during her
sickness, and in getting well she had made herself stop thinking
about it at all. And one night in the grass country she woke up
thinking about it and she got up to make sure it was still in her
trunk. It wasn't. The Indian boy had it, along with all their money.
So she tried to think what to do, and she thought of a thousand
things that were totally impossible and of one that seemed easy
and entirely just. The Indian boy had ignored her warning and
lied to her. What would a man in that country have done to him
for that? She lay and thought, and anger and dread rose in her till
she could stand it no longer. She rode out into the grass and waited
till she heard his mowing-machine rattling. . . . "That was all,"
she said. "I'd already given him all the chance he was entitled to,
so that was all. It didn't help much. I sent the Howell money back
then, but I had his. I had to take it so people wouldn't tie it up with
the horse-race too close, and I didn't know where to send it. Some
day maybe I'll go back there and find out from somebody. Now I
haven't got any more to tell you. Some men are waving at you from
the wagons."

She went and knelt over the dead stallion and drew her fingers through his long mane. She didn't feel afraid. Once she would have been; she would not have wanted him to know those things about her for fear he might misjudge her by them. But he had seen her afraid, he knew what fear could do to her, and even if they were through with one another it was better for him to know them, if only to know what he was through with. He waved back at the men, watching her. "There's more to tell," he said. "Your father got caught trailin' horses in a blizzard, and then what? You made out all right after that?"

She said no, and told him about winter in the mining-camp with frost drawing nails in the empty shacks and wind blowing across the old tunnel-mouths in the night so it sounded like voices when she tried to sleep, and about traveling alone against this shift of people from the land to the railroads; all belonging to some community, she belonging to none of them. In their prosperity she hadn't wanted to belong to any of them. Prosperity brought out everything in them that was childish and pompous and ridiculous and wasteful. But adversity brought them down to cases; it made even the simplest of them get in together and get work done. Getting the wagons down over the slide was work. Their bad management of it had cost her a horse, but they were getting it done. And they had crowded her off camp-grounds, but they would take her wagon down when they came to it, along with their own. They were worth belonging to.

"I know it," he said. "I wanted to settle down in one place and stay there, and then I looked over the people that had. They're all right, but they don't amount to anything. These people do. If enough of 'em was to take to the road all at once, they could stand this country on its head. You can't tell what they might do."

Nobody could tell what they might do. Once enough of them had taken to the road all at once, and they had conquered half the continent. It seemed a pity that they never seemed able to do such things until they got starved down to them, but it might have been worse. There were people in the world that didn't do anything even then. "Well, we're in it," he said. "I ought to tell you about the things that I've done. There was a jail-break that I'd helped with across the mountains, but it's done with now and it wouldn't matter in a stampede like this, anyhow. That's one good thing about it. Nothing counts except what's goin' on around you."

"That's the way I've been trying to live ever since I saw you," she said. "Sometimes I almost managed it, and then something would spoil it."

"You'd better move your wagon over with ours," he said. "We won't be out of this place before morning. The people know you're here, and they'll expect you to be with me."

There was no ceremony of reconciliation. None was possible, because people were watching them from the road; none was necessary, because the country was going through a shaking-up that overshadowed any need for it. Even her old habit of trying to protect the people in her own outfit against any outside risk was shed off. She showed that when the Burnt River men came down to get Clay to help them on the slide.

"They want us to put up a horse-handler for them wagons now," old Carstairs explained. "We've scared up an old derrick-horse for one side of the neck yoke, and we thought that mare of yours could pack the other one if you took charge of the drivin'. You'd better come on now, or they're liable to put another Cherry Creek man at it and slaughter another team for us."

Clay waited for her to answer them, remembering what she had said once after Clark Burdon had enlisted him in a dangerous expedition for the public welfare. "I might git bunged up a little," he told her. "It wouldn't be these people's fault, but you might think it was. I want to go, but anything you say."

"You won't get hurt," she said, strong and confident. "If you do, I'll take the wagons down in your place. Go on, show those bush-settlers that our men know how to handle horses."

THE END